Reasonable Joy

A novel by

Lauren Sanders-Jones

REASONABLE JOY Copyright © 2011 by Lauren Marlene Jones. All rights reserved.

Printed in the United States of America. No part of this book may be used or reproduced in any manner whatsoever without written permission except in the case of brief quotations embodied in critical articles and reviews. For more information, address Lauren Marlene Jones, c/o lawn819@yahoo.com.

www.lulu.com/reasonablejoy

THIRD EDITION

Designed by Lauren Marlene Jones

Printed on acid-free paper

Library of Congress Cataloguing-in-Publication Data

Jones, Lauren Marlene., 1958 -- .

Reasonable joy / Lauren Sanders-Jones – 3rd ed. -- 2011

Reasonable joy / Lauren Sanders-Jones – 2nd ed. – 2005

Reasonable joy / Lauren Sanders-Jones – 1st ed. -- 2004

ISBN 1-4116-4540-5

1. African American women – Fiction. 2. African-American life in the South – Fiction. 3. Women – Fiction. 4. North Carolina – Fiction. 5. Washington, DC – Fiction. 6. Southern United States – Fiction.

DISCLAIMER

Although one part of this story is based upon actual events, this is a novel, and is, therefore, a work of fiction. Names directly connected with the actual events have been changed. Beyond that one part of the plot, any resemblance between the characters herein and real persons living or otherwise is purely coincidental.

Dedications

tO MY PRECIOUS Mama:

I'll be seeing you in all the old familiar
places
That this heart of mine embraces all
day through
In that small café,
the park across the way
The children's carousel, the chestnut
trees, the wishing well
I'll be seeing you in every lovely
summer's day
In everything that's light and gay
I'll always think of you that way
I'll find you in the mornin' sun
And when the night is new
I'll be looking at the moon
But I'll be seeing you. [1]
My late, priceless mother,
**Marlene LYNCH Sanders Jones
(4/3/32 – 12/28/02)**
told me South Park Stories, which were the
thread that bound this novel together!

♥

Kristen Danielle Fuller, Adrienne Carol, and
Justin Charles Tucker:

"Ayana," "Ngambika," and "Kayin," [2] you
are
the three who brighten up my place!

♥

Ernest Lenwood Sanders, Sr.
"Granddaddy" 10/6/09-10/6/89
"And gladly would he learn, and gladly
teach."
-- *The Canterbury Tales*, Geoffrey
Chaucer
This is satisfaction: a full life lived well and a
startling intellect fully enabled.

♥

Ollie Mae Killebrew Sanders
3/21/12-11/15/96
Grandma was the embodiment of grace
and wisdom. She was, at the end, a
brilliant star enshrouded in fog.

CHARLES ROBERT JONES
10/13/32-6/7/83
"Daddy"
An Unrealized Genius of the South,
whose talent burned, bright and
powerful, for a brief time and then,
like a quasar, was extinguished.
Stars
I often like to stand and watch
The twinkling stars at night,
And see just how they shoot from
space
It's such a wondrous sight.
A sparkling little diamond,
It resembles in the sky,
It gives off rays of bluish light,
I sometimes wonder why.
Now, if I was a little star
That shines high up in space,
I'd twinkle with distinctive poise;
I'd brighten up the place.
But since I'm not a little star,
And exist not in the air,
I guess my place is here on earth
To watch the stars up there.
-- Charles R. Jones, 1947

♥

Six men stand above all
Others in my life as **PHENOMENAL
MEN.**
They are my maternal uncles.
To **Ernest; Robert; Carl (1939-
2009); Frank; Maurice;** and
John Sanders:
Thank you a million times: for
being in my life, for believing in
me as a writer even when I was a
child, for your constant and
uplifting support, and for your
fabulous families!

Frank Thomas Sanders, Jr.
11/29/64 – 10/21/03
BELOVED. ALWAYS.

Cornelia Rand Sanders Haywood
2/7/13 – 1/30/94
No words can ever adequately express the
encomium to graceful, loving wisdom that
Aunt Cornelia's life was in our lives.
She is eternal.

†

Reginald Ann Smith White
8/19/46 – 1/7/94
**Rogers Mae Powell Smith Evans
7/31/24 – 11/22/97**
Blessed are the women who have the
courage to be kind, the fortitude to care, the
wisdom to love deeply, and the presence of
mind to stand strong and fight the good
fight. Blessed then were Reggie Ann White
and her mother Roger Mae Evans. And
blessed are we who knew and loved them.
Roger Mae experienced a dove visitation
after Reggie Ann's death.

†

**Yvonne Jones
8/14/59 – 6/1/93**
Her brief walk upon this earth was
accompanied by the congas of royalty.
Every step was a graceful musical interlude
that bespoke pride, joy, and the infinite
wisdom of motherhood.
Yvonne's walk was Willia's; Yvonne's birthday
was Willia's.

†

**Cheryl Gerard Dinkins Gatling
10/4/62-2/18/98**
Every morning she awakened early, ready
and eager for the adventures of the world.
Rest well, sweet, beautiful Cheryl.

†

To all the mothers and all the fathers who
preceded me in the **Emerson, Morgan,
Williamson, Sanders,** and **Jones** families,
thank you with love for bringing me here.

---

[1] **I'LL BE SEEING YOU by** Irving Kahal / Sammy Fain, 1944

[2] Ayana: beautiful flower; Ngambika ("Nam-BEEKA"): help me to balance
or carry this load; Kayin: Joyous or celebrated arrival of the long-awaited
son.

Acknowledgements

I devoted many hours to the research of this book. Without the invaluable help of the following folks, I could not have told you an authentic, though fictitious, story of Raleigh, North Carolina as it was during the time of Rainey.

Marlene Lynch Sanders Jones, my late, great mother, was my dearest friend, my favorite person on the face of the earth, and my number one fan. She told me historical facts about Raleigh, most specifically, Raleigh's black community in general and South Park in particular, with such flair that I felt myself transported to those times. I thank her especially for details about life for African-Americans who lived and worked in Raleigh. My fond memories of and lessons learned from her help propel me through a life made barren by her passing.

A final word about my mother: "She has achieved success who has lived well, laughed often, and loved much; who has enjoyed the trust of pure women, the respect of intelligent men, and the love of little children; who has filled her niche and accomplished her task; who has left the world better than she found it, whether by an improved poppy, a perfect poem, or a rescued soul; who has never lacked appreciation of Earth's beauty or failed to express it; who has always looked for the best in others and given them the best she had; whose life was an inspiration; whose memory a benediction." – from "He Has Achieved Success" by Bessie A. Stanley

Sarah Bell, Bill Brown, Boyd Cathey, Paul Kiel, and **Sarah Minor** represent the North Carolina Archives for me circa 1992 – 1994. They were all extremely helpful and knowledgeable, going out of their way to provide me with sources that they thought might enhance my search. They were extremely patient as I did my research on old Raleigh. They embody the genuine nature of combined Southern competence and hospitality.

Bernice Borden, who worked in the Wake County Clerk of Superior Court in 1992 – 1994, opened a vital door for me by taking the time to look up the court records of the actual 1960 murder case that is fictionalized in this text. Thank you, Bernice, for being such a helpful and kind professional.

Special thanks to **Dyanne Boone Baldwin**, *my Hampton University classmate and treasured friend, for her astute and thorough eyes as an editor!*

To my family and friends: *THANK YOU! You are the world's greatest cheerleaders! You were the first to believe that this story was embraceable. In addition to my late, great mother, who eternally wore pom-poms and cheerleading cleats on my behalf, my six favorite uncles and my maternal grandparents always thought I was a great writer even when I was scribbling on the wall at my grandparents' home.*

I want to give special acknowledgement to my cousins **Gloria Haywood** *and* **Leonidas "Sonny" Haywood**, *children of my late aunt Cornelia Sanders Haywood, and my dear friend* **Jennifer Cherry Hinton**, *three very picky readers who were the first people outside of my immediate circle of influence to be excited about my story.*

It is my pleasure and honor to offer special gratitude to **Samuel and Effie Merritt**, who believed in my work and offered valuable assistance to me to get the book out to a wider audience.

Finally, I want to acknowledge the enthusiastic support of a courageous woman whose short life was also "...an inspiration; whose memory a benediction...." **Laura Beth Oberkircher** fought the good fight against inflammatory breast cancer until her journey ended on Wednesday morning, June 22, 2005. She was an avid fan of *Reasonable Joy*. More importantly, she was a proactive champion of healthy living for all mothers and all children, and an excellent and beloved friend to my children and me. We will always cherish her 42 years in this world.

An important historical note: Shaw University's law school closed in 1914. I have extended its life in this book.

1960

She sank her slim feet into the warm heavy sand along the shoreline in back of their house. She stopped at each moonstone, inching it out of the wet sand with her toes.

Moonstones.

She stopped and looked up at the bright sky. Sea gulls circled and flew over her. Their cry, once a source of joy for her and a confirmation of Tesima's natural beauty, was now a plaintive lament. The sun had burned off the morning clouds, and the breeze that wafted past her was like so many silk scarves wrapping themselves around her thin frame. The waves, at low ebb, washed over her feet like chilling but soothing memories. And she remembered...

Another soft breeze waltzed across her face. It, too, felt like a piece of silk, cool and soft and shimmering, caressing her with loving brevity. She closed her eyes; sighed. Far away, waves rolled against the shore. That sound, which had always given her such joy, now brought back such remnants of pains past.

She burst into tears suddenly, an explosive sobbing coming upon her with vicious persistence. She wept, she sobbed, she screamed briefly. Her face was aglow with her tears.

What manner of woman had she become?

And just as suddenly, she stopped; stood straight and still; closed her eyes. Breeze again.

So many thoughts assaulted her weary mind. She had much to consider. And much for which to account.

Composed now, she looked up into the brilliant, cloudless sky. May, for all her 60 years, had been the month that reminded her to celebrate how good her life was. After this dreadful May, there would be no more celebration. There would only be commemoration.

Rainey Elizabeth Clark Herndon Davis, a believer in the concept of one's deeds coming back to haunt or bless one, did not know in 1960 that she fully embraced principles of karma. But she did know that there was a possibility that some of her actions over her life had brought her to this sorry state of hopelessness.

Had it started from her origin as a "foundling" (I wonder if I really count as a foundling, she often mused, when I was found on my real father's doorstep)? Was it her maternal legacy to want what was not her own? Was it the total recklessness of her birth mother Nettie Ann rising up within her?

Could it have been her move to Washington, DC? She had immersed herself into that life in ways that still sometimes made her gasp in shocked recollection. During her days in DC, she had convinced herself that she was fundamentally all she had in the world. Had those sins, however unintentionally committed, brought about this horror?

Step....

Laurence sprinted through the valley of her thoughts. She felt anguish, and closed her eyes more tightly. Even so, she felt a stirring of passion that she squelched almost instantly.

If I close my eyes real tight, you can't see me, Mommy. And if I squeeze my eyes tighter like this, you won't be able to hear me neither.

Willia's childhood voice echoed through her mind and Rainey flinched.

Her mind went gray for a moment, and she sat still and straight, grief draped unevenly around her shoulders, until she could stand to think again.

Willia.

She shut her child away from her thoughts quickly. Not right now. Not just yet.

But a glint of metallic blue, polished to a high sheen, sparkling underneath a stately bed of flowers, wafted across her mind. She forced her mind to numbing grayness. She breathed again, and turned back toward the shore.

Her mind's caricature of the moments after the monster had eaten his final dessert zoomed up and into her line of sight.

She imagined it was not a pretty sight, that he had probably lost control of all of his bodily functions. This pleased her ever so fleetingly.

And then she wept again. Another cloudburst that ended as rudely as it had started.

Willia.

There was really nothing she could do but consider the whys of how she had come to this stage in her life. She hugged her arms against her chest and waited anxiously for the easing of the ache of Willia's memory.

Her mind raced back to yet another caricature: her own beginning. Perhaps she was a foundling after all. Found on her father's doorstep... found herself to be an orphan . . . found in Washington, DC with people she had never known...found in a marital farce that would warp her perceptions for years. . . . found to be a possible murderer?

Found . . . finder . . . foundling.

Foundling, Rainey's Prologue

1899 - 1922

Let Us Proceed By Looking Back....

December 15, 1899

A heavy branch from the old sycamore tree out back had sashayed and shimmied against their bedroom window all night. Occasionally, he could feel a bit of spray from the windy drizzle outside that forced itself into the room through the tiny holes in the walls of this inadequate house. His wife had probably never been gassier in all their marriage than she was that night. But Rufus Clark would not have slept at all anyway. Now, weak fingers of daylight played across his fevered eyes. Throughout the night, he had looked over at Evie, who slept, as always, like the dead. Neither the weather conditions nor her snores nor her flatulence disturbed her. He truly envied his wife. With the weather like it was, he could not breathe when he lay down, and his temples throbbed when he sat up. Somewhere far away he was sure he could hear a baby crying, but how could that be? A baby would surely die in weather like this.

Every now and again, he could hear a floorboard creak. It had taken him several hours to get accustomed to the possibility that it was just the house settling.

Worst of all, the same tune kept running through his weary mind: Has Nettie Ann had that baby yet? Ain't it time for Nettie Ann to have that baby? I bet she done had that baby. . . I wonder if that baby is mine. . . I bet that baby ain't really mine . . . she so damn fast she probably don't know who the papa is.... And the mewling sounds of a baby somewhere kept the beat of this tune. And on it went, this annoying ditty that he could not get out of his brain, swirling 'round and 'round in his mind until he was sure the words had swelled large enough to cause his skull to explode.

Nettie Ann Houser had been an invisible resident of his home for the past year. Both he and his wife knew that she was there, silently brooding, swelling larger every day, looking at them sadly, trying with some success to be a final wedge between the childless couple and any remnants of joy they might be able to hold onto. Evie had been his faithful wife for 15 years. She was his helpmate and his loyal companion.

Rufus Clark found faithfulness, devotion, helpfulness, and loyalty stifling and boring.

Nettie Ann had been the heat he thought he'd needed in his life, but now the flames had begun to sear at his flesh. He needed a way out. Well, he reasoned with his conscience, she at least won't bring the baby around here. She surely won't. Even Nettie Ann wasn't that bold . . . was she?

Rufus was glad to know that the day was going to be a rainy, muddy mess. No ditch-digging endeavor could be successful under such conditions. His boss wouldn't want to be outside; since it was Friday, he'd much rather start his 48 - hour drunk a few hours early, so that he would have more time to run behind some whores. To get to his activities quickly, the boss would send the workers home for the day. For once, Rufus was grateful to lose this day's wages. He could envision his boss's mottled, bloated face as he told them to "get the hell on home, you sorry darkies." The man was ten years younger than Rufus, but looked 15 years older.

Rufus's own life was a shambles, he knew, and he had no idea what to expect next.

He jumped when Evie gasped and turned over onto her other side. As daylight continued to brighten into the gloom of their tiny bedroom, Rufus realized that he would soon need to brave the elements to go to the outhouse.

Evie stirred and threw back the blankets on her side of the bed. She sat up and looked around for a moment, trying to remember where she was.

"'Mornin', honey," she murmured through a yawn. "I'm-a go get dressed and fix us some breakfast."

"All right then," Rufus said, dismayed to hear the slight tremor in his voice.

In the kitchen, Evie had allowed a kettle to simmer all night so that they would each have warm water for their morning wash-ups. She felt sad as she poured her allotment of hot water into the deep bowl they used each morning. Evie knew it was about time for Nettie Ann to have that baby. What would happen now? How would this child affect her home? Why didn't Rufus want her the way he so obviously wanted Nettie Ann? Would he want to leave Evie to be with Nettie Ann and the baby?

A slow, cold procession of tears promenaded down Evie's cocoa colored face. She knew she would stay with Rufus; she had nowhere else to go, and you just didn't up and leave your husband in those days. She had tried to make him happy and to be a loving wife. It was not her fault that they had never been able to have a child. She supposed, as she had all along, that one of her many childhood illnesses had left her barren.

Evie wished, for one brightly desperate moment, that maybe, somehow, she could rear the baby herself. She knew from her scant contact with Nettie Ann that the girl was not ready to settle down and be a mother. Evie felt sad for the child that Nettie Ann would have, and for that moment, her sadness for the child overshadowed her bewilderment at having a husband who took his intimate love elsewhere.

Rufus decided to lie back down for a moment to give Evie a chance to use the outhouse. He drifted into a chaotic nap from which he was awakened a few minutes later when Evie came back into their room to dress for the morning.

"Whew," she said quietly, for she did everything quietly. "It's a whole bunch of little kittens being born out there by the Wilson's outhouse. I reckon that's the racket I heard all last night. I couldn't sleep a wink."

They had both taken their baths the night before, so she was ready quickly. Rufus must have dozed off again because he could smell sausage from the kitchen.

He hurriedly pulled on some pants and stopped at the front door for a moment before stepping outside. The scene before him was bewildering.

Icy drizzle. Biting choking winds whistling through nude trees. Dull gray clouds rolling across a mournful sky. Dead leaves swirling about.

On mornings like this one, Rufus Clark was in a foul mood. With his sinuses clogged shut by the gray morning drizzle, he always felt as if his head should just be unscrewed from his neck and emptied of its annoying contents. He was a sallow complexioned man with an abundance of wavy black hair that had strands of gray weaving their way back from his hairline. This morning, his clear gray eyes held in them some of the clouds that moved in a funeral procession across the darkening morning sky.

He was of average height, with the sturdy build of a man who enjoyed working outside. Rufus Clark was a firm, hard-working man who did not suffer fools. Period. And this weather, to him, was just like a fool.

So it didn't help that on this morning, when Rufus Clark stumbled forward onto his creaking front porch, he nearly fell, clogged head first, over a soggy bundle. He glared down at the pale green rags, which blocked his path to the necessary. He lifted his right foot to kick them off the porch. The color drained from his olive face as the pile moved. Soon he could make out the shapes of tiny thighs and knees kicking and squirming. He snatched the bundle into his arms just as a mewling squawk emerged from it. He looked around frantically.

Evie was singing some shanty spiritual or other back in the kitchen.

Rufus opened the top of the bundle with a gentleness of which his callused and cracked hands seemed incapable. Inside, he beheld the tiny, fretting face of his indiscretion.

Pinned to the inside of the blanket was a crudely written message.

The note, written by the woman he had brutally taken as his mistress, read:

Rufus this little gal is your. She jus bornd last nite. You taik her I can not. No money. Nettie Ann.

Suddenly the chilly morning was cold steel. How had he gotten himself into this mess? He knew how, and he shut away the memories of that particular series of messes. Evie didn't deserve this, but he knew full well he deserved whatever fury might be about to rain down upon his sorry head. He knew his wife was no fool, and he also knew that she had to have figured out what was going on between Nettie Ann and him.

Rufus remembered, his face reddening, that all that summer and fall, Nettie Ann made sure she paraded that big belly in front of him whenever he was with Evie. Nettie Ann was mad as fire by then; once she had told Rufus they were going to have a baby, he didn't bother with her anymore. She came to church at First Baptist every Sunday, told everybody her husband had been killed in the war (Rufus could see them wondering to themselves 'What war?'), and that now here she was all alone with a baby. She always managed to look directly at Rufus whenever she was selling this poor story to the vaguely suspicious members of the congregation. Still, the church members seemed to take pity on this poor helpless widow woman, who was uncommonly lovely. Her dark caramel skin had an exotic touch added to it with the combination of honey - colored eyes, straight black hair that hung to the middle of her back, and high cheekbones. She was a tiny woman, barely five feet tall, and the pregnancy caused her to walk sway - backed as if her spine might be in danger of snapping. She offered a rather pitiful sight for anyone who would stop to talk with her after morning service.

Rufus's skin was so pale that when he blushed, he looked just like an apple. He was Macintosh an awful lot over those months.

Rufus gulped now and prepared to take the baby in to his doting wife. He walked slowly to the back of the rickety shotgun house to the kitchen, which was full of the scent of baking biscuits and the acapella strains of a voice that was more sincere than sweet. Every step he took seemed frozen in time, every step sped him to the inevitable. When he stood looking at Evie and her pretty chocolate face atop her slender tree limb of a body, he felt he had gotten there much too quickly. He took a minute to contemplate her face as he gathered his thoughts. She was an elegant beauty, blessed with perfect teeth, almond shaped eyes, a vibrant smile, and a figure that would get a white woman a job modeling for the Sears Roebuck catalog. He wondered now why he had ever gone astray.

Still, even in the face of this huge lie he must tell, Rufus could still remember the smoldering moments in which he and Nettie Ann had probably produced this child. Legs intertwined, stifled moans, ecstatic . . . hot . . .

He stopped himself, ashamed.

But, what kind of woman would give up her child?

He cleared his vision now, and looked squarely at his wife.

"Evie. Look what I found on my way to the necessary." He offered the child to his wife, who hurriedly wiped her hands against her frayed apron.

"Rufus, what in the world...? What's this, Rufus?" Evie gasped and soon burst into a delighted chuckle. "Wonder can we keep it?"

"Well," Rufus began, and his voice hardly faltered. "The note says that the mother can't take care of it." Rufus's tongue felt thick and dry as he launched into his tall tale. He was grateful to some indulgent god that Evie had only passed by the one-room schoolhouse on her way to pull tobacco. "It says here that it's a little girl and she was born last night. Ain't this something, Evie? We thought we would never have us young'uns, but God has blessed us with one."

"The Lord works in mysterious ways, Rufus." A dry-eyed Evie looked steadily at her husband for a long moment before bending her face, that deep well of wisdom, to her new daughter's sleeping one. Rufus felt another chill that sent blood coursing to his cheeks.

"Lord Jesus," Evie was saying now, "You has blessed us this morning and I thank you!" She checked the child to make sure she had all her fingers and toes. Rufus felt tears begin to pool in his eyes, but it was the harsh pinch of his guilty conscience that put them there.

"Evie, I got to get to that necessary right this minute or I'm gon be wet like that baby!" Rufus ran from the house and hurried to the lopsided outhouse. As he relieved his throbbing bladder, Rufus Clark made a vow to his God: "Lord, never let her find out what I done and I swear I'll serve You long as I live. I swear, I will serve You and be a faithful husband to her long as I got breath."

When Rufus got back to the kitchen, he found Evie sitting in the chair with the most cane left in its bottom, crooning in her achingly poor voice to this child, whose bottom she had dried and wrapped in a dishtowel. "Rufus, I am just so thankful this morning. I don't care how she got here," she stopped rocking back and forth with the baby to look deeply into Rufus's eyes. "I'm just so glad she can stay." Evie rocked the child some more, humming her broken melody. At last, she said, almost as if to the baby, "What we gon name her?"

Rufus looked around his kitchen with new eyes and a renewed spirit. Suddenly he remembered a very special ancestor in his family. "There's only one name to fit a tough one like this. Rainey."

Many, many moons before night light first sifted through the darkness beneath it to rest upon the loveliness of Rainey Elizabeth Clark, there lived, in Mecklenburg County, North Carolina, another Rainey whose son was set free because his features were a stamp of the features of his father. This son, who was called Rufus-Earl Clark, worked, with quiet devotion, in the large, grand house called Felicity, the home of his father, who was a very wealthy planter, and of his father's wife, the mistress of the great house. He called his father "Master," but his father feared him, for this son was a reminder of a time he wanted never to remember, but could never forget. He called his father's wife "Madam," but his father's wife hated him, for the son's face was a mark of embarrassment for her, the beloved and precious mistress of Felicity, that great and grand house.

Now there was one person the mistress of Felicity hated even more fiercely than she loathed young Rufus Earl. That person was Rainey Hollins, and she was the mother of that son who worked with quiet devotion in the grand house of the Master. The mistress had urged the master to sell Rufus-Earl's mother, Rainey Hollins, to her brother-in-law at his fine Georgia plantation. Rainey Hollins was much too impudent to be worth anything as a slave. Rainey Hollins needed to be tamed, the mistress insisted, and the fine Georgia plantation of her sister's husband was just the place for a taming. Mistress Clark hated Rainey Hollins for looking directly into her own face as if her skin were as lily white (and flawless) as Mistress Clark's skin! Why, Rainey Hollins had even smiled at her, the brazen heifer, and no slave gal was going to get away with smiling at the mistress of the plantation. And every time Mistress Clark spied Rainey Hollins looking at her husband, Mistress Clark knew that she and Rainey shared some secret knowledge. And Mistress Clark could not abide sharing **anything** with Rainey Hollins, with her queer gray eyes and her lemony skin and all that hair piled up on her head.

Josiah Clark did not like to upset his wife. When his wife was agitated, the whole system of that finely tuned plantation was set upon its head, and eventually all things productive ground to a halt. And so, soon after his wife's latest display of tears and fury, Josiah Clark had brought Rainey into the big house from her work station in the fields to inform her that she was about to be sold to a new house. She had stood up to him and insisted that she ought not be separated from her son. This statement enraged Josiah Clark. Rainey Hollins had several other children, and he had sold all of them away from her. And each time she had wept and complained as boldly as she dared. But only this son, Rufus-Earl Clark, did she share with the master. She had less of a right to question his judgment about that son or her self than with any other slave on the place. Or so he reasoned with his feverish conscience. And so he had ordered the overseer to whip Rainey... perhaps because she had **more** of a reason to try to appeal to his heart than any other slave still on the plantation. He would sell her away at a lower price, if he had to, if she were damaged from this punishment.

Soon enough, she was no longer at the place called Felicity.

Still, it was perhaps Josiah Clark's overactive conscience that had beaten him into emancipating Rufus-Earl Clark immediately after Rainey Hollins, of broken and bleeding body, but defiant and unbent mind, was shipped off to Georgia. Rufus-Earl, now a freedman, had stayed on at the plantation as an indentured servant and as a reminder to his biological father (and his biological father's wife) of his own evil deeds.

Josiah Clark dared not offend Rufus-Earl in any way; it was a secret, nearly unconscious pact he had made with Rainey Hollins. But Young Rufus-Earl did not know that his father, Master Clark, did not want to offend him. Behind that slight smile, deep within that sculpted chest, were a mind and a heart dedicated only to the goal in front of him now, and he thought of it and its twin prizes without interruption or detour every waking hour of his day. Rufus-Earl Clark had a higher calling: to emancipate his mother and his betrothed, Sissie Bell Lewis.

The larger part of Rufus-Earl Clark's calling was fulfilled after five years, when he left Master Clark's place and headed south, to a certain Georgia plantation. It was there that he found his mother, nearly a skeleton, laboring in a lush cotton field with other cadaverous automatons. He purchased his precious mother for a dear price from Mistress Clark's brother-in-law, and they set out for North Carolina. Three perilous weeks after they left Georgia, mother and son found themselves once again at the spot where the son's life had begun.

Rainey Hollins's return to Felicity was a glorious day, one that seemed to reverberate victory, triumph, quiet vengeance. Rufus-Earl drove onto the plantation in a ragged wagon that was on its last wheels, literally. His sole purpose now was to purchase the freedom of Sissie Bell Lewis, the woman he would marry. But Rainey Hollins had a more urgent debt to settle. Though her body was weak, she was still a relatively young woman. (According to the records of the Clark plantation, Rainey Hollins was 12 years old when she came to that house as a part of Mistress Clark's dowry from the Dobbs County plantation of Mistress Clark's father. So, the family would later estimate that she was 45 years old when she returned from her season in hell, Georgia style.)

On that glorious afternoon when she returned to Felicity, Rainey Hollins was armed with her emancipation papers, and she felt no fear. Trepidation was no dweller in her soul after the torture of her Georgia existence. Rainey Hollins seemed to float up the stately, rounded steps of the plantation house, fairly sailed into the front door and directly into Josiah Clark's library, where he sat nursing a snifter of brandy and writing his monthly bills. Rainey Hollins stood straight and proud in that doorway, an emblem of an oak tree rooted in endurance. The breeze from the adjacent windows billowed lovingly around her as if welcoming her back with silken and luxurious arms. At last, Josiah Clark noticed that someone was looking steadily at him. He turned toward the door and jumped back in his seat, his face pale and beaded with sweat.

"I'm back," Rainey Hollins said softly, and the quiet power of her voice wafted to him with the clarity of a church bell.

Josiah Clark was, for once, speechless.

"But I ain't here to stay," Rainey Hollins continued, her chin high, and her bony cheeks giving her a regal air. "I'm a free woman, and me and my son just stopped by here for him to pick up his bride."

Josiah Clark found his voice then and said to Rainey Hollins, "You ain't got no right to come back here!" But his voice was tiny and carried no resonance.

"I got a right to do anything I please now. I'm a free woman. You just remember that you will never forget. Do you hear? You will never forget to remember me."

Rainey Hollins turned and walked out of the house and climbed back on to the splintery, wobbly wagon that had brought her back to this place.

Josiah Clark, in a frenzy of guilt, accepted the money Rufus-Earl offered for Sissie Bell's freedom. It looked to many of the slaves that day like Old Master had seen a ghost. It was a specter that would haunt him, hunt him down, unto his last days, which would come so swiftly now.

Together, Rufus-Earl, Rainey, and Sissie had left that part of North Carolina, Rufus-Earl and Sissie as common-law husband and wife. They traveled carefully by night, armed with letters of emancipation, because bounty hunters lurked at every tree trunk, it seemed, ready to take them back to a master who no longer owned them. Rainey Hollins, Rufus-Earl, and Sissie had tried to move away to the North, but they only got as far as Kinston, North Carolina, where the wagon fell apart beneath them. They settled in Kinston, laughing at the fact that the first kindling for the fireplace in their new hovel had traveled all the way from Georgia.

From the tree that Rainey Hollins had become, her one surviving branch saw three limbs thrive. These limbs were named Addie Rose, Rufus, Jr., and Mittie Jane. Of the three, only Rufus, Jr. would bring forth a child, Rainey Elizabeth Clark.

And that child, like her great-grandmother before her, endured.

Evie stood up now, nodding her head in agreement, and laughed softly as she walked toward Rufus.

"I reckon that's just the right name for this little sweetheart. She had to be pretty tough to stand all that rain and cold out there this morning."

In this shimmering moment, here in her arms lay the child she'd believed God for, even in her apparently barren state. This child was for Evie a miracle, no matter the facts of her origin. Evie thought of another barren woman, a heroine of the Bible, who had become a mother despite all logical evidence against her.

"Rainey Elizabeth Clark, welcome to our home."

After Evie lay the baby down inside a fortress of pillows, she let her husband in on something.

"Rufus."

She walked into the parlor and stood in front of him as he reacquainted himself with his dusty Bible. He looked up, his eyes wide, his face going to crimson. Evie cleared her throat. Her eyes never left his, and when she spoke, her voice was clear and unwavering.

"Rufus. I've loved you all these years. . . . And I believe I've been a good wife to you. Wait – let me finish. It hurt me that you snuck out to be with that – that gal when you ought to have been home with me, your one and only wife. It hurt me to look at her walking around carrying your child when I couldn't give you one. But I can still love this baby girl you brung in here because she's part of you. And I can love her because I believe that God makes a way out of no way, and He makes a way out of strange ways. I want you to know I can forgive you, and I can raise that little darling in there like she came from me, but I can't put up with this from you again. You understand what I'm saying, Rufus?"

"Evie, I made a promise to God that I wouldn't ever hurt you again. I made a promise to be a good husband to you."

"Then I reckon that's enough for me."

Rufus, having never heard such a declaration of love nor such fierce conviction from his wife, felt a new respect for her . . . and a surge of deep passion he had never felt for her. Where once there was cool acceptance and predictability, he finally saw symptoms of the flames and deeper feelings he sought in Nettie Ann's bed.

There were a few days when, try as she might, Evie could not bear to have Rufus touch her. In those odd days, she cried herself to sleep alone in their marriage bed while Rufus made a pallet for himself on the frigid floor of the parlor. Little Rainey's frequent wails from her newly constructed cradle kept him company those nights.

Gradually, Rufus and Evie became newlyweds again.

The new Rufus had been tried by the now dampened fire of his loins, and had come out of the inferno renewed, with a never before seen passion for Evie and for staying at home with his family. Whenever he left the house, he reported to Evie his expected whereabouts (and she could actually find him there), his expected time of return (and he was rarely late), and ended his recitation with a warm and intimate embrace (which felt to her like a sunny afternoon at Lake Johnson).

And he taught Evie to read.

†   Soon enough, the Clarks started showing up at church, and all around town, with a new baby girl who was left, just by coincidence, on their doorstep, and who, also just by coincidence, looked an awful lot like Rufus Clark himself.

Hmmm..., some of the busier brains in the congregation got to thinking, whatever happened to that pretty little war widow? They couldn't be quite sure, but many of the church members thought they had seen her lovely eyes peering from the face of the Clarks' new baby.

Nettie Ann could be seen around old Raleigh at all times of night, on the arms of different unsavory men. She was usually as drunk as they were, and Eddie Houser, her younger brother, just had to make up his mind that he wasn't going to try to defend her honor. She just didn't have any more honor.

It was Eddie Houser who represented the good that lay buried, beneath crusty layers of corruption and wrecked sensuality, within Nettie Ann Houser. Nettie Ann Houser might have decided to drop out of little Rainey's life, but Eddie Houser made up his mind that he would not.

When Nettie Ann started carrying on with Rufus Clark, who was 37 years old, and graying, she was 19 years old, two years older than Eddie. Why they had to want what they wanted from each other was beyond Eddie's comprehension. Sure, Nettie Ann was a pretty little girl, even her younger brother could see that when they used to race down to the branch behind their shack outside Lumberton. But Eddie could also see from early on that she just never did have good sense.

The best thing she ever did was to give birth to Rainey.

Eddie had always shouldered his share of the blame for Rufus and Nettie Ann getting together in the first place. Eddie was always the responsible child in a gloomy household that consisted of a desperately ill, widowed mother (later Eddie would understand from her symptoms that his formerly energetic mother died a slow, tortured death from breast cancer), a serious son who would have given most anything to restore his mother's health, and a wild daughter who, lacking the nurturing from a mother who would have had a profound effect on her had she been physically able, wanted only to search for the next party. After his mother died, Eddie came looking for work in Raleigh, any kind of work, really, because there just wasn't much for him to earn money doing in Lumberton.

As for Nettie Ann, Eddie had never voiced his suspicion, but he was almost sure that she sold her favors to a contingent of the local men in Lumberton. Nettie Ann was a source of great disappointment and shame for Eddie. It was not in the nature of Croatan women to act like Nettie Ann insisted on acting, and she had been brought up by their mother, until illness hindered her, to be a lady in the tradition of all Croatan women. Nettie Ann had no peers in their hometown; she had brought disgrace upon the honor of Croatan women, and she had probably had times of lurid intimacy with too many of the Lumberton men to be trusted by any of the women there.

After their mother's death, Eddie moved to Raleigh in search of a better life. He ended up working and living at First Baptist Church, Colored, the premier Negro church in Raleigh. It really turned out that he was working for his room and board, because they didn't have much money to pay him a salary. He did everything around that church: he patched here, he swept there, he drove the pastor's buggy, which was attached to a lone mule too old to live, let alone pull a puny carriage. That buggy was used not only to take the pastor around the little city, but also to pick up the children -- in shifts -- for Sunday School.

He ignored the children when he overheard their hoarse voices whispering "Indian Eddie." Eddie had always been proud to be a Croatan, and later, toward the end of his life, when his tribe was renamed Lumbee, he was equally as proud of that name. He was glad they could tell he was an "Indian."

Soon after Eddie moved to Raleigh, Miss Nettie Ann's welcome in Lumberton had worn dangerously thin. She decided she wanted to see what Raleigh was all about. One Sunday, Eddie asked Reverend J. J. Worlds, his esteemed pastor, to announce that his sister was moving to Raleigh, and would anybody know of jobs and places for her to stay? After service, Mrs. Evie Clark came up to Pastor Worlds and told him that the factory she used to work in always had openings for seamstresses. There was even a rooming house for young colored women over on Swain Street that wasn't too far from the trolley stop. Eddie thanked Mrs. Evie that afternoon. She'd always been mighty nice to Eddie, just as she was to everybody else.

Not too long after that, Hurricane Nettie Ann blew through old Raleigh. And the day that Eddie took her by to meet Mrs. Evie so she could thank her for her kindness, Rufus was at home, too, on one of his days off. Weary of digging ditches, Rufus had recently become a porter at the train station. He wouldn't go on the rails for a few more years. They took one look at each other, and Eddie knew trouble was on the way. Eddie was certain that Mrs. Evie saw it, too; she got so quiet after Nettie Ann came into their little shotgun house. Although Eddie considered Mrs. Evie a "right good-looking woman," with her smooth dark skin, those almond shaped eyes, her ever-present smile, and her good figure, he knew that she was no match against Nettie Ann, who was what many might call exotic looking.

Suddenly, Eddie could never find Nettie Ann when he wasn't working. He finally found her at home in that rooming house one day, maybe six weeks after she'd moved in.

"Nettie Ann, where have you been," Eddie asked her on that rare day when she was there to receive him in the guests' parlor.

"I've been working and having a time," she said, tossing her hair and pretending not to blush.

"What kind of time you been having, girl," said Eddie.

Nettie Ann looked at Eddie as if he were her partner in crime.

"A Rufus Clark time," she said.

"Look, Nettie Ann, don't be no fool."

"I ain't never been no fool, Eddie-boy."

"Oh, don't get me started on that," he replied.

"Look, I ain't gon' sit here and let you try to boss me no more, Eddie-boy. I know what I'm doing and I'm definitely liking it. Besides, who's the oldest of us?" She stared up at her brother with a challenging boldness in her amber eyes.

"I don't think it's right for you to go behind Mrs. Evie's back like you doing."

"What I'm supposed to do? Get in her face? Evie don't know what's going on no how. Don't worry me no more. I can handle myself, thank you."

If handling herself meant getting herself in the family way, then Eddie Houser's older sister did a fine job of things.

Never mind that the circumstances were embarrassing, and that Nettie Ann herself became more and more of an embarrassment. At least, Eddie Houser reasoned, Nettie Ann thought enough of the baby to take the child to her papa, who had at least come to **his** senses. Eddie never could get mad at Rufus; he'd seen many men get dragged under by his sister's charms. Eddie Houser bore no ill will toward Rufus Clark, especially since his devilment had brought about the birth of his darling Rainey.

But Rufus thought the mountain of a man had come to settle a score with him on that momentous day "Uncle Eddie" showed up at the Clarks' front door. Mrs. Evie was in the back of the house, in the kitchen when he knocked on the door. Eddie would always remember that it was unseasonably hot outside that afternoon, and he thought he might look a bit frightening with his swarthy, sweat-shiny face. Rufus came to the door, took one look upward at Eddie Houser, who stood six feet, five inches and towered over most people in the world, and the fear of God apparently came over him. His face reddened to Macintosh once more, and his eyes widened.

Eddie made sure Evie was not in the room before he spoke. "Now Rufus, I ain't here to hurt you, so calm yourself down. I want to meet my niece."

A relieved Rufus, still looking pretty shaky, invited Eddie Houser in, and practically ran to the kitchen to summon Evie. When Mrs. Evie came up front, carrying baby Rainey, who was about seven months old at that time, Eddie Houser fell in love with his niece immediately, though he was careful to show himself to be a happy church member coming to wish the Clarks well.

"I just thought I'd come by and say 'hello' to your little bundle of joy," Eddie Houser said to Mrs. Evie, trying to sound both detached and unaware of the reality of the situation his sister had helped to create. But even as he spoke his "white lie," he saw his sister Nettie Ann's eyes in Rufus Clark's face. Eddie bent down to let Rainey play with his fingers. The baby smiled and made little noises at him. He must have stayed there for hours that first day, playing with little Rainey, and talking to her. At one point, Eddie looked up and saw Mrs. Evie looking at the two of them as they sat in that old cane bottom rocking chair she kept in her front room. She just smiled and nodded her head.

"Yes, Eddie, she's gonna call you 'Uncle' when she can talk." And they smiled at each other, their friendship further cemented by their mutual love for an innocent child conceived in lustful deceit.

"Please come see the baby any time, Eddie," Evie said before she went back to her kitchen, from which the wafting, seductive aromas of johnnycake and collards and baked hen and sweet potatoes caused Eddie nearly to drool.

"And you're welcome to stay to dinner if you'd like."

Eddie stayed, and over time, Rufus learned to breathe easy again.

Eventually, Eddie Houser was a frequent and welcome visitor in the Clark household.

Nettie Ann Houser remained an annual caller.

Eddie thought on that first afternoon, the only nut in your family tree, little Miss Rainey, is your mother Nettie Ann.

Eddie made a vow to himself that he would do for little Rainey, not the least of his motivations being the harsh fact that Nettie Ann hadn't had sense enough, or maybe backbone enough, to rear her own child.

Rufus, and later Evie, taught Eddie how to read. They spent golden hours sitting on the tiny front porch of Rainey's first home, fine-tuning Eddie's reading skills. Later, on the larger, but still wretchedly small porch of the East Street home, or in a Sunday School classroom at First Baptist Church, they continued to praise his valiant and successful efforts. Under Rufus's tolerant tutelage, Eddie slowly learned how to recognize letters and then words and then full sentences from the Bible.

He finished his "schooling" and went on to college. When he started at Shaw University, he knew it would be a painful process; he had left school in what was probably the equivalent of the second grade. There he learned the very basics and went on to full training as a primary school teacher.

But Eddie was determined to be the kind of man his father had shown him he could be during his own short life, and the man his mother had taught him he should be. Perhaps above all now, he wanted to be somebody of whom his little Rainey could be proud. It took about seven years, but he believed he had Rainey to thank for giving him the motivation he needed to get a college education.

The day of Eddie's graduation from Shaw was as proud a day for the Clarks as it was for the graduate himself. He looked out on that lawn and saw little Rainey smiling and waving a white handkerchief at him to show him her pride and her love for him. Even Nettie Ann had shown up at the ceremony, though she was not all there; she was dressed as if she were going to some sort of cabaret, she was leaning heavily on some dandy's arm, and she constantly shifted her attention to Rufus and his family as if her presence on the lawn of Estey Hall was sure to cause Rufus some sort of remorse. Despite Nettie Ann's odd presence, Eddie could not lose his joy or pride that he had met his goal to become an educated man.

Over the years of Rainey's childhood, Eddie put away a little money here and there: a little here for himself and his future family, a little there for his beloved Rainey. By the time Rainey herself enrolled at Shaw, Eddie proudly paid for her first two years' tuition.

Eddie went on to become probably the only Indian man to teach elementary school in the Negro school system in Raleigh. And all those little young'uns stopped calling him "Indian Eddie" -- at least to his face.

On the evening after her twelfth birthday, Rainey was summoned into the tiny parlor of their cozy East Street home. Her mother, who in those rare moments of leisure usually sat in her rocker knitting socks or reading the Bible, was seated on the sofa, with its springs protruding through its worn upholstery. Papa motioned for Rainey to come and sit between them.

Mama cleared her throat and put down her knitting. Outside it was darkening and chilly. They heard crows cawing and dead leaves rustling mournfully past their front porch.

"We think it's time we let you know something that is mighty important." Papa's gray eyes clouded over for a moment, but he soon continued.

"We need to tell you about that lady who comes to see you for your birthday."

Rainey had wanted for years to ask her parents why Nettie Ann Houser always came to see her once a year, but their awkwardness at her presence had silenced her. Rainey had heard what kind of woman Nettie Ann Houser was, and she had seen for herself Nettie Ann Houser coming out of any number of liquor houses that lined the route from Rainey's house to Crosby-Garfield School. Each time, it seemed, Nettie Ann, either pregnant or thin as a bed slat, was on the arm of some new and unsavory looking character. Rainey could not, for the life of her, figure out why the woman came to see her every year on December 14.

Deep down in her heart, perhaps she knew . . . .

Rainey remembered the awkwardness of last evening's lightning fast visit. During that visit, as with all others in the past, Nettie Ann came to the door and asked, timidly, if she could "see the baby." Rainey had sniffed; she was not a baby anymore! When "the baby" appeared in the parlor, Nettie Ann made a quiet to-do over how much Rainey had grown, and how pretty she was. Then she would just stare at Rainey for a while, as the child stood awkwardly and politely waiting for the next phase of the quick visit. "Won't you have a seat?" Evie would invariably say to Nettie Ann, who would always look at Evie as if she couldn't believe she was there.

Nettie Ann always declined, saying she had to be going; she just wanted to take a look at the baby.

While Rainey wasn't particularly upset or anxious about it, she was puzzled. At last, she was about to find out what was going on.

Mama spoke now.

"Sometimes what looks like evil is God's way of bringing a blessing into your life. Do you know what I mean, sugar?" Rainey nodded, basking in the warm and sweet rhythms of her mother's voice. Though she and Rufus had often teased Evie about her poor singing voice, there was no denying the lilting beauty and soothing comfort of her spoken words.

"Well, a long time ago, it looked like your Papa had made a mighty big mistake with Nettie Ann Houser, but from what looked like a mistake came the greatest joy in my life." Did Mama's eyes mist over for a moment? Rainey was unsure until Evie leaned over to give her a kiss on the cheek, and she could see a tiny teardrop balanced upon her mother's eyelash.

"Yes, I wasn't the best husband to your mother back then." Papa seemed more relaxed now. "I reckon you know that she means all the world to me now." Rufus squeezed Evie's hand on the high back of the sofa behind Rainey's head. They smiled at each other. "I treasured your mother then, but I just didn't have good sense." Rufus shook his head slightly so that the gray in his ample head of hair seemed to shimmer in the dim light of the kerosene lamps.

"But anyway, for a time I was acting a little like Nettie Ann Houser was my wife."

Rainey stifled a gasp. Despite her youth, she was certain she knew what was coming next: the confirmation of her distant, veiled fears. But it just couldn't be!

"Papa . . . you trying to tell me Nettie Ann Houser is my real mother?" Horror grasped at Rainey's slim throat and threatened to drag her away from this place of comfort. Her amber eyes grew large.

It had to be, she thought now. She and Nettie Ann did favor a little bit.

Evie's smooth voice pushed away some of the pain that threatened to engulf Rainey, who was a mirror image, most days, of Nettie Ann Houser.

"Yes, sugar, she is the person who brought you into this world . . . ."

For an eternal brief moment, colors shifted and blended together before Rainey's face.

"Oh, no! Mama! Nettie Ann Houser is one of them . . . women! She can't be my mother! She hangs around with bad men, and drinks spirits, and keeps having different babies that don't look alike, and she doesn't keep ANY of her children and --"

"But see," Papa interrupted, rubbing his daughter's hand to calm her. "Out of that bad deed --" his voice faltered ever so slightly -- "your mother -- " nodding his head toward Evie "--and I got you. And you are our daughter, no matter who brought you into the world."

"Yes, baby, Nettie Ann knew we were the best parents for you. That's why she left you on our little porch so we'd find you."

Rainey wanted desperately to stop her ears. First, she had to hear that Nettie Ann Houser, a bad, nasty woman, was her real mother. Then she had to learn that the woman didn't even want to be her mother! It was too much. The dam burst, and tears shot out of Rainey's eyes to flow in torrents down her cheeks.

"Oh, Papa! I don't like that lady. She smells like kerosene, and she is forever wiping her mouth with the back of her hand. She can't be my mama!" The amber eyes pleaded with Rufus to confirm that this was all some wild misunderstanding.

Evie held her daughter and rocked her gently back and forth. Rufus, his face a disturbing Macintosh red once again, rubbed Rainey's back and murmured nonsense sounds to soothe her.

At last, the storm of Rainey's grief subsided. Her eyes grew stony for a moment.

"Well, you'll excuse my saying it, please, but I'm not gonna go live with her, no matter what."

Both her parents gasped. "No! Of course not!"

"She can come see me on my birthday if she wants to, but that's all."

"All right, sugar."

"Because y'all are my parents. Not nobody else."

"That's right, baby."

"May I please be excused to my room?"

Rainey tried not to run out of the room, but she had no choice. She would surely vomit right in front of her parents if she had to stay in the parlor another second. In the newly completed bathroom off the back porch, Rainey slumped against the toilet and wept inconsolably. A most certain footing was now less secure under her feet. Well, she reasoned long after her last hiccupping sob had subsided, at least they weren't going to give her back to Nettie Ann. She could just see herself, forced to live with the likes of Nettie Ann Houser, and having to escort her "mother's" menfolks to her. She'd be forced to baby-sit her little brothers and sisters, whose names she would be incapable of remembering. It would be slavery times all over again. Rainey imagined herself being successful in aiming her mother Evie's spindly legged skillet (appropriately called a "spider") at Nettie Ann's head. She relished the phantom sight of Nettie Ann's head, bashed in and gushing blood as the sorry mother figure sank to the floor, dead as a doornail.

With that thought, Rainey began to giggle sheepishly, almost to the point of hysteria, and, wiping her puffy eyes, she went out to her parents, who waited anxiously in the parlor, and kissed them both.

Coping with the true facts of her parentage would be a long time coming for Rainey Elizabeth Clark. She invited Martha Alice Chestnutt, who had been her best friend since first grade, to be present on her next birthday, and she invited the entire Chestnutt family over to sample her first cake, which she had successfully created with much loving help from Evie. Still, when the knock came at the front door, Rainey felt her heart grow cold. Evie answered the door to admit Nettie Ann Houser, and she, pregnant and almost disarmingly lovely, stepped carefully into the tiny parlor of the Clark home.

"Hey, there," she said to Evie. "Mind if I see the baby?"

The impenetrable fortress around the heart and soul of Rainey, guarded so well by her parents and Uncle Eddie, was completed by a powerful trio: her lifelong best girlfriend, Martha Alice Chestnutt, her cousin Laurence Ragland, and his longsuffering wife, Miriam were guardians of the gates.

Martha Alice Chestnutt was the only girl out of four children, the youngest at that time, and, in her own mind, the least looked after. The first day of school for Martha Alice marked a high point in her lonely life. Here comes this little bouncy girl, an only child with her curly pigtails, to sit beside Martha Alice in Miss Lillie June Peacock's first grade class at Crosby-Garfield School. She looked over at Martha Alice and smiled.

"Hey! My name is Rainey Clark. What's your name?"

"Martha Alice Chestnutt." She felt shy and looked down before she spoke again. "Are you six already?"

"Uh-huh, and I'm gonna be seven in December."

"I'm still five and I won't be six until October," Martha Alice replied mournfully.

"Do you have a big sister," Rainey asked, and Martha Alice shook her head no and felt all alone again. "Well," Rainey said as if it were all settled. "I'll just have to be your big sister, okay?"

"Okay."

They were inseparable from that first day of school; theirs was a bond that was never severed.

More often than not, Martha Alice was big sister and protector to Rainey, whose potentially "smart mouth" could have brewed many episodes of controversy. Martha Alice grew to a commanding height of five-feet-ten inches, towering like a mothering oak over Rainey, who remained a diminutive five-foot-two. This height contrast influenced people's perceptions of the strength of each girl. Ironically, it was Rainey's razor tongue that was more likely to cause trouble, had the opportunity ever arisen. From Rainey, Martha Alice would learn to "dish out trash talk" when she needed to. But folks assumed that Martha Alice's height matched her toughness.

"Rainey Clark, I heard you was half injun," Sadie Burton said to Rainey one afternoon in their third-grade year. Sadie couldn't stand Rainey because she assumed that Rainey "thought she was cute" because of her captivating looks. Sadie's feet, encased in run-over shoes, were itching to kick some part of Rainey Clark's body. Rainey looked at Sadie's paper-bag wrapped plaits and her ashy face. Any number of sharp retorts strutted through her mind in those moments, and her amber eyes sparkled. ("Least I ain't wearin' no grocery bags on my head . . . It don't matter if you use lard or lotion, just grease your ashy face, gal . . . .")

Martha Alice saw that wicked gleam in her friend's eyes and moved closer to her.

"That's right, Sadie Burton. She is half Indian. So?" Martha Alice, who towered over Sadie, too, gulped as quietly as she could; she hated confrontations. Still, she kept her face set in an expression of deadly seriousness. Sadie Burton gulped, too; she didn't want to tangle with Martha Alice Chestnutt.

"I was just askin'," Sadie Burton mumbled, ducking her head and shuffling away from the girls, who giggled quietly as they continued home, mocking Sadie's speech. Little did Sadie Burton know that Martha Alice stood between Rainey and her to protect Sadie – and Rainey – from Rainey's lethal mouth.

Rainey measured all boys (and later, men) by her cousin Laurence, who was a sweet, if slightly jaded reflection of her father: did he work hard? Could he dance like a dream? Could he make a party out of a cup of tea and some toast? Was he kind to his relatives? Was he blessed with sparkling eyes and a slow, easy smile? What about naturally curly hair? (Did he have a wife whom everyone, including Rainey, thought was a saint?) Though he stood five foot seven, Laurence Ragland was the tallest man she knew, next to Papa and Uncle Eddie. Ah, if only . . . .

Laurence, five years Rainey's senior, was Evie's nephew. He had assigned himself the responsibility of acting as Rainey's protector since she could walk, practically. He had been the one to confirm that they were not blood relatives when seven-year-old Rainey had told him 'I love you, Laurence. I want to marry you when I grow up.'

It had been, on her seventeenth birthday, Laurence who showed her how to kiss a boy, about two years too late for them: he was by then married to sweet, docile Miriam.

Miriam wasn't comfortable at the raucous gatherings of the Clark and Ragland families, though she admired the easy, natural liveliness of the active participants. She smiled and laughed as if she were enjoying herself fully.

And of course, there was Rainey.

Laurence was passionately devoted to his "cousin," to whom Miriam knew he was not related by blood. Miriam saw the fire in her husband's eyes each time he looked at Rainey, the light upon his face when he spoke of her. Rainey was fire and light about Laurence, too. What Miriam always saw in Laurence's eyes when he looked at her, his own wife, was respect, slightly detached lust, and fondness, but no passion. There seemed to be no illumination strong enough to blot out the rivulets of flame that passed unconsciously between Miriam's husband and his adopted cousin.

But then, there was really no one quite in Rainey's league, Miriam knew, and she sometimes yearned for that certain inviting quality that Rainey possessed, even in her youthful innocence, which drew everyone to her.   There was no doubt that Rainey was a pretty girl – for she would always be something of a girl in Miriam's eyes – and Miriam was more than a little flattered that people sometimes mistook them for kinswomen.   Yet, Rainey's looks seemed totally unimportant to the beauty herself.   Miriam had likely never met a sweeter person than Rainey.   She'd heard of Rainey's genuine goodness before she had met her.

"Oh, you're gonna love Laurence's family, especially his cousin Rainey," Miriam had been told on more than one occasion. "She's as good as gold . . . She'll do anything to help somebody else . . . She likes everybody . . . She's a funny girl . . . She's a character."

Ironically, Miriam could be counted among those forever devoted to Rainey. She would love Rainey for her entire life for the extra time the younger woman had taken to be kind to her at the beginning of her life with Laurence.   Miriam would never shed the girlish shyness and timidity of her own youth.   She was by nature a quiet woman who, at the beginning of her marriage to Laurence had instantly begun to fade into the background at the rambunctious Clark-Ragland gatherings.   To Miriam's dismay, even the usually retiring Aunt Evie was spiced up and lively at these gatherings.

In the beginning, when she and Laurence were newlyweds, Miriam sat silently in the background during a Ragland family gathering at the home of Laurence's mother. Deborah Ragland grabbed Rainey when she arrived, a white shawl draped neatly over her arm. Deborah hugged Rainey, and then pushed her away, holding the girl by the shoulders as if she wanted to shake some sense into her.

"That's a pretty girl right there!" Deborah Ragland said, smiling lovingly at Rainey.

"Thank you, Aunt Deborah." Rainey smiled and kissed Deborah's cheek.

"But tell me something, Sugar." Deborah put her arm around Rainey's shoulders. Although there was much laughing and talking in the room, Miriam listened carefully for clues about how to talk to her daunting mother-in-law.

"It's hot as the devil outside. How come you always carry that shawl with you?"

Rainey looked at her mother Evie, who had walked in behind her with Rufus. She smiled at her mother, who smiled back and put her hand on Rainey's arm.

"See, Aunt Deborah, Mama gets hot all of a sudden. And she breaks out sweatin'. Then she goes to fanning herself and breathing all funny. So I keep this here shawl with me so I can fan her whenever she needs it." She turned toward her mother Evie and began to fan the shawl at her as if she were a harem girl.

"See?"

"Gal, get on 'way from here," Evie said, her eyes brimming with tears of amusement. "You so silly!" Both Deborah and Evie laughed heartily as they hugged Rainey's shoulders and sent her on her way. Miriam longed to have the nerve to be so funny and lively around these folks.

Later, young Rainey had come to sit next to her.

"Hey, Miriam," Rainey grabbed Miriam's hand that first day and looked at her. "Do you sing?" Rainey's tone was calm and engaging.

"Well, sort of –"

"Alto?"

"Yes, but I –"

"What's your favorite song?"

"Oh, uh –"

"Do you know Amazing Grace?"

"Yes. . ."

"Come sing it with me?"

"Oh no, Rainey! In front of all these people?"

"Oh, Miriam, these are your folks, too! Aren't you and Laurence married now?"

"Well, yes, but --"

"That's right! So, let me tell you a little secret: better make a mark now or they won't notice you later."

Miriam was puzzled.

"You better let 'em know what you can do now so they'll have something to remember you by. You wait too long and try to do something, they'll just look at you like you done gone fool. They'll say, 'Hmmph. That Miriam must-a took herself a beau or something, putting on all them airs and carryin' on.'"

Miriam giggled tentatively as Rainey chuckled. "You want to sing alto with me?"

"Okay!"

"Come on!"

Miriam's voice had faltered a bit at first; she'd never sung before Laurence. But soon, with guidance from Rainey's powerful soprano and beautiful piano playing, Miriam's voice grew wondrously strong.

From that gathering on, the Clarks and Raglands remembered that "sweet Miriam sure can sing."

Rufus Clark had come so very far from his 1899 self, when his loins seemed heated to the temperature of molten lava. Once he understood that God and Evie had forgiven him for his indiscretion, that Rainey really could stay with them, and that Eddie Houser had no intention of maiming him with those hands that could crush the skull of a hog with the ease of a finger snap, Rufus settled into his role as provider.

Rainey could depend on his greeting to her when he returned from his run on the Raleigh & Gaston Railroad. Evie and Rainey managed always to be in the kitchen, which was at the back of the house, when Rufus returned. Each time, he burst into the front door, and called out:

"Evie! Rainey! You don't know who's here, do you?"

"Now, let me think. It ain't my bee-eyed sweetie, is it?"

"Mama, do you think Papa sent somebody else to live with us?"

"Well, I don't care about that. All I want to know is, did he bring us a coconut sweet?"

At that Rufus burst into the kitchen, and laughing loudly, picked up his wife first, and then his daughter, as if he had been away at sea for years, rather than on the railroad for three nights. Then he showered them with their favorite sweet coconut candies. Life with Rufus was that way; he insisted on making their family life wholly pleasant and joyous. Even during that difficult time later when he disagreed with Rainey over what college she would attend, he insisted that she understand that he loved her and wanted what was best for her.

She watched her father crush her dreams under the weight of his well-meaning caution: she wanted to go to Nashville to be among the famous Fisk Jubilee Singers. No, that was just too far away; what if something happened on the road? She compromised. What about the nearly as famous Hampton Singers? Now everybody knew that Hampton was a port for lusty sailors and soldiers with just one thing on their minds. Why, wasn't Fort Monroe practically in Hampton's backyard? Besides, hadn't he been hearing reports of Klansmen attacking poor helpless colored folks on the roads between Raleigh and Hampton?

Okay, then, Papa, she reasoned with him, I'll go to Shaw University. She bit back a harsh question: now, what's wrong with Shaw? Rufus could think of no appropriate protest to this request. From their house on the corner of East and Worth Streets, they could see the campus on its princely hill. Shaw was bordered on its east side by Person Street, which intersected with Worth Street, and South Street, which was at the other corner of their block. On a leisurely walk down Worth Street, Shaw University was about three minutes away from the little house they had called home since Rainey's fifth year.

So she, along with Martha Alice, started at Shaw University, and those first few weeks weren't so bad after all. The music professors were really skilled and the choirs were quite good. She even got a couple of solos during her first two months in school. She was meeting interesting young men, some of whom were like Laurence, and some of whom were either hideously unlike him or surprisingly more exotic. These young men were law students, medical students, or divinity students. She even dated one incredibly handsome law student on several afternoons – when Rufus was on the rails, of course -- but William Davis was just too serious for her immature nature. A date for William was a church concert, or on rare occasions, attendance at the speech of some great Negro leader or other with an early dinner afterwards at the Arcade Hotel's restaurant. While she was mightily impressed by the ease with which he escorted her around black Raleigh, her assessment of their dates was a shrug and a yawn.

She settled into her life as a college student, and she helped to pay for her books and sheet music by working a few hours a day at Barbour's grocery store on Bloodworth Street at Worth Street, which connected directly to the back of Shaw University. Her life, except for her occasional dates, was confined to a straight path up and down Worth Street.

Suddenly, a major foundation crumbled beneath Rainey's delicate feet.

Rufus Clark was often away as a porter on the Raleigh & Gaston Railroad line, and when the influenza epidemic of '18 started, Rainey would later think, he was bound to catch it. But she never expected him to die from it. And the end came so quickly: he came home from his normal run of three nights out, and when Evie and Rainey ran to him to greet him, he held out his hands to stop them.

"I've got it," he said weakly, his sallow face flushed, his gray eyes a watery and feverish red.

"I've got the influenza. I've got to get to a bed."

The two women nursed him diligently. They sent for Dr. Chestnutt, Martha Alice's father, who rushed to the Clark home, Martha Alice at his elbow, to examine Rufus. He came away from Rufus's sickbed with a grimness that he had quickly acquired over these last few months, having seen so many people fall victim to this dreaded disease.

Dr. Chestnutt pulled his surgical mask wearily from his lean face, and then slowly removed his gloves. He sighed.

"You all need to give him plenty of liquids to drink, and be sure to wash his linens and glasses in the hottest water you can, because he is very contagious."

Evie, usually calm, was as agitated as she ever got. "What must we do, Doc Chestnutt?"

"Is he gonna get well?" Rainey chimed.

"See, that's all a matter of chance right now. He's mighty sick, and we'll do all we can, but we got no guarantees that he'll make it. It's going to take time, and a lot of prayer. I'll be back in the morning to check on him."

But Rufus didn't make it through the night. His fever climbed higher, sending him into delirium. Rainey ran frantically to Dr. Chestnutt's house just a few blocks away down Person Street. Dr. Chestnutt listened intently to the symptoms that Rainey recited to him, and called for an ambulance from Saint Agnes Hospital to get Rufus to the hospital immediately. By the time Rainey and the doctor returned to the Clark house, Rufus's body was in total rebellion: his diarrhea was completely out of control, he was vomiting bile, and sweating as if water were being poured onto his body. Evie calmly cleaned Rufus after each bout of sickness, patting his hand and murmuring soothing words to him.

Rainey fought fiercely against her own hysteria as she worked with her mother to comfort her father in what were to be his final hours. She sang his favorite spirituals to him in her smooth, powerful voice, and he seemed calmed by the sounds. Rainey worked hard not to think of all the wonderful years she had had with her father, tried not to remember the ways he had always let her know he treasured her.

Dr. Chestnutt was outside Rufus's room now, waiting anxiously for the ambulance to arrive. When the ambulance finally struggled up East Street, on a flat tire, Rufus Clark had taken his final breath ten minutes before this so-called help arrived. Evie and Rainey let loose the wrenching hysteria that both had held at bay during these terrible hours leading up to Rufus's death. Dr. Chestnutt administered a weak dosage of laudanum to both women to calm them, but even then, when the ambulance attendants put Rufus's emaciated body on the trundle, the women threw themselves across his lifeless form to prevent his being taken away. Gradually, though, they resigned themselves to his death. Instead of holding on to his corpse, they held on to each other, clung also to Martha Alice, and, by now, cousin Laurence, as the ancient ambulance rumbled away to Mr. Doll Haywood's Raleigh Funeral Home.

Rainey would always feel the chill of unreality that illuminated the wake or "sitting up" at their little house three nights later. All that was left of her beloved father lay in a solemn pine casket, his cheeks afire with rouge to cover up the sunken, emaciated state of his face, his gaunt torso encased in his only suit, a slightly frayed black jacket and pants with a frequently boiled shirt his to wear through eternity. Mr. Doll brought two gaslight torchieres to place at either end of the casket, and the surreal, upward slant of their lights bathed the tiny parlor in an eerie golden light. Rainey felt lightheaded, seeing the world go slightly beige in front of her. She didn't take her eyes from the coffin that night. It was as if she alone could guard all that was left of him in this world. Next to Rainey and Evie sat Rufus's two sisters, who had traveled in separate train cars and in separate taxicabs to Rufus's house.

Adele Clark Connelly, a willowy woman who seemed custom-built for a life as the wife of a Washington banker, had temporarily forsaken her plush life as a white woman to mourn her only brother's passing. Tears flowed unchecked from her gray eyes as she rested her head on the pillowy shoulder of her baby sister, Mittie Clark Gaines, a powerful merchant in Georgetown's Negro community. A substantial woman in bulk and the local power she wielded, Mittie Gaines patted her weeping sister's damp hand and stared fiercely at her brother's casket – as if, a bemused Rainey would later reflect, she dared him to stay dead.

Directly behind them sat Rainey's guardian angels, her cousin Laurence Ragland and his wife Miriam.   And then there was, as always, Martha Alice Chestnutt, ever a solace to Rainey.

All through that grueling night, church members, neighbors, and friends walked up to the casket, a few murmuring about how "good" Rufus looked,   paid their respects to Evie, and squeezed Rainey's shoulders or kissed her feverish cheek.   She responded by rote, mustering all the genteel politeness she could into each greeting. Toward the end of the sitting up, she heard someone singing quietly, almost as an undertone,

Blessed assurance, Jesus is mine.

Oh what a foretaste of glory divine.

Heir of salvation, purchase of God.

Born of his spirit, washed in His blood.

Gradually, she felt her own lips moving, realized that she was the lone singer.   She squeezed her eyes shut and put the entire force of her powerful lungs behind:

This is my story, this is my song!

Praising my savior all the day long!

The second time she sang "This is," she lifted her voice to a grand height and held the "is," remembering that her father liked to hear her sing it that way.   She sang clearly through her tears, raising her hands in supplication to her Savior for His help.   By the time she sang I in my Savior am happy and blest, those sisters from the church who were so inclined launched into their familiar shouting routine.   And on the final chorus, all the mourners joined in with her.   But it was her power that carried them on home –

Praising my Savior all the day long.

-- and carried her through the night.   She forgot to be angry with that same Savior for taking her father away from her.   She could only remember that Rufus got a peculiar look of pride and awe on his face when she sang. Everyone else appreciated her voice, and leaned forward expectantly to hear her sing, but Rufus seemed to hear something more in her voice. Whether it was the gift he felt she had, or just an overabundant fatherly pride, she sang only to him and in memory of him on that night of the "sitting up."

After she was finished, Rainey felt like a soaked dish rag. She had no more strength. She moved to the chair closest to the casket and sat down heavily. Mr. Doll and his assistant came to close the casket then, and she felt an ecstasy of hysterical grief come over her. Martha Alice, her life's protector, helped her to her tiny bedroom when she became unable to stand the sight of her father being closed away. She forgot to comfort her mother, or to say goodbye to their visitors. Laurence and Martha Alice assumed those duties. (It had, after all, always been Martha Alice and Laurence who stood between her and the dangers, toils, and snares of the outside world.)

Rainey cried herself to sleep that night.

Evie was much like a glassy-eyed doll throughout those terrible days. It was as if she were also dead. Rainey remembered reaching out to comfort her mother and was alarmed that her mother was now completely out of her reach. Later, Rainey understood that her mother Evie had already left her at that point, never to return.

At her father's funeral, Rainey felt no hesitation in setting things right with Nettie Ann Houser, who was sprawled at the back of the sanctuary, veiled in blue, weeping in a blubbery haze of gin and self-pity. At her mother Evie's side, Rainey paused to glare at Nettie Ann, this woman who had granted her life, blessed her with beauty, and who had offered her nothing beyond her genetic contributions to her existence.

"Stop it," Rainey hissed at that moment, shocked within herself at her own audacity. And Nettie Ann stopped, her eyes going wide with surprise. "Just stop it." Rainey walked on, never looking back, dismissing Nettie Ann from her fevered mind.

Rainey pulled herself back together and returned to school. She spent her (daytime) free time studying diligently and tending to her mother, who, though calm on the outside, had apparently not returned from that netherland of grief. She simply collapsed inside. During those daylight hours, Rainey found herself mothered by her own Martha Alice, her confidante, comforter, and shelter from the stormy shards of grief that were liable to pelt her fiercely at any time.

Still, Rainey, in the throes of a hell-raising streak she'd inherited directly from her mother Nettie Ann, managed to sneak out to a weekly speakeasy party after she'd made sure her mother Evie was comfortable -- and sound asleep -- for the night. She tended to be well known at several of the jumpingest juke joints in colored Raleigh. As the daughter of a dearly departed preaching deacon and his grieving widow, she honed to a fine art her sunlight role as a demure lady; however, as that hell-raising ingenue by moonlight, she did her exploring incognito, usually in the company of her cousin Laurence, who was a surprisingly clean-cut devotee of the jaded nightlife.

Laurence loved to sneak away from Miriam -- who wouldn't dare cabaret on any day of the week -- and go dancing. Inevitably, Rainey was his dance hall partner after her father died. She loved the way they would slink out of their houses and meet at a certain spot to, as Laurence put it, "light out for the territories." (He was a big reader of Mark Twain, and so of course Rainey – like Miriam before her -- become an avid Twain reader, too.)

Rainey often donned a pair of her Papa's work pants and a work shirt, shrugging away her tendency to fantasize that he was truly spinning in his grave over the current occupation of those clothes. With Laurence as her escort, she eased about town to check out the sights at the joints and liquor houses that thrived in the underbellies of South Park and Fourth Ward.

More and more over the next three years, Evie sat in their tiny parlor staring at the front door of their little house as if she expected Rufus to come in from work. At night, Evie slept with alarming soundness, never budging from one position from 10:00 at night until about 7:00 the next morning. The only spark of life Evie showed in those last days was during Rainey and Martha Alice's graduation from Shaw University in May of 1922, when mother and daughter clung to each other, weeping for joy and sorrow at this great occasion. She had even shown genuine joy at Martha Alice's wedding, the following Saturday, to Arthur "Red Art" Seaton, a barber who already owned his own shop across from the University. After those glorious and triumphant May afternoons, Evie's gradual fading sped downward into a rapid decline. She faded away until by late June there was literally nothing left of her but a fragile shell of a woman.

And so Evie, too, passed out of Rainey's young life.

At first, Mittie Clark Gaines had not approved of Rufus marrying such a sooty black stupid - looking gal as Evie Ragland. But in very little time she had come to respect Evie as a loyal and steadfast wife to her brother. Gradually Mittie had grown to like Evie as an industrious and kind person in her own right. Finally, understanding all that Evie had suffered during the years before Rufus's conversion, Mittie grew to love her, although the love was tainted with pity and more than a little guilt about her first opinion of the woman. She knew that she never could have tolerated her husband trying to pass off his love child as a "foundling." Every time she thought of Rufus trying to pretend Rainey was somebody else's child, she snorted contemptuously; he could have spat Rainey out, they looked so much alike.

Now, as Mittie came home to Raleigh for the funeral of her sister-in-law, she thought only of her niece's welfare. (Addie Rose, who had been widowed just one year after Rufus's death, begged to be excused from making the trip. She felt too "blue" to travel.) Mittie brought her own thriving enterprises to a halt so that she could see to her niece. Rainey and Mittie were virtual strangers, but Rainey asked Mittie if she could live with her in Washington for a while. Mittie, only too eager to act as a mentor, agreed with Rainey so quickly that both women were startled.

Later, Mittie wondered how her business would be affected by this sweet bumpkin's presence, but decided that, as the boss in her own home, she would handle any changes that came their way.

With Martha Alice's solemn help, they closed up the little yellow cottage on East Street.

Rainey walked across the newly paved road to say good-bye to Mr. Doll Haywood and his family, then up the street to the Harrisses to bid them farewell. Neighbors up and down the block stepped out on their porches to wish her well, and to help Mittie and Rainey load their suitcases into the backseat and trunk of beloved cousin Laurence's ancient jitney.

Miriam stood tearfully by, her cherubic face softened in sentimental misery. Meanwhile Martha Alice, with her new husband, Arthur "Red Art" Seaton, hugged Rainey tightly, told her she'd better write every week. Both women tried to smile at each other as they said good-bye. Rainey's farewell to Laurence at the train station was outwardly restrained. Inside, she was a screaming, hysterical mess. When will I see dear Laurence again? Will I ever meet anyone like him who can be just for me?

Soon, the two Clark kinswomen, aunt and "foundling," and their legion of luggage, boarded the train bound for the nation's capitol and what would be for Rainey a new and uncertain life in Washington, DC.

Goodbye, Raleigh! Goodbye, Martha Alice! Goodbye, Laurence (and Miriam)!

1960

Rainey walked slowly up the back stairs of their beach house, slamming the door behind her. She collapsed on one of their prized Adirondacks, all the strength drained from her. She sat, breathing heavily, until she could handle the intensity of the beach memories. She had to force out other more poignant memories. They would have to wait for another time. She could feel them, and all her grief, jockeying for position inside her damaged psyche: there was anger, there was despair, and there were so very many questions. She had held so much of her emotion back for so long, trying to be strong for her husband and for her children. She had not yet screamed the scream that was tearing at her insides. She had worked off some of the anger when she ... when she ...

Part One: To Dream Of The Stars

1922 - 1925

The heart of a woman goes forth with the dawn,
As a lone bird, soft winging, so restlessly on,
Afar o'er life's turrets and vales does it roam
In the wake of those echoes the heart calls home.

The heart of a woman falls back with the night,
And enters some alien cage in its plight,
And tries to forget it has dreamed of the stars
While it breaks, breaks, breaks on the sheltering bars.

-- Georgia Douglass Johnson▲

―――――――――――――

▲ *Johnson, Georgia Douglass. The Heart of A Woman and Other Poems. Boston: Cornhill Co.,*

1918.

1960

She had left Raleigh a little girl lost, desperate to reclaim the love that she believed had abandoned her when her parents died. Right now, today, she still felt the bottomless emptiness of her soul on that day she moved to Washington with Aunt Mittie. She shivered and draped a light blanket around her shoulders, grateful that she kept several blankets in plastic in a storage bin on their screened porch. She sat back against the wooden slats of the Adirondack.

Step Herndon cakewalked across her mind now, and she squeezed her eyes shut. He would haunt her forever, she supposed, though he had been a barely visible spectre in her life all these years. Until now.

Seagulls cried, and waves crashed. Before her now, all she could see was her time in Washington, and she searched for clues from that time to help her understand why her life had taken her onto such a desolate path.

Chapter One

Going Forth With The Dawn

Smudges of an unusual mid-July rain wiped querulously across the blackened train window, leaving behind pellets of sharp, icy water. Rainey pulled her shawl close about her shoulders and turned her back to the onslaught. Beside her on the aisle seat, Aunt Mittie slept soundly, and loudly. For a gloomy moment, Rainey gazed into Mittie's round pale face, so like her Papa's face. Even after four years, the sting of his death was a keen prick at her heart. Poor Papa! He worked so hard and loved them so deeply right up to the end. And now Mama was gone; she had just pined away after Rufus's death.

At 22, Rainey was an orphan.

In this odd July, when Rainey no longer had a _real_ parent to call her own, Aunt Mittie rescued her from the little house on East Street where she had spent her happy, formative years as the apple of her parents' eyes. Now they were both gone, and she couldn't imagine feeling more lonely.

Looking across the expanse of the years, Rainey understood now, as she gazed unseeing out the sooty window, that her mother's heart had simply ceased to beat regularly after her father's death. She grieved quietly, feeling tears itch down her face.

Even Uncle Eddie couldn't fulfill the role of parent.

Rainey sighed. She knew she would be forever grateful to Uncle Eddie for his love, his patience, his financial support, and perhaps especially, his ability to help her remain respectful toward her biological mother in the face of sometimes overwhelming evidence that she may have deserved a swift kick in the hips.

When Evie died, Eddie promised Rainey that he would find a house where they both could live, or he would even stay there on East Street with her.

But Rainey was ready to go somewhere new, perhaps explore the teeming night life of a new, larger city.

So she had readily agreed that she should go to live in Washington with Aunt Mittie and her husband Mason Gaines. "That's a good place for colored folks to be right now, child," Mittie told her as they dismantled the household of Rainey's youth. And Rainey paraphrased those same words to Uncle Eddie as she sadly explained to him her decision to move away from Raleigh. He was devastated by her decision (did he, perhaps, feel slightly betrayed?), but agreed that she should probably go live with Mittie. Rainey could see his tear-filled eyes now in the grimy glass before her. She turned away from the window, once again, and stared at her aunt, this stranger with whom she shared family ties.

She thought fleetingly of her beloved Laurence, and quickly pushed him away from the bloom of her internal vision. She forced her higher mind to chant: He is my cousin, he was Mama Evie's nephew, he is my cousin . . . .

The ragged, bumpy little car had a moldy taint to it, and the smell made Rainey feel slightly sick to her stomach. The rainy weather had heightened the dank odor so that it nearly overpowered her. She knew they had to be pulling into Union Station soon. She asked the conductor the time on each of his trips past her tattered seat. After her seventh query, he rolled his eyes heavenward in mock exasperation and smiled kindly at her as he answered her unspoken question. The conductor, James Estes, reminded Rainey of her father, paternal and protective. She would never know that to him she was an erotic dream that he dare not fulfill. After all, as he was painfully aware, this little dream's father, the unforgettable Rufus Clark, had been James's mentor when he had begun his career on the N&O in 1903.

It would have to be Mittie Clark Gaines guarding this beauty. James Estes knew that damage could surely be done to him through the female incarnation of Rufus Clark who sat, with watchdog intensity even in sleep, next to Rainey. James Estes shuddered when he thought of the fact that Mittie didn't need a bouncer to protect her interest in her basement. She could whip the ass off any man, no matter how tall, wide, or strong he was. Estes knew enough of Mittie Clark's history to know that she was actually more of a guardian hellion than a guardian angel.

And now she's going around calling herself Mittie Clark Gaines, he sniffed derisively. Estes had known Mittie since she had moved to Washington in the mid - nineties. He knew good and damn well that Mittie wasn't any more married to her "husband" than she was to the chair in which she slept so loudly. But he humored her anyway; it was the lesser of two evils. If he didn't call her Mrs. Gaines or Mittie Gaines, she would lay a cursing on him that would put a soldier to shame. Only now when she cursed someone out, she spoke quietly and smiled with genteel grace as she carefully pronounced every syllable and inflection of every filthy word that sprung forth from her elegantly painted mouth. James also knew that Mittie Clark -- Mittie Gaines's -- left hook was about as deadly as Jack Johnson's.

Unlike her older brother, Mittie Clark Gaines didn't use the Bible as her guide. Estes did know, just like anybody else who spent any time in DC, that Mittie's basement was the place to be after hours if you wanted some good hooch.

Estes glared at Mittie's round mound of a body, being careful in his self-righteousness not to remember the intimate pleasure of her company in his bed not too many years ago. He wondered if she let her Georgetown neighbors know that she actually dipped stuff. He doubted it, and sniffed at Mittie Clark Gaines's bulk as if she had a foul odor about her, though he admitted grudgingly to himself that Mittie Clark Gaines's hair looked mighty fine. She had one of those pineapple bobs, and it fit even her big face with an easy elegance. The chic "v" cut at the nape of her neck almost hid the roll of fat beneath it.

Rainey's stiffly straightened hair clung tightly to her scalp and then cascaded to her shoulder blades in careful, slightly greasy waves. He noted with disdain that even down South they had discovered the process of the straightening comb and the marcel iron. He understood that women wanted to straighten those naps; he just didn't like the way they smashed their hair to their skulls like they wanted to pretend it didn't belong to them or something.

Despite her unfortunate hairstyle, the pretty young Clark girl had an engaging speaking voice. The few times he had heard Rainey speak, Estes felt as if his ears had been unstopped to hear sweet, flowing melodies from a fountain of sound. Rainey Clark had obviously been educated somewhere in the ghastly terrain of the South. In sharp contrast to many of the other passengers, she formed every syllable impeccably, and the clear enunciation of the words enhanced the refined lilt of her drawl. She smiled politely at him each time she spoke to him, looking directly into his red-threaded eyes with her potent amber ones. Those eyes were the showcase of a face frosted in pale caramel beauty. Estes noted with shivering pleasure the smooth and kissable lips, the glow that came off the flawless skin like radiant beams of sunlight. Like her aunt, Rainey was short, probably about five-foot-two or so, but she had quite a petite and inviting figure, unlike Mittie, who now seemed to Estes to be dumpy and greasy looking – except for her magnificent hair.

In the early morning hours of this trip, Rainey was reading a newspaper voraciously. She stopped to ponder the implications interwoven throughout the words she had just read. She stared out the window, its pane, like the others, stained with coal soot, and thought about how the world events of 1922 might affect her own quest for freedom -- to sing, to dance, and to cabaret as she pleased.

Above all, she wanted to be in a place where she would be able to hone her craft as a singer. It wasn't so much that she was keenly interested in the world's goings-on; she wanted all obstacles to her search for singing fame to be removed.

Rainey set foot in a Washington, DC mud puddle and the event pretty much marked her life there for the next three years. Rainey's cotton stockings were soaked and they sagged off her puny calves, but her spirit was unbroken. Mittie, a stout, sallow-faced woman, more honeydew than lemon in complexion, patted her pineapple bob into place and stifled a yawn as she waddle-stepped off the train behind Rainey. A dainty protrusion to the right side of her mouth was lessened when she spat priggishly into a small cup she kept stashed in the recesses of her cavernous carpetbag purse. While Rainey looked around the Union Station platform in quiet awe, Mittie Clark Gaines stepped to the end of the platform and emptied the contents of her cup onto the rails. She wiped the inside of the cup with an old handkerchief, and stuffed the emptied cup into her purse. She grabbed Rainey by the elbow to steer her to the inside of the station.

"Lord, seemed like we wouldn't ever get here!" ("Get here" was only slightly audible as "getchair.")

"Yes, ma'am, it's good to be off that train."

Despite her muddy, soaked stockings, Rainey was thrilled to be in Washington. People hustled past her, and she enjoyed the feeling that she was a part of the throng that was surging forward into the heart of the city. Never before in the little capital city of Raleigh had Rainey seen so much life, felt so much vitality. Finally, Mittie and Rainey arrived at the front of the station, where all manner of automobiles and more horse-drawn carriages than she had expected to see zipped or trotted past them. Taxi drivers leapt from their vehicles. "Taxi, lady? Taxi?" But each time, Mittie shook her head. Rainey was too thrilled by all the activity to care that the dampness was beginning to seep into her skin. For the first time since she had buried her mother two weeks earlier, Rainey felt hopeful, as if she could count on becoming a singer even south of New York, where all singers ought to be.

Right in front of her, a young man did an elaborate step. (He danced like a dream!) He had the deepest waves in his hair she had ever seen. (What about that naturally curly hair!) His (sparkling) brown eyes never left her awestruck amber ones as he tapped, stepped, swirled, and dipped through the drizzle, finally executing a modified cake walk toward the two women. Finally, this dynamo swooped into a stylized bow, sweeping his arm before him. Delighted, Rainey clapped her hands together. A smile dawned across the dancer's face, slow and easy. (Where was that tea and toast?)

Aunt Mittie's hunk of a hand snatched at Rainey's bony forearm. The pursed-lip look of admonition on her face pushed the girl into confused silence.

"Cab, Miss Mittie?" The young man spoke in stylized, cultured tones. He was the most enchanting harlequin of a man she'd ever seen.

"Yes, Step, and kindly stop all that showing off to my niece." Mittie was a stylization, too. Rainey looked at her sharply. As they had traveled up from Raleigh, her aunt had spoken in a decidedly less clipped dialect.

"Yes, Lawd, yo' papa was som'n else in his day, gal," she confided to Rainey at one point. "He needed to preach 'n' carry on, cause he was fixin' to buss hell wide open if he didn't." Amused, Rainey snickered to herself and shook her head now as she listened to the contrast.

"And just who is this vision of a niece?" Step said, averting his crimson-threaded eyes from Rainey in mock humility.

"Never mind, boy. She is weary and we need to go to my house. Now."

"Yowsuh, boss," Step muttered, being careful that Rainey, not Mittie, caught his sarcasm. "Q Street here we come!" Rainey's little bumpkin heart swelled as "Step" deftly transferred her damp carpet bags into the back seat and trunk of a jalopy that had fought more than a few battles in Washington traffic. The two women sat up front with Step, and Mittie made sure she sat between the dandified driver and her niece.

The seating arrangement was fine with Rainey. When she wasn't stealing glances at Step Herndon, she was looking at this new hometown of hers. All around her, the city rushed: cars puttering to and fro, folks bustling along on sidewalks, their faces set in stone-faced determination. Here at an intersection, a car had given up the ghost, and other drivers behind it honked their comical horns impatiently. While their car was stuck in the merging traffic next to the car, Rainey got a good look at what was going on. Oblivious to the confusion he had caused, the driver leaned under the hood, his face fully submerged in the thick white fog that emerged from the ailing car. He rubbed at his chin, a professor at work on a complex problem, and laid his hand on his belt to contemplate the dilemma. Finally, the exasperated driver directly behind the car threw open his car door and stomped up to the preoccupied driver. They began to talk animatedly, and finally the driver of the dead car pushed the second driver. Rainey never saw how it all turned out; traffic up ahead finally began to move off.

Far off on the horizon, Rainey could see the Washington Monument. Her heart jumped. Hadn't she heard of that place all her life and seen only drawings of it? She realized that those drawings could not capture the majesty of the building itself. She told herself that she would go to see the genuine article as soon as possible. The cab made a sharp right turn, sending its occupants leaning into each other. And suddenly, on the right, was the White House! Rainey gasped; in all her bumpkinish awe, she didn't expect to see the White House on the very first day she arrived.

"Goodness," she exclaimed now, and Step and Mittie chuckled softly, remembering their own first days in Washington.

By the time the motorcar sputtered up to the curb of Mittie's Q Street rowhouse, Rainey found herself fully smitten with Step Herndon.

When he could finally talk to Rainey away from Mittie's earshot, he told her that he was 26 and a South Carolina native. He had been in Washington for about five years, he told her, trying to make a name for himself as a dancer while working as a driver and a runner for Miss Mittie in order to save up for that big move north to Harlem. "'Cause if you plannin' to be in the business, you gotta plan on being where the business is," he explained broadly to Rainey despite Mittie's icy scowl toward him. Rainey only giggled a little. She was awestruck. She could also tell he found her to his liking. She decided that he would be her first date in Washington.

He wasted no time in making sure they had that date, and he spoke to her in his best po' suthun boy drawl to prove his sincerity. They were in Mittie's foyer, and Step was about to move their luggage to their respective bedrooms. Rainey was speechless at the opulence of the place: white wallpaper with raised curlicues; rich mahogany chair rails and crown molding; Persian rug on a dazzling dark wood floor; Louis XVI loveseat on one side of the wide mahogany staircase and a Queen Anne table on the other. Step's honey-dipped voice pulled her slowly out of her trance as she stared up at the five-tiered crystal chandelier that hung, peacock proud, from the twelve-foot ceiling.

"Mason, honey," Mittie called out in a voice that was suddenly dipped in essence of gardenia. "We're home! We'll be down in a few minutes!"

Rainey followed Mittie upstairs to her new bedroom, a gorgeous baby blue chamber with a bay window seat, high ceiling, and a four-poster bed. She was there, mouth agape the whole time, long enough to wash up and change out of her muddy, travel - soiled clothes.

She and Mittie met at the base of the stairs. Mittie wore a beautiful purple silk kimono and some soft slippers to match. Rainey's buttery yellow outfit was identical to Mittie's.

Piano music wafted up to greet her at her heels from some mysterious source below her. She could feel it tinkling at the soles of her feet, warming her legs. The tune was not remotely familiar to her, and it captivated her. It was delicate and fleeting, like the tantalizing aroma of cinnamon buns cooling at Mr. Jiggetts's bakery back home. Rainey thought of white lace curtains billowing softly against a sweet breeze into a sun-drowned white room, a room with dazzling hardwood floors, bookshelves, and lush plants --

Rainey's reverie was postponed when Uncle Mason rushed down a long hallway to greet them now, his eyes alight with joy at seeing his Mittie after so long.

As Mittie and Mason embraced now in the foyer, Step got his mo-jo to working on Rainey.

Aunt Mittie spoke into a mesh-covered hole cut into the side of the grand staircase. "Reeves," she said. "Come meet my niece."

"Say, Miss Rainey," Step began, moving closer to Rainey with a flourish of decorum. "How'd you like to see me dance after you get yourself settled in? Now Miss Mittie, don't say nothing. Let the girl make up her own mind. She grown, ain't she? You know where I dance ain't nowhere but up the street to Boney's. So what do you say, ma'am?"

"Well," Rainey began, and allowed her thick eyelashes to brush against her high cheeks. "If you keep calling me 'ma'am' I'm going to feel like an old maid. But I would like to see you dance. When?" Rainey blushed at the eagerness that forced that last word out of her mouth, but she ignored Mittie's nudge.

Mason stepped between Rainey and Step, and handed Rainey a neatly folded piece of lavender stationery. Rainey turned aside to read Mason's note, and blushed with grief – tinged emotion and a dollop of irony; she still had one mother left yet.

Dear Rainey:

Your aunt and I are very glad to have you come live with us. We want you to feel right at home. We both love you already. I was looking through my poetry books (you will find me in the library whenever I am at home but missing), and I found this poem by Thomas Hardy. I do not want to make you sad, but I do want you to know that I understand what you are facing now.

To An Orphan Child
A Whimsey
Ah, child, thou art but half thy darling mother's;
Hers couldst thou wholly be,
My light in thee would outglow all in others;
She would relive in me.
But niggard Nature's trick of birth
Bars, lest she over joy,
Renewal of the loved on earth
Save with alloy.

The Dame has no regard, alas, my maiden,
For love and loss like mine –
No sympathy with mind-sight memory laden;
Only with fickle eyne ♦.
To her mechanic artistry
My dreams are all unknown,
Any why I wish that thou couldst be
But One's alone!

Dear young niece, I think the poet wants to express, as I do, his sorrow about a young lady who has lost her mother at such a tender age. I wish things for you had been different, and that your mother had not been taken from you in your youth. Even though I do not speak, please feel free to talk with me. I will listen carefully to everything you say, and I will offer my guidance on paper. Yours truly, Uncle Mason, your "father" in Georgetown

Rainey smiled (she had to find a dictionary quickly; what kind of word is niggard she wondered, amused and perturbed) and hugged Uncle Mason from behind as he hugged Aunt Mittie. She was, for just a fleeting moment, a

---

♦ The old English word for "eyes."

little girl again, turning her parents' romantic moment into a family gathering.

From an oak door, also cut into the side of the grand staircase, an odd-looking man appeared before them. He wore a starched white shirt that was buttoned to its top, leather suspenders, and high-waisted black trousers. His skin was sallow and pockmarked, and somehow the cigar he chewed made his huge eyes seem bigger. He was bald, with sparse remains of hair around his ears and above his neck. Rainey couldn't tell how old a man he was, but she was struck by his delicate hands, which rested patiently in front of him. The nails were neatly clipped and filed, the cuticles were pushed back, and the skin on those hands looked soft, despite the network of veins rippling just below their surface.

He was Joseph Reeves, who, at 34, had been in Washington for 15 years. His gig as a pianist in the Gaines's "other business concern" was but a part-time fulfillment of his lifelong passion for music played well. He was a full-time butcher at a popular Georgetown slaughter shop, and he was most proud of the fact that he was a local officer in Marcus Garvey's United Negro Improvement Association. He was also proud of his wife's association with the Movement. Her father, Curtis Thornhill, was a high officer in the national Association.

He smiled expectantly at the Gaineses and their niece. Rainey thought she noticed the slightest scowl when the man's eyes chanced across Step Herndon. Had Step moved every so slightly behind Rainey when everyone turned toward the oak door?

Aunt Mittie motioned for the man to come toward them. Uncle Mason motioned everyone into the parlor at the foot of the grand staircase. Rainey was enchanted. This "parlor," which her aunt considered small, was twice the size of her parlor back home. It was adorned in pale yellow wallpaper, and it had eight sides. Its ceiling was, like the foyer's, twelve feet high, and the chandelier that cascaded downward from its flawless ceiling was fabulously draped in crystal, or something like it. The door of the parlor was at an angle and had a small wall to itself. To the left of the door an upright piano waited, its surface alive with the cool gleam that accompanies many hours of loving care. A banker's lamp sat at the ready atop the piano, but a doilie separated its base from the piano's surface. (Rainey noticed that doilies were abundant throughout this room, a touch that seemed both excessive and pleasing to her eyes.) To the right of the door was a captivating fireplace with a marble mantle. Above that mantle was a smoky mirror built into the wall, and, above it, yet another mantelpiece, this one also of marble. Directly across from the fireplace, heavy summer air oozed into a floor-to-ceiling bay window set deep into the wall behind a cushioned window seat. A Queen Anne couch sat regally to the left of the bay window, and on the other side of the window, another Queen Anne held court. On either side of each Queen Anne couch, tiny tables, doilies dripping from them, sat waiting to hold the beverages of guests. At the small wall to the right of the first Queen Anne couch were Aunt Mittie's treasured brick-a-brack shelves. To the left of the second Queen Anne were another three windows through which summer breezes wandered absently. At the floor was a burgundy, blue, and gold Oriental rug that added a dazzling contrast to the sedate and elegant room. Rainey knew she would spend most of her time here after she'd gotten settled in.

When they were all seated (Step stood awkwardly by the parlor door), Mittie said:

"This is my little niece I was telling you about. Rainey Clark, meet Joe Reeves. He plays piano for us part-time. This gal can sing, Reeves. You'll want to hear her sometime."

Rainey stood and offered her hand to Reeves, who rushed to receive it. His palm was as soft as the kid leather gloves her mother had gotten one Christmas from one of her "boss ladies."

"Hello, Mr. Reeves. You play mighty nice."

"Thank you, sweetheart. Friends call me Joe. And since you're Miz Gaines's niece, you're a friend." This time Rainey knew Joe Reeves looked pointedly at Step Herndon, who blushed and looked closely at the curlicues in the pale yellow wallpaper.

Rainey was enchanted by Joe Reeves's rough voice. It was gravelly and smoky and welcoming. Fatherly. She liked Joe Reeves.

"You know," Joe Reeves was saying now. "I got a little niece about your age. She's been like a sister to me." In front of her and to the right, Step Herndon stood awkwardly at the parlor door. Suddenly he was a connoisseur of fine furnishings as he perused the silk wingback chairs, the marble front fireplace, the tiered chandelier, the Chinese rug on the gleaming hardwood floor, and the stunning lace draperies at each window. Still aglow about her initial encounter with Step, Rainey allowed her own eyes to follow the path his eyes took. It really was a gorgeous room, but why was Step so uncomfortable right now? He was standing in that doorway as if he needed to excuse himself to the bathroom. A perplexed Rainey shifted her attention back to Joe Reeves.

"Well, I better get on back downstairs to my piano. Pleased to meet you, Miss. Let me hear you sing soon. I need some help downstairs, don't I Miss Mittie?" Both laughed, and Uncle Mason smiled.

"Reeves is one singing man, Rainey. He's got a lovely voice, but our friends who visit us in our other concern" -- it sounded to Rainey as if that last phrase had quotation marks adorning it -- "request songs from him all night long, and they **never** give him a break."

"Well, okay, then, see you all later." Reeves gave a little salute to Rainey and the Gaineses. Step gave him a wide berth, and seemed to mumble "Goodbye, Mr. Reeves" as Joe Reeves brushed past him. Soon, Rainey heard his delicate music again, and she drifted upward with it for a time, floating along on its elegant streams, lulled into near restfulness by its easy beauty.

"Now, that's one nice fella," Mittie said, pitching a look in Step's direction. "Married to a sweet gal. They got two beautiful young'uns. . . . Well, I reckon I better go in and see about dinner. And then Missy, you and I have got to do something about that hair of yours!" Rainey blushed; she had noticed that Aunt Mittie's hair was not grease laden like her own. She longed for a change in her look.

Uncle Mason stood up and shook his head "no" vigorously. He motioned for them to follow him to the dining room. On the way down the hall, Step followed behind them, his head hung and his eyes averted, the thick falseness of his humble and meek air a smelly shawl at his shoulders. He picked up a thread of conversation that had been postponed by Joe Reeves's arrival.

"Now, Miss Rainey." He was back in his dandy mode now. "What about you coming out to see me dance sometime?" Step's smile was a brilliant star. Rainey forgot the music.

"What did I just tell you, Miss Rainey?" Aunt Mittie's voice was sarcastic, and Uncle Mason looked back at Rainey with a strong expression that echoed his wife's displeasure with Step's forwardness.

"But, Aunt Mittie --"

"Rainey, I know you grown, sweetie, but take it slow." Mittie's look, had it been fully empowered, would have sent Step to his grave. They stood at the dining room door now. Mason, rarely one to offer any negative opinion with his facial expression, scowled briefly.

"Besides," Mittie continued, "you need to get to know folks 'fore you start going places with them." Those eyes! Such daggers they shot at Step Herndon, a bullseye in a fully exposed target.

"But Aunt Mittie, I was going to ask you to go with me, too." Rainey allowed those disarming eyelashes to go sweeping again. She saw Mittie's scowl soften with her left eye. She allowed her right eye to close ever so quickly, with just the slightest hint of seductiveness, so that only Step could see her. His disappointment disappeared immediately, and he hastened to agree with Rainey.

"Now that's a good idea. Miss Mittie ain't seen me dance since I don't know when. What do you say?"

"Well, ain't no harm in me going with her. We'll let you know. You finished putting our bags up? Good. Here's a little something for you -- " Rainey swallowed a gasp as she saw that Mittie handed Step a five-dollar bill. Most folks didn't make that much in a day! "Now, I need you to go take care o' that other delivery I told you about for today."

"Oh, yes ma'am, I did that first thing yesterday morning. It's already in."

"Good. Good. Let me pay you for that." Step earned another five dollars. Rainey felt light-headed. Maybe she didn't want to try to teach after all!

The dining room was lovely. The walls were a deep royal blue, an unusual color in Rainey's limited experiences with dining rooms. The buffet, china closet, table, and chairs were mahogany, and the color of the walls complimented the suite in such a way that the furniture looked almost as if it were floating over the blue Oriental rug beneath its claw feet. Uncle Mason had set an incredible table. He had apparently learned well from Aunt Mittie, who was always a stickler for correct table etiquette. Each piece of tableware was exquisitely placed. The china he had chosen held subtle hints of the royal blue of the walls, and both the flatware and the crystal goblets were trimmed in gold leaf.

Uncle Mason's eyes sparkled as he motioned for the women to go and wash their hands. He disappeared through a swinging door, through which Rainey glimpsed glass kitchen cabinet doors. Mason set out steaming bowls of collards, snap beans, mashed potatoes, Rainey's beloved rice ("How did you know," she beamed, delighted), sweet corn, and a baked hen that looked absolutely mouth-watering. He even had biscuits tucked away inside a basket stuffed with royal blue napkins.

"Oh, Mason, honey, this is simply gorgeous!"   Mason blushed and motioned for everyone -- including Step, who declined and left quietly -- to sit down. He went over to another small enmeshed hole discreetly placed near the kitchen door and cleared his throat. Soon Joe Reeves was sitting with them in the dining room. They laughed and talked, all enjoying each other's company.

"Uncle Mason, I can't believe you cooked all this! I didn't even know you could cook."

Mason, Mittie, and Joe laughed heartily.

"Now, baby, you know Mason ain't cooked none of this. We got us a old woman who comes in here to cook about once a week. She must have cooked fresh today, right honey?" Mason nodded.

"That way," Mittie continued, "we can act like we having ourselves a night off away from the house. No, Mason ain't no kind of cook."

Rainey had begun her new life and she couldn't have been happier . . . unless Mama and Papa had been there with them.

Later, in Aunt Mittie's beauty parlor, where smells of marcelling irons commingled with aromas of lingering perfumes and the various pomades and potions that well-groomed colored ladies allowed onto their scalps, Rainey saw herself transformed into an elegant woman. But not before Aunt Mittie laid a tongue-lashing on her such as Rainey's delicate and genteel ears had never heard.

"Now gal, who told you you needed to put all this here grease in your head? You got soft, straight hair. It ain't no better than nobody else's, it's just what it is! You see me with any of this shit in my hair? Hell no you do not! I got straight hair just like you do! I'd look like a fool sittin' 'round with a pile of grease all laid up in my head! Now you got to remember you got you a Indian for a mama, and us Clarks is damn near too light to live! Why you can almost see blue veins under your Aunt Addie Rose's skin. Now I ain't all that crazy about bein' mistook for no white woman, but, hell, it worked for Addie Rose. Now you just gon' have to face facts, gal: you cain't do your hair like everybody else you know, no sir. We gon' fix you up good!"

By the time Mittie took her first breath -- and that was well into her soliloquy -- Rainey was wiping tears -- of hurt? of anger? of shame? She had no idea which -- from her face. Finally Mittie looked down at her niece to see the tears streaming down her cheeks.

"What the hell you cryin' for, gal? Aunt Mittie ain't meant you no harm. I just tells things as I sees 'em! Ain't got nothing to do with you. You could ask Mason, and if he'd open his mouth to speak he'd tell you I'm a little on the sharp-tongued side. But I don't mean you no harm." Mittie turned Rainey's chair around to face her. Rainey wept openly now.

"One thing I want you to keep in your mind always. You are my brother's child. I loved my brother--" and here Mittie's voice broke, but she continued. "-- and I mean to look out for you, girl. But when I say what I got to say, I just come right out with it. I don't mean you no harm. You are my blood, and I don't mess over my blood, and I don't let nobody mess over my blood." Mittie kissed her niece precisely on the cheek.

"Now you hush crying. Ain't me and Aunt Addie Rose all the family you got, 'cept for your Uncle Eddie?"

Rainey, consoled, nodded. "Well, then, give us a smile? That's a sweet girl. Now. Let's get this hair fixed up."

Rainey was now initiated into the scalding love of Mittie Clark Gaines.

Veiled Histories & Thundering

Tapshoes

The people with whom Rainey now made her life were haunted by shadows of selves they had discarded at various ditches along their life paths. What Rainey came to know of them she could only see through the prisms of finely cut glass they had themselves crafted and polished to a high sheen. Rainey would perhaps never know the true genesis of any of these new significant folks in her life; perhaps she would always dwell in a state of darkness about them. In at least one instance, the glaring truths she was destined to uncover about one of them would scald her innocence forever. For now, though, those who would be most important in her life -- Mittie, Mason, Mittie's sister Addie Rose, and Step Herndon, had created new selves that worked, more or less, in the stylized world of George Town, Washington, in the District of Columbia.

Mittie Jane Clark came to Washington to get away from a married beau. He had been married all along; but had neglected to let her in on that little secret. Amos Williams was 25 years older than Mittie. But when Mittie started working as a maid at the Yarborough House in downtown Raleigh, Amos was the best looking colored man working on Fayetteville Street. When they met, he was a frustrated bellman at the Sir Walter; he felt that he had to beg, practically, to get white folks to tip him. So he was talking even then about taking the railroad job that would eventually separate him from life in Raleigh forever. In the meantime, he courted young Mittie (so young, she often reflected), never bothering to tell her about his wife and eight children until the Sunday there was no longer any way he could have denied his real life.

Mittie was coming from the Yarborough, and he and his brood were coming up Fayetteville Street. They met head on: Mittie was pondering her life, head down, walking determinedly toward the little house she shared with Rufus and Evie. Amos apparently saw her before she saw him and he tried to turn away from her path.

Mittie picked his face out from among a small crowd of faces, and she smiled expectantly. Then she took in the whole picture and that olive face fell. She never slowed down, but Amos's wife, a short, fat and greasy looking woman (as Mittie noted with deep and comforting satisfaction), saw the looks that passed between them. As she hurried away from the family, Mittie could hear Amos's wife questioning him loudly about "jes' who the hell was she?" And just as they left her earshot, Mittie heard what might she hoped was a large purse making contact with a block of a head.

This episode was the final straw for Mittie who had, it seemed, always been mistreated by every man with whom she had ever fallen into bed. From that moment on, she resolved to move away from Raleigh to some place where colored folks were allowed to make some real money. She knew how to do hair, so she could make a living anywhere.

And there was Addie Rose, her older sister, who had always expressed her wish that she and Mittie could live closer together. She finally decided on Washington, DC because Addie Rose had lived there for a number of years -- passing as a white woman with her colored husband, who was also passing.

Addie Rose, now known as Mrs. Adele Connelly, was ecstatic that her baby sister would come to live with her, as her personal maid. Addie Rose's husband David was also anxious to have Mittie come start a new life with them. The door had always been open for Mittie to come to live with them, though she would have to live her life as the live-in hired help.

The Connellys were a childless, reasonably wealthy "white" couple in what was a strange, lily-white enclave of a largely black community called Georgetown. Mr. Connelly was a prominent banker in the city, and Mrs. Connelly, whom Mittie called, with barely a straight face, "Madam," was a powerful force in Washington's social circles. Adele Connelly soon recommended her new maid as hairdresser for all the other society ladies' colored maids.

Before long, Mittie had a full clientele of satisfied customers, who recommended her to their friends and family. Mittie's intention was to save money for her great hair salon. This dream would see daylight since Addie Rose and David insisted that she put every cent they paid her in a special account they set up for her at the Riggs National Bank.

Mr. and Mrs. Connelly were kind enough to let Mittie remodel their upper basement into an efficient hair salon.

Meanwhile, when the saintly Mrs. Connelly wasn't making sure that her new colored maid was well taken care of in her second profession, she was in that colored maid's quarters, giggling and reminiscing about their growing years. It wasn't long before the Connelly's cook began to notice that Madam and the new maid were not only very chummy, but that they bore a striking resemblance to one another: both were pale women with those "queer" gray eyes. Cook began to talk around to the other hired help, and soon it was necessary to let cook be on her way. Mittie was, for a time, maid and cook to the Connellys, in addition to her growing hairdressing business.

After cook's abrupt departure, Mittie's only other co-worker was an oddly silent man named Mason Gaines, whose deep-pool eyes drew her to him. Mittie was appalled, initially, that she would be attracted to a "cripple";

but she found him so easy to talk to. He always looked at her as if he appreciated every word that emanated from her well-worked mouth -- even when the words were directed against him. Though he was no greatly handsome man, he certainly was easy enough to look at.

She gathered from his gestures that he was about 30 years old at that time, and she knew that when he wasn't working for the Connellys he worked as a mime down near the Willard Hotel or the Capitol Building. He made quite a bit of money in this part-time endeavor. No one had ever encountered a Negro who could mime with the same technique as the French mimes. The social-climbing white Washington elite prided themselves on their capacity for vulgar over tipping towards performers whom they considered worthy, and that vulgar excess paid off beautifully for Mason.

The gossip started by cook persisted throughout the servants' quarters of that strange, lily-white enclave, and before it could find its way into the servants' quarters of the households of other prominent city bankers, the Connellys decided to build a breath-taking Queen Anne home out in Virginia, away from the wagging tongues, and away from this now all-Negro neighborhood. The Connellys quietly deeded their lovely brownstone to their loyal maid, and disappeared into the lushly elegant woods of Arlington, Virginia.

On the day the Connellys moved away, Addie Rose went into her baby sister's room and cried bitterly about their very necessary separation. Mittie understood, and was not a little envious of the fact that her sister, at 33, had had opportunities that would never be open to her just because the olive in her skin stood as a far stronger proof of their shared heritage than it ever would in Addie Rose's skin -- or in David's, whose own skin, like Addie Rose's, was not just pale, but even blue-tinged where his veins showed through.

The opulence of the Connellys' new home turned out to be a fitting compensation for Addie Rose's separation from her blood relative. Occasionally, the Connellys' former city maid would come out to their nearly palatial country home to orchestrate their many dinner parties, soirees, and barbecues. As had been the case in the city, many of Adele Connelly's most loyal friends slipped over to Mittie to tell her how honored they would be if she would consider coming to work for them. After all, they could probably pay her better than Adele; she was rather stingy about wages, wasn't she? These devoted friends of Adele's promised that they could offer more luxurious quarters than Adele could, and that their decorating tastes far surpassed Adele's. They believed that David probably didn't give Adele quite the household allowance that their own husbands gave them.

Mittie, with great effort, held her tongue during these "secret" sessions. It went against everything within her to allow someone to speak ill of her kin; however, she could be quiet in these instances for several reasons. First and foremost, she was not going to give away the Connellys' most precious secret, and beyond that, she had heard from the help of these devoted and loving friends that most of them were not nearly as well off as the Connellys. Further, Mr. Connelly didn't paddle his wife's ass when he had had a bad day at the bank, did he? Many of these lifelong friends of Adele's would die if they knew that their husbands' abuses and infidelities (usually with the maids) were common knowledge among the hired help. Mittie had seen nothing reprehensible in her brother-in-law's behavior toward Addie Rose. If he had any secret goings-on, neither she nor Addie Rose was aware of them. Besides, Mittie knew enough about David to know that he was far too afraid of being found out as a Negro to do anything that might cause undue scrutiny.

Finally, Mittie merely smiled and demurred to these sisterly friends of Adele's. She could hardly wait to get Addie Rose by herself and tell her, word for hateful word and mannerism for bird - brained mannerism, all that they had uttered. And how they laughed at these pretentious, silly women!

The brownstone became a sweet comfort for Mittie. Suddenly she was landed gentry, so to speak, and she would always have a security blanket on Q Street. And she hadn't had to lose her sister to gain that security. Mittie couldn't remember having been happier.

As Mason prepared to move into humbler quarters, he gazed at Mittie's then voluptuous self from crown to corn with those amazing orbs of his as he handed her a poem he had reproduced in his spiraling, beautiful handwriting. At the beginning of his message, Mason explained that this poem was called "Mary Donnelly," by a poet named William Allingham. He had found it in a book of poems in the Connelly's well-stocked library.

Mittie Clark

O lovely Mittie Clark, it's you I love the best!

If fifty girls were round you I'd hardly see the rest.

Be what it may the time of day, the place be where it will,

Sweet looks of Mittie Clark, they bloom before me still.

Her eyes like mountain water that's flowing on a rock,

How clear they are! How grey they are! And they give me many a shock.

Red rowans warm in sunshine, and wetted with a shower,

Could ne'er express the charming lip that has me in its power. ♦

The usually sharp – tongued Mittie, now struck silent by her attraction to Mason, wrote a heartfelt message to him,

_____

♦ This poem is paraphrase of a portion of "Mary Donnelly," by William Allingham (1824-1889), an Irish poet who was acclaimed in Great Britain during his lifetime.

thanking him for the beautiful verse, and telling him that she really needed him to stay in the house with her; she simply couldn't live there alone. And it was true; she had never lived alone in all her 25 years. When Mason accepted her offer, Mittie's heart jumped and faltered. She wouldn't have to live in that beautiful home alone, yet, she would have the full run of it! But did she have to have sex with Mason? But one strange and steamy night in Mason's surprisingly luxurious bed showed her that he really wasn't a cripple; he just wasn't much of a talker.

And so Mittie had settled into her life as the "wife" of Mason Gaines, and she celebrated the commencement of their life together by framing the beautifully penned verse and placing it over their "marriage" bed.

Mittie felt that she couldn't have gotten luckier: the house had four levels. They used the top two levels for their living space and the first lower level for her beauty salon. The bottom most level Mittie and Mason had renovated for a purpose that would take at least two more years to realize.

If there was one unifying factor among the Georgetown residents for whom church attendance was a mandatory showing of one's piety (finery), it was the drink. Mittie understood this soon enough after taking over the brownstone, when many of her customers brought their own "teas" and "toddies" to sip on while their hair was dressed. More than a few of her customers left her chair well satisfied with their hair and nearly crawling from having imbibed their own concoctions.

Mittie, ever committed to making more money, understood immediately that if she could offer "teas" and "toddies" in a polite setting, she could cash in on the unquenchable thirsts of some of Georgetown's most prominent Negro citizens.

On a humid and lightning plagued evening in the middle of her first summer as mistress of the house, Mittie went down to the sub basement to contemplate the space and its potential. The day had been long and steamy hot, and the customers had come to her in a steady stream from the time she had opened her door at 7:30 that morning until she had closed her door on the back of the last very pleased customer at 6:15 that evening. Her ceiling fan had droned lazily, and only the cool basement locale had saved them all from sweltering under the intense glow of stagnant natural heat compounded by curling irons and straightening combs. Mason was still downtown at the Willard earning his keep, as she liked to tease him.

This lower basement was the length of the brownstone, which was, on its top two levels, a rambling 4,500 square feet. It was a maze of passageways, trapdoors, and stairways. Addie and David had long suspected that this brownstone had a secret history. They had convinced themselves that their house was a way station on the Underground Railroad. When Mittie had first moved to Washington, her sister and brother-in-law had taken her on the secret tour of their home one evening after all the truly hired help had left for the night. They had begun their tour on the bottom most floor and worked their way up to the attic.

It had been a fascinating trip then and on the day that Mittie re-acquainted herself with the passageways, she continually gasped in gleeful amazement.

On the bottom most floor, the future site of the saloon, there was a trap door in the middle of the floor of what would become the seating area of the saloon, and another trap door behind the future bar. Those doors opened up to a short staircase that ended in a dank, cool room that would soon be in use as the storage room for the liquor that Mittie and Mason hoped would flow freely each night. There was still likely to be enough floor space in the room for about ten people to stand huddled together. One bald light bulb illuminated the concrete slab floor.

A mirrored bookcase behind the future bar would conceal the small doorway through which one could quickly move toward a second staircase. At the top of the staircase, another small doorway opened into Mittie's hair salon. That door was already hidden behind a supply cabinet in the shop. Mittie decided to have that cabinet nailed the door so that the door could be opened if necessary.

There were two more hidden staircases leading out of the basement, which fascinated Mittie. Addie and David had discovered that one of these staircases, a long and narrow horror, led straight up to the very top floor, while the second staircase plunged into darkness on the other side of the brownstone and led directly to a tiny doorway that opened onto P Street. This invention seemed to be a stroke of genius developed by some brilliant engineer on the Underground Railroad, perhaps? The doorway did not seem to open onto anything more involved than the side of an abandoned building.

At the brownstone's end at the corner of Q Street and Wisconsin Avenue, which was not connected to another brownstone, Mittie could envision a door in a portion of the brick wall. Her customers would have no reason to enter any other part of her house, and they could be escorted off the premises if they forgot their mothers' home training as they sampled her products. As Mittie studied the potential of the layout, she knew that she was doing the right thing for herself (and Mason too, of course). People always wanted to get high; why not give them a nice little place to do it in? There was no harm in her making some money off the folks's thirst. It was all legal, after all.

Within a month, Mittie and Mason had hired carpenters and electricians and plumbers to come in and transform the dusty open space into an elegant little saloon, and to fortify the secret stairways. You never knew, Mittie supposed, when you might have to use them for some quick get away.

It took nearly a year, and not a few headaches, for the transformation to be complete, but when Mittie stood back to survey the finished product, she sighed contentedly. In the middle of the tiled floor were twelve round tables, and at the side away from the door was a bar with a massive, sterling-framed mirror behind it. A piano -- a gleaming mahogany baby grand -- was stashed away at a corner near the doorway. Mittie knew just the person to play it, too: that young butcher named Joe Reeves who worked full time at the Downing Butcher on M Street. She'd heard him play for one of the choirs at Metropolitan AME Zion Church, the elite gathering place for Negroes to enhance their spiritual lives. Metropolitan was not only her church, but the place from which most of her saloon clientele would originate. Joe Reeves was mighty good on the piano, so Mittie decided to hire him as her part-time pianist and part-time bouncer. Joe Reeves was also mighty tough.

Business flourished in both of Mittie and Mason's basements for the next ten years. Mittie and Mason's little unnamed saloon was the beginning and ending point for many a night out for black Washingtonians. . . . until the fateful day when the government decided that, beginning in January, 1920, it would be illegal to sell alcohol.

Mittie and Mason were furious. Although Mittie's hairdressing salon was the place to go to get one's hair done in Georgetown, their biggest profit had come from the saloon. They had established a very good rapport with their distributor, James Felcher, who had overcome the usual odds associated with being immersed in both Negrohood and manhood simultaneously to become quite the entrepreneur. Mittie's volume of business had been so strong that Felcher had, years ago, arranged for her to receive a substantial discount on her supply.

And now Uncle Sam was going to come along and mess up her good thing.

"Hmmph. I'll be damned," she declared to Mason one night in their lust - fortified bed. "I know it's got to be a way around that bullshit the government just shoveled in our door."

Mittie hadn't slept that night, working through her own particulars, ironing out her problems, and overcoming the current challenges.

First she refreshed her memory about the extra stairways and tiny alcoves throughout the brownstone.

Over the next few days, Mittie discreetly made inquiries of key people in her Georgetown neighborhood. Otis Faulcon was the police officer whose beat included Q Street. The Gaineses and Faulcon had enjoyed a very friendly relationship over the years they had all known each other. Because his unique ceremonial position on the Washington police force was little more than tattletale, Officer Faulcon always had the time to stop in and say hello, and Mittie, ever the astute and farsighted businesswoman, always made time to talk with him. So, their relationship was almost as solid as a friendship by the time the Prohibition law became a looming reality. One November afternoon, as they sat in the parlor sipping hot apple cider -- Mittie's was always "unlaced" with her product; she never touched the stuff -- Mittie asked the token policeman casually:

"Officer Faulcon, what you think about the government outlawin' liquor sales?"

"Well, if I can beg your pardon, Miz Gaines, I think it's sort of dumb myself. Folks ain't gonna stop drinking just 'cause Uncle Sam says so."

"So, what you plannin' on doing if you catch somebody breakin' this new law?"

"Well now it depends on who it is. Say for example it was Nannie Bostic. That lady runs Madame Calico's? She can forget it. I'd turn her in before she could draw her next breath."

"Why?"

"'Cause she's a snob. Turns her nose up any time she sees me. Won't even speak. Now other folks speak to me and treat me like I'm a human being, so I'll look out for them. Folks like you and Mr. Gaines, y'all know how to treat folks with respect, and y'all the kind of folks that knows that good service is something that deserves some appreciation. It ain't too many people offering really good service nowadays."

"I see what you mean, Officer Faulcon. You made a good point there, and you won't hear no complaints about that from me."

Cal "Boney" Bertrand, the proprietor of Boney's After Hours Supper Club, was Mittie's next interviewee. Tall, dark as sweet chocolate, and thin, except for a slight gut he covered with stylish jackets, Cal "Boney" Bertrand was as elegantly refined as Mittie was unfailingly direct.

Cal was a hard-drinking, night-loving man, whose age never showed on his body or face. He had appeared on the DC scene, claiming to be a part of its native population. Oddly, nobody knew him before he opened Boney's in 1902 as a strange, ramshackle juke shanty near Georgetown. He glibly and deftly avoided answering specific questions about his past. Soon his patrons and associates shrugged and forgot that he was unknown to them. They decided about him what a famous Harlem evangelist would someday proclaim about himself: that he had combusted himself to life on the site of Boney's After-Hours Supper Club just in time to get the place up and running.

In fact, Cal Bertrand was born Calvin Bertrand Ellington in 1870 to parents who were a part of a rare breed: a Negro upper class. Father was a physician and Mother was a physician's wife with full involvement in charitable organizations. Father did not have the desired physical characteristics to qualify for membership in the Blue Vein Society of his community, but he was the chief doctor for all those elite blue-veined movers and shakers. Calvin Bertrand Ellington was the youngest of two sons whom their parents loved easily as much as their Waterford crystal. Calvin was a great embarrassment to his parents, who were well respected in all parts of Buffalo. They spent far too much time in the police station tending to Calvin, who had a youthful lust for drunkenness, attempted rape, and shoplifting.

Dr. and Mrs. Ellington hoped that by sending their son to Howard University, where he would be under the watchful eye of his older brother Whitman, a medical student there, he would calm down. Calvin was reasonably responsible as a student at Howard until December of his junior year. An unfortunate mishap with a local girl, a wine bottle placed in the wrong orifice, and a knife landed Calvin in Lorton for a brief and brutal stint. Father and Mother washed their hands of their son with irrevocable sadness, and their social life continued as if they had only ever had one son.

Calvin Bertrand Ellington became Cal Bertrand, a man who had learned his con man's savvy, his cooking trade, and a few other valuable skills during that brief period of incarceration. When he was paroled, he returned to Washington, found the unfortunate local girl, Jeanne, married her, taught her to cook food that would make anyone "stand up and shout," and began a life of lawful crime as a charmer. He immediately charmed his way in as head cook for an excessively wealthy Washington society couple whose fortune had been made in the jewelry business.

The aged jeweler took a liking to his new cook. He took this smooth-skinned, finely muscled young man under his ample wing. The feathers on that wing were secret cash donations, secret wardrobe enhancements, and no shortage of secret rendezvous. Cal Bertrand was promoted to this gentleman's personal valet, and accompanied him on jewelry procurement trips abroad. On these trips, Cal laid out the man's plush clothing, and drew his baths in the fine accommodations aboard the luxury liners and in the fine hotels of Europe.

Cal was well trained by his employer in the arts of intimate friendship that can only be shared between men. Cal was well trained, and a quick study indeed. And because he didn't have to spend any money, Cal Bertrand stashed away every penny the gentleman bestowed upon him. When the gentleman died of natural causes in 1900, Call Bertrand was quietly one of the wealthiest black men in Washington, and he had broken only the most obsolete, rarely enforced sodomy laws to amass his wealth.

Cal knew that his life on the sunny side of the law was much more to his liking than the horrors of the endless brutality of the chain gang. He settled into a polished, affected life as a gentleman entrepreneur. The shanty in which he began his successful career as proprietor of Boney's (the late gentleman's pet name for a certain part of Cal's anatomy) gradually became an elegant, two-story brownstone. By the time the club gained its popularity, he had his quiet and devoted wife Jeanne to thank for the high quality of the food that kept his customers coming back.

On a morning when she had blocked out about an hour between hair dressings, Mittie stopped in at Boney's After-Hours Supper Club to speak with Cal about this new government Prohibition business. They were seated in Cal's office, encased in the harmonious smells of a dinner that had kept his club filled with satisfied patrons for so many years.

"Jeanne is one good cook," Mittie remarked as she settled into her chair across from Cal's plush desk. "It always smells like a little taste of heaven in here." Mittie was one of the few people who knew that Cal's chef was also his mysterious, rarely seen wife. Mittie was also one of a tiny handful of folks who knew that the rumors were true about Cal's insatiable appetite for the tight flesh of young men. Theirs was a solid relationship because they understood and respected each other, for better or for worse. Their camaraderie was as solid as a friendship.

"Thank you, Mittie," he smiled now, settling back into the deep cushions of his chair. "I'm always proud of Jeanne's work. But do you know what she serves me at home? Leftovers."

They laughed easily. He and Jeanne, his wife of more than 20 years, were rarely at home to enjoy a meal – or much else – together.

"Cal, how you thinkin' about handlin' this Prohibition business?"

"I'm not going to deal in the hooch trade any more. That's simple enough. I can't be bothered with the complications. So, come January, I shall let my patrons know that if they

want their own liquor, they need to bring it in themselves --
without my knowledge."

"What if one of your customers still wants a drink and didn't
bring his own?"

"Now what have you always done when some of your
customers still want good food and didn't bring any food to
your place?"

"I always send them to you."

"That's right. And what have I always done when my
customers want some high quality liquor or some exotic
drink mixtures?"

"They always tell me 'Mr. Bertrand told me to come here if I
wanted some high class spirits.'" They chuckled at Mittie's
overdone imitation of Cal.

"Then I don't see how that's going to change, do you?"

"Well, no, and I'm mighty glad to hear that. How would
you like to make a little extra change?"

"Oh, I never object to that."

"How about if I let you know the password each day, and
you sell that information to your customers who want to
know."

"We got ourselves a deal, Mrs. Mittie." They shook on this
new deal, and Mittie left, satisfied that she had at least one
ally in the entrepreneurial world of Georgetown. She would
later make a similar, though less cordial, arrangement with
Nannie Bostic, the owner of Madame Calico's.

All Mittie's bases for illegal alcohol sales seemed to be
covered, save one, which nearly caught her off guard.

Daniel Brown was a tall, skinny 25-year-old ex-convict. He
had hit the ground running -- straight back into a life of
crime -- as soon as he had been released from Lorton after
having served a sentence for involuntary manslaughter. He
had gotten his long, rat-like fingers into every excess of
human corruption available to him since he had become a
free man six years earlier. He was a pimp who beat his
whores as if they had run away from his plantation during
slavery times. He was a numbers dealer who oversaw at
least ten numbers runners. He was a drug dealer for a tiny

but growing population of drug addicts. He was a slum lord, having bought one dilapidated tenement after another as he could afford them, only to rent apartments to extremely poor people for prices just slightly too high for many of them to be able to afford. His strategy was always to evict these unfortunate folks from their homes while they were at work. He could then sell their furniture (or burn it if its condition was too deplorable) before they returned home to find their front doors padlocked.

Mittie had also heard through several grapevines about Daniel Brown's special friendship with Cal Bertrand.

So it was no surprise that Daniel Brown would involve himself immediately in the quickly souring business of illegally providing liquor to speakeasies. As he did in most of his business dealings, Brown recruited customers by intimidation, strong-arming, and lying.

Daniel Brown steered clear of direct business contact with people like James Felcher, his chief competitor in the liquor business, because they were people whom he could not intimidate at all. But he didn't know Mittie Clark Gaines, so he assumed that, because she was a woman who lived with a mute ("dumb") man, he could force her to do his bidding.

Daniel Brown began his interview with Mittie using his version of cordiality.

"You know who I am, don't you?" He said after having burst into her hair salon at a rare moment when she was there alone.

"Look like to me you somebody ain't got no home training."

"Don't talk sharp to me, old woman," was his retort to the 55-year-old Mittie.

"And don't you bring <u>your</u> little skacey tail into <u>my</u> shop talking like you ain't got good sense!"

"Look, don't you know who I am or not?"

"Looks to me like I see a rat name of Daniel who just slithered out of a jailhouse, trying to mess with the wrong woman."

Daniel Brown responded to Mittie's statement by walking up to her quickly as if he were going to assault her. Mittie stood up to meet him, taking a swift step forward that caused him to stop short and lean back away from her.

"What you plannin' on doin', boy?"

Daniel, taken aback by the fierce, almost maniacal look on Mittie's face, took another step back and decided to change his tactics just a bit.

"Look, Miss Gaines, I can tell you a smart woman. Why don't you just go ahead and get your liquor from me and save yourself some trouble?"

"Why don't you save <u>yourself</u> some trouble and get the hell out of here? I already got my business taken care of. And let me tell you something else. I'm old enough to be your mother, so don't you ever think you can come in here and talk to me like I'm one of them 'ho's you be whipping up on down there on M Street. And I also know that you need to leave now."

"Suppose I don't?"

More swiftly than Daniel Brown could ever have expected, Mittie Clark Gaines was upon him. She raised her ample knee, encased in white support hose beneath a demure white smock, and aimed it successfully at his groin. As he lay on her floor doubled over in pain, Mittie pressed her foot into his abdomen just above the point of original contact, leaned her face down to his face, and said,

"Let me get somethin' straight with you right now, you long turd. I handle my business my way. Ain't no snot-nosed sissy gonna come in my shop or any place I do business and try to mess with me. You better <u>know</u> I know who you are! Matter of fact, I was expecting you." Mittie's back grew tired, so she stood straight and looked down at him, her surprisingly dainty - looking foot still pressed into Daniel Brown's heaving abdomen. With each word that she spoke, Mittie pushed Daniel Brown a little closer to the door of her shop.

"My lawyer, the police, my husband, my pastor, my customers, and even my sister-in -law down South know about you because they all have letters saying that if anything ever happens to me for them to come looking straight for you. If anything happens to me, my husband, or James Felcher, or anybody I know, you will be back in the jailhouse with all your little twisting boyfriends. Now carry your narrow ass on out of here, and learn how to treat a lady!"

By the time Mittie had finished her discussion with Daniel Brown, Nanette Winston stood at the door, her eyes wide open in surprise, her feet nearly covered by the now - sniveling Daniel Brown. Brown stood up quickly, despite his still-piercing pain, and beat a hasty retreat from Mittie's shop doorstep, which he would never darken again.

"You better remember what I told you," she yelled out of her door, "'cause if anything happens to any of us, they gon' come looking for you!" Mittie slapped her hands together, wiping them briskly to indicate that her garbage was now discarded. She was ready for her startled customer. Her smile was like a radiant beam of sunlight.

"Hey, Miss Nanette! Come on in! Let me just wash my hands."

Having thus successfully disposed of her last ounce of real trouble, Mittie Clark Gaines continued, only more discreetly, in the liquor selling business. She made sure that a letter identical to the one with which she had threatened Daniel Brown was in the hands of every person she had mentioned after winning this latest championship bout. The speakeasy continued to thrive as the Gaines's biggest source of income.

Certainly, Mason Gaines, Mittie's silent partner, was more of a mystery than his straightforward common-law wife. His past, with its rocky paths and jutting secrets, had more of a stain about it than Mittie's.

Mason Gaines, a native of Chase City, Virginia, had been named Jethro Gaines at his birth. He and his little sister Maude had come to Washington together, along with

Maude's tiny daughter Ellen.   They were on the run from their father's fury at Maude's early motherhood. And so they had set out for anywhere north of Chase City. Jethro was 16, and Maude was barely 14, but Jethro was suddenly burdened with the sense of responsibility that some long grown men could only wish for.

After a brief stop in Richmond, the heart of post-Civil War resentment and oppression, Jethro, Maude, and Ellen headed for Washington, DC in search of better opportunities and real distance from their enraged father.   Once in Washington, Maude had somehow made herself scarce from Jethro and headed for parts unknown to him. As for Ellen, he could only hope that the little girl was safe and happy.

For the next three years, Jethro Gaines had no earthly idea where his sister was or what had happened to her or his niece.

Jethro Gaines was a brick mason by trade, training, and initiation.   He grew tall into bearded, muscular manhood in the District of Columbia, and soon he hardly resembled the country boy who had fled Chase City. He fine tuned his once deficient reading skills, and began to read The Washington Post every morning before work and during his lunch break. Soon he began to write letters to the editor, and those letters were often featured on the paper's Op-Ed pages. Jethro smirked each time one of his letter appeared; they would probably just die of a stroke if they knew his letters signed by "J. Mason Gaines," were the masterpieces of a lowly colored day laborer.

On his 19th birthday, he and some of his lodge brothers decided to celebrate his coming of age.   Down in Southeast Washington, there was a steamy little Negro dive stashed away from "civilized" folk. It didn't even have a name, just a number; regular patrons called it "the 805" as if it were a regular train exiting the city. Well, trains were running all night in this little dive, and, though they never actually left the city, they arrived all night long.

Reasonable Joy

The 805 was an ideal spot for a manchild to sow the wild oats of manhood, or so it seemed when Jethro Gaines entered the club. There were beautiful -- or at least well made up -- dancing girls on the stage in the building's shabby but aggressively decorated great room. These young ladies danced with threadbare suggestiveness to a lone drummer's beat. The drummer was accompanied occasionally by a shrill, ear-shattering trumpet whose input hardly made a difference in the overall performances of the women. Besides, the men in attendance at The 805 were rarely interested in vertical entertainment.

Soon, Jethro and his three lodge brothers reconvened to the more exciting terrain of the rooms above the rickety great room. Lena Lyons, the proprietress of The 805, had made special arrangements for the birthday boy to sample one of her most popular girls, Topaz.

"You'll find her to be a rare jewel, fellas," Lena promised them.

Jethro would never forget, nor would he ever tell, the ambiance of the room in which he found this rare jewel, Topaz. Incense burned a thick, pungent fog into the room's atmosphere. Flames from a candelabra flickered lazily on the farthest side of the room from the bed, which was draped with stunning white eyelet and lace covers. Jethro squinted to see more clearly in the dark, smoky chamber as he approached the bed.

And in the middle of that dazzling whiteness laid a candlelit vision. Tiny and shaped to perfection, Topaz sprawled, completely nude. Her jet-black wig cascaded around her heart-shaped face, obscuring her forehead and curtaining her heavily made-up eyes. She moaned softly as she caressed her breasts lovingly, and stroked her clitoris invitingly, her hips writhing in rhythm to her hand strokes. Jethro's long neglected manhood responded immediately.

He had been to a prostitute before, but the one who had serviced him had been, at best, a necessary evil. Now before him lay a dream come true. Jethro disrobed quickly and as he moved close to Topaz, she felt around in the air near him until she gently grabbed his erect penis and took it into her warm mouth.   Soon, he fell to those stiffened nipples, the bejeweled navel, and that fragrant neck, his hand grasping the heart - shaped valley of pubic hair.

Topaz moaned beneath him, and his desire grew to a fever. He entered her in a panic, thrusting into her as if he were some sort of rabbit in heat.   As he approached orgasm, she seemed to be getting there with him.   She arched her chin upward, and as her head thrashed left and right, her wig pushed back from her forehead. . . and there underneath him, and surrounding him, was his little sister, Maude.   They both yelled, horrified, and Jethro climaxed violently. His entire body shook as he tried in vain to fight off the deep ecstasy that engulfed him. He pulled out of her and hurried into his clothes. He gasped for breath as he ran from the room.

Downstairs, Lena managed to block Jethro's path as he ran for the front door.

"What happened, birthday boy?"

Jethro tried to speak but no words came out.   He somehow got around Lena Lyons and ran from the 805.

He never again saw anyone connected with the club.

He immediately turned to a new line of work. When he sought employment with the Connellys, they asked him his name. He did not spell out the name Jethro, but he spelled Mason, along with his last name.   From that moment, he ceased to be Jethro and became Mason. He never again wanted to think of himself as Jethro, because Jethro Gaines had a sister named Maude. What Jethro had done with Maude was immoral; but what Mason had done with Maude seemed a little less objectionable.

He never spoke again, because he feared that he would be compelled to tell somebody what he had done.

Mason was as avid a sleep-talker by night as he was a silent presence by day. He had awakened Mittie many a night discussing his liaison with some woman that he called Topaz or Maude. In just over a month, Mittie learned that

Mason was not his given name, and that Topaz/Maude was a prostitute in southeast Washington. Further, she learned that this woman was probably about 28 years old by the time Mittie began to live with Mason, that Mason sent her money to be used only for her daughter's welfare. He called this little girl Ellen, and he also referred to himself as Uncle as if he were talking with the child. It didn't take long for her to know how Topaz/Maude looked, as Mason described her vividly, as if he needed to purge his spirit of her memory, for several nights in a row. By the end of the second week of frantic talking, Mittie knew that Maude was one of the whores who got her hair dressed at the Bouvier Salon on G Street, near Capitol Hill. Mittie made it her business to learn the fine points of the Negro hairdressing trade at the Bouvier Salon.

As for his "natural ability" as a mime, Mason Gaines did in fact see a French mime on a Georgetown street once. Blessed as he was with a photographic memory, Mason was able to mimic that performer almost effortlessly. He began his career as a mime in front of the Willard Hotel with hardly a second thought one sunny March afternoon. Before his feet as he performed, white men began to shower the sidewalk with silver coins. Mason knew immediately that he had a good thing going there, and began to mime at least three times per week from that day forward.

When he was not at work for the Connellys or miming for his own fortune, he was in their fascinating library, hungrily studying the contents of every book they owned.

✾

From the tiniest spare corner of her consciousness, Rainey noticed the stark differences between her two aunts. The contrast between the two elder Clark women was startling. Aunt Addie Rose, though only about eight years older than Aunt Mittie, looked far older. By 1922, Addie Rose was a 65-year-old widow walking tentatively with a cane. Mittie, at 57, walked swiftly, as if she were avoiding any number of

Adele Connelly

offending obstacles as she made her way, get there or bust, to her destination. Addie Rose was as rail thin as Mittie was pumpkin round, and though she was still strikingly pale, Addie Rose was beginning to show the blush of her heritage. She covered her darkening face with powder so that in certain shadows, her face looked disembodied, as if it were floating into the room detached from her body. Addie Rose wore spectacles by now, and kept her hair pulled into a huge bun. Mittie, whose pineapple bob haircut kept her looking fashionable, needed spectacles for faraway sights, but, as she had always been a vain woman, Mittie refused to surrender to her retreating eyesight. Addie Rose had lost her spirit when David died in 1919. Mittie had enough spirit to buoy them all through any storm.

Even Aunt Addie Rose had a history that Rainey would never fully understand. Born a free child to newly freed parents in April, 1857, Addie Rose was the oldest child of Rufus and Sissie Bell Clark. Her adult life had been plush but strangely antiseptic and tinged with loneliness. All her life, until she married David Connelly, Addie Rose Clark had been in search of a sweeter existence, a less "colored" way of life. It wasn't that she didn't like being a Negro; she enjoyed her family and her friends. They were all precious to her and a joy for her to know. If only she could have the colored way of life without having to be (mis)treated like a colored woman.

As the oldest child of the Clark family, she was the one who remembered their father, a man who was, unfortunately just a bright specter to Rufus and Mittie. Physically, Addie Rose had taken after their father: her skin was whiter than the skin of some people who identified themselves as Caucasians.

Addie Rose was 14 years old when her father never came home again. It was early in 1872, and the South was in the heat of the Reconstruction. His body had been found, beaten savagely, and hanging from a bent and ancient oak tree deep in a forest, down by a sleepy ravine where he sometimes took his family for joyful afternoon picnics, or where he slipped away with his sickly wife, on her good days, to court her like he did when they were newlyweds. Hope of real reconciliation between black and white folks was fading away to hellish depths for freedmen, freedwomen, and freed children. The Southerners wouldn't budge on issues of equality for Negroes and the Northerners were beginning to show open hostility.

The entire Clark family was devastated by the loss of the head of their household. Sissie Clark would never again have any well days now that she was a widow, and her impact upon her younger children grew fainter until they came to regard Addie Rose as their mother. Mittie Jane grew into a young woman who was tough with everyone and rather shrewish to boot, while Rufus the younger quietly but completely turned against all people who were not Negro or Indian. But perhaps no one was more strongly affected than Addie Rose, who, having suddenly been put in the position of being mother and head of household, wished only that white people would refrain from hurting Negro people. She knew her father had not hurt anyone; yet, she knew in some ways that his death was inevitable. She just wanted to be done with a life that would cause her such pain.

Addie Rose Clark walked out of her life in her rural community one afternoon after her mother wasted away unto her death. Rufus and Mittie were now old enough nearly to fend for themselves, so she escorted them to the home of their mother's sister in Raleigh, where they grew into adulthood. She sent money and postcards to her sister and brother and their aunt. But she would never again be seen in their company, except on her own terms in the distant future. She was, from the moment she left her brother and sister behind, a young white woman named Adele Rosa Clark.

Addie Rose headed for Chapel Hill, where she quietly worked her way through school at the university by scrubbing floors in classroom buildings. By day, she diligently studied the principles and procedures for teaching elementary school children the three Rs. By night, the newly re-invented Adele Clark scrubbed those floors carefully. In one careless moment, she did manage to scrub the soft leather shoes of a young Economics student named David Connelly, who walked along her corridor that night, unaware that someone was cleaning there. He was deeply involved in his textbook, and when Addie Rose scrubbed his shoes, he looked up absently as if someone had tapped his shoulder. He looked down and smiled at Addie Rose, who blushed and stood up. He was of medium height, with slightly curly dark hair and green eyes. His smile was open and inviting, and she liked him immediately.

"You're pretty, and you're working pretty hard, aren't you?" She returned his smile, and offered her hand to him when he introduced himself. They talked for just a minute, and he was on his way. But from that point on David Connelly walked along that corridor each evening, stopping to chat with his new friend, Adele Clark, who was deeply flattered by his attention.

Soon enough, this David was as taken with her as she was with him; but, she was not about to risk her cover as a young white woman from meager beginnings to court this white boy. Soon enough, though, David confessed to Addie Rose that he wanted to take her home to meet his family.

David was from a "typical" family of comfortable means. His father was, as he would be, a banker, and his mother was a housewife who did more work than her maid, who was a pale, elderly Negro woman to whom Addie Rose took a liking immediately. The lady sat around in the parlor during their first visit, cuddling David as if he were her own, and receiving the affection of all the family as if she actually were their kinswoman. Addie Rose dared not comment on what she saw as a heart-warming scene between a family and their beloved servant. She was afraid she might betray some stray emotion that would reveal her identity.

So many times over the months of their courtship and over the first year of their marriage, Addie Rose made up her

Adele
Addie Rose
married David

mind to tell her beloved David about her real background. If he loves me, he will accept the truth, she would tell herself. But when she looked into his face and saw the way his eyes sparkled at the sight of her, her courage fled from her so quickly that she could feel a draft wrapping itself around her body.

About a year after their marriage, David came home from his apprenticeship at the bank one evening, sat down at their tiny kitchen table, and wept. Addie Rose was alarmed and ran to him.

"What's wrong, sweetness?"

"It's Grandma! She's dead!" David leaned over to his wife and wept as if he were five years old.

"I'm so sorry, honey! I wish I'd met her. You always talked so highly of her."

Suddenly David looked up at Addie Rose. His face was flushed, yet he looked deathly pale. Addie Rose had never before seen anyone look so odd. She drew back from him, holding her breath. Had she said something wrong?

"Adele. Adele. . . ."

"What, David?"

"You . . . have. You have met my Grandma."

"No, I didn't! How would I forget?"

"The woman you thought was our maid. She was my grandmother."

They stared at each other for a long, breathless moment.

"Then what are you saying?"

"We are a family of Negroes," he stammered. "We have lived as whites for my entire life. My grandmother didn't have the features to pass, so my mother and father pretended she was our live-in maid." David looked at Addie Rose as if he expected her to spit on him. Addie Rose smiled, and with that smile came a deep breath from her tense chest. It was as if she could finally breathe easily.

"Thank you, Jesus," was all she could say at first.

"What, my darling?"

"David, we have been keeping secrets from each other when we could have been living our lives together in total truth. I am colored, too."

Despite David's deep grief at the passing of his grandmother, he laughed weakly, said "Thank you, Jesus" too, and kissed his wife gratefully.

Two years after their marriage, David got a position with the Riggs National Bank of Washington, DC. They headed north, looking back only long enough to say goodbye to their families. Though they lived their lives as whites, they vowed never to forsake the welfare of their loved ones.

William "Step" Herndon had worked diligently to forget his own beginnings in 1887 as Willie Junior Bivens in a town that was more ditch than village in the sovereign state of Georgia. The fourth of twelve children, Willie hated his father who wandered, zombie-like between being in a dead asleep drunken stupor or beating the shit -- sometimes literally -- out of his mother, and Willie and his brothers and sisters. Willie despised his mother (but loved her for trying anyhow) for being a cheap whore who sold her body to feed her brood. It was, literally, a lousy and stinking existence he lived. There seemed to be no hope for any of that Bivens crowd, as they were known on the outskirts of Acworth, Georgia. None of them seemed barely able to form whole sentences that anyone outside of their hovel could comprehend. And as for home training? There didn't seem to be enough of that, or food, or lye soap, to go around in that Bivens crowd.

Willie got some pretty bizarre ideas about sex, and from that education took a rather sleazy delight in the male anatomy. He stole a cracked hand mirror from his mother's side of the big room all 14 of the Bivens crowd existed in. When he wasn't chasing his younger siblings around the piss-poor yard (because none of them went anywhere near school), he was in the nearby woods looking at a distorted image of his changing body structure. He decided he liked the look of his engorging penis, but decided that it was right, based on the pathetic empirical data that he had at his disposal, for him to like to look at girls.

So he tried to like looking at girls, but he more often found that looking was simply not enough. Worse, girls' bodies just weren't all that interesting to him. Finally, Willie Junior Bivens had to flee Acworth, Georgia when he got caught, at the age of 14, masturbating while fondling a slightly older white girl (while thinking, almost unconsciously, about her brother) in the back of the town's general store. The white girl, his secret reading teacher, was enjoying herself just as much as Willie was, but the owner of the general store, being the cousin of that white girl, saw only that the black boy's actions were an offense to unsullied true womanhood.

Willie's hegira out of Georgia began and ended without announcement. His family never knew what became of him, and none of them were overly concerned. His parents covered their relief with a mask of hope that Willie had been hired on by some migrant farmer or some outfit that could help him make a good living for himself. The eleven other Bivens children hoped that they would get to share in Willie's portion of their meager rations and Willie's portion of the hand-me-down rags they had to wear.

The Bivens crowd filled the gap left by Willie's sudden absence like water seeps into the groove left by a shell removed from wet sand.

Willie Junior Bivens was next sighted near Cowpens, South Carolina, where he was known as Will Bivens. For those next three years, Will had his share of the girls in Cowpens, both during and after his hours as a farm hand on the McKinney farm, though he always felt that the pickings there were rather slim.

Will Bivens thought he was happy in Cowpens. But then a troupe of traveling colored minstrels stopped through town for a few days' rest. Will saw them dance and was immediately enthralled. The world, and time, seemed to disappear from his consciousness as he watched the men and women caper and prance and cake walk. He felt a strange stirring in his soul when the small crowd cheered for this group. For the first time, Will Bivens felt love, though he could not decide to whom or what this love should be directed.

He decided to try a few steps with them. He was a bit raw, having never danced before, but the leader of the troupe gave him a few lessons. By the end of their stay in Cowpens, the dancers had decided to take Will under their wing as an apprentice.

He traveled with the troupe to the various shanty communities in South Carolina towns, and for the next few months, Will's life was peaceful. Will knew he was happy. He also knew that he was turning out to be one of the better dancers in the little group, which drew, not surprisingly, the envy of the former principle dancer, a wisp of a man named Chester. Will stayed out of Chester's way. He really didn't want any trouble, he just wanted to dance.

Will even had a little girlfriend among the dancers, a reluctant lover named Saluda. They got on quite well, at least by his standards -- he did what the hell he wanted to her and she didn't complain, because she thought he was extremely handsome. Unbeknownst to Will, Chester had designs on Saluda, too, and apparently was making some headway -- until Will joined their group.

When the troupe arrived in Charleston to perform, their audience was so overjoyed to see other black folk dancing -- and so intoxicated, in some cases -- that they became a bit too rowdy. Soon enough, in the midst of one of Will's solo performances, somebody in the audience brandished a knife at another patron, which was justification enough for some of the other drunks in the audience to exact revenge upon their enemies in attendance. The atmosphere changed in a flash from festive to lethal, and many of the fighters spilled onto the dance area. Before Will knew what was happening, Chester was upon him with a knife of his own. Always one to have quick reflexes, Will snatched the knife away from Chester and plunged it deep into his taut chest. Chester's eyes bulged for a moment before he sank to the ground. His last words were, "I won't gon' kill you, Will."

Horrified, Will dropped the murder weapon and fled to the dance troupe's makeshift dressing area. He searched frantically through all the belongings piled in a heap there, in search of his things. Along the way, he found several extra dollars, a cheap old diamond engagement ring, and several other trinkets that would help finance his flight. He gathered together all his poor belongings (and everybody else's money) and ran away, neither looking back nor stopping to take a breath until he found himself at the colored platform of the Charleston train station. The conductor told him that based on the money he was showing him, he could make it as far as Washington, DC, and then he would have to get off the train. He paid his fare and sat still as a statue, bug-eyed with fear of discovery, until he arrived at Union Station. Will decided to become "William" because he could never get used to a name that didn't sound like Willie. Most fortuitously, Herndon was one of the towns the conductor called out as they passed through before arriving at Union Station. They sat at that town's stop long enough for Will to copy down the letters of the town's name and pronounce it over and over again.

William Herndon stepped off that train from Charleston, South Carolina and stumbled into a completely new existence.

Still a shuffling bumpkin when he emerged from a train just in from points south, William Herndon was wearing shoes that were laughably cheap and run over, and his hair was a matted and kinky mess slicked down by some smelly pomade. Cal Bertrand, proprietor of the wildly successful "Boney's After-Hours Supper Club," saw a finished product in the poor boy that day, and, nearly forgetting the shipment of supplies he had come to retrieve, he stepped forward immediately to claim his prize.

"Young man, are you new here?"

William Herndon looked around frantically, like a trapped animal. Cal wondered if he was on the run from some hometown law enforcer.

"You talkin' to me?" William's diction that day assaulted Cal with the force of hot nails being spat from his full lips, but Cal Bertrand could hear melodies waiting to emerge from the boy's voice.

"Yes. I'm looking for a man to help me with my business concern."

"For real?" William's eyes lit in eager anticipation of instant employment. Cal's chuckle was confident.

"Yes, for real. I take it you might be interested."

"Oh, yes, sir!" William straightened to attention then, his well-developed chest bulging beneath his faded and worn shirt.

"Tell me. What brings you to Washington, Mr., uh...?"

"Oh, I'm William ("Weeum"). William Herndon. I come from South Carolina." William pronounced his "home" state "Sousca-lahna."

"How do you do, Mr. William Herndon. I am Calvin Bertrand, proprietor of Boney's After-Hours Supper Club." Cal enjoyed seeing the obvious impression he had made upon this young prospect. "I am always looking for new help or new young talent. Now. What brings you to my hometown?"

They were inside the terminal now, the dapper Negro businessman and the pitifully bumpkinish con man who claimed South Carolina as his home. From the right corner of his line of vision, Cal could see that Watts, his delivery man, had procured his latest supply of factory-preserved foods and was trundling the load toward him. He turned to give blunt but pleasant instructions to Watts, telling him that he would meet him at the wagon.

"Now. Go on, William."

"Well, I'm up here because I can't make no kinda living down home. I really wants to have a chance to tap dance on the Broadway stage, but I figured I'd start out right here. 'Sides, my money ran out here."

Cal chuckled magnanimously. "Well, thank you for your refreshing honesty! And today must be your lucky day. You see, I'm always looking for good dancers to accompany my excellent stage band. Do you have somewhere to stay?"

"Nawsuh. I was just taking my chances."

"Fine. You won't mind coming with Watts and me to my club. You can audition there to be a dancer with my band."

Once at the club, William danced enthusiastically a cappella. His time with the dance troupe had lain a solid foundation for him as a dancer, and Cal saw the raw talent emanate from the boy like a cool but brilliant light. William's potential as a great dancer was obvious.

Cal applauded William with genuine praise.

"You're quite a hoofer there boy. You might as well call yourself Steppin' William." Both men laughed heartily. Cal grew solemn.

"Now you'll need some lessons to refine that talent, Step." He saw that William was thrilled that this important man had already addressed him by his new nickname.

"I have just the teacher for you. Mrs. Lessie Kearney is the best dance teacher Negro Washington has ever produced. I will set you up with her immediately. You should be ready to perform within six weeks or so. In the meantime, I will put you on my payroll as a delivery boy. What do you say?"

"I say, when do I get started?" Again the men laughed. Again Cal grew solemn.

"Now I will help you with your wardrobe and your, uh, diction."

"Diction?"

"Yes, the way you talk."

"Do I talk funny or something?"

"Well, yes, the way you talk is a little strange for this part of the world."

"Okay, then. Whatsinever you say."

"Now, I happen to have a little flat -- apartment? -- some rooms? -- over on M Street. You said you didn't have anywhere to stay. Let me take you over there and get you settled in. You can come on back to the club with me and we'll get you started on your new life."

"Thank you, suh."

"Mr. Bertrand will do."

"Huh?"

"You may call me Mr. Bertrand, not sir."

The 1912 Step, even at 25 years old, was so overwhelmed by the entire Washington experience that nothing about Cal's approach seemed suspicious to him. He was grateful to have gained so much in so little time. His matted hair was now elegantly shorn, and never before had he had so many changes of clothes. And his new home! It was the nicest place Step had ever lived in. He did have so much to be thankful for (relieved about).

Goodbye, Willie Junior!

Still, it didn't take Step very long to resent -- silently, of course -- the utter control that his employer Cal Bertrand had over him. Now that he had enjoyed the meteoric -- and ultimately truly deserved -- rise to principle dancer at the club, he had little else to do during the day. After about five years of living exclusively as what he called "Cal's dancing circus bear," Step approached Mrs. Mittie Clark Gaines at her speakeasy one night when he and Cal went there on the pretense of tending to business matters. He asked (begged, really) Mrs. Mittie to let him take care of all her deliveries. He knew that she had been hiring various hobos to get her supply of liquor for her on the promise that they would get to sample the product. At that time, it was still legal to operate a saloon. Step assured her that he hardly drank at all; so what she paid him in salary, she would also save in product. Mittie, ever one to see a beneficial business deal, agreed.

Later, when the nation's governing powers shut down legal and official drinking, Step's discretion and his apparent indifference to alcohol paid off handsomely for Mittie and Mason, and ultimately, for Step, whose part-time salary at Mittie's increased as his responsibilities grew.

Through his association with Mittie Clark Gaines, Step was able to retain a modicum of freedom. He rarely discussed his business dealings at Mittie's with Cal; and as Cal didn't see a conflict of interest, he didn't complain. From that night in early 1918 until Rainey came to Washington, neither Mittie Clark Gaines nor Cal Bertrand had any reason to be disappointed in him.

There was only one person in the world whom Cal Bertrand loved other than Cal Bertrand: Step Herndon.

The two had been lovers since the second day after Step's arrival on the DC landscape, when, as Cal helped him adjust a brand new high collar shirt and a sporty new tie, Cal Bertrand placed a light kiss on Step's lips. Step dimly interpreted the gesture as the "Northern" way of friendship between men. In fact, Step liked the firm feel of this man's lips on his own; the pressure was much more to his liking than the soft and reluctant caresses of his South Carolina girlfriends. So Step Herndon smiled across at Cal Bertrand. Taking this smile as encouragement, Cal kissed Step again, this time gently forcing Step's willing lips apart with his tongue.

Step had often kissed his South Carolina girlfriends like this, but he had always been the aggressor. He liked this kiss even better than the first, and to his surprise, responded eagerly to Cal's seeking tongue. Cal stood back from Step and studied his face.

"You liked that, eh?"

"Yes, Mr. Bertrand, I did."

"Good. This could be the start of a great life for you." Cal turned away from Step and then with lightning speed, whirled back toward him, striking him across the face with amazing force. Step fell back, stunned.

"And if you ever tell anybody about what goes on between us behind these doors, anyone at all, I will kill you, do you hear?"

Step's view of Cal was blurred by tears of pain and shock.

"Yes, Mr. Bertrand."

"And when we're here alone together, you may call me Cal."

"Okay ... Cal."

Cal Bertrand smiled then, relieved. He locked his fingers together and turned his palms outward so that the knuckles cracked loudly.

"Now, Step. Let me see that you know how to hang up your clothes when you get undressed. I don't want to see any of these clothes --" Cal swept his hand in a semicircle across the veritable wealth of clothing that lay on Step's bed "-- laying around as if they've been thrown away."

Step undressed and felt a surge of passion arouse in him the deepest feelings of lust he had ever known. Some time later that day, he cried out in an agony of glorious pain as Cal Bertrand rammed away at the last vestiges of his bumpkinish innocence.

Much later, Step lay on his stomach, basking in the afterglow of his first truly violent, truly sincere eruption of passion, as Cal gently cleaned his anus, kissing at it to help ease the pain he had inflicted. Step hissed softly, caught in a maelstrom of newly awakened feelings.

"Are you all right, Step?" Cal turned Step over, deeply concerned. "I didn't hurt you too badly, did I?"

"It was worth it ... Cal. I didn't have no idea it could ever be like this." And Step sat up then, oddly thrilled by the throbbing soreness, and kissed Cal deeply.

And so began Cal's possession of Step.

From Cal, Step got money, new clothes, and what Step admitted only to himself was "real loving." From Step, Cal got well-feigned attentiveness, well-feigned affection, and genuine passion. Step was a very quick study, and was possessed of what Cal regarded as "divine lechery" – he not only learned quickly, but he soon taught Cal some things. No one had ever made love to Cal the way Step did.

Step could barely stand the sight of Cal outside the bedroom of their little hideaway. To Step, Cal was the ugliest trained seal he had ever laid eyes on. He couldn't stand the way Cal's face seemed to protrude from his head. Even those whiskers he called a mustache had about them the look of sea mammal. His slanted eyes looked far too desperate for Step to feel anything more positive than tolerance towards him.

To Cal, Step was an Adonis, a golden gift from some distant automaton of a god. He had managed to convince himself that Step's loyalties were real, and that those loyalties were devoted only to Cal Bertrand. He treasured every aspect of Step: the lovely and luminous heart shape of his face, the delicate bulges of his muscled torso, the lovely shape and relentless steel of his magnificent penis. He managed, usually, to ignore the sly looks of contempt that Step slid his way when he thought he was unobserved. He ignored the stark reality that if he were not showering his lover with all that kept his interest, his lover would be a glimmering memory in his life. Cal Bertrand convinced himself that he didn't give a damn that Step had affairs with women. He only cared that Step was there at their little M Street hideaway at his beck and call. He regarded Step's female dalliances as passing fancies; surely Step's love for him was as great as Cal's own love for Step.

The one reality that he could barely ignore about William "Step" Herndon was that he could always be bought. He constantly farmed himself out to the highest bidder. Step Herndon had no loyalties beyond his next free meal, wardrobe or sexual encounter. And Cal knew, and reluctantly admitted to himself, that he had probably created this monster. He had to face the reality more often than he cared to.

Step Herndon was a whore.

And Cal Bertrand, self-made man in an elite Negro community, was but a helpless john, hopelessly addicted to the charms of the accomplished young gigolo. But, oh, what accomplishments!

Step Herndon's fount of inconsistencies and erratic behavior flowed deeper still than most of his associates knew. He was dapper to Rainey, deadly and irresistible to Cal, useful to Mittie, and addicted to a potent combination of heroin and laudanum called "The Max" exclusively by his circle of addicts, who were the only aficionados of this mixture. Step had first been introduced to laudanum alone by a cute little dental office assistant he used to keep company with (steal from). The girl's name was Mary Fisher, known by all her cohorts as "Little Mary." She was a cute sweet little gal, not much taller than a ten-year-old, with the deceptively innocent face of a child. That face masked a totally debauched wreck of a woman who used her appearance and the outward façade of orderliness to steal or coerce whatever she chose from whomever she designated as her prey.

Despite her cold and calculating nature, Little Mary must have been loopy on the stuff most of the time.

She walked up to him that first night holding in front of her a dainty white handkerchief with blue-scalloped edges. She was smiling her usual dreamy smile and Step smiled at her, expecting female sex from her. She leaned up to him as if to kiss him. Step readied his mouth only to have it socked full of wet, alcohol-dampened handkerchief. Before he could protest, Step Herndon felt a sensation he had never felt before. He was blind, he was deaf, he was devoid of speech, his nostrils were stuffed full of sparkling nothing -- and then sweet weightlessness that lasted for an eternal thirty seconds. As he descended to earth, his head, arms, and legs felt as if they were the weights pulling him downward into bland reality.

"Girl, gimmee some more of whatsinever that was," Step breathed when he swayed back into sobriety. "And what was it, anyway?"

"Laudanum," Little Mary breathed, sliding down the foothill of her own intense high. "It's what Dr. Goins uses for the real difficult cases. You like it, eh?"

"Hell, yes. I want some more."

"Nah-uh-uh.   Gonna cost you.   The first time was free."

"Well, shit! How much?" Step grabbed his billfold.

"Oh, no, baby, just drop them drawers for me one time."

Soon after Little Mary's handkerchief trick, one of Step's fellow dancers showed him how to put a dab of a new and exotic powder inside his nostrils and sniff it. The dancer called this powder "white horse" and told Step that only the most chic people even knew about it. Soon, it was Step who introduced the potion of heroin and laudanum to Little Mary in Dr. Goins's office, and later, to their growing posse of like-minded cronies. He named this concoction "The Max" because he could not imagine a feeling that would be more maximum in its intensity than laudanum and heroin together.

He felt so totally alive, so much the captain of his own destiny, that he didn't see the hollows that had carved into his cheekbones, or the haunted vacant gaze in his once alert and searing eyes. For his now baggy clothes, which seemed to swirl around him as he danced lately, he credited his constant movement and boundless energy as a dancer.

What he didn't understand then would later become for him a frigid reality: he was now a dope fiend.

CHAPTER THREE

A Bumpkin In Love

---- Q Street
Washington,
District of Columbia
October 20, 1922

My Dear Martha Alice:

I hope this letter has arrived in time for your birthday! Happy Birthday, my darling friend! How does it feel to be as old as me (smile)? I hope you like the little charm I've placed inside this letter. It's a 10 karat gold image of our church, Metropolitan AME Zion Church here in Georgetown. Of course, we are there every Sunday, no matter how late we have worked the night before. According to Aunt Mittie, "anybody who <u>is</u> anybody goes to Metropolitan!" Aunt Mittie is <u>so</u> funny. She dips snuff, sells hooch <u>and</u> she tries to be holy right along with the high society colored folks! Still, Aunt Mittie is a lot nicer than I expected her to be, and she is rich, too. You must come up here and see Auntie's house. It is the most beautiful place I have ever seen.

But that is not the most exciting thing that has happened to me. I will get to it all in time, don't you worry. I am <u>very</u> happy here in Washington.

How is Uncle Eddie? He should have gotten my letter by now. Does he seem sad since I left? I miss him so much! Look after him when you can? Do you see much of Laurence and Miriam? I <u>really</u> miss Laurence, too, and Miriam, of course.

When I got here, Aunt Mittie had already arranged for me to teach at Delicado High School, will wonders never cease! It seems she knows the principal, Mr. Belton, very well. It is such a thrill to teach there. It's about five blocks from Aunt Mittie's house, so I get to walk there. You know how I love to exercise! Remember how our mothers used to tell us that all that jumping around wasn't ladylike? Well, just so Aunt Mittie won't say anything like that, I deliberately set my watch ahead fifteen minutes so that I can pretend that I am late for work. That way I can practically run without being accused of conduct unbecoming. At any rate, Aunt Mittie is usually asleep at that early hour of the morning (7:30).

And, of course, Uncle Mason never says a "mumbling word." Oh, forgive me. I'm being wicked. He's a nice man, but he's so quiet, he scares me! Aunt Mittie says she has never heard him speak!

The school is huge! Can you imagine a school with 500 students? And they all want to sing! I am the second music teacher, and I work with all the girls' choirs. There are four girls'-only choirs, Martha Alice! There's the Freshman-Sophomore Girls' chorus, the Junior-Senior Girls' Chorus, the Girls' Glee Club, and the Nightingales, twenty of the singingest girls I have ever heard in my life! It's like a dream come true for me. I see so much potential there with all the girls. Many of them never knew just how well they can sing.

I hope you can understand why I haven't written you so much lately. I have simply been so busy! All the choirs are practicing most of Handel's Messiah for Christmas. Now that is hard work, but I believe it's going to be absolutely beautiful! Will you and Arthur please come up to hear them? I miss you so much! I will never have a better friend than you, Martha Alice!

The lead teacher is Professor Charles Willis, the most wonderful man, and he is a master organist for Metropolitan when he is not teaching. His wife, Mrs. Helen Willis, teaches Language Arts at Delicado, too. She's such a sweet lady. They are the nicest couple. If I ever get married, I hope to be as happy as you and Arthur and Mr. and Mrs. Willis are.

Professor Willis has been very gracious to me and seems to respect my own talents. He tells me I have one of the most beautiful singing voices he has ever heard. He has encouraged me to go on with my education. So come this summer, I'll be taking up master's courses at Howard University. They have a special program for teachers who want to earn master's degrees. I'll be finished in the summer of '24. How about that? No, I don't expect to meet any eligible doctors or lawyers there, thank you very much.

One thing I've done that I never thought about at all is join a sorority. There's a brand new sisterhood at Howard called Zeta Phi Beta Sorority. It's the newest Negro sorority, and all summer long I talked to Mrs. Willis and her daughter, dear Alouette, about joining. They've both been Zetas since it began in '20. About two weeks ago, I, too, became a Zeta! The next time you see me I will be wearing lots of blue and white -- Zeta colors!

My hair is now marcelled! Have you tried that at your shop yet? If not, maybe you could come up here and let Aunt Mittie show you how. Any old excuse for you to come up, okay? I love having my hair like this. I only have to bother with my hair once a week now.

My skirts are now much shorter than they were in Raleigh. Well, short skirts -- and hair -- are really all the rage in Washington right now. Now, I have to dress like a school marm by day (except for the marcel), but by night, honey! Whee!! Please come see me soon? Arthur won't mind, will he?

Now for the big news. Are you ready? I think I am in love! Now don't faint. His name is William Herndon, but everybody calls him "Step." He's 26 years old and very distinguished looking -- he has a tiny bit of gray hair around his temples. He's from South Carolina, and he works for my Aunt Mittie when he's not dancing at Boney's After-Hours Supper Club. And my goodness, he can dance!

Sometimes I can hardly see his feet, they're moving so fast. He's teaching me how to tap and he says that maybe someday we can tap together at Boney's because I'm what he calls a "quick study"! Let me describe him to you: he's about Arthur's height (isn't he about six feet tall?), extremely muscular, skin the color of a butterscotch brownie (appetizing!), dreamy brown eyes, and his hair is naturally wavy. He dances like a dream, and he treats me like I'm his dream come true. He kisses better than any fellow I have ever kissed. (Maybe one day soon, we will do "other" things, my dear!) I think I want to spend the rest of my life with him, Martha Alice. He's so smart and romantic. He always brings me nosegays, and, every once in a while, a rose. He tells me how pretty I look, smells my hair, kisses me on my neck, and oh, so many other little things that make me feel so special. I know he could have any other woman in Washington, but he chose little old countrified me. He seems to spend every free moment he has with me. And he has never, ever tried to be fresh or mannish with me. His patience makes me that much more eager, if you know what I mean. Step just makes me so very happy. I can hardly wait for you and Arthur to meet him.

When we first got to DC, Step came to get us from Union Station in Aunt Mittie's old car. When we got to the house, Aunt Mittie not only tipped him ($5!!!) for bringing our bags in, but she also paid him another $5 for some kind of delivery. He must be <u>some</u> hard worker! He actually swept me off my feet right there in Aunt Mittie's foyer, but of course, I didn't let <u>him</u> know it. He was so debonair! For some reason, Aunt Mittie was really dead set against me going out with him, but I guess she saw that we were determined to be together, so she gave in. It has taken her the longest time, though to give in and go with me to Boney's to see him dance. We are finally going this Wednesday night! I'll write you as soon as I can to tell you all about it!

Now let me tell you about how Aunt Mittie got to be so rich. Remember I told you she paid Step for some deliveries? Well it didn't take too long for me to understand about these "deliveries." Wait until you get a load of this. Those deliveries were NOT hair products! Are you ready? She has a SPEAKEASY downstairs! (Remember I told you she sells hooch? Well!!) It's a very elegant establishment, with a three-tier chandelier in the center of the ceiling and wall sconces and fresh flowers on each of the tables (there are 12 little tables). She's got bouncers to keep troublemakers out, and she pays a "tribute" to the police in the neighborhood to make sure they don't raid the place. The people who come in there are decked out in furs and tuxedos. They stop off at Mittie's on their way to places like Boney's or Mr. Blues or Madame Calico's Supper Club. Aunt Mittie trusts me to the point where I wait tables in there now -- every night this summer and on weekends now that school is open. (Nice extra change, by the way. I'm putting it away for a rainy day that I don't believe will ever come!) She has a piano bar and this wonderful man named Joe Reeves plays any song customers want to hear for a small tip. Sometimes I get to sing with Joe, who has a lovely baritone voice. I think we sound marvelous together, but of course, I like to use any excuse at all to sing anywhere (smile). Joe Reeves is a good friend, Martha Alice, but he worries about Step and me more than he needs to. Step cares for me, no matter what some seem to think.

Anyhow, the funny thing is, I was able to get the job teaching at Delicado High School because Mr. Belton, my principal, comes into the speakeasy real regularly. He gets looped, too, most nights. I don't see how he holds down a job, Martha Alice! But somehow or the other, he always conducts himself with great dignity. Will wonders never cease?

The thing I like about Aunt Mittie's place is that there are no troublemakers coming in there. You have to know a password, which changes daily, and you must pay a fee to Reeves, who splits the take with Auntie, to find out what that password is. It's all very low-key and calm.

Oh, darling, you have to come and visit. I am truly living the life here. Well, I must close now. I will try to write you really soon. I miss you so much. Give all your folks my love!

Hugs and kisses, Rainey-bear

****

(Picture postcard of the Governor's Mansion, Raleigh, NC)

October 27, 1922

Dearest love Rainey-bear:

You be careful, you hear? I am in the family way, expecting in March. More details later. Happy news about your job! I had a wonderful birthday!

The charm is simply <u>gorgeous</u>! I shall think of you each time I look at it dangling from my bracelet. You always did spoil me, you know!

Aunt Mittie sounds like a character!

We love you and miss you. Come home for Thanksgiving? We'll really put on the dog for you, girl! Yes, I'm marcelling here, too.

Miss Rainey E. Clark
c/o Mrs. Mittie Gaines
----Q Street, NW, 09
District of Columbia

YOU BE REAL CAREFUL,
ALL RIGHT?
  Much love,
  M-A-Bear.

   Rainey stared at the picture of the Governor's Mansion with its sharp turrets and its recessed porches. She pondered the rare beauty of its corner gardens and its simple brown brick as she had never done on those lazy Sunday afternoon strolls past its Person Street side. She sighed and was surprised to find tears spilling onto her cheeks. She didn't know until that moment that she really was homesick, that she hadn't allowed herself time to grieve for her mother's death, that she hadn't even allowed herself a single longing thought for her father. And dear Uncle Eddie! What would become of him?

   Rainey wiped the tears from her silken cheeks finally, turning the card over once more to read Martha Alice's note. She was thrilled to know that she was to become an "aunt" in March. But "Be real careful"? What in the world was Martha Alice talking about? Rainey pushed her fist into her waist in consternation. Careful? With Step and Aunt Mittie looking out for her, what in the world did she need to be careful about?

Boney's After-Hours Supper Club was, for Rainey, three months after her arrival, well worth the wait. The Club was the showcase of Negro society in Washington. Of course, by then she was deeply in love with Step, and everything about him had a golden glow attached to it. Later, the heavy burgundy velvet drapes, delicately arranged at windows that were actually brick walls, would show their frays and frazzles to her. It wouldn't be too long before the elegant twinkling of the heavy chandelier would reveal itself to her as faulty wiring, which would also explain the slight singed smell that Rainey always dismissed as a cigar burned overlong in someone's ashtray. Not too long from then, the cool brass sheen of the chandelier would reveal that it had long given itself over to clots of paint gouged from its surface. Someday in the not too distant future, the ample Persian rugs covering the burgundy carpet in the lobby would themselves wear through to reveal a warped and scarred floor with several missing boards. The now musical raindrops tinkling onto the roof above them tonight would later beat out the rhythm of her misery. The rarefied air in which she thought she could thrive tonight would someday mean to her nausea born out in the moldy atmosphere of the club. And those unevenly cushioned seats that forced patrons to remain alert while the jazz bands jazzed and the dancers jammed and the singers crooned would, in their own sweet time, chafe against her spare behind.

All those revelations were for a distant future dawning on a horizon of bitter understanding not so far away. Tonight, on this first night she would see her beloved perform, Rainey could see only a gala opening, a "happening" as her granddaughter Honey would someday call such an event. And what a happening!

At exactly 9:00, when the lobby clock chimed the hour with soft elegance, the band leader tapped his baton on his music stand. The room darkened immediately, and at the precise moment that the first trumpet note growled forth, a greenish spotlight glowed on the 10-piece orchestra. For several minutes, the band rendered an amazing, peppy tune that sounded vaguely like some spiritual Rainey had sung both at First Baptist and at Metropolitan. She was pleasantly shocked by this apparent blasphemy; it just confirmed for her how far she had come from the tiny town life she had left behind forever. She was instantly swept away by the drama of it all. As each player soloed, he stood up, expressed himself eloquently and sat back down, wiping his drenched face with a blindingly white handkerchief.

Rainey felt a scalding tingle course through her body: this was excitement. All around her, patrons were idly sipping their drinks, their heads leaned together in conversation. Their tapping feet and their snapping fingers and the rhythmic nods of their heads revealed their true absorption in the music. A cross between hot jazz and Bessie's blues, this music was infectious, irresistible. Rainey swayed helplessly in her chair, wishing she was on stage engaged in a frenetic tap with Step. Almost involuntarily, her heels slammed against the carpeted floor in time to the beat. No sharp look from Mittie tonight: she was, like her niece, caught up in the music.

The song ended with a crash, and Rainey felt let down somehow, as if a draft had suddenly invaded the warm room. But before she could adjust herself to the emptiness, the green-glow spotlight was back on the stage again. A single trumpet, in bold, poignant falsetto, held the room hostage for a languorous, breathless moment. B flat, Rainey thought. That's an odd note to start off with. Intrigued, she leaned forward expectantly in her chair. She was not disappointed. After the long note, the band launched into yet another frantic, foot-stomping rhythm. Dancers leapt onto the tiny stage.   They seemed to come from everywhere, and their feathered costumes swirled blindingly around their flailing arms and legs and their questing hips. One lone figure seemed to materialize in the midst of the bandstand. Clad all in black, even down to the mask that covered its face, this figure mirrored the moves of the other dancers in half time. The effect was stunning: all around this dancer, band members sweated and bounced, dancing girls jumped, executed flawless burlesque caricatures of curtsies, kicked and clapped.

And in the midst of frenzy, masked cool.

Suddenly, the music roared to a jagged halt. Every patron in the room seemed to lean forward, and an expectant hush spread from the stage outward. The band leader stepped into the spotlight with the figure, whose back was turned to the audience. The band leader wore a self-satisfied smirk, and paused for a too-long moment before projecting his voice, basso profundo:

"Ladies and Gentlemen! Hold on to your seats. It's Step time."

Rainey gasped. With dizzying speed, her beloved whirled around, removed his mask, and launched into the most amazingly executed set of taps, pirouettes, and leaps, his manic, sharp taps in stunning concert with the improbable beat of a high hat. The audience cheered and whistled; the band members stomped their feet in grateful time to the drummer's rhythm. The other dancers, barely visible on the edges of the stage, occasionally kicked their long legs outward to the periphery of the spotlight. At the climax of his magnificent performance, Step somehow leapt onto the top rafter of the bandstand and then executed the most tremendous leap forward to the front row of the now screaming audience. The music cleared its own way through the wild applause and as Step took bow after bow, the band completed the frantic, b-flat beat it had begun a delicious eternity ago. The crowd was on its feet now, cheering and begging for more. Step moved away from the stage and strutted toward Rainey's table. Her heart beat faster: what in the world was he going to do now?

As he got closer to her table, Step suddenly began to leap and pirouette again. In an instant he was in front of her, and she felt eyes burning into her from all over the smoky room. Step grasped her trembling hands in his callused ones. He planted a deep, lingering kiss on each upturned palm before kissing her primly on her hot cheek.

The audience roared its approval as Step disappeared backstage.

Meanwhile, in the wings, the proprietor stood silently, watching, fuming.

Rainey had never met a more charming and affectionate man. He was so romantic that she was hopelessly swept off her feet soon enough. He always had a flower for her. He always kissed her left cheek and her supple wrist. She was intrigued by the gleam in his sleepy eyes. He always seemed to be just a half-world removed from her and from his surroundings.

And she was so enamored of him that she hardly minded that he had a sniffle all the time. She would gently offer him the stack of newly starched white handkerchiefs that she had bought for him. She had embroidered his initials, including the "S", in an antique blue in the lower right hand corner of each handkerchief. It was all right that he went through most of them each visit. She kept a dainty little basket at the ready for him to deposit the used ones. And the next afternoon after his visit, she would hurry to the laundry to have them washed and ironed in preparation for his next visit.

And what a love he was, she thought now. In each month since they had met, Step had brought excitement into her line of vision. (He really could have made a party out of tea and toast.) In July, though Mittie would not let her out of her sight, he had taught her to do his remarkable three-step dance routine. He'd made it up himself, he had told her proudly, and each time he executed it at the Supper Club, he had gotten wild screams of approval from his audience. Rainey had learned this step quickly, her slim feet sweeping through the air with nearly as much grace as Step's. He had rewarded her with the most tingling French kiss of her life. She hadn't had so many opportunities for that kind of romancing, and she nearly swooned against his solid chest. And she'd been utterly tickled to realize that they had barely missed being discovered by Mittie, who came bustling into the parlor scant seconds after the kiss. Rainey was happy for the swelter of July; Mittie would think nothing odd about the deepened circles of perspiration beneath the sleeveless bodice of her dress.

In August, Step accompanied the family on a Sunday afternoon picnic at Aunt Addie Rose's house. He lurked about them like a troubled shadow, to be more accurate. He was careful to keep his distance from Joe Reeves and his family.

Joe's wife, Irene, was a sweet-faced woman with merry eyes, a ready laugh, and a body that was a testament to her hearty appetite. She dwarfed her husband in height and width. And as if in genetic echo to their parents, the Reeves' daughter, Claire, at 12, was tall and round like Irene, and nine-year-old little Joe was just that -- little, and powerfully built -- like his father. Both were pleasant and well-mannered; why, the adults hardly knew the children were there. After dinner, they played in the southwest corner of the massive backyard. Claire was the domineering teacher to Little Joe as the attentively amused pupil.

On that August afternoon in 1922 when Rainey visited Aunt Addie Rose's mansion for the first time, Adele Clark Connelly put on her best face for her sister and her niece. She had sent her servants away for that day, and she and Mittie and Rainey cooked in her dark and cavernous kitchen. Outside, Mason and Joe prepared the fire in Addie Rose's barbecue grill, while Step fetched anything they needed, and they roasted pork and chickens enough to feed them all well for the rest of the week. The family dined on Addie Rose's screened back porch, laughing and talking and singing. Addie Rose commented that she was happy to live in such seclusion so that she could visit with her people in peace, but she was getting lonely now. While Addie Rose and Mittie argued gently over whether Addie Rose should just give up and move into a wealthy widows' home, Step moved quietly to Rainey's wicker chair and whispered,

"I'll race you to the edge of the yard!"

Rainey stifled a giggle and asked Aunt Mittie if she minded her taking a walk around "Aunt Addie Rose's beautiful yard." Mittie, embroiled in an intense discussion with her sister, waved her away. Rainey and Step walked demurely off the back porch and into the huge landscaped playground that they would make of Addie Rose's breathtaking yard. Once the screened porch was out of their sight, they took off running, Rainey holding her annoyingly long skirt with one hand and waving after Step Herndon with the other. Step Herndon had removed his spats, which Rainey reluctantly acknowledged were inappropriate for this outing, and his shirttails flapped joyously behind him. It seemed to take them an eternity to reach the edge of Addie Rose's yard. But they finally reached the ivy-draped, wrought-iron fence, through which they could just make out the back yard of Addie Rose's nearest neighbor (whom they would of course never meet).

This corner of the yard, like the whole expanse of it, was enchanting. There was a gazebo through which birds swooped and sometimes landed (and sometimes left their vile souvenirs). In the middle of the gazebo, on a raised platform, a white iron loveseat beckoned to them. Step and Rainey sank into the chair, careless of any dust (or leavings) that might assault their bottoms, and fell to each other's mouths. Rainey had by now perfected the art of the French kiss, and was one of its premier connoisseurs. Step was pleased with the progress his pupil had made. In his debauched heart of hearts, he believed that she would soon open unto him more than just her willing lips, and, ultimately, her purse strings would open freely unto him.

"Sing to me, Miss Rainey," Step commanded after an endless bout of kissing. And she sang to him, disturbed vaguely that she only knew church songs. But he looked enchanted, and soon got up to engage in a little soft-shoe in time to one of her spirituals. Rainey quelled her horror. She had never been allowed to dance on Sundays, so dancing to a spiritual on a Sunday was almost too much for her to bear. But bear it she did, for the sake of her blossoming love for Step Herndon.

Inside himself, Step Herndon was miserable. It had been far too long since he had boosted the Max stupor. He was beginning to feel sick, and he was beginning to get restless. He had brought a little of the Max with him, and was desperate to get into a secret place alone and return to himself. He stopped dancing suddenly, turned toward Rainey, and excused himself. He pretended to blush.

"I hate to do this, Miss Rainey, but I need to, uh, you know, and I don't think I'll make it back to your aunt's house!" Step quickly chose a spot behind a curtain of trees far enough away from Rainey that she would not hear the snort of his dosage or the splash of his relief. Rainey looked uncomfortable with his admission, and lowered her eyes modestly to give her assent.

Step slipped away, and when he returned, eyes a-droop, lips sagging slightly, he fell into the loveseat next to (Yvette? Donna? oh--) Rainey and took her hand into his callused palms.

"You are beautiful," he said, and laid his head against her shoulder. Soon he was snoring against her chest. At first, Rainey was moved beyond words by what she thought was a gesture of his trust in her. But soon, she found she had to nudge at him repeatedly, until he sat up, wearily, and wiped drool away from his loose lips.

"We'd better get back to the house, Step," she said, rubbing at her sore shoulder, startled (disgusted) by the stain of bergamot left there by his "naturally wavy" hair.   Ah, Laurence . . . !

"Huh? Oh."

As they made their way back to Addie Rose's screened porch, he stumbling and she bewildered, Rainey wondered where all Step's energy had gone all of a sudden.   Still, she'd had a wonderful afternoon with Step, and, despite the slight gloom she felt for a brief moment in September of that year, she looked forward to many more.

It was Rainey's September memory that caused her only reservations in her happiness with Step. As she practiced with Joe Reeves one Saturday morning, Joe suddenly slammed his hands on the keys he usually treasured. Rainey, startled, cut her singing mid-warble. Outside, the day was golden, and she had wondered what Step was doing, and where he was. Was he missing her, too? Would he hear her sing after he danced at Boney's?

Joe Reeves stared at her now, and for Rainey, his look was inscrutable.

"What's the matter, Joe? Was my singing off?"

"No, Rainey it wasn't. But if you keep on like you been doing, it will be off, and that won't be all!"

"Joe! What in the world!"

Joe Reeves stared at her for a long time. She felt nervous and worried. What had gotten into Joe? He was usually so serious about his music, and he usually concentrated on it totally. She had never seen him angry, and could not imagine what she had done to offend him.

Finally, he took a deep breath, crunched once on his ever-present cigar, and pulled his pocket watch from his vest.

"Sit down a minute, gal. Let me tell you a story."

Rainey, still worried, obeyed Joe Reeves's command, and took a seat next to him on the long piano bench.

"Not too long ago, there was a pretty little girl, lived right here in Georgetown. She looked a little bit like you, Rainey.

But she was mighty hardheaded. You'd tell her to come straight home from school, and she just had to stop by the store, for some MaryJanes, or she had to go to her friend's house to put a bow on her hair just the right way. And no matter what you did to her, didn't matter if you punished her, or sent her to bed without her dinner, she just kept right on doing what she wanted to do.

"You know, at first it was cute. 'That little gal's got a mind of her own, ain't she?' That's what all her people would say about her. But when that pretty little girl got to be a young lady, and she still wouldn't come home when she was told to, it got to be a real problem for her people. See, by the time she got to be a young lady, she wasn't stopping by candy stores any more. She was stopping by speakeasies, you know, the kind that's open all times of day or night. Her people started having to go into these speakeasies and pull her out. Oh, she'd poke out her lips something awful, she'd be so mad. But her people didn't care if she was mad or not. They wasn't gonna have her out in the streets of Washington like some lowlife woman.

"It got so bad, she had to be walked to and from school by some of her kin. Her people thought this was working, but they didn't know that she had already met the fellow who was going to be her undoing. It turns out that after she got walked to school, this pretty little girl would find a way to sneak out into the play yard at that school and slip away with this devilish fellow. While all the nice girls were sitting in the play yard eating their homemade lunches and talking about hair styles and baby dolls and all that other stuff girls like to spend their time talking about, this pretty girl would be in some alleyway with the devil, doing things that only married ladies ought to be doing, and then only in the privacy of their own homes with their own husbands.

"The next thing her people know, and you can just about expect this, the pretty little girl was in the family way. And where was that devil? Well, after he slapped her face black and blue, that devil left that pretty girl high and dry and having HIS baby!"

Joe Reeves's fist slammed through the air, but stopped short of attacking the ivory keys he loved. He was silent for a few moments, struggling to calm himself.

"The pretty little girl's people went looking for this devil after he sent her home crying like her heart was broken and looking like she'd run into Jack Johnson's fist a couple of times. And she led them right to him, where he worked nights. Her people were ready to kill this devil, but she begged them to spare his life. Maybe he would come to his senses and take care of his child. And, since she was gonna have the baby, she didn't want to have to tell her child that her people killed his papa. So the devil's life was spared. And he still lives right here in Georgetown, working at his jobs, and charming the young ladies. I hear he might be one to charm other folks, too."

Rainey had barely taken a breath during Joe Reeves's tale. She blinked now, and cleared her throat.

"Where is the pretty girl?"

"She's up in Delaware now, with her little boy. The devil has never seen his son, and he ain't NEVER, NEVER asked how that pretty girl is doing, or if she needs anything. She's been hurt to her heart 'cause of this devil and I don't think she'll ever be right again. She won't go out, except to work, or to take her little son to school. She's still mighty pretty, and young men always try to court her, but she refuses. That devil ruined her."

Joe Reeves turned to Rainey now, and his big eyes became pools of truth.

"So I'm telling you, Miss Rainey, I'm begging you and I'm warning you. Be very careful about the company you keep."

"I am, Joe. You know who I go around with --"

Joe Reeves's eyes narrowed slightly, and his nod was almost imperceptible.

A January wind nudged the striking man into her shop, and Mittie Clark Gaines stopped her marcel iron just long enough to glance toward the door. It was only Cal Bertrand. She smiled politely and continued her work.

"Yes, Cal, how are you today?"

"Hello, Mrs. Gaines." Cal stood just about ten feet away from her, and his face was in shadow in the meager light of the overhead lamp. But she knew that he was here on business; he only called her Mittie or Miss Mitt at any other times.

Uh-oh. "Let me finish this gal's hair, and I'll be right with you."

Within ten minutes, Mittie had completed her latest masterpiece and sent another satisfied customer on her way, adorned with a lovely head of hair and relieved of a few dollars from her purse.

"What in the world is wrong now, Cal?"

"I think we've got a little problem. I believe Step has been seeing a lot of your niece?"

Mittie's face darkened. "Hell, yes, and I don't like it one bit."

"Nor do I."

"I'm just so afraid to come out and say anything to my Rainey about it, 'cause that might make her want to be with him that much more."

"I understand your position, Miss Mitt. I definitely believe that Step will be a problem for you and for your niece. And on top of that, I don't know how, but it seems that his involvement with your niece has had some effect on his work."

"How do you mean?"

"Oh, now it's not her fault, but he's not rehearsing as much or as well as he used to. Sometimes he doesn't even come to rehearsal."

"Okay, but I don't see how that can have anything to do with Rainey. She's at work during the day. You know they don't get any free time."

"I didn't think she could be seeing him during the day."

"So what does Rainey have to do with Step being a no-good crank?"

"Well, nothing, I'm sure, but I thought you needed to be aware. I plan to talk to him, persuade him to stay away from your little niece."

"Thank you, Cal."

"Oh, the pleasure is all mine."

And so the months melted into one another, bringing her 'round to that January, where Rainey, seated in front of her aunt's marble fireplace, still thought she was ready to give herself to Step Herndon.

"But, Rainey, dearest! You and I have been so very close for the past six months now. Surely you can trust me," Step said, nearly moaning into Rainey's tousled hair.

Although Joe Reeves's story had haunted her since September, she continued to see Step, and to wish fervently for a long life with him. As she spent more time with him, Rainey found it more difficult to believe that Step could possibly have been the devil of Joe Reeves's story.

January. Outside, snow raged from a soft gray sky. Trees bent against the onslaught, and people bent away from the blizzard as they hurried inside. Lights from living rooms and businesses cast upon the glittering snow the only semblance of warmth out there, out in the elements.

Inside. A crackling fire raged in the marble and stone fireplace. Mittie's parlor was the place for perfect unions between friends, acquaintances, and lovers. They were cuddled together on the Queen Anne couch in front of the little inferno. They shared her lovely black shawl -- a Christmas gift from Aunt Mittie and Uncle Mason. Rainey loved the shawl; it had been knitted in the mysterious design of a spider's web. It was terribly elegant, and very cozy.

It was about 4:00 in the afternoon. Mittie was with a customer. Mason was taking care of business in their "other concern." Step was free from the Supper Club and the speakeasy until 6:00.

Rainey was alone with the love of her life -- or so he seemed. On this snowy January afternoon, when all elders were away, and she sat, courting on a Queen Anne couch, Step Herndon allowed her the luxury of seeing his beautiful bronzed chest. Rainey gasped and marveled: it was, to her like chiseled stone. Step was the most beautiful golden caramel color. To her mind, he was a god.

"Don't you love me, Miss Rainey? Haven't I shown you all my love?"

"Yes, Step, I do love you! How could you think I didn't?"

"We are both grown, ain't we? Don't you want to express love to me like I do to you?"

And suddenly, she was ready, so very ready, for this expression. They had been together quite a long time, after all. She had never had a beau in her life for so long a time. And this beau was her marching band and her gospel choir. He was every shout "Hallelujah" she could recollect. So what was the harm? She had met the man of her dreams, and she was going to spend the rest of her days with him.

Why, Martha Alice and "Red Art" had only courted for six months before they married. And Laurence and Miriam seemed to have gotten married rather instantly. She carefully ignored the fact that, in the Seatons' case, their families had known each other for all their lives before the courting, that those families had practically pushed them together into the courting. It was just a happy accident that they had truly loved each other. As for Laurence and Miriam, theirs was a very peaceful and contented relationship; there were no opportunities for parties, of the tea and toast variety or any other, with the tranquil and retiring Miriam. All those facts were for them; her situation was different. She had been lucky enough to meet her love on her own.

And though she decided on that January afternoon to give herself to Step, she thought she had better take a precaution.

On that afternoon, as the fire crackled in the marble fireplace and snow raged outside, Rainey Clark sat up away from Step Herndon's bronze chest, gently pulled his shirt together, and looked deeply into his eyes.

"You're asking me to do with you what only wives should do with their husbands, Mr. Herndon," she began, though her body was screaming to be taken.

"Miss Rainey! I don't mean you any disrespect! I just love you and I want to love you more."

"But it would be disrespectful of myself to give to you what is promised to my husband, whoever he may be." Rainey sat back inside herself and laughed, amazed. She didn't really embrace such stodgy morals, but she understood how they could work for her, even with this man whom she loved so well. If Step Herndon was Joe Reeves's devil, she wasn't about to be left high and dry with a baby!

"Miss Rainey," he was saying now. "I am terribly hurt that you would think that I want to hurt you, of all people. You are my sunshine and my starlight. I only want to love you more."

"There are other ways to show love, Step."

Suddenly, Step looked at his watch.

"Lord, look at the time! I'd better make tracks down to Boney's! I've got a rehearsal! Uh-- can you lend me a little? I don't get paid until the weekend."

Rainey went upstairs quickly to fetch her purse, and found three dollars there. She rushed back downstairs, where Step stood in his fully buttoned overcoat, and his pants stuffed carelessly into his galoshes.

"I only have three dollars --"

"Oh that'll do just fine! Thank you, Miss Rainey!"

He kissed Rainey chastely on her now burning cheek, and hurried away (to get in the Max) to Boney's.

After he left, Rainey cried for an hour; she was sure she had lost him. And she now had no extra money until her own payday at the end of the week. Despondent, she went upstairs to her bedroom and cried herself into a short nap.

She awakened with a start. I really am broke until the end of the week, she thought as she looked at her puffy face in her hand mirror. She adjusted her clothes, washed her face in her basin, and hurried down to the sub basement. Maybe she could wait tables tonight, though Mittie and Mason frowned on her working during the week. She knew, despite her deep love for Step, that she would never see those precious three dollars again.

Spring in 1923 was, as is its custom, glorious. Rainey found herself singing aloud mornings as she sprint-walked to work. Step was back in her life, and with him came excitement that was almost too much for her to bear. He was a marching band; indeed, he was a full-length parade to her. He brought more laughter and singing and dancing to her in one visit than she thought she'd had in her entire life. He made no further noises about wanting to "love her more."

Charles Willis, the lead choir teacher, noted her renewed joy, as did his wife, dear Mrs. Willis.

"Why, Miss Clark, I do believe you embody joy lately," he commented one afternoon as she prepared to leave the building, and he prepared to meet his wife for their short trip home.

"Why yes, Mr. Willis, I am happy, but springtime always brings me joy."

"Ah, but my wife thinks she sees something else in your eyes, young missy."

Rainey laughed and blushed. "I hope I'm not that obvious. But I do have a special beau."

"Well won't you come with me to Helen's classroom, and tell us all about him?"

"Yes, sir."

In Helen Willis's classroom, the couple teased Rainey gently about her new beau, cajoling her about his name and his occupation. Helen offered Rainey a homemade oatmeal cookie, and Rainey begged her for the recipe; she had never tasted a better oatmeal cookie.

"I'll make a deal with you, young Soror. If you tell me your beau's name, I will give you my secret recipe." They laughed. Rainey adored the Willises, who had always treated her as if she were their young kinswoman.

"Well, his name is William, but everyone calls him Step. He dances at Boney's After Hours Supper Club, and he also works for my auntie."

Suddenly, the cavernous room was a tomb as the Willises looked quickly at each other and then away. Rainey, puzzled, stopped crunching her cookie.

"Is something wrong, Mr. and Mrs. Willis?"

Helen Willis was suddenly totally involved in grading a few last papers. Charles Willis studied the oak tree outside his wife's classroom window. Finally, after endless minutes, Charles Willis spoke to Rainey.

"Mr. Herndon . . . has made quite a name for himself here in town, Miss Clark . . . ."

Helen Willis spoke up now. "You be mighty careful, Rainey. He's a bit older than you --"

"Oh, only about four years!"

Again, the Willises exchanged looks. Finally, Charles spoke in a voice softer than his usual jovial boom.

"Miss Clark, Rainey, you know that Helen and I have grown to care for you a great deal. We just don't want you to get hurt. We are just asking you to be very careful, and to go slowly with Mr. Herndon. We hope that you understand our concern."

"I just don't know why everybody is telling me to be careful!" Rainey was near tears. Joe Reeves's story, Aunt Mittie's glares, and Uncle Mason's disapproving stares all haunted her now. Add all that to the Willises dire reaction to Step's name, and she felt that her beloved was perhaps the most misunderstood man in all Georgetown.

"Because we care about you, sweetheart." Mrs. Willis spoke now, gently. "Don't want you to go and get yourself hurt, that's all." Helen Willis put her fingertips lightly underneath Rainey's chin and delicately lifted the young woman's face to her own. "Now, dearie, here is Mrs. Willis's recipe, just like I promised!"

Rainey smiled, but inside she felt all cloudy. How could Step be so badly thought of, and yet be so wonderful to her?

Still, she took one look at Step later, and all her clouds burned away under the awesome power of his sun-bright charisma.

She drifted through that spring and summer, a graduate school co-ed at Howard University, admired by all sorts of handsome and upstanding Negro men. Yet, Rainey Elizabeth Clark remained afloat on her Step Herndon constellation just above the heads of those awestruck young men, ecstatically attached, yet blissfully untouched.

"Man, the Max is gettin' to be mighty damn expensive!"

Step sprawled across the damp old sofa in the basement apartment of Jimmy Best, one of his drug partners. It was by now the end of November. They had just barely put together enough money to pay Little Mary for the extra tank of laudanum she always ordered along with Dr. Goins's other supplies. Now, pulling together the funds for the horsey was going to be another challenge.

"Looks like we can't get our horsey supply this time, Jimmy."

"Can't you get some money from one of your, uh, sources?"

They were high at that moment, so the immediacy of their next dosage seemed a bit remote.

"That lil' ole country gal ain't got shit to give me," Step breathed contemptuously. "Looks like I'm a have to marry her ass to get any of her pappy's pension!"

Step had no idea if Rainey's father had even left her a pension, but that had been his hope with her all along.

Jimmy laughed. "You? Get married? Much as you likes to sample new meat? Shit!"

"Hell, I ain't even had a chance to sample this meat! She one of them proper bitches."

"Why you callin' her a bitch? Why you got to be disrespectful like that?"

"You got a helluva lot a nerve, talkin' about somebody bein' disrespectful! The way you be whippin' up on yo' women?"

"I don't be callin' 'em no nasty names, though. Ain't none o' yo' other gals got no funds, Step?"

"Yvette got married herself couple of months ago, and Donna done got the Holy Ghost."

"I reckon you drove her to it."

"Man, kiss my ass. We still got to find us a way to keep our supplies comin' in regular. Let me see if I can talk to my boss man about a raise. I'll see you tomorrow evening after I get off work."

"Yeah."

Step, though floating off on his own rhythmic cloud that night, danced well -- in his mind. To Cal Bertrand, Step was becoming more of a stumblebum than an accomplished dancer. He noticed with a mixture of alarm and jealous pleasure that Step's audiences, including tonight's, were no longer as enthusiastic about his performances. They had a date for that night, and Cal was determined to make Step understand that his work was suffering.

After a lovemaking session that was, as usual of late, less than inspired, Cal rolled over toward Step and took him into his arms. They kissed for a long time, and then Cal began, "Step?"

"Hmmm?"

"I need to talk business with you, baby."

"Okay, Cal, 'cause I need to ask you something, too."

"Step," Cal said now, leaving the disheveled bed, and beginning to dress. "Your dancing is not like it used to be . . . and for that matter, nothing much else is, either."

"What you talkin' about, Cal? I thought I danced my ass off tonight. And as for other things --"

"Step, you used to take a lot of pride in everything you did. You took pride in how you looked." Cal, now clad in his underwear, walked over to the dresser and picked up a hand mirror.

"Have you had a good look at yourself lately, Step? You're starting to look like a ghost."

"Cal, what the hell are you talking about . . . .?" Step, now sitting up in the bed, looked at his reflection in the hand mirror Cal now thrust before his haggard face. He was stunned. He hadn't taken a good look at himself. He was pale, thin, and his eyes looked like they were peering out of tiny hollow caves. Damn! No wonder his girls had dropped him. Only Rainey had stayed loyal to him, and that was probably because she didn't know any better.

Still silenced by his reflection, Step looked into Cal's eyes. He saw disappointment and hurt and concern there. He saw deep, wounded love. Step felt disgusted. He didn't give much of a damn for Cal Bertrand beyond the man's money, which supplied him with the Max, the man's club, which gave him a chance to express himself creatively, or the man's sex, which was the only kind he couldn't do without. The man himself, unadorned with those treasures, was useless to Step Herndon.

"I didn't know I was looking like this! I have been mighty troubled lately, Cal."

Cal, all concern now, sat next to Step on the bed. Surprisingly, Step's face was mysteriously beautiful and almost achingly enticing to Cal in the dwindling flicker of candlelight. He touched that still beloved face now.

Step fought the urge to recoil from Cal's clammy touch. "Well, you know I've been keeping company with Miss Mitt's niece."

Cal's stomach tightened. He couldn't stop Step from being with women, but he hated them all for their ability to attract any of Step's attention.

"Well, I'm awful worried." Step swung his long legs over to the side of the bed, his feet searching for his slippers. "I think she's in the family way," he lied.

Cal stood up and backed away from Step.

"How could you be so careless, Step?"

"When she finally gave herself to me, I won't prepared. I just took it because it was there for me to have. I think I'm gon' have to marry her."

Cal turned away from Step then, turned away to the wall and wept silent tears of enraged devastation.

The next evening, back at Jimmy Best's flat, Step stood anxiously in the middle of the tiny living room. Other dope fiends sat around that night too: Little Mary, Jesse Sloan, Ronald "Do-Run" Potts, Andy Phelps, Moses Turner, Abe Smith, Willie McKnight, and Hezekiah Baldwin. They were all under the influence, and they were all getting nervous about the fast vanishing horsey stash.

"Man, Cal ain't gonna give me shit for a raise. He say I ain't dancin' up to par no more."

"What about your little country gal, Step?" Little Mary batted her eyes with false innocence. She'd worked with that little countrified bitch occasionally at her part-time job with the Gaines's, and although she had to admit that Rainey was a tireless worker, Little Mary had disliked her on sight.

"What about her?"

Moses Turner spoke up. "She makin' a livin', ain't she?"

"Yeah, but she really ain't got no money. I can't get but a few dollars from her at the time. I don't believe she can touch her pappy's money 'til she gets married."

"Well, then, I reckon you know what you got to do, huh, Step?"

"Yeah, I reckon. But that's gonna take time. We'll have to sign papers, and get the money up here. We needs us some money now."

Jesse Sloan, who had been quietly enveloped in his euphoria, cleared his throat slowly, as if he were floating around in a jar of thick fluid. The others turned toward him, and waited. Jesse didn't talk much; he had to think about what he would say for a long time before opening his mouth.

"I don't think we got to wait at all. We just needs to roll somebody's place." Jesse looked pointedly at Step.

"Why you lookin' at me? You know I ain't got no place."

"Yeah but you works at some pretty rich 'stablishments, don't you?"

"Yeah --"

Do-Run picked up Jesse's line of reasoning.

"Yep, we pick the right nights, we can make a killing. Have us enough money to be in the Max for a good long time."

Jesse cleared his throat again. "And Step's jobs pull in some mighty long green, I do believe."

"So, how we gonna pull it off?" Step offered this question as a challenge. He felt a cold claw of fear at his throat. How the hell was he going to help pull off robberies at Boney's and Mittie's and they not suspect him?

Andy Phelps, a thief to his heart who would steal his grandmother's bloomers right off her if it meant money, took the lead at this point.

"I ain't got a doubt in my mind we can pull this one off. Step, you need to give us the layout of both places. Now, this is gon' take a lil' bit o' plannin', but . . . ."

Christmas, 1923.

Rainey, still in the full glow of her abiding love for her ever-attentive Step, sat before the grand tree with her beloved man and her dear aunts and uncle. They were spending the afternoon together, and Aunt Addie Rose had quietly come into the city overnight. Rainey couldn't stop looking at her left ring finger. On December 14, Rainey's 24th birthday, Step had placed a beautiful diamond ring there. He had asked her to become his wife. Rainey's amber eyes still grew misty when she thought of that tender moment . . . .

I think teaching agrees with me, Rainey smiles at Step as she leads him into Aunt Mittie's parlor. Those girls just would not pay attention, and then I understood why. They were waiting for Mr. and Mrs. Willis to bring in my birthday cake! That was so sweet for all of them to remember. And look, Step! The girls put together the sweetest little charm bracelet for me. She holds up her right wrist before his sleepy eyes. Now I've got all their names to remember!

Step pulls a tiny box from his pocket. It is covered with (frayed) burgundy velvet. Now, Miss Rainey, you know your Step didn't forget this special day. Open.

Rainy practically snatches the box from Step's rugged fingers. She opens the (creaky) box. And there it is! The ring of her dreams, though any ring will do as long as it comes from Step. Two smaller diamonds adorn the one larger square diamond. They are set in white gold. Though the ring is slightly snug as he slips it (pushes it) over her knuckle, Rainey is ecstatic.

Oh, Step! Does this mean . . . ? Step nods.

I want you to be my wife. I want to grow old with you. And Rainey bursts into tears of joy, and hugs Step and kisses his entire face.

(Step Herndon is relieved, though Ralney will never know it. He had lifted that ring the night he'd stabbed Chester in Charleston. He thinks now that the ring used to belong to the mother of one of the girls in the troupe. He had found that little pitiful box in a trash bin out behind Boney's the other day.)

This was my (eyes puddling) departed mother's ring. So you know you're mighty special to me, Miss Rainey.

Rainey begins to talk about their wedding: of course, Martha Alice will be her matron of honor.

You'll love Martha Alice and Red Art, Step. Now do we get married here at Metropolitan, or do we go home to --

Step places his fingertips gently over her lips. Your Step has already took care of our wedding, baby.

Rainey is stunned. You have?

Step nods. December 31, 1923 at 10:00 in the morning. We going to Reverend Moses Turner's church, First Unified Congregational Church of God in Christ, just you and me, and we are going to become Mr. and Mrs. Herndon.

Rainey is disappointed. She has always wanted a big church wedding. She opens her mouth to protest, but Step presses his fingertips to her lips again.

Now see, Miss Rainey, I'm trying to save us a little money starting out. I done already started paying Rev. Turner. Maybe later in the New Year we can talk about having a nice reception. How's that?

Rainey is quite disappointed, and ready to protest having so much of her life decided by someone else -- as if she is a child. Still she can't help but be impressed with Step's take-charge attitude.

She wavers between deep annoyance and the lure of the intoxicating feeling of being comforted and pampered. Ultimately, the pampering overcomes the annoyance.

I can't wait, Rainey says now, and throws her arm around Step's neck.

It's gonna be our little secret, okay? Now, now, now! It's just that Reverend Turner isn't really supposed to be performing any marriages without his supervising pastor being present. It'll be legal, but he still in the last stage of his training. But his supervisor is so busy, he can't hardly be so bothered. So we'll just slip down there to the church, get married, and then we'll tell your folks about it. Okay?

Rainey, again disappointed that not even Aunt Mittie will be at her wedding, manages to smile and say, Okay. . .
.

And here she sat this afternoon, bursting with joy, remembering her birthday, yet unable to share that joy with anyone until after the fact.   Rainey understood that Reverend Turner, whom she still had not met, could lose his place at his church if he were found out. Step had taken care of the license and everything. As the family sang The First Noel, Rainey thought of her wedding night.   She felt a thrill of fear and what she would soon be able to identify as lust.   She was swept away on a wave of anticipation as they launched into an enthusiastic rendition of God Rest Ye Merry Gentlemen.   By the time they sang Deck The Halls enroute to the soothing blue dining room, now bedecked with lovely crimson baubles and soft white candle glow, Rainey was about ready to reveal her secret joy to everyone. But one look at her beloved's sleepy face, and she knew she dare not tell a soul until after the fact.

It was a day of agonizing ecstasy.

Moses Turner was hardly a reverend by any stretch of the imagination. Although he was not as avaricious as Andy Phelps, Moses Turner did not mind performing services if he was going to be paid for them.   And Moses Turner liked the way Step Herndon was paying for this "wedding ceremony": in the Max and in cash.   The Max had already started coming in, but the cash would have to wait until after Step was married and could get his hands on his "wife's" money.

While Moses was performing the bogus ceremony, Ronald "Do-Run" Potts shuffled humbly into the business concern of Mittie and Mason Gaines.

"Ah, excuse me, ma'am, I'd be willing to do any kind of work you need done 'round here."

"Well," Mittie began imperiously.   "You're in luck this morning. My regular dishwasher is sick and won't be in this evening." That sorry Hezekiah Baldwin was out sick again.

He didn't miss much, but it seemed as if he always managed to be out on the busiest nights.   "What's your name again?"

"Ronald Potts. But you can call me "Do-Run," Miss Gaines!"

"I'd rather not, thank you, and it's MRS. Gaines. Can you be here at 5:15?"

"Oh, I'll be here at 5:00, you want me to!"

"Well if you do come early, I'm sure Mr. Gaines and I will have something for you to do. Now we don't pay all that much and it's part-time, but it is steady work."

"Yes, ma'am! You don't know what this means to me, ma'am."

"Come knock on the back door there when you get here, and we'll let you in."

On schedule, the wall telephone rang, its bell an intrusive clanging.

"All right, well, let me get this phone, Ronald. I'll see you this evening at 5:15!"

Yes, ma'am! 5:00!"

Mittie turned away to answer the phone. Ronald Potts turned away from her toward the service entrance. He slowed at the doorjamb just long enough to stuff cotton into it. He left quietly.

"Mrs. Gaines, this is Mary Fisher."

"Yes, Mary. You're still going to be working with us tonight, aren't you?"

"Oh, yes'um! I was just making sure you needed me tonight."

"Oh, more than any other night of the year, I reckon. New Year's Eve is always busy. Bet you'll get a nice load of tips this evenin'."

"Good! Well, Dr. Goins is closin' up shop early tonight, so I'll be there right at 5:00."

"All right, Mary. See you this evening."

Meanwhile, across Georgetown at Boney's, Cal Bertrand supervised the artistic renderings of his wife

Jeanne, as she prepared the ever-popular baked chicken and potato dinner that had helped put Boney's dining room on the map in colored Washington. As he tasted and complimented the usually silent Jeanne on her outstanding preparations, Cal felt and heard the opening of the door leading from the kitchen into the dining room. Andy Phelps sauntered into the kitchen, much as if he were entering his own mother's kitchen. Cal stared at him for a second or two before looking back to Jeanne's pots and pans.

"Uh, Mr. Bertrand?"

After a long moment, Cal turned toward Andy Phelps as if coming out of a trance.

"Yes?"

"I'm Andy Phelps?" Cal looked at the younger man blankly, though he assessed him in that brief time and deemed him not as desirable as Step -- his eternal measuring stick.

"I'm a friend of Step Herndon's?"

Still, blankness on Cal's face, and then, slowly, the dawning of vague recollection.

"Oh. Yes. How may I help you, Mr. Phelps?"

"Well, Step asked me to come in here and tell you that he should be here by about 1:45 today. He had to take care of some business and he didn't want you to think he was going to be late."

"Oh, well, it was mighty responsible of Mr. Herndon to have you let me know." Cal's voice dripped with sarcasm; it was easier to count the number of times Step had actually arrived at rehearsal on time than to count his tardy arrivals. "Thank you for informing me." Cal started to turn away from Andy Phelps and toward Jeanne and her cooking, but did a double take in Andy's direction as if he were surprised that Andy had not disappeared as soon as he had delivered his message.

"Oh." Andy seemed surprised to find himself still there, too. "I'll be on my way. I've got to get to work myself."

Andy sauntered to the service door as Cal launched into a light conversation with Jeanne about the evening's offerings. The ever-suave and cool Andy Phelps looked around calmly to make sure that he was unobserved, pushed some cotton into the door jamb of the service door, and turned to leave, pushing the door gently closed. Although Andy Phelps had not been gainfully employed in nearly two years, he was always about his business.

"I now pronounce you man and wife. You may quickly kiss your bride, Mr. Herndon."

Step left a chaste and hurried peck upon his "bride's" tear-softened lips. The bride was humbly adorned in a modest cream colored dress, her slim shoulders draped in a spidery black shawl. The groom looked dapper despite the cheapness of his shiny brown suit.

"Now you two must depart. I must be about my day's work."

"Thank you, Reverend. I'll have the rest of your payment to you in the morning."

"That'll be fine, St -- Mr. Herndon." Moses was practically pushing them along the aisle out of the sanctuary, hurriedly unbuttoning his boss's robe as he walked anxiously behind the "newlyweds."

The Reverend Dr. Sherman Jones arrived at the door of his tiny office at the back of the sanctuary just as Moses Turner, the trusted custodian, neatly draped his robe across a hanger, buttoned it meticulously, and placed it upon the Rev. Dr.'s coat rack. Moses Turner could have wet his pants when he heard the Rev. Dr.'s familiar whistle of "Blessed Assurance." Moses needed some of the Max!

CHAPTER FOUR

Some Alien Cage

In Step's tiny flat, upon his spare and unyielding bed, Rainey Elizabeth Clark Herndon marveled at the feel of her husband's body, smooth and nude and solid and warm, atop her own body, smooth and nude and soft and warm.   She   nearly   swooned   at   the   melting commingling of their flesh as the much celebrated French kiss extended to a full body massage and collage; the smell of his manliness beneath the hurried scrub of lye soap and the careless application of cologne; the squeak of springs beneath the crisp white sheets; the song of joy in her head. Oh! It was worth all the wait, all the anticipation of the solution to an eternal riddle.   Her body was primed and seeking and urging her on --

But she was not prepared for the relentless, steely pain of initial penetration. Shocked, Rainey's hips pulled back from Step, her knees, of their own accord, tried to push him away, and she looked up into his clouded eyes to plead with him to stop. But she wasn't there for him any longer, or so it seemed. She was some sort of vessel, perhaps, from which he would not be denied his portion. And he pushed in relentlessly, tearing away at her hymen.   She felt the tearing, thought she felt a splash of moisture that could only be blood, and then he was, suddenly, finished. She felt him go slack inside her, and he rolled over and fell immediately into a deep sleep.   Disappointed, Rainey sat up in Step's bed and looked at her husband, who had already fallen into a self-indulgent stupor.

Yet,   she   understood   somewhere   within   her   new womanliness that there was more, much more to this act than this man had given her. For now, he was a supplier of some nameless nectar that could be the only quencher of the thirst that had grown within her. She would force him to supply it well, though on this, her wedding day, she had no idea how she could coerce him.

Rainey looked again at her husband, his body curled into a fetal position. She had just been introduced to a world that held for her the potential of shouting intensity, and her tutor could only respond with a snore? She looked down at her new self. Yes, there was a spattering of blood, and some other thick fluid oozing languorously from her onto the sheet beneath her. She felt vaguely offended, though she did not know why. Perhaps it was his instant departure from her when she would explore other continents in this new world. Maybe it was the detachment in his eyes when they were engaged in the act.

Suddenly, all the evidence of her first experience grew cold and clammy beneath and upon her. She had to bathe immediately. Rainey hurried to the cold clear water of Step's wash basin, intrigued by the intense, sticky soreness between her legs as she moved. She found a clean wash cloth in the top drawer of the chest upon which the basin rested. Though she could find no soap, the sting of the cold water was like some strange baptism to her.

Mittie stammered and fidgeted, the full power of her rage subdued by the red hot curling iron she held poised over Helen Willis's head. Helen Willis simply stared, her smooth hands curled tightly against the arms of her chair. Her lips quivered at their corners; they knew not whether to roll upward into a forced smile or to fold downward in consternation or grief. She could only imagine what Charles would think about this new and hideous development.

After all, Step Herndon was exactly the reason for their niece Angela's nervous breakdown.

It still hurt them to think about Angela, Charles's elder sister's girl. She was not a very bright girl anyway; consequently, boys tended to take advantage of her, and girls tended to be unkind to her. So a dandy like Step

Herndon pretended to be kind to her because she lived with Uncle Charles and Aunt Helen, and cousin Alouette. It was likely that Step thought they had money. Well, they didn't, any more than too many other colored people in their time; they had just had their one child early in life.

Alouette was as unlike dear Angela as night and day. Their girl, who was effortlessly brilliant and endlessly patient with Angela, was now teaching literature at Howard University. Meanwhile, Step Herndon had "loved" Angela to a breaking point that had sent her screaming into the street. The Willises, at a loss about what to do with the seemingly permanently hysterical Angela, had taken her to Dr. March in southeast Washington. He had assigned Angela to stay for a short time at the home of Mrs. Rachel Mellon, a retired nurse who was known to be especially helpful in cases of "women's hysterics." Angela -- and Mrs. Mellon -- had lasted one month before Angela had to be moved to the hospital at Howard University, where she had remained until her mother, who was hardly able to care for the girl, had taken her home to Williamston, North Carolina.

"Charlie, I don't blame you," Deborah said to her brother as she hugged her unresponsive child. "I guess the city is just a whole lot more wicked than any of us could have guessed."

The Willises, devastated, had watched Angela, Deborah, and Deborah's husband Jimmy return to the colored car of the old, old train, enroute back to North Carolina.

Step Herndon had never bothered to see about Angela again after her breakdown. He was, in the Willises' estimation, a monster to frighten Mary Shelley's creation.

And now he was the husband of one who had become like another daughter to them. What curse had been visited upon them, Helen Willis wondered now, that would have Step Herndon as a constant thorn in their sides?

The women looked at this sweet girl now standing before them, all aglow, so hopeful of her dismal future. She waited for their acknowledgment, for their blessing. And neither woman could give it.

Rainey felt her insides begin to collapse beneath the intense looks of disappointment on these two women's faces.

December 31. 7:00.

All joints that were so inclined were preparing to ring in 1924. Black folks all over Washington, anxious to celebrate, had saved their pennies for months for this very night. Ladies and gentlemen for this evening alone, ditch diggers, maids, cooks, teachers, doctors, and lawyers adorned themselves in finery that ranged from the laughably cheap to the kind of finery for which they would exist just short of starvation to keep until the next December 31st. Washington was curtained in rain storms on that evening, but the would-be celebrants would not be denied their revelry. Tomorrow they might shout contrite "hallelujahs," dressed in wardrobes of sackcloth suits and alcohol-ashened faces as they prayed for forgiveness before the Lord, but tonight they were hedonistic slaves to their desires.

Still ensconced in her aunt's home -- Step had told her he would move her into his apartment during the first two weeks of January -- Rainey Clark Herndon touched at her marcelled hair as she adorned her lovely face with various powders and potions, glassy baubles dangling at her ears and glowing at her throat. She wore a lovely turquoise frock that evening with spaghetti straps beneath a bright white stole. Her outfit, though of the cheap finery variety, was most becoming to her slender frame. She had even borrowed her aunt's best perfume, and, as she spritzed it at her neck and elbows, she heard a commotion downstairs in the foyer. Rainey stood from her dressing table, and hurried downstairs, but not before giving herself one last approving look in the old mirror.

As she got closer to the top of the staircase, she could hear Mittie's harsh staccato pummeling away at

Step's slurred voice just below the tinkling chandelier, and she hung back from their sight, certain that she had some role in the disagreement.

"Step Herndon, carry your ass right on back over there to Boney's. Rainey is still living in my house, and until she moves out of here, I'll decide if she's gonna stay home or not!"

"Miss Mittie, she don't need to be going out this evenin'! Niggers is crazy out there! Ain't you heard how crazy they act on New Year's Eve?"

"Oh, yeah? When did you get the inside report on the niggers in this neighborhood? You got a special pipeline or somethin', tell you that this year is gonna be crazier than any other year?"

"Matter of fact, Miss Mittie, I do. It's already three or four fights done broke out in front of Boney's since nightfall! Just let me talk to my wife."

"Don't let me get started on THAT bullsh--"

"Miss Mittie, this really ain't no longer none of your business. I'm going upstairs to talk to my wife. She ain't goin' nowhere tonight."

Rainey appeared at the top of the stairs then, a vision of shimmering innocence. Both Step and Mittie stared up at her for a second before they began to state their cases. Rainey, who truly felt like a woman now, held up her hand, and they both fell silent.

"Good evening, y'all. What is all this noise down here?"

"Rainey, you can't --"

"Rainey, Mason and I think you should --"

Again, Rainey held up her hand and descended the stairs, her movements deliberate and graceful. She spoke again only when she had reached the foyer.

"Step, darling, you know Aunt Mittie and Uncle Mason have been making plans to take me out for months now. They've got the other business in good hands tonight, and we're going to Calico's for dinner, then we're coming to see you dance. After that, we're all coming back here to work downstairs. I don't see anything wrong with that, now, do you?"

"Yes, ma'am, I do! You know you're my wife now, and when I say you ought not do something, then that's just how it's supposed to be."

Rainey felt conflicted for a moment. It was an era when husbands did direct their wives' movements. Papa had been the boss in his home, but he had never been rude or pushy with Mama. She had never seen Aunt Mittie allow Uncle Mason to boss her around. While Rainey didn't want to be an overbearing battle ax, which is how Mittie often conducted herself, she decided after a moment that she wasn't going to allow Step to run roughshod over her, either. She stood silently looking at her new husband, her face a blank wall of stone.

"Well? Go on back upstairs, Missy!"

Both Rainey and Mittie inhaled sharply, and stood side by side, looking at this man like he was some sort of fool who had just grown horns and a tail.

Rainey spoke finally, her voice grown small and quiet and deadly.

"I'm going to Calico's with my auntie and uncle, sweetheart. I don't want to quarrel with you about it, and I don't have anything else to say about it."

"What??" Step lunged at Rainey as if he would grab her by the neck. Amazingly, as if on cue, Joe Reeves and Mason Gaines, both of whom had been waiting in the shadows for just such a moment, appeared near the foot of the steps and behind Mittie, respectively. Step retreated immediately. Rainey, recovered from the shock of her husband's impending attack, decided to take the high road in this one; maybe he was simply nervous about being a husband. She knew he loved her, and she had certainly shown him much love.

"Hadn't you better get to Boney's now, darling? I'll see you tomorrow. I really appreciate you caring about me, sugar. See you in the morning?"

Step looked down at the floor, his rage at a boiling point beneath his subdued demeanor.

"Okay, sweetie. See you in the morning." They embraced briefly, and Step hurried away to Boney's where he should have been warming up for the first show thirty minutes earlier. When I get that bitch by herself, he seethed, I'm gonna show her who's boss!

It was 11:55 PM at Boney's After-Hours Supper Club. The standing-room-only crowd was practically dancing in makeshift aisles as the band played and swayed in time to the high kicking, staccato-tapping, pirouetting dance troupe led by the ever-amazing Step Herndon. The air in the club was aswirl with commingling cheap perfumes, cigar and cigarette smoke, and bodies in various stages of cleanliness.

Four figures, clad all in black and wearing fedoras pulled low over their faces, blended themselves into the surging crowd. All four wore watches, and all four watches had been synchronized. Their presence barely warranted a second glance from the revelers around them. Quietly, one of the phantoms moved to the back of the room, to the fuse box. Another stood just behind a table of overly dressed, overly scented single women.

One of those women, Flora Washington, glanced at the figure in black from head to foot, as was her habit when she thought she saw an eligible bachelor. This fellow looked familiar, even if he was all doozied up like a convict or something. She noticed the socks on this one more than anything else. Damn, she thought, those look like the socks I gave Moses for Christmas. They had the same black and gold argyle pattern.

"Moses," she whispered after she had turned her head away from him. Flora Washington saw the figure flinch slightly but remain still. Stunned and fascinated, Flora Washington watched Moses Turner's every move until midnight.

The third figure moved effortlessly through the crowd and stood near the bandstand, in close proximity to Step Herndon. And the fourth figure stole into the kitchen, which was teeming with the clean up process of a successful night of dinners and desserts. The thief instructed the workers there to lie down on the freshly scrubbed floor. He went straight back to Cal Bertrand's office, where the proprietor, whose back was to the door, sat figuring the evening's receipts. The black-clad figure smashed Cal Bertrand's head with a paperweight from the man's antiseptic and ordered desk, and tied Cal's arms behind the chair.

The countdown to 1924 began then, with a pastel balloon floating upward from the bandstand with each count. As the crowd yelled "Happy New Year," Step Herndon was yanked from the bandstand, the lights throughout the club vanished, and screaming women were roughed into sniveling silence. All patrons were made to place their billfolds or handbags on tables and lie down on the floor. The man in the kitchen was now joined by Step Herndon and the man who had snatched him. Together, the three of them made for Cal Bertrand's inner sanctum, his office, the home of the club's safe. Step had, of course, coerced the combination from the ever-trusting Cal years earlier, and now, he deftly unlocked and opened the heavy door. Inside, the thieves found $850 neatly bundled and stacked; waiting for them, waiting to be in the Max. The men had rehearsed their actions enough to do little but gasp at this incredible windfall as they stacked the money into sacks that Step Herndon had earlier hidden behind the safe.

In the main ballroom of the club, as patrons tried to keep quiet in the tense, darkened room, Moses Turner and his accomplice moved with lightning speed from table to table, collecting cash from purses, billfolds, and pockets.

It was 11:55 PM at Mittie and Mason's place. Little Mary Fisher was swamped with last - minute orders from patrons who, in their typical states of dignified, maudlin, or leering drunkenness, wanted fresh champagne to start the new year. She was assisted in her efforts by two other waitresses: Flossie Dunn, who was, to the 25-yea-old Little Mary, an elderly woman at the age of 46, and Rainey Clark, when she wasn't singing with Joe Reeves. Miss Rainey had breezed in at about 10:45 with her aunt and uncle, dressed to the nines, looking like she wasn't about to lift a finger. To Little Mary's surprise (though she had to admit that Rainey was a very hard worker), her majesty had tied an apron over her dainty frock and gotten right to work. Little Mary was intrigued by the ring on Rainey's left ring finger, and fumed at the thought that Step was now fully Rainey's.

Each time Reeves summoned her, Rainey pulled off the apron, rushed over to the piano, and put forth a solo or duet with Reeves that sounded as effortlessly beautiful as if she had nothing else to do that evening. Then, as soon as the song was sung, Rainey donned her apron once again, and was back at her third of the twelve tables, politely taking orders for drinks and hors d'oeuvres, and graciously accepting tips. Little Mary, who loathed Rainey for her place in Step Herndon's life, felt a grudging admiration toward the girl.

The rarified air of the speakeasy was alive with a blend of cheap perfumes, smoke, and bodies in various stages of cleanliness.

Three figures, clad all in black and wearing fedoras pulled low over their faces, blended themselves into the surging crowd. All three wore watches, and all four watches had been synchronized. Their presence barely warranted a second glance from the revelers around them. Quietly, one of the phantoms moved to the back of the room, to the fuse box. Another slipped into the tiny business office where Mason Gaines frowned and stuck his tongue out of the side of his mouth, a study in concentration, as he added and re-added some figures. The black-clad man slipped behind Mason, and, before Mason could react, pressed firmly at the base of Mason' skull, rendering him unconscious, but otherwise unharmed. Mittie came bouncing into the office then, and the black-clad figure quickly gave her the same treatment. She puddled immediately to the floor, also unconscious.

A third phantom stood in close proximity to Little Mary, whose station near the club's exit gave the thug nearly instant access to anyone who might try to leave. Little Mary continued to work frantically as if he wasn't there. The figure mirrored her moves and never stayed more than thirty feet away from her.

The countdown to 1924 began then, with Joe Reeves playing a grand flourish on his cherished piano with each count. As the crowd yelled "Happy New Year!" Little Mary was yanked from her station, the lights throughout the club vanished, and screaming women were roughed into sniveling silence. Somewhere out on the floor, a drunk relinquished the contents of his stomach on a tabletop. All patrons were made to place their billfolds or handbags on tables and lie down on the floor. The man in the kitchen was now joined by the new dishwasher, Do-Run Potts, Little Mary, and the man who had snatched her. Together, the four of them made for Mittie and Mason's inner sanctum, the tiny office, the home of the club's safe.

Little Mary, who had been a trusted employee of Mittie and Mason's since the speakeasy opened as an underground enterprise, had learned the combination quite by accident from Mittie, who had, in a rare moment of carelessness, left the precious series of numbers on her desk for one fateful moment as she had given Little Mary some specific table-waiting instructions. Now, Little Mary deftly unlocked the heavy door, but needed help from the three men to pull it open. Inside, the thieves found about $750 neatly bundled and stacked, and waiting for them, waiting to be in the Max. Mason and Mittie had, over their years together, squirreled their money away in various banks around the city, thanks to Addie Rose, and in at least two banks overseas. No one would know their true financial worth for several more years to come. But tonight, these robbers were satisfied that their windfall would enable their tawdry little group to be in the Max at least through the spring. They bagged the money hurriedly in sacks they had brought in with them and left the office.

Rainey, cowering beneath Joe Reeves's piano, was frightened and furious. Who were these rogues and why had they decided to ruin a perfectly good evening? She hoped that Aunt Mittie and Uncle Mason were all right; however, she dared not move just yet. She had no desire to cry as she could hear so many other women doing. She was angry and wanted to hurt the people who had caused this trouble.

"Ladies and gentlemen," one of the bandits yelled after an eternity. "You have been robbed but are unharmed. Please consider this in the near future. Don't anybody get up or move until ten minutes from now. Good evening and happy 1924."

When the ten, molasses-dipped minutes had passed, Little Mary screamed from around a gag. She sat in a chair with her arms bound tightly behind its swerved back and her legs bound to the legs of the chair. Several patrons rushed, in a drunken haze, to her aid, and when Little Mary did not immediately cease her histrionics, one of the drunks slapped her with a half-hearted, unfocused blow. Little Mary immediately grew calm, and sat rubbing absently at her wrists and her ankles.

Rainey ran into the tiny office to find her aunt and uncle just regaining consciousness. They both complained of headaches, and had trouble standing on their own.

"What happened, Rainey," Mittie demanded.

"Some rogues came in here and robbed the place! I can't believe it."

Mittie looked pointedly at Mason, who blinked, though Rainey did not notice the exchange.

"Should we call somebody?" Rainey was near tears now.

"We'll take care of it, baby. Help me stand up, sweetie."

Taking care of it for Mason and Mittie meant one simple solution: Cal Bertrand. Mittie knew for sure, without even conferring with Cal, that he had been hit, too. And it would take less than a second for either one of them to figure out the source of the hit: Step Herndon, whose days were now numbered.

"Cal, you know we can't go to the police, but somehow or another, you've got to make them understand that it was eight or ten people involved in this mess, not just four." Mittie was angry, though not at Cal; she understood that the employee they shared -- and the nephew-in-law who had been forced upon her -- was largely responsible for the New Year's Eve robberies. Four months had passed since the robberies, and the police seemed to have no interest in Cal's case at all. Of course, Mason and Mittie were over a barrel, as it were, since their enterprise was on the far outskirts of the law.

Even Cal's legal business was not a priority for the authorities. Police nonchalance had both Mittie and Cal convinced that they would have to handle this situation on their own.

Mittie had fired Step as soon as he made a mistake. The opportunity came about 48 hours into the New Year when Step dropped -- and shattered -- a bottle of whiskey right in front of Mittie, Mason, and Joe.

"Boy, get the hell out of here! You ain't worth shit in a toilet stool no more!"

"So what you saying, Miss Mittie? You firin' me?"

Mittie spread her hands wide, and looked expansively at Joe Reeves and Mason, who stood nearby.

"What do you think, gentlemen? Did it sound like I just fired him to y'all?"

Mason nodded, and Joe Reeves said, "Yes, ma'am, that's what it sounded like to me!"

"Now, go on, get out of here, Step Herndon."

Mittie regretted her decision to fire him when she got a good look at her niece a few days later.

Cal was furious, too, that he had allowed Step Herndon to earn such a trusted place in his life. He was certain that, though Step had been found tied to a chair in the middle of the bandstand, he had shared the safe's combination with the bandits.

A very nervous Flora Washington, one of his most regular patrons, had stopped by his office about the middle of January to tell him that she was certain Moses Turner was one of the robbers at his club that night. She had told him about the socks she had seen, how he had flinched when she called his name, and how the police had practically ignored her tip. Flora had allowed as how she wasn't positive about the identities of the other robbers, but she knew the men with whom Moses was often seen. She had named Andy Phelps, Jesse Sloan, "Do-Run," whose last name she didn't know, Jimmy Best, Abe Smith, Willie McKnight, and Hezekiah Baldwin. Flora intimated that they all had a bad habit that she thought they called "maxing," and that it kept them high or drunk most all the time.

"I hate to tell you this, but I tried it with them a couple of times when me and Moses was goin' together. I believe I seen Little Mary there -- you know the gal works over to Miss Mitt's sometimes? -- and Step Herndon was over there, too."

Cal Bertrand thanked Flora Washington profusely for her valuable information, wrote her a coupon for a free dinner at Boney's, and sent her on her way. Alone in his office, Cal brooded to the boiling point. So Step probably had more than a little to do with both robberies, and that damnable trollop Little Mary who used to go around with Step was in on it, too.

Now, to make matters worse, Step's smoldering smug coldness toward Cal had sprung to the surface like a long dormant boil. Worse still, perhaps, every time he saw Step now, the boy seemed to be stumbling and mumbling worse than the time before. His once magnificent body had wasted away to a virtual skeleton: his eyes were sunken into dark and frightening hollows, and his once proud posture was now concave on a too-thin frame.

And Step Herndon had the nerve, from what Cal had heard, and Mittie had confirmed, to be a wife-beater. From what they had both heard, Step had taken to slapping the now-pregnant Rainey around.

"She's trying to hide it, trying to make out like everything is okay," Mittie fumed to Cal. "But she ain't fooling' us. She comes over here sometimes; acting like everything Is hunky dory, with all this pancake make up on her face. You know Rainey won't never too much for putting on a whole lot of make up. Oh, Cal, it just breaks my heart," Mittie sobbed loudly. "I just want to KILL that sumbitch!"

Cal sighed. "Miss Mitt, I really hate to agree with you on this one, but sometimes, ever so often, I just want to kill the sumbitch, too."

"Looks like there ain't a thing I can do to help Rainey except wait this out," Mittie sighed.

"Now, Miss Mitt, I want to tell you that I have a certain very loyal patron who has given me some very valuable information about the robbers --"

"You mean we might be able to find out where these turds are?"

"Yes, ma'am, that's exactly what I mean."

"You don't mind if I bring Reeves and Mason into this, do you?"

"I was just about to ask you if you would."

All the promising strength that Rainey had shown on her wedding night evaporated the first time Step Herndon punched her in the face. Poor, naive Rainey thought that she and Step would have the kind of marriage in which they could talk out their differences. If she disagreed with his position, she believed, she could talk with him and iron out the details so that they could move on in their idyllic co-existence. In fact, she had been trying to do just that over some insignificant something when he sighed loudly and rammed his knuckles into her face.   Shocked, Rainey had stared at him for a long time as he stood over her, his fist at the ready to strike again. Finally, this woman who had only been spanked by her parents on the rarest of occasions, and who had always been adored by everyone around her, stood to face her husband, her attacker.

"Why did you do that?" She asked quietly, in a small voice that would have melted the hardest of (humane) hearts.

"You talk too damn much. Just hush, and you won't get more of the same." They had turned away from each other, one feeling betrayed and the other feeling like the true victor. Rainey had felt enraged suddenly, and had flown at Step's slightly rounded back with all the force she could, ramming him face down onto the bed. She pinned him there on his stomach.

"You are not supposed to hurt the person you love! You are not supposed to beat your wife!" She was sobbing, hysterical. Step had simply shrugged her off his back and pinned her down, facing him.

"I am the head of this household, Rainey! I run it, and I will do to you whatever the hell I want." He had dealt such a flurry of slaps and punches to her face that Rainey was unable to leave their flat for three days. When she finally returned to work, she was heavily made up with cosmetics that a contrite Step had hurriedly bought at her sullen request. Step was full of apologies and promises to his wife after that first incident. Despite his promises, Rainey was, indeed being used by her husband as a punching bag.

As the business owners' investigation of the robbers proceeded with the pristine speed of a snail's progression -- and trailing the same amount of slime, it seemed --Rainey's beloved husband's temper grew ever more hair trigger, and most anything could set him asail on his lake of ire. She quickly learned that resistance from her would only heighten the intensity of the inferno. So Rainey trained herself to dance gingerly around Step. She began to work diligently to accommodate him, though in her pregnancy, she hardly felt like being nice to anyone sometimes. To his sleepy self, she was nurturing, always ready with her comforting bosom for his rest. To his amorous self, because all traces of her own desires evaporated as her pregnancy progressed, she was a willing partner for his rabbit-punch lovemaking. Maybe today, she always hoped, maybe he'll give me more today! But he never did. To his lively, playful self, Rainey was all sprite. She ended each day in a state of near panic and total exhaustion. She never knew what to expect from Step Herndon, but she felt that this was simply a bad time for her husband, and it was her duty as his wife to stand by him, and be as supportive of him as possible, particularly so that her child would know his or her father.

To her family and few friends, Rainey enacted a plan of evasion, urging them with her eyes, please, not to acknowledge that, yes, she was wearing too much make up, but please, pretend with her that she was not. Those amazing amber eyes sent the message to her worried students and co-workers that, yes, sometimes she walked like an old woman, but, please, no, don't act like you're concerned. Just play along with the charade. It will be okay. It's just a bad patch.

Rainey couldn't understand Step's cruelty to her, and she pondered the change in him for a few moments. Had it really begun when she explained to him that there was no pension left from her father? Or had it begun much earlier, in quieter ways? She explained to him carefully that she had gotten the last of the meager allotment when she'd graduated from Shaw. He had cursed her and reviled her that night, ridiculing her for being a college graduate ("with some useless piece of paper, trying to act like you so important!"), for pursuing her master's degree ("trying to get some worthless degree! You better not let me catch you walking around at Howard with some other nigger! I'll kill both of you!"), for looking so bad and so plain ("you look like shit, girl! You act like you don't mind looking like a hag."), for being so dependent upon her aunts and uncle ("they must do your thinking for you!").

Rainey had never had a chance to retort that her worthless degrees kept food on their table and their rent paid, that she had stopped looking so attractive any more because now all her meager earnings went to keeping them housed and fed. She didn't get the opportunity to voice her suspicions that he was taking money from her, a small portion at a time, and that he acted as if he himself were not employed at all. There was no leeway for her to insert these concerns because Step Herndon punctuated every breath he took with a punch to some part of her now tender face or body. By the end of their "discussion," Rainey was cowering on the other side of their bed, nearly afraid to blink. She'd considered fleeing his home that night. The Willises lived only two blocks away. But she didn't want to explain her troubles to anyone at so early a stage in her marriage, which at that point was but a month old.

And so she had stayed with Step, despite her real trepidation about living with him.

She stayed with him when she learned, quite by accident, that Moses Turner was no more a reverend than her "husband" was married to her legally. Rainey saw Turner walking through the halls of Delicado one morning, in search of his niece, who had forgotten her lunch that morning. Rainey remarked to the colleague standing with her, "There goes Reverend Turner."

The colleague had looked at Rainey in shock for a moment before laughing aloud.

"The only gospel Moses Turner is preaching is 'the gospel of getting more liquor and some more of that dope.' He works at First Unified Congregational Church of God in Christ as a janitor, but that's the only churching that fool does." Rainey forced herself to laugh along with her co-worker, but her stomach was knotted and her heart was in turmoil. She had never felt so confused in her short life.

Rainey opted to live the charade of the sham marriage because by the time she discovered Step's lie, she was pregnant with their child.

And so she'd remained, locked away in misery, sometimes limping, sometimes overly made up, trying to make sure that her child had a legal name and would not be considered a bastard. Though he or she would be just that in the eyes of moral judges, Rainey Elizabeth Clark [Herndon] would never reveal the child's true status to anyone.

It had been a bad patch indeed for the thieving disciples of the gospel according to the Max. Those left unscathed by whatever pestilence had rained down upon them had to wonder if their New Year's Eve activity had brought about some sort of curse.

In June, Hezekiah Baldwin had, at his wife's request, gone to the Downing Butcher Shop on M Street to purchase a pound of ground meat. His usual butcher, Joe Reeves, had served him with his characteristic joviality. "Let me throw in a little something extra, just for you, Hez. You've been a loyal customer." Hezekiah had thanked Joe Reeves profusely; times were hard, and money was tight. Any little bit helped.

Two days later, Hezekiah was dead, and his wife was clinging to life. The doctor could find no trace of a problem from looking at Hezekiah's ashen corpse, and, when, his wife died the next day, the doctor remained clueless. The couple were buried together in a pauper's grave.

Just two months after Hezekiah's untimely death, Moses Turner and Jesse Sloan were killed instantly in a bizarre hit-and-run accident at about three o'clock one morning. They waited at an intersection to see if the truck at the intersecting street was going to move off. It looked as if the truck had come to a complete stop, so the men made their way across the street. But as they stepped off the curb, the truck barreled ahead, plowing into them, and sending them flying about 50 feet into the air. By the time they landed on the ground, the truck was gone, and the men were no more.

The rest of the gang would follow suit over the next months.

In the swelter of July, when Rainey Clark Herndon was a rotund six months into her pregnancy, a tiny firebrand of a woman flew into a Virginia barnyard, the featured performer of the Virginia state fair for colored people. The firebrand's mission: to amaze and dazzle her devoted fans while raising money to achieve her goal to open a flight school for Negroes. Bessie Coleman, at age 32, was not only the first black licensed aviatrix in America, but remained the only black woman in that closed and unwelcoming fraternity of American pilots. She was flamboyant, brilliant, and lively, a petite beauty who could hold her own in the sometimes crude company of men, yet look like a movie star when the occasion presented itself. Bessie Coleman, a world traveler who was respected in Paris, adored in her adopted hometown of Chicago, but reviled by her colleagues, had decided, with no provocation or encouragement from anyone else, that she would excel in a field that, except for Amelia Earhart, excluded women from its male-dominated stratosphere. There were no women like Bessie Coleman in the air, though, and she was determined to blaze that heroic trail. From her home base in Chicago, this lively Texas native raised money by traveling the country performing as a fearless barnstormer and lecturer.

Rainey idolized Bessie Coleman, not because she herself wanted to fly, but because Bessie Coleman embodied and enlivened all the traits that Rainey thought she herself possessed: perseverance, courage, self-confidence, grace, and tenacity. But Bessie Coleman refused to temper any of those positive traits to please some other person or to fit some other person's mold. Rainey sometimes blushed in shame at the thought that she had, unlike her idol, compromised herself in order to have a reasonably placid life with her man.

When Rainey got the word through Aunt Addie Rose that Bessie Coleman would be barnstorming at the Virginia State Fair for Colored out in Prince William County that July, she simply had to see her perform. Addie Rose and Mittie, staunch believers that a pregnant woman should not be denied what she wants, were determined that their niece would see Bessie Coleman. Rainey wanted all her loved ones to see Bessie in action, and begged Step to be her "date" on the long excursion. It was sure to be great fun; not only was she going, but her other favorite folks were going along too. Her aunts, her uncle, Joe Reeves's family, and the Willises seemed as eager as she was to witness Bessie Coleman's remarkable performance. They would spend the night at Aunt Addie's and head out early that next morning for Prince William County so that they could get a good spot on the grounds near Bessie's scheduled performance.

But Step, in one of his moody stupors, refused, and in fact, demanded that she stay at home with him that weekend.

"When is the last time you and I have been here alone together?"

Yesterday, Rainey thought, glaring at her husband from behind a mask of placid wifeliness.

"Sweetheart, Aunt Mittie and Uncle Mason are waiting downstairs. Come with us? Please?"

"Hell, no, and if you were any kind of wife, you'd stay home with your husband. Why, I bet we ain't even got nothing to eat!"

"Darling, I cooked this morning. Remember? I cooked for the week. Plenty of food in the ice box." Rainey stood looking at her man for a long moment. She was vaguely conflicted; she felt a twinge of guilt about leaving Step, but she had been at home with him every night and every afternoon all summer. Her life revolved around her studies at Howard University and Step Herndon. She had not even been a loyal Zeta since her marriage, and her sorority activities had always been a solace to her.   Her overworked mind cried out for respite.

And, after all, Bessie Coleman was about to barnstorm!

That July Sunday was hot, still, and overcast. Clouds hung, dark and ominous, though ultimately impotent, just above the quietly excited crowd.   Rainey, her ever-throbbing bladder in a state of rest and repose for the moment, sat on a well padded, upturned barrel, so that she reclined slightly above her family and friends, who sat comfortably on outspread blankets.

"Can't let that gal stand up in her condition," Aunt Mittie and Aunt Addie Rose agreed many times over that weekend as they made extra provisions to comfort their niece.   Now they all fanned themselves with picturesque paper fans from the DeGraffenreidt Funeral Apartments, the premier colored funeral home in Washington. Mrs. Willis had brought along oatmeal raisin cookies, and sugar and plum cakes. Alouette had made chocolate morsel and pecan cookies.   Aunt Addie Rose and Aunt Mittie brought along the requisite fried chicken and potato salad and a bucket of string beans. Rainey's biscuits, her mother Evie's recipe, were a big favorite among the group.   They sipped warm lemonade along with the dinner spread.

Rainey thought of Step intensely several times, and she wished she could call him.   But, like most folks they knew, they didn't have a telephone in their tiny flat.

Today, Rainey intended to live vicariously through Bessie Coleman, who had never been beaten down by some man, who had never allowed problems to do any more than challenge her, and who had come out the victor every time.

And triumph Bessie Coleman did on that still, heavy day in July. When she first appeared before the awestruck crowd, "Brave Bessie" wore her usual full-combat military style uniform, complete with puttees, a long strip of cloth wound round the lower leg and worn as part of a soldier's uniform, and a Sam Browne belt, a sword with a support strap over the right shoulder and also worn as a part of the uniform.   She proudly displayed the skills she had learned abroad each time she performed.   Her plane burst into the leaden sky, a sprite of many colors, with strips of rainbow - colored ribbons fluttering from each wing.   Accompanied by an able assistant, "Brave Bessie" zoomed up into the sky, taking control of it, mastering it, her plane trailing a thick plume of smoke as she climbed.   When it seemed she could go no straighter into the air, Bessie Coleman executed an amazing series of loop-the-loops, figure eights, and Richthofen glides, which sent the crowd below her into a frenzy of applause and catcalls. The most breathtaking of her executions came when Bessie Coleman made her plane go into an apparent nosedive. The crowd began to gasp in horror; but just when it seemed that she would surely crash, Bessie Coleman executed a perfect loop upward, followed by several smaller, more delicate loops.   At the end of her five - minute performance, Bessie Coleman apparently let her assistant take over the piloting.   She next appeared before her adoring fans as she wafted to the ground in a delicately colored pastel parachute.   Safely far away from Bessie and the crowd, the plane glided into a perfectly executed landing.   As the parachute cascaded down behind her, the aviatrix executed two curtsies that would have done any debutante proud.

Rainey was in tears as Bessie Coleman delivered a stirring lecture about her life as a pilot and her quest to open a flying school for Negroes.   She felt vindicated and affirmed by this one woman and all she represented.   She jumped and cheered nearly as hard as the rest of the crowd.   For Rainey, her summer was now complete: she had seen a genius in flight.

CHAPTER FIVE

A Break From The Cage

The trips back to Aunt Addie Rose's house and then back to Georgetown were lively and happy for everyone. For Rainey, the travel was the culmination of an absolutely perfect time away from Step. She hadn't been so happy since the day she married him. Her hugs goodbye to her family, the Reeveses and the Willises were tinged with genuine sadness.

Rainey ascended the stairs to her flat with despair resting its heavy arm around her shoulders. She had no idea what to expect, nor how to react to Step's mood, whatever it might be.

The blinds were all closed in the little flat as she entered, a sure sign that Step would not want to be bothered with her at all. Rainey tipped into their bedroom, bracing herself for a surly or belligerent Step, hoping that she would find him asleep.

She found him slumbering, bronze god's body nude and entwined with the slightly paunchy but equally nude body of Cal Bertrand.

She must have screamed because both men sat upright suddenly and looked around them in the daze that is particular to people forced out of a deep sleep. Cal Bertrand's face fell, his slightly jowled cheeks jiggling gently as his look of surprise slid into despair and resignation. He seemed unable to accept that he had been discovered in his true state after all these years of careful concealment. He looked sadly at Rainey's shocked face, and, rendering her invisible in his mind, turned away from her as he began to dress himself slowly and meticulously. When both his shoes were tied, Cal Bertrand gave one last look at Rainey, who stood, still as a statue, her eyes darting from one man to the other. He placed his bowler on his down-turned head and left the flat.

As soon as the door closed on Cal Bertrand, Step Herndon flew at Rainey.

"Bitch! What the hell were you staring at? Huh?" A slap on the face, which brought her out of her terrified trance.

"Why you looking at me like that? Huh?" A punch to her chest, which started her gasping.

"You surprised? You think any man wouldn't turn to somebody who acted like he cared? You ain't cared for me one damn in a long time!" A series of slaps, through which Rainey grabbed at her purse, found her keys, grabbed for her toothbrush, and backed out of the flat.

He didn't come after her.

Rainey moved as quickly as her heavy body would allow her. She didn't stop moving until she stood at the Willises door. When Alouette Willis opened her parents' door, Rainey collapsed in her arms, hysterical and barely able to breathe.

"Rainey? Oh, my Lord! Mama! Papa!"

The three Willises helped the nearly unconscious Rainey into their parlor. They would never forget the sight of the poor girl's wild hair, which had just minutes earlier been neatly pinned into a bun. They could see violet and blue bruises beginning to bloom on her face and arms. Rainey's eyes were glassy. It would probably be a while before she could tell them what had happened.

Alouette Willis put on a kettle of water. When Rainey felt more coherent, Alouette would insist that she drink some chamomile tea.

Eventually, Rainey told the Willises everything -- except the farce of her marriage. She admitted to them that she was beaten by Step at least every two weeks, that he was becoming more and more cruel to her, and that worst of all, she wasn't his only lover. The Willises told her gently that they had known most of this all along, and that she was perhaps the last person in Georgetown to know about Step's many faults.   They assured her that she certainly had a place with them.

In a rare still moment, Mittie Clark Gaines sat down on one of the prized couches in her parlor.   She thought at length about her niece.   Something wasn't quite in place with Rainey lately. The first couple of days after they'd seen Bessie Coleman's show, Rainey had made herself scarce. Usually, Mittie could expect to see Rainey after she had completed her classes and made the long trolley ride from Howard back to Georgetown. Rainey was nearly finished with that graduate program, Mittie knew, so she must be working extra hard to get finished. Mittie shook her head and clasped her hands across her ample abdomen.   She knitted her fingers together and twiddled her thumbs.   That wasn't it.   The girl didn't have any trouble handling her studies.   What was it?

Rainey seemed to have gotten solace from spending quiet time with Mittie and Mason. But during those first few days -- that whole first week, really -- after their excursion to Virginia, Rainey had been oddly absent from their lives.

When Mittie finally saw the girl again, she could tell that bruises were beginning to lighten around Rainey's eyes, nose, and mouth.   Mittie worked valiantly to quell the hot fury that flew through her at the sight of those healing evidences of Step Herndon's punkery.   She reminded herself to let the girl come to her own understanding about that sorry piece of shit she called a husband. She told herself once again that Rainey really did have good sense; she was just young. But if this dried up, wastrel of a human turd hurts this gal of mine any more, I'm just going to have to kill his stankin' ass. . . . . Come on, now, Mittie, she told herself, she's going to see the light soon enough. You just keep a calm head. (Kill, kill, KILL . . . .)

As the summer progressed, Mittie watched Rainey's transformation from a sad, pitiful urchin to a resolved pitiful urchin. After those July bruises faded, Rainey's lovely face took on a distant shadow of its old glow. She still wore her hair in that hideous bun that she'd resorted to when she'd married that crank, Mittie noted, and no amount of cajoling or fussing on her part could persuade Rainey to let Mittie do her hair.

Rainey seemed less troubled now. Could it be that Step Herndon had finally decided to act like a man (and it was about time, with his old ass --!) and treat her niece as she deserved? Mittie didn't think so, because any time she asked Rainey about Step, the girl's eyes would dart away from her face, and she would mumble something like, "Um-hmm," or a sheepishly soft "Aw'n know" and quickly change the subject, usually to their favorite topic: the baby.

"Now, I hope you know you comin' to stay with us when it's time to have this baby, Missy," Mittie said to Rainey one afternoon as the younger woman reclined on a couch in the parlor.

"Oh, yes, ma'am! I can't wait for you to spoil me." Rainey and Mittie laughed.

"Hmmph! I ain't studyin' you; I'm thinking about that young'un of yours. After you have that child, you can go on 'bout your business!"

But soon Mittie grew serious. "What's going on with you, baby? Everything all right?"

"Oh, yes ma'am," Rainey replied too quickly, the clouds in her eyes closing her aunt out once again.

Mittie sighed. Well, since the little gal wouldn't tell her, she'd just have to find out for herself.

The Maxers, including Step, continued to meet regularly at Little Mary's in the months after Rainey left Step. There was no further need for Step to sulk about his home when he wasn't working, he reasoned. Rainey was barely speaking to him now that she had moved in with the Willis family. She'd moved up higher on the hog, or so Step assumed Rainey thought. He missed her in obscure, self-centered ways: she was a good cook who was getting better and more creative; she kept the house -- and him -- clean; she at least tried to be pleasant toward him, which, in his sparse seconds of remorse he had to admit was more than he'd offered to her. But most importantly, she had kept money coming into the house.

On those occasions when he'd needed an extra hit of the horsey, her purse or her "hidden" stash of emergency money was always readily available to him. Now, with Rainey gone, he guessed for good, he had no such luxury.

One early October evening, as the outside air took on an almost sinister chill, Step and the four remaining members of his dwindling gang of maxing thieves sat around in Little Mary's "parlor," which was really just a tiny open space between her kitchen and her bed. Soon after Moses and Jesse had died, Abe Smith had disappeared, and Willie McKnight had died in his sleep. The survivors felt damned lucky and a bit haunted now. They had never seen so many folks die so close together. It couldn't have been anything but a mighty bad patch of luck that had hit them.   The survivors, feeling as lucky as they did, had shrugged off their apprehensions and continued with an enlarged stash of the Max.

Step was unemployed and about six weeks behind on Cal Bertrand's rent. It had been a hideous few weeks for Step. He had stumbled badly twice during two separate, relatively simple routines. The second stumble had caused the once-adoring crowd to gasp and then titter nervously. Step had flown hot with anger, and had stalked off the stage, leaving the band, the other dancers, and the audience in a lurch.

Cal had never been harsh with Step before, but that night, his fury knew no bounds.

"If it wasn't for those people you're so upset with, you wouldn't have a job!"

"Yeah," Step countered, "and if it hadn't been for me all these years, you wouldn't have a full house!"

Reasonable Joy

"We'll just have to see how we make out without you, William." Step looked at Cal sharply. The older man was visibly shaken by his own decision.

"'Scuse me?"

"I'm going to have to let you go, William. You've become quite a liability to the club lately. Maybe when you find yourself a cure for whatever it is that ails you . . . ."

Step didn't want to hear anything else from Cal. He ran from Cal's office, feeling betrayed and hopeless.

He pulled himself away from the memory slowly now as he sat with his motley gang of dope fiends.

"Say, Step," said Doo-Run Potts now, wafting down from his high for a moment. "Ain't it 'bout time for your woman to be having that baby? Where she at, anyway?"

"She ain't livin' in my house no mo'. Got too triflin' and I had to put her ass out."

Little Mary cleared her throat, contemptuous of Step's claim. "Step Herndon, you's a damn lie. One thang that gal ain't is triflin'. I might don't like her, but she works mighty hard."

"Yeah, that's in the public eye, but 'round home, she ain't never do shit." Little Mary gave him the evil eye and settled into the intensity of the Max trance.

"Oh, yeah, right." Jimmy Best roused himself from his own stupor to join in. "I bet you don't even know when that baby s'posed to be born, do ya?"

"I believe October, 'round 'bout Hallowe'en. I seen her other day, look like she was 'bout to bust wide open."

"Why you gon' turn a woman out in the street, and she fixin' to have your child?" Doo-Run Potts looked at Step with disgust. "Man, that shit ain't right!"

Even the usually nonchalant Andy Phelps took part in this increasingly heated discussion.

"I believe she left yo' ass! What you doin' for this gal anyway, Herndon?"

"Now look, this ain't none o' y'all's business! I ain't tryin' to sit here with no house full of niggers, talkin' shit to me about my business. I'm fixin' to get the hell up outta here!"

Andy Phelps halted Step's exodus, and the calls for his departure, with a chilling pronouncement: "Folks, we got a little problem with the Max." His words, spoken in a near whisper, rendered the room eerily silent.

"What you mean, Andy?"

"I mean, in case you haven't noticed, we's just about finished up our stash."

Jimmy Best stopped himself in the middle of a particularly satisfying scratch of his testicles to exclaim: "You don't mean it!"

Andy Phelps, who had taken to spending extended, intimate nights at Little Mary's after the others departed, felt that he was an expert on the amount of the Max left. He sat up straight to defend his claim. "Yes the hell I do. We probably got another good month of the shit left, ain't that right, Little Mary?"

"Little Mary, since you was elected the caretaker, tell us what the hell's goin' on."

"Look, y'all know good and well it's been almost a year since I ordered that big stash of laudanum through Doc. We been maxin' like crazy! It seemed like a lot of money when we got it, but that $1750 went away from here mighty quick. We been buying horsey like it was 'bout to go outta style. Now all the money's gone, and the shit's 'bout gone, too."

The junkies huddled together now, considering their own financial straits, and the horrors of a life without the Max.

"I got an idea, though," Little Mary offered after a few anxious minutes. The men looked at her, eyelids lifted with real effort.

"See, what really cost us so much money was that laudanum I had to buy through Doc. We could save us a lot of money if we just went with something like the straight horsey."

The dope fiends considered her proposal for a while before Little Mary continued.

"I know where we can get a substitute real cheap, and regular. Doc knows how to get morphine for a few of the real bad cases that come through there.   This stuff is a little bit different from what we're used to, but it'll save us some money."

Doo-Run Potts sat forward nervously.   "What you mean different?"

"You got a problem with hypodermic needles?"

"What!"

"That's the best way to take it.   I know how to give the shots.   Take a few seconds, and you'll be feeling right as rain!"

Step spoke up.   "I'm game, but we ain't got no money, Little."

Little Mary spoke in drawn-out tones: "Look I don't think hitting es-tab-lish-ments again is a good idea.   Y'all work out how you want to pay for it.   I won't be joining you, 'cause morphine'll put you out for most of a day.   But if you get me the money, I'll order it on the sly for you, and I'll even shoot you up."

Step couldn't live with the idea of having no place to go, no up in his life.   He didn't know about the others, but he made up his mind to get Rainey, his little dividend, back home with him as soon as possible.

Jimmy Best was shot to death that night as he walked past an alley, absently floating along in the Max world and smoking a cigarette.   He never saw his assailant, but was killed instantly by a gunshot wound right between the eyes. Doo-Run Potts enjoyed a ground steak sandwich made of the finest cut of meat that could be prepared for him by Joe Reeves, and within twelve hours of his last meeting with his gang, he, too, was a dead man.

Three weeks later, Little Mary Fisher didn't show up for work at Dr. Goins's office.   Dr. Goins was concerned.   Little Mary was always at work before he could get there, but this morning, his office was still dark, the furniture and equipment gleaming from his valuable office assistant's attentive loving care.   He left a note for his patients, and headed for Little Mary's flat.   Once there, Goins knocked repeatedly, but got no answer.   At last he was able to rouse the superintendent of the building. Goins begged the man to open Little Mary's door. Something had to be wrong; it was not like her to miss work.

Dr. Goins followed the superintendent into the apartment, but the super stopped short and gasped, "Oh, Jesus!" Dr. Goins stepped around him to see what the man saw, and he, too, gasped.

Little Mary lay sprawled across her bed on her back, completely nude, next to an equally nude man, whom Goins could later only identify as "Andy." He, too, lay on his back. Both their necks were slit open from ear to ear.

Later that same day, a desperate Step Herndon, unaware that his last two partners in the Max were dead, headed to the Willis home.

Over the last three weeks, he had alternately been moderately intoxicated by the depleted stash of the Max, staggering under the weighty influence of the tiny portion of morphine he had been able to purchase, or violently ill when he could have neither. He was haggard, and his cheekbones pushed through his ashen skin. Now he had to make some changes in his situation, he resolved as he stared at the hollow-eyed skull that gazed back at him from the mysterious recesses of his mirror. His mission: to entice Rainey, his little dividend, back into his arms, and his own hands back into her pockets.

CHAPTER SIX

Arrivals and Departures

Oh, when I was in love with you,
Then I was clean and brave,
And miles around the wonder grew
How well did I behave.

And now the fancy passes by,
And nothing will remain,
And miles around they'll say that I
Am quite myself again.

-- A. E. Housman, 1896

Helen Willis rushed to her front door. The insistent knocking alarmed her, and sent pangs of anxiety coursing through her. She could see a short, squat opaque through the white glass. She stopped short for a minute. It had to be Mittie Gaines.

Oh, Lord, Helen thought. I know she's come looking for Rainey. Helen took a deep breath and pulled open her door to face Mittie.

It was early November now, and the sky seemed awash with fluttering and dying leaves. The sun was a bright beacon above the determined head of Helen's hairdresser. Helen took a few seconds to examine all the glory of autumn before sweeping her eyes downward toward Mittie Clark Gaines.

"Hey, there, Mittie!"

"Hello, Helen. Where's my baby girl?"

"Come on into the parlor --"

"--Said the spider to the fly. Is Rainey here?" Mittie stepped into the foyer and followed Helen into a parlor that was nearly as inviting as her own. Helen waited until they were both settled before she spoke again.

"She's upstairs having a nap. Mittie. Please don't be angry with us. We wanted to tell you where she was, but she made us promise not to --"

"I went to see her at that nab's apartment, and the sorry dog couldn't hardly make it to the door. He was drunk or something, like always. Anyway, when I asked where Rainey had gotten off to, he looked at me like I was crazy. Talkin' 'bout, 'now you know good and well she at the Willises'. Girl, I could have throttled him right then and there, gon' try to get smart with me!"

Mittie sat back on the couch now and eyed Helen for a long, rather baleful moment. Helen began to squirm. She really didn't want a Mittie Gaines-style tongue-lashing. Such a blessing from Mittie was a hotter pepper than she intended ever to taste! Helen had managed to avoid that scalding in the 25 years she'd known Mittie, and now was no better time to become a beneficiary than any other. Mittie cleared her throat, and Helen's eyes widened, alarmed.

"Now about you. I can't believe all them times you sat in my chair -- under my hot combs, mind you -- and you didn't tell me where my baby girl was! I wouldn't have made her come home right then . . . ." Mittie's voice trailed off and she looked at Helen. After a silence that brightened from chilly to warm, both women laughed.

"Yes you would have, Mittie Gaines! Don't try that with me! But seriously, she's been in mighty good care here. She's been a pure joy, even though she's been mighty down. We can't get her to fix herself up, but at least she can rest away from . . . him."

"Helen, you and Charlie have had your times with that no-good crank, too, so I reckon I don't need to be all that upset with you. You meant well. Tell me what he did to her to make her leave?"

By the time Helen explained the incident that had driven a hysterical Rainey into the street, Mittie was fuming.

"I'm mighty glad I fired that turd now, Helen. Oh, excuse my language, honey. I could just kill that -- rascal for what he did to my Rainey. Well, I tell you what, Helen. Let her sleep, and then ring me up when she's awake. I want her home with me tonight. I got the baby's things all ready, you know."

"Do you? Isn't it exciting?" The women chatted for a few minutes about Mittie's preparation for the impending arrival. Both women had their own speculations about the baby's gender, but they agreed that the child had a chance to be healthy away from Step Herndon.

"You've got Mamie Belk for her midwife, right?"

"I wouldn't think of letting anybody else do it. I'd better get going. Mason will be looking for me sooner or later, I reckon. You ring me up, hear?"

"Okay, Mittie, I'll do that."

"Gimmee a hug, gal. It's a mighty sweet thing you done for my baby."

"Mittie, we love her, too. She's been like a second daughter to us."

The women locked arms as they strolled to Helen's front door. Outside, the joyful sunshine and the playing leaves were a stunning affirmation of their friendship and their shared love for Rainey.

Just around the block, Step Herndon waited to make his move.

On this early November afternoon, Step felt a need that could not be fulfilled by food, or by an apartment, or by Cal's lovemaking. He needed to be doped. His body cried out for relief. And the only person who had what he needed -- money -- was Rainey.

He waited in the alley next to the Willis's brownstone, until he saw the light go on in Rainey's room. She was finally awake from her nap.

He sauntered around to the front of the Willises home with a nonchalance that was the farthest thing from his turbulent mind. He knocked purposefully on the door and waited.

Step had dressed carefully for this event. He wore the shiny brown suit he had worn to his sham marriage ceremony. He hoped that this gesture would endear him to Rainey somehow.

After a long wait, Rainey, who had heard the knock as she came out of the upstairs bathroom, answered the door. Upon first glance, she was a pitiful sight to Step, though he couldn't have cared less about any discomfort she might be feeling at that moment. She wore a shapeless white shift that strained over her amazing bulk. A spidery black shawl, which seemed somehow familiar to him, was draped about her scrawny shoulders. She seemed to be cocooning herself in it. To Step, Rainey looked as if she might be about to give birth to twins, though to the caring eye, she merely looked as if she were overdue to give birth. Her once vibrant hair was now pulled back into a careless bun, and sandy wisps draped her sallow face. Her amber eyes were cloudy with weariness, and she hadn't bothered to clear the sleep from them. Her back seemed swayed against the weight of the child.

When she opened the door, she gasped, and Step felt heartened. She probably missed him enough to give him what he wanted.

"Step!"

"Hello, Miss Rainey. May I come in, please?"

"What do you want, Step?"

He felt confused for a moment. She didn't sound glad to see him, and she was looking at him as if he were the chief suspect in a murder.

"Oh, come on, girl. You know you miss your man! Don't you?"

Rainey was ecstatic to see him, horrified to have ever laid eyes on him again. Her mind was truly jumbled now. She'd managed just fine without him since July, and, while she missed him terribly, she was so relieved not to have to deal with his alarming mood swings. She felt slightly nauseated looking at him now, after all these months: here was the man she had loved most of all, the man who had hurt her and could have hurt her child.

He interrupted her reverie by pushing past her into the parlor.

"Wait --"

But he was sitting down already, patting the seat beside him, beckoning her to him. Ultimately, she sat in a wingback chair across from the couch.

"I'd better let Alouette and Mrs. Willis know I'm awake first, though. I've been asleep all afternoon."

"No, no, wait. Talk to me for a minute."

Reluctantly, Rainey continued to sit down across from her "husband." He looked at her fondly, his eyes seeming to linger over her face, her hair, and her prominent belly. He spoke at last.

"When is our baby coming?"

Rainey sighed. "Our baby was supposed to have been born about a week and a half ago." Rainey patted her belly, exasperated. "I don't know what's keeping him."

"Well, be patient, sweetheart. It's just getting stronger in there."

"I try not to call the baby 'it'."

"Well, excuse me. I'm sorry. I just wanted to know how you've been. You got away from me so fast that day, I never really knew where you'd been all this time until today."

Rainey stared hard at Step Herndon. He made it sound as if she had left him on some sort of lark, just for the hell of it. And he had known from the second day after she'd left where she was. He had come past the Willis home that very afternoon, at the time she would have returned from Howard, just to see if she was there. And sure enough she'd been waddling down the block with Alouette Willis, who was carrying her books and helping her to make her way. Rainey had looked up to see Step, but he had turned away from her before they could make eye contact.

Indeed, Step Herndon had a knack of some sort for coming past the Willises' house at the most significant times. Rainey had seen him out of the corner of her eye the afternoon she had earned her master's degree. She and the Willises were out on their front porch, sharing a pitcher of lemonade and a batch of cookies to celebrate. Shortly, they would all travel, very slowly and carefully like a line of pachyderms, to Mittie's to have dinner. They needn't worry that Mittie would find it odd that they all arrived together since they lived so near each other. Rainey sat in a Boston rocker that afternoon, sipping leisurely at her lemonade, when a slight movement caught her attention ever so subtly from across the street. Step was behind a tree over there; she'd seen the left side of his face just as it slipped behind the pale trunk. Rainey didn't react outwardly then. But she felt a wave of cutting disappointment undulate across her belly. The Willises never knew he was anywhere near them.

The evening of Mason's birthday was a chilly October night. Rainey and the Willises and the Reeveses were laughing uproariously in Mittie and Mason's parlor. A shadow oozed by the bottom of an eggshell colored window shade. Rainey knew immediately that the shadow was but the specter of her estranged husband, who probably needed money, or dope. Mittie saw the shadow, too, and hurried to the front door to shoo him away from her property.

"You ain't got no business comin' 'round here no more, Step Herndon," she whispered fiercely. "I don't care if you are still married to Rainey, me and Mason don't want you 'round here! Go on 'bout your business!" And he left, his head and shoulders bowed as he shuffled away.

Rainey's hardened heart flowed like molten lava, and she bowed her own head to hide her tears.

And now on this chilly November afternoon, Step Herndon sat here with her in her overstuffed state, sitting upon Helen Willis's overstuffed couch, trying to act as if what had transpired between them was nothing more than some silly misunderstanding.   Her eyes overflowed again, but the reservoir was a-boil in deep fury.

"I . . . got . . . away . . . ?"

"Well, yeah --"

"You knocked the fool out of me, and all I did was get away?" Rainey stood as quickly as her bulk would allow her and stood face to face with this man for whom, even now, she felt a deep, pricking love. She pushed his chest with every few words she uttered now.

"You get out of here right now, Step Herndon! You don't give a damn about me or my baby!   You stay away from us!"

"Aw, come on, Miss Rainey! Please!"

For Step Herndon, the slight needy throb he'd felt until now suddenly bubbled up into desperation.

"Get out!"

"I just need a few dollars --"

"I am not working, because I am getting ready to have our baby! Get out!"

And suddenly, Step's desperation took hold of him, and he was out of control. He flew at her, and before he could stop himself, he slapped her. She pushed him, and as usual, she made to turn away from him, in anticipation of his next assault.   But a new bubble of desperation welled within Rainey, and she turned back suddenly, filled with a new rage, and slapped his sallow face with all her might. As if someone else had control of it, the sole of his spat-covered foot lifted up and pushed itself into the abdomen of the woman who bore his latest child. The kick brought Step back to conscious thought as if cold water had been dropped upon him from the sky.

I guess I ain't gonna get what I came here for, was the clearest thought wafting through his fevered mind.

The Willis women stood in the doorway of the parlor now, and Alouette was growing hysterical. The slender but solidly built younger Willis woman flew at Step Herndon. Helen ran to Rainey, who lay moaning on the floor, an inverted pyramid of dark warmth brewing on her shift. Alouette slapped and kicked Step Herndon with such fierceness that he would be bruised and swollen for several days after her attack.

"Alouette! Go call Miss Mitt!"

Alouette, still holding Step Herndon by his high collar, dragged him down the narrow hallway to their telephone, where she frantically dialed Mittie's number. By the time Mittie answered the telephone, Alouette's breathing was ragged.

"Miss Mitt! Step kicked Rainey in the belly! Come quick!"

"Let . . . me . . . go!"

Alouette Willis pulled Step up to her face by his collar.

"You monster! You will not go anywhere until Miss Mittie tells me what to do with you!"

In the parlor, Rainey lay in a thick haze of misery. She felt agonies shooting through her entire body, radiating outward and upward from her womb. She could never have imagined such pain, and she couldn't quite recollect what had brought it to her. She was pretty sure, though, that the baby would need to be born in the next few minutes or hours.

"Mother Belk . . . Mother Belk. . ." was all she could utter before a wave of pain took her under, her moans bubbling from her whited lips.

"Alouette!" Helen never left Rainey's side, and hardly noticed that she had dispensed with her usual quiet demeanor in her frenzy. "Call Mamie Belk right away!"

Alouette complied, though she never let go of Step Herndon's collar. By now, he, too, was breathing raggedly. As Alouette spoke with Mamie Belk, Charles Willis came in through the front door. Relieved, Alouette dropped Step Herndon roughly to the floor.

"What in the world . . .?" Charles Willis began, and dropped his book bags in a corner of the foyer. Helen Willis quickly explained the situation to her husband, urging him to watch after Rainey while she ran and got some towels and a blanket. Rainey had begun to shiver violently by now. Charles Willis complied immediately, but not before striking a blow to Step Herndon that rendered him unconscious, and bloodier than he had been after his encounter with Alouette.

"You gon' stay here and face this music, boy!"

Mittie's house was about a ten-minute walk from the Willises, but Mittie, Mason, and Joe Reeves were knocking on the front door of the Willis home within five minutes after Alouette's call.

Mamie Belk followed them by about six minutes, her unruly, mostly gray hair already wrapped in her usual "birthing bandanna," and her everyday spectacles, in all their stylishness, were forsaken for some aged, cracked glasses that she wore only when engaging in her profession.

Within three hours, a very serious, bright-eyed infant made his first appearance in his mother's world. This manchild was pale and chestnut brown-eyed. His tiny fists remained tightly clutched at his chin unless they were forced away from it. His lips were puckered thoughtfully as if he were in awe of the world he had just entered. From his first tiny cry and his long stare up into Mother Belk's eyes, he was instantly adored by everyone in this wretchedly small universe. Mother Belk cleaned the baby gently, diapered him, wrapped him tightly in a clean, sweet-smelling blanket, and placed him at his mother's breast. He drank greedily, after a few seconds' hesitation.

"What you gon' call him, baby?" Mamie Belk asked Rainey gingerly, as she cleaned the new mother, and bound her carefully.

"William Rufus Clark Herndon," Rainey said drowsily, but decisively. Mamie Belk's eyebrows inclined slightly; she'd be damned if she would have named her child after that demon.

Rainey seemed to hear her midwife's thoughts. "No matter what kind of Papa he's got, I want him to know without a doubt who that Papa is. Besides, I didn't have time to think of much else," she said with a weak shrug. "I'll call him Will." Rainey turned her undivided attention to her son, whose beauty and utter helplessness pulled at her heartstrings, and he claimed her for his own.

Later, Mamie Belk presented the new manchild to Rainey's loved ones, and her still unconscious "husband." The family cooed and fussed over the baby, while Mittie sent Mason home to get the bassinet.

"When can they come home, Mamie?"

"Oh, give them about two days, and then make sure she don't do no whole lotta walking. Make sure they ride in a car over to your house, Mittie."

"Sure, Mamie. What did she name the baby?"

"William Rufus Clark Herndon."

"Well, I will just be damned," said Joe Reeves and Mittie and Charles Willis, all at the same time.

"Yeah, say she gon' call him Will."

"Lord have mercy," said Helen and Alouette Willis.

From a corner of the parlor, which had, by now, been righted of its recent upsets, baby Will's father moaned, still wasted in the oblivion of his fist-induced coma.

Two days after he was born, Will Herndon and his mother went home to Aunt Mittie's house. There they had hardly a finger to lift in the huge pale blue bedroom that had once been his mother's alone. While they got adjusted to each other, Mittie and Mason got adjusted to so much late-night hullabaloo ("Seems like the child stays hungry," Mittie muttered contentedly one night).

Cal Bertrand brought a silver rattle to baby Will, who grasped it tightly as he considered it, before letting it drop onto the cool, lavender-scented mattress of his bassinet. Will smiled, but Mittie said it was probably just gas. They all laughed, which startled the baby, and he was, for a few seconds, a tiny cloudburst that suddenly stopped at a sleepy junction.

Step Herndon languished in his apartment, badly wounded by his assailants on his son's birthday, and too fearful to leave the relative safety of his bedroom. He had no desire to see his child, because seeing him would mean facing the danger of people who hated him. He had only a hazy memory of that afternoon.

He had gone to see Rainey with only the purest intentions: he wanted to make sure his wife and child were safe (he denied to himself now that he wanted to palm some money off of Rainey), and she had gotten mad at him. For no reason. From that point, Step had very little recollection of what had occurred. He only knew fear, and that he'd better stay the hell away from Mittie Gaines's house. In the days after his latest son was born, he usually dealt with those waves of fear by falling into a turbulent, pain-racked sleep.

As the months passed, William Rufus Clark Herndon thrived. He was clearly the handsomest, most intelligent child the world had ever witnessed.

And his father had yet to lay eyes upon him.

Rainey settled into her life as a housewife without a husband. Going back to work was out of the question, no matter how she might sometimes long to return to the classroom. Aunt Mittie would have pitched a fit if she even thought Rainey missed teaching. So Rainey submerged herself in the joys of cooking (Aunt Mittie's kitchen had rarely seen so much attention), cleaning, and tending to the demands of her growing son. Every afternoon, the Willises rushed over to spend time with Rainey and baby Will. Every evening, Aunt Mittie and Uncle Mason rushed in to dote upon baby Will for an hour or two, giving Rainey a little time to nap, or even just stare into space, if she wished. It was a seemingly endless cycle, but Rainey was content through it all, just to have her Will with her forever.

Step still had not seen his (latest) progeny.

Early in April, when baby Will was just at the point of sitting up alone in the corner of a couch, the Gaines household was startled into alertness by a strange visitor.

She stood at the door that April evening, a study in aged living. She was stoop-shouldered, nearly bald, and almost toothless. She knocked humbly at the Gaines's front door, and stood waiting patiently.

Mittie recognized her immediately. It was old Jennie Hankins, who had worked as a maid for one of the wealthier families in the white section of Georgetown until she was simply too old to engage her much-abused body in any more strenuous work. Jennie and her husband Bob had never had children, but had always been very kind to any youngsters in their care.

"Hey, there, Miss Jennie," Mittie greeted her now, surprised beyond measure at seeing this woman at her door.

"How-do, Miss Gaines. I come to see the baby."

Mittie was taken aback. Jennie Hankins had never been to her house even for Christmas caroling, so why would she come to see the baby as if she had some kind of right?

"Beg pardon, Miss Jennie?"

"I come to see the baby. That Herndon boy over there on M street told me to come by here."

"For what? He ain't never seen no baby in this house!"

"Well, he told me to come have a look-see. Mind if I come in?"

"No, ma'am I don't, but you got to tell me a little bit more than what you just said."

Once they were situated in the parlor, Miss Jennie told Mittie a story that made her see many colors of the rainbow at once as her rage swirled in front of her.

Cal Bertrand had recently hired Miss Jennie to keep his M Street flats tidy; just light housekeeping, really, which was how she had come to know "that Herndon boy." He was always in bed or slouched over in a chair, his hair kinked and standing all around his head, his face badly in need of a shave. He was always very sad, and finally after about a week of Miss Jennie coming in to find the boy in such disarray, she asked him what was wrong.

"'My wife and I just had us a baby'," Miss Jennie repeated, trying to approximate Step's speech, "'and we cain't afford it. Wife's living over there with her auntie, and I cain't find me no kind of work.'"

According to Miss Jennie's version of Step's tale, he believed that they really ought to go ahead and put the baby up for adoption. Such a statement was apparently the spark they needed to get excited about life again. So Miss Jennie expressed interest in adopting the child, and began to ask questions about it. How old was it? Boy or girl? Healthy? Even-tempered? Step answered Miss Jennie's many questions eagerly, and Mittie surmised that he figured he had found himself a big sucker just ripe for the licking.

And take a licking Miss Jennie did, apparently, because she had paid him $200, which she now admitted to Mittie had been pieced together from a "whole lotta different places," in order to "adopt" baby Will. Miss Jennie had misunderstood Step's instructions apparently, because she repeated that he had told her that "I need to go over there with you, because I have to let my wife know that we have a good family to put the baby with. But they live over on Q Street. Go by there so you can see where the house is." When Miss Jennie realized that she should not have come in to the house without Step, she was horrified. She had disobeyed his orders, and she could tell that the folks in the Q Street house were not prepared for her.

Mittie also thought, and she ain't playing with all her marbles either, forgetting stuff that's supposed to be important!

Mittie thanked Miss Jennie for coming over, but assured her that not only was the baby not for sale, but that Step Herndon had never even laid eyes on his son.

"I'll make sure you and Mr. Bob get your money back, you can believe that! You just give me a couple of days, hear?" Mittie hugged the weeping Miss Jennie lightly as she escorted her to the front door.

"Don't say nothing to that Herndon boy, hear? I'll take care of him. Just go 'head and clean his place just like you-all never talked, all right?"

"I sure will, Miss Gaines. I sure appreciate you setting me straight. I can't believe I fell for a trick like that."

Mittie went downstairs to dust off the rope that lay coiled in a corner of the storage room of her speakeasy.

Later, she called Cal Bertrand, and asked him to please come over as soon as he got a chance. He heard Mittie's story and went home to load his pearl-handled revolver. That evening, as Joe Reeves tuned his piano in the speakeasy, and as Mason Gaines stood silently by, fuming, Mittie told them what Miss Jennie had said.

At the Reeves's home, long after midnight, steel made contact with stone. Joe Reeves was an artisan of the truest form.

Was he dreaming? Cal had burst into his flat, but there was hardly a strand of light seeping through his blinds. Outside, the sky was midnight blue. Cal must have stopped by on his way home, where he <u>had</u> to be, making like a good husband. Surely, Cal stood over him in this icy midnight hour. Step could smell that unique (disgusting) blend of cologne and body musk that no amount of soapy lather seemed ever to erase from that body he knew so well.

Cal never said a word, just stood there, glowering at him, wild-eyed in the halting light of the one kerosene lamp that still functioned. Step had never seen the man look so mean, and he recoiled in horror, just as Cal lifted his right arm to show it draped in a white towel. Suddenly, Step heard a muffled grunt, and the towel had a smoky hole in its center.

And Step knew pain on the right side of his chest, and he screamed, lapsing into a semi-conscious state, where he wallowed in red agony.

An eternity later, it seemed, another man stood over him. He could not see this man's face, but what he could make out was the harsh but fleeting gleam of steel in the growing light of dawn. This man said nothing; he kept his hat pulled low to obscure his features. The last time Step saw the glint of the steel, it seemed to be floating rapidly downward toward him. And again he knew pain, this time in his torso, as the steel ripped downward for a hellish second and then removed itself from his body.

Step Herndon's life forces drained away from him, and he fell away into anguished misery. He was unable to speak now, but when the heavyset figure entered his apartment some time later, when whispers of morning danced through his dusty blind slats, he knew it was probably Miss Mittie. She methodically unfurled a length of rope that draped her arm, and then rewound it viciously around his neck. When his eyes began to bulge out of their sockets, she laughed softly and removed the rope.

"You ain't worth all this, Step Herndon. You gonna get yours, though." Mittie backed out of the flat, smiling maliciously, while the mortally weakened Step grabbed hopelessly at his rope-burned neck.

Later still, as the sun arched higher in the morning sky, Rainey slipped into the flat and stood over him, brooding. He looked up at her, and lifted his hands weakly, in supplication. She recoiled, but spoke in a fierce, determined whisper that tore through the fetid air of the room like a flood.

"Step Herndon, how could you? You have never laid eyes on my baby, but you sold him to some old lady off the street? You cannot live! You cannot live!"

Rainey snatched a pillow off the filthy bed, hardly noticing that blood was everywhere upon the mattress. Somewhere in the back of her mind, she thought it odd that Step's bed would be so bloody, but in the forefront of her mind, she couldn't have cared less at that moment. She hardly noticed, when she lifted the pillow that his hands had fallen, that his eyes had closed, that his mouth hung at an oddly slack angle, a tiny trickle of blood clotting its way down his stubbled chin. She lifted the pillow and brought the pillow down over his face with all the force she could muster. Perhaps he put up a weak struggle. Rainey would never really know. She came to her senses suddenly, and pulled the pillow off her once beloved husband's face.

His face was forever locked into a final gasp. His chest and stomach were a slumping ruin, and blood had begun to dry all around him. He was the picture of decadence gone permanently and irrevocably wrong. Rainey dropped the pillow, proclaimed herself a murderer, and ran all the way home to Mittie's, her hand clamped across her open mouth to staunch the flow of the scream that would launch its maiden voyage there.

She was a widow, and she had caused her own widowhood.

Part Two: Echoes Of Home

1925 -- 1934

The heart of a woman goes forth with the dawn,
As a lone bird, soft winging, so restlessly on,
Afar o'er life's turrets and vales does it roam
In the wake of those echoes the heart calls home. . . .

CHAPTER SEVEN

Those Echoes The Heart Calls Home

Rainey Elizabeth Clark (Herndon), 25 and a common-law widow, hoisted her six-month-old son higher on her bony hip and walked diffidently into the colored waiting room of the Raleigh train station. She carried a worn, hurriedly stuffed carpetbag in her free hand. (Aunt Mittie had promised to send the rest of her things as soon and as often as she could. "But right now, gal, you better make tracks. Remember, Aunt Mittie loves you.") Water drained generously from the ceiling, clattering to the ancient floorboards, and Rainey adjusted the baby's bonnet, pushing his trusting little face to her neck. Where were Martha Alice and Arthur? What about Laurence (and Miriam)? They knew the train was supposed to let her off at three o'clock. She sighed, realizing that this was probably the first time the train had arrived into Raleigh on time since at least '16.

Unable to go on further, even to the rickety pews in the middle of the floor, Rainey leaned against the doorway leading to the tracks. An insistent stream of icy rain cascaded boldly down her caramel face, pushing a lock of hair into her line of vision. Now, perhaps, the blood upon her weary head would be nullified by this torrent. Rainey rolled her eyes heavenward, willed her arms to continue to carry her baby, who seemed heavy as a man, and trudged to the sturdiest looking bench. She wrapped her spidery black shawl around her son and herself as if it had the power to protect them from their uncertain fate. A shiver, perhaps of guilt, attacked her thin back. What must I do now? she asked herself as she fought against the memories that crowded in on her.

She was awakened by a light touch on her shoulder. She thought she had been mulling over her future; apparently she had only been drooling onto her dozing baby's bonnet. She looked up, expecting to see Martha Alice's welcoming face. A moment of horror. Step? Instead she gazed into the eyes of a man she hadn't given a thought to in at least five years.

"Well, hey, William!"

William Davis had been a first-year law student at Shaw University when she had enrolled there as a freshman music student. He had persisted in expressing his potential for ardent devotion to her and to her well-being, but during her time as a childless young innocent, she had found him too sedate for her tastes. While his desires for companionship ran toward a quiet evening lecture on the potential of the talented tenth, or a piano concert, or even a few hours in the reading room of the library, Rainey was occasionally reprimanded by the Dean of Girls, or worse, the Chaplain's wife, for being too forward. William Davis would have been shocked, she thought.

In reality, William Davis knew, and yet he still loved her from afar. For him Rainey Clark was marching band, orchestra, gospel choir, and percussion section. She was and, he was determined, would be, the music in his life.

Looking at his smiling face now, Rainey remembered that she had thought of William as a good looking man. She'd always regarded him as a masculine beauty; secretly she'd felt that all that beauty was wasted in the serene company he liked to keep. When she'd last seen him, she had been looking for a man who could help her burn life's candle at both ends, a man who loved music and dance as much as she did, a man who could rescue her from the drabness of Raleigh, North Carolina. She had found more than she'd been looking for in Step. The shiver that jumped into her this time caused baby Will to stir, and he pushed his little fist against his nose as if a fly had lighted there.

Frantic thoughts flew through her mind, despite her efforts to push Step out of her still fevered mind. Surely Step Herndon had run, bug-eyed and short of breath, from the sharp clutches of some South Carolina Klanners or Legionnaires. Had he winked at some willowy blonde? Or had he been caught pinching the backside of the son of some rich and manly town power? Did he steal some trousers off the clothesline of some redheaded, waddling housefrau? Or did he steal that housefrau's husband and/or his money? Whatever the source of the fleeing, Step was no port in any storm.

She finally succeeded in pushing the newly departed Step away from her damaged psyche, refused to see his bloodless, twisted body on their bed, hands bent into one final, grotesque attempt to grasp at her sympathy. Still, she was oddly comforted by the thrill of horrified delight that shot through her at the thought that she was free from his obtrusive presence.

"Rainey. I thought it was you. How have you been?" William's handshake, so like a welcome hug, warmed her, made her feel hopeful for the first time since before Step's untimely exit. The look in his eyes said he was still ready to offer his devotion, and that he really did care how she had been.

"Not so good." Rainey felt as if she would choke on the words, and for the first time since leaving Washington, she allowed herself to feel as beaten and used up as she actually had been. She decided not to let the tears fall from her eyes. "I'm waiting for Martha Alice Chestnutt and her husband. Do you know them?"

"You talking about Arthur Seaton? Yes, he's my barber. Good fellow. His wife always speaks real highly of you."

"She's been like my sister since we were little bitty girls. Well." Rainey stopped searching the waiting room and looked into William's face. "What are you doing these days?" She felt possibilities with this man, possibilities that she could not decipher just yet, and she nuzzled little Will's head against her neck.

"I've got my own office down on Hargett Street. I do all kinds of law, and I sell all kinds of insurance, too. Doing pretty well, I reckon. Got me a little house over on Cotton Place, not too far from Saint Augustine's."

"Good. Well, as you can see, I've been a little busy. I guess you knew I was living in Washington."

"Yes, I heard about your ... tragedy. I'm sorry, Rainey."

Not even Martha Alice knows the whole story there, Rainey thought, relieved.

"Thank you. It hasn't been easy. I reckon I'll find myself a teaching job somewhere around here. I can't just give up." She tried to keep her eyes down to mask the sudden relief that flooded her heart.

"Matter of fact," William was saying now, clearing his throat in order to allow a clear passage for the lie he was concocting, "I believe I saw Arthur's old car down to Woodson's Garage. It didn't look so good. Why don't I give you a lift to Arthur's shop and then we can see what's what?"

They smiled at each other as Rainey stood. She knew he was lying and that the Seatons had permitted him to do so. He knew that she knew and was glad.

Arthur Seaton, the premier barber of South Park and husband of Rainey's best friend, was putting the finishing touches on a particularly close shave of William Davis's rather unruly beard stubble. William had kept this Wednesday afternoon appointment with Arthur just like clockwork for the last three years. When Arthur mentioned that Rainey Clark was going to be waiting for them at the train station that afternoon, William volunteered to get her from the station so fast that Arthur stopped shaving him to have a look at the crazy man in his chair.

"Ummph, I forgot you was sweet on her!" He laughed and chucked William's arm. William felt silly, and he blushed, which really made him feel foolish. "So you've heard what happened with her, then?"

William, alarmed, sat straighter in the well-worn barber's chair. Arthur continued.

"She was married and her husband got killed. She buried him about two, three weeks ago. I don't know much more than that, but she <u>does</u> have a little baby boy. I <u>do</u> know that much.

"Me and Martha was supposed to get her, but I reckon we can just think up a reason why we can't ---"

"Let me think up what we'll tell her. Any chance I can get to talk to Rainey alone, I'll take it."

William felt so happy, he guessed it was a little like a drinking man feels when he engages in his hobby. So with his newly cut hair and his clear calendar that day -- it was one of the few times William could remember being grateful for a clear calendar --the youthful attorney stepped out onto Blount Street and headed toward his jalopy.

As William drove toward the train station he remembered how he went and bought his old Ford used from an elderly Spanish-American War veteran over in Mordecai. William could have afforded to buy a new motorcar, but in those days, a gang of white folks would likely beat a colored man for walking on the same sidewalk with them. He probably would have signed his death warrant as soon as he signed for a new car. And he just could not bring himself to wear a chauffeur's cap in his own car, the way some Negro men did. So William got into his rickety but dependable Ford and headed downtown to the colored entrance of the train station at Nash Square.

Who'd have guessed he'd ever have cargo as precious as Rainey Clark in the front seat with him!

When William saw her, it was just like the first time all over again. There was still something of the wild speakeasy ghost in her even now. But today dark circles haunted her lovely face. Her long lashes really called attention to the puffiness lingering just beneath her amber eyes. Her face was now extremely thin and slightly yellow; William worried immediately that she (had been mistreated by her late husband -- and he grew livid) hadn't been taking care of herself -- and he felt sad. William stopped himself from touching her hair, once so lovely, and now so limp and dull. He remembered that the first time he saw Rainey, she wore her chestnut brown hair parted down the middle and pulled loosely back from her face by a satin ribbon. The ponytail hung between her shoulders. The effect of the hairstyle, which framed her face in a slightly fuzzy triangle, was that she looked rather saintly, which was ironic.

The first time William saw Rainey was at the Shaw University chapel. She was a member of the chapel choir, and her solo that Sunday was "His Eye Is On The Sparrow." And did she sing! In that dignified gathering, one or two in the congregation even got in a good shout. Rainey took command of the song that day, and from that day, William never heard another version of the song to satisfy him unless Rainey was the singer. She looked just like an angel that day, and somehow William felt himself falling into an infatuation with her. And such a fall was no easy feat for him.

William Macke Davis was an old law student by the standards of the day. Born in 1890 in Goldsboro, North Carolina, William spent his boyhood working in tobacco side by side with his mother, his father, and his four brothers and two sisters. His parents were extremely hard-working folks who saved all their pennies while they lived on the property of Feston Wallace, a big-time cracker farmer down in Wayne County. When they were able, and with Mr. Wallace's permission, of course, they built a small A-frame house on the property. You never saw a cleaner, more lovingly kept place than that little house! Several years later, at Mr. Wallace's insistence, William's parents began paying what they thought was a mortgage on the property so that they would eventually own it.

When they tried to rent a portion of "their" land to his mother's brother, William's parents got quite a jolt from old man Wallace. All of a sudden, they had to face the reality that they had only signed a 15-year lease on the property. ("Y'all's got it all wrong," he remembered the old man saying, and he had so much glee in his croaking voice. "Leasin' doesn't mean buyin'! Nosiree!") Never mind that all of his actions and all of his words indicated to the entire Davis family that his parents were buying the land. They now had no choice but to work from sunup to sundown on the hateful, rented piece of land.

Now his parents became more determined than ever to see to it that as many of their children as possible went to training schools or college. William was third in line to go to college. When his turn came, he chose the State Normal School for Colored in nearby Fayetteville, which would some day be renamed Fayetteville State Teachers' College, because it wasn't too far away from his parents.

William completed his teacher's training there in 1912 and took a teaching job in a little town called Bayboro, North Carolina. William was certified to teach high school history, but he, along with the two other teachers at the Consolidated High School, taught everything he was told to teach. Like all his brothers and sisters, William sent home as much money as he could to help his parents pay off as much of that cursed lease as quickly as possible.

While William was in Bayboro, he met a man about his age who sold insurance policies to the colored people in that county. William believed Lester Thompson was an honest man, but he saw this insurance business as just another way to keep people in debt. Thompson explained it to him that families didn't have to be wiped out if the father died on the job. All their funeral bills and living expenses could be taken care of if they paid their premiums on time to the insurance company. William felt a bit more comfortable with the idea and he bought policies for his parents. Pretty soon he was selling insurance, too, working as Thompson's apprentice. For those five years that William lived in Bayboro, he taught, sent money to his folks, and sold insurance.

He kept company with a sweet little girl during his last year down in Bayboro. She was just a little bit younger than William, and when he asked her to marry him, she said yes eagerly. They were all set to be husband and wife, sweet innocent little Daisy Burton and kind, calm William Macke Davis. And then his number came up -- literally -- in the great lottery of 1917, which pressed many a young man into service as a part of the American theater of the Great War.

Off he went back to Fayetteville for basic training in the Army life and the worst of Jim Crow at Fort Bragg. William never left that wretched place during the entire time the United States was involved in the war. He engaged in basic secretarial work, taking dictation and typing letters for various commissioned officers, making coffee, and sweeping floors because it was easier just to keep his mouth shut and comply. How he wished that Jim Crow was just a cute sweet recipe. Those commissioned officers weren't especially rude to him; they just didn't see him. They saw a darky in a uniform who was there for their menial jobs. Such was the plight of the Negro, and in so many ways William saw few changes in the years afterward.

William decided to make some changes in his life. He faced the cold realities of unrequited love -- Daisy Burton had become the wife of Lester Thompson and the mother of his firstborn son with amazing speed (William had to remind himself that it took women nine months, not six, to give birth to healthy infants) with bemused calm. With amazed exasperation, he stared down the grim realities of Jim Crow, which seemed amplified by the urgency of the Great War as his "darky" status only got more apparent to him. He knew by then that the way for him to keep other poor folks from suffering like his parents had was to become an attorney-at-law. So when 28-year-old William finished his duty at Fort Bragg, he headed for Raleigh and the law school at Shaw.

He was taught by his parents always to go to church on Sundays, so, being new to Raleigh, William went to the chapel on campus. Even if he hadn't been in the habit of going to church regularly, the chapel would be where William went most often, because it was in that sanctuary that an angel waited for him.

On that first Sunday, the angel sang to the heights of her vocal range and then sat down in her designated place in the choir loft. And on that first Sunday, after she sang her breathtaking solo, the angel devilishly passed notes to the girls on either side of her, stifling giggles as she wrote notes and as she read the replies of her friends. Twice, the minister of music whispered something sternly to her and twice, the angel retreated into contrition -- for a few minutes. But her solemnity never lasted long. William was intrigued, for beneath the girlishness, he detected a staunch, elegant fierceness.

After church William introduced himself to Miss Rainey Elizabeth Clark and immediately invited her to go for a walk with him. She was compelled to be polite; William could almost see how she had looked as a little girl as her voice softened and she kept her fascinating eyes averted.

"Why, thank you for the offer, Mr., uh, Davis, but I need to get on home to my parents. They're expecting me for dinner." Rainey Clark smiled at him and as she wafted away from his presence, William called after her.

"May I walk you home?"

She looked surprised, and a peachy blush stained her cheeks.

"Well, I reckon that would be okay. But you can't walk me all the way because my Papa will be upset to see a man as old -- I mean, who's so much older than I am -- walking with me."

On their walk down Worth Street, toward Rainey's family's yellow shotgun home, they talked about all the polite things, the weather, school, and their families. And underneath all that she said, William could tell that Rainey Clark was full of life and ever ready for fun. She told him a little about how her father tried to stop her from going away to college, launching into a mischievous mockery: "Baby you cain't go downtown to the trade school. You might get run over by the trolley. Might come up on the sidewalk and just run ye down."

William laughed until tears welled up in his eyes. He was amazed that this tiny innocent looking girl would be so comfortable with him that she wouldn't mind opening up to him so easily. Based on the way Rainey talked about him and how hard he worked, she clearly loved her father, so her imitation was merely a gentle poke at his overly protective approach to rearing her. William's heart warmed for the first time since he had been jilted by Miss Daisy.

What was it about this young woman that appealed to William? She was lively, for one thing. She clearly had a mind of her own, knew how to have fun, and was mischievous. While William had a mind of his own, he realized that he never was able to instigate much in the way of fun. He had always been the serious type who admired people who understood how to play and why it was so healthy, as Rainey Clark so obviously did.

As he got to know her, William understood, too, that Rainey was also very kind. He witnessed her show genuine charity to many people who seemed to have been forgotten by others. There was one lady who sat near the front entrance of Shaw who seemed to have lost everything; she didn't seem to have any place to live, and she carried some old cloth bags with her everywhere she went. Sometimes she cried while sitting there in front of the school. Sometimes she sang spirituals or the blues in a rather incredible contralto voice. She never, ever smiled. And she never begged anyone for anything. Some mornings as William walked to class, he saw Rainey talking with her. Each time, the woman's face was alight with the biggest smile, and she and Rainey were apparently having a really pleasant visit. Rainey had some packages wrapped up in waxed paper, and she handed them to the woman, whose smile got even bigger. With great dignity, both women sat on the low wall in front of Shaw and had breakfast together. They talked as if they had always been friends. William could not adequately express how this sight touched him; he almost looked forward to seeing Rainey talk with that woman more than he yearned to seeing her walking alone.

One day, William asked Rainey about the woman.

"Oh, you mean Mrs. Andrews! She's so sweet. She lost everything when her husband got killed in the War."

"Have you known her for a long time?"

"No. She came to Raleigh thinking she could get a job, and she's been down on her luck."

"How'd you meet her?"

"Oh, I just started speaking to her. She's a sweet lady. She won't come to my house or anything. Says she doesn't want to be a burden. I wish I could help her."

But William could see that Rainey had helped the woman by not only showing kindness to her but also by sitting with her and fellowshipping with her.

From that first Sunday afternoon walk, William asked Rainey to accompany him to any lecture, piano recital, or concert he could discover. And William was particularly proud that he had been able to show Rainey's Papa that he only had her best interests in heart and mind. Yet, after Rainey's father passed away, William understood that when she wasn't being tied down by him -- for surely, he believed, he tied her down with his calm pursuits -- she liked to go to juke joints and drink a little. She wasn't morally unclean; that word would have gotten out right away. No, she just liked to dance and drink a little. William felt he was no match for the juke joints because he had to be about his studies. So he had gradually drifted out of her life. But she had never left his heart. His hopes about Rainey lay simmering below the surface of his daily life.

And now, on this glorious day in May, William Davis had a chance to see her smile again, maybe to coax an anecdote from her steely wit . . . to win her heart, perhaps?

She looked so tired, so cast away sitting on that old raggedy bench holding that adorable child. William's heart melted all over again. When he saw little Will, he felt like it was a sign from God that they had the same name.

William felt a sudden surge of confidence that no matter what had happened with her late husband up in Washington, he could make her forget it all and move on to a good life with him. Why, they could become a family with no trouble at all. William found himself imagining what it would be like to come home every night to Will and Rainey. He couldn't stop smiling; he had to push his face into a sympathetic look with his hands before he got to her pew.

She was asleep when he walked up behind her, so he stood in front of her and tapped her shoulder. He waited for her to wake up. Now William understood what it meant to look at a vision. For just a minute, her eyebrow arched up, like she was going to be angry for being awakened, then she smiled and it was like the sun had come out from behind a cloud. She opened her eyes and then, after she got through looking confused, she called his name. William was determined not to let her get away from him this time.

When Martha Alice Seaton finished her last customer that day so that she and her husband could go and get Rainey, she was so excited because she hadn't seen her best friend in almost three years. From inside the shop, Martha Alice could hardly tell it was raining, even though she would remember later that the streets looked as if they were about to flood. Martha Alice loved her husband, but there was nothing like a best friend. Rainey had always been like a godsend in Martha Alice's lonely life. They had had no secrets or awkwardness between them, except, perhaps, for the shameful details of this bad time that was just ending in Washington. Lord, so much grief and so much sadness, Martha Alice thought as she swept the floor on her end of the shop. Why did that girl have to suffer through all of that? Even Martha Alice's miscarriage of her first child couldn't compare to Rainey's misery. Martha Alice's heartbreak had been mended with the birth of Arthur, Jr. last year. Martha Alice understood that Raney had been kind of on the wild side, but she'd never hurt anybody. Rainey had told her very little in her letters, just an antiseptic explanation that Step, her husband, had been killed, and she would be coming home.

Martha Alice had canceled all her hair appointments for that afternoon. She looked across the room at her husband, who was finishing up a customer. They were telling some pretty funny jokes because Arthur was laughing loudly and wiping at his eyes. The room was so big she could hardly ever hear what folks were talking about over on Arthur's side. The Seatons had their areas set up diagonally from each other. It was cheaper that way, and they actually doubled their business: husbands and wives, boyfriends and girlfriends, parents and children came in together to get their hair done. The best thing about that setup was that Martha Alice could look at her "sandy-headed" man all day. (It was a funny thing about Arthur's hair. The term "red-headed stepchild" was never so comical to him because all his life he had been burdened with caramel brown skin and light, almost dirty blond looking hair. When Martha Alice met him at beauty/barber school, he was very sensitive about his hair, and wouldn't stand for any teasing about it. Over the years, he got used to his weird coloring. On the other hand, Martha Alice had liked it from the very beginning; she thought it made him stand out from the crowd.)

Martha Alice walked across that big floor to Arthur's side, where he stood grinning at her.

"Guess what, baby? We ain't going to get Rainey."

Martha Alice's heart fell to her knees. She assumed immediately that Rainey had decided not to come home after all. So why in the world was her husband grinning like that?

"William Davis was just in here. When I told him that Rainey was coming home, he 'bout broke his neck volunteering to go get her from the train station."

"Oh." Martha Alice was disappointed for a minute. Then her memory got to work. "Oh!" She grinned, too. William Davis was just the kind of man Rainey needed!

Martha Alice had figured from Rainey's too cheerful and infrequent letters that "Step" Herndon was quite a rascal: "'Step's kind of moody . . . Step likes things just so . . . Step is between jobs . . . Step and I are having a cooling off period . . . Step was found dead . . . ." What she had gathered about Rainey's life with him was none too good.

Together, Arthur and Martha Alice waited for William and Rainey to arrive.

By the time Rainey and William arrived at the Seatons' style shop, two amazing things had happened on that May afternoon. The sun blazed down on the dampened street as if it had never gone away. The day had suddenly become as it should have been in May: gorgeous and uplifting. And, miracle of miracles, Arthur's jalopy was back from Woodson's Garage, apparently right as rain. Rainey expressed her amazement at the car's miraculous recovery and looked pointedly at William. They chuckled together, and knew they had a joke between them. Rainey felt comfortable with William Davis, the kind of comfortable that prompts you to take your shoes off and rub your toes against the warm earth. This was an amazing transformation for a young woman who had vowed never to trust or seek the company of a man again in her existence.

Oh, God, thank you! I'm free! I'm back home again! Rainey's heart sang and her legs wanted to dance for joy. But for now she walked calmly into the shop, anxious to see her best friend, whom she had not seen in nearly three years.

They stepped into the style shop, one dapper figure in a well-cut beige suit, and one bedraggled soul in a gloomy black wool dress and a rain-soaked hat suitable for wear at a November funeral. Rainey carried a lively child who was, despite the sogginess of his bottom, ready to crawl about and explore the carefully swept floor beneath his kicking feet. Martha Alice yelled, and, with a little jump, ran to Rainey, crushing mother and son to her chest.

The women stared gratefully at each other, Rainey's amber eyes gazing into Martha Alice's brown ones. Sisters reunited, the links of time and space mended, the bond of friendship renewed. They hugged again, and tears crept unchecked down their lovely faces. Crushed between them, baby Will squirmed.

Momentarily forgotten, William sat down in Arthur's empty barber's chair and sighed, still grinning. His face flushed when Arthur nudged playfully at his shoulder.

"Oh, girl, look at you," Martha Alice said as Rainey changed Will's diaper. "You need to gain about ten pounds, and look at your hair!" Martha Alice shook Rainey's ruined hat on the floor and clucked over the state of disrepair into which Rainey had fallen. She couldn't know that Rainey had stopped giving a damn about how she looked shortly after Step had demoted her to the rank of punching bag.

"Come on over to my side, Rainey, and let me do something with your hair. It's on me. I've even got some diapers and a little space made up for the baby to play. William, can you come around here to the shop at about 5:00 to carry Rainey to our house? Okay, thanks. Come on here, then, sweetheart, and let's get you fixed up."

Dear Mama and Papa:

I don't know if I'll ever be able to thank Martha Alice for what she did for me that day. It had been so long since I'd cared about anything that didn't have something to do with Will, that I'd just stopped looking into mirrors. When Step broke my heart, I just lost all consciousness of myself. I would wash my hair with the same soap I bathed with, and just let it dry by itself. It was a mess,

of course, but I was so grateful to Martha Alice for not laying me

out for letting it go like I had. (Aunt Mittie had, of course. I was

making her look bad, and on and on she would fuss. I reckon

she thought a tongue-lashing would bring me back to my old

feisty self, but I just didn't care any more.)

Just before Martha Alice sat me down at her shampoo

bowl, I got a good look at forgotten me in the mirror. I didn't

know it was me at first: I saw a skinny girl with these great big

eyes staring back at me. Eyes the color of honey, but glassed

over somehow. She was in a ragged old black dress with a

spidery black shawl hanging off one shoulder. Her hair was just a

big fuzz, and the part that was too long to stand around her head

just drooped over her curved and slumped shoulders. I noticed

that her mouth fell open in shock at the same time mine did, and

when Martha Alice put her arm around that girl's shoulder at the

same time she put her arm around mine, I realized who that little

urchin was. I began to weep, and as I wept I was healing from

all those months of horror I had endured. I felt all the crust of

worry begin to peel from my body and from my mind like

calluses finally cut away from overworked feet and hands.   I

buried my head on Martha Alice's shoulder and I wept.

Five o'clock came and the urchin was no more. Martha Alice kneaded and massaged Rainey's neglected scalp, and clipped and snipped at the damaged length of her hair until the hair was flattened into a slightly longer version of the Louise Brooks bob, with a square, layered cut and short bangs, and the added chic of a smart little "v" formation at the nape of her neck beneath the bob.

After the initial tears, Rainey began to ask about life in Raleigh, about all the people she'd missed seeing over nearly three years. Finally, she said, "In a way, I guess I'm glad Mama and Papa can't see me like this, huh?"

"Oh, girl, Mrs. Evie and Mr. Rufus would have been happy just to see you back home. "'Course you know you wouldn't have gotten out of the house if Mr. Rufus was living." They laughed.

The tiny bell at the top of the Seatons' style shop door tinkled and William came in. Outside, the sun had the glaring brightness of a summer sun after a thunder storm. It took William a few seconds to focus his eyes upon the vision that Rainey had once again become.

Rainey looked at herself in the hand mirror that Martha Alice handed to her. Once again her mouth dropped, but this time she was pleased.

"Well, Mama would have said that hair is woman's glory, and I should have left it long, but I reckon the only glory I need is a crown up yonder." Rainey looked up at Martha Alice with deep gratefulness and affection.

"I know, sweetie." Martha Alice patted her friend's hand. "Now come on, let's go home and change clothes. In fact, let me throw this mess you wearing in the fire tonight when I'm cooking." They laughed and Arthur joined them. In perfect harmony with their laughter, baby Will squawked about his wet diaper, and Rainey hurried to him. While she was there with her son, he decided he was hungry, too. Rainey excused herself to Martha Alice's bathroom long enough to get the baby settled on her right breast.

"Has Mama's baby dined sufficiently?" Rainey asked baby Will as she held him up. Their eyes sparkled at each other. Baby Will cooed and smiled his satisfaction.

"Yes, that right, Mama's baby has dined sufficiently! Let's go back with all the big people, honey."

Mother and son returned to the main room of the shop.

William remained silent as he gazed at the beautiful Rainey carrying her kicking, cooing son. A soft smile played across his serious face.

"Say! May I tag along to your house for dinner tonight, Martha Alice?" He tried to keep his tone light, but everybody understood that he wasn't willing to be away from Rainey for too long if he could help it.

"You know you're always welcome," Martha Alice beamed. "Even though I know you're not all that anxious to taste my cooking, huh?" William and Rainey blushed, Martha Alice and Arthur chuckled.

"Why are you laughing, sweetheart?" Martha Alice nudged her husband gently and they laughed heartily.

The Seatons cleaned up their sides of the shop, with a lot of help from Rainey, and closed up.

Outside, Eddie Houser stood across Blount Street, still as a statue, gazing at them. Rainey's face brightened even more. She asked William to wait for a moment, please, and carefully crossed the bumpy road.

"It's so good to see you!" She hugged the giant man with her free arm. He smiled down at her, and his still-black hair sparkled in the sun. He returned her hug, and kissed her forehead. "I still miss your ponytails, Uncle." Rainey smiled at Eddie, touching at his close-cropped locks, and continued, "This is little Will, Uncle Eddie. Will, say "how-do" to Uncle Eddie!"

Eddie Houser took the newest member of his family into his massive arms.

"I think he likes you," Rainey said. "I'm glad you got my letter in time!"

Martha Alice sauntered over to them. "Hey there, Mr. Eddie."

" How-do, Martha Alice? Little Rainey, even if I hadn't gotten a letter, don't I always know when and how to find you?"

"Yes, you do, and it's amazing." Rainey's smile faded slightly. "How's Nettie Ann," she asked cautiously.

"Oh, she's still wallowing in her pigsty."

"Excuse me, y'all, I don't mean to interrupt, but Mr. Eddie, you are still coming to dinner tonight, aren't you?"

"I wouldn't miss it for the world, Martha Alice." Rainey looked up quickly into her uncle's eyes. She saw how deeply grateful he was to be included in her life. His was a lonely existence. She knew he desperately wanted a wife and children of his own. These treasured gifts would not come to him for several more years, but even so, Rainey would always be his favorite person in the world. Rainey loved Martha Alice even more at that moment for understanding how much her uncle meant to her.

She looked across the road at William, who stood awkwardly next to his car, still holding the ancient carpetbag she used for baby Will's diapers and clothes. He was talking at Arthur, but his eyes slid constantly over to Rainey. She knew that he was wondering who this big handsome man was who had stolen Rainey's attention away from him. He looked up to see her motioning to him, and he hurried across to them.

"William Davis, this is my uncle, Eddie Houser." William looked confused as he shook Eddie's huge, still callused hand.

Rainey's amber eyes twinkled. "He's my real mother's younger brother."

That night Rainey helped Martha Alice with dinner, their baby sons played on blankets, and their men chatted in the Seaton parlor. Laurence and Miriam came over, too, and the festive occasion was complete.

Eddie wandered contentedly among the three groups, chatting with the ladies, smoking at a cigar with the men, and cuddling and entertaining the babies. Eddie Houser's life was complete again, now that his baby girl was home at last.

CHAPTER EIGHT

Reasonable Joy

"Thus would the whole business
of your interceding with us be concluded
with abundant and most reasonable joy."
-- from CHAPTER III, Letters of Saint Augustine,
"Letter 104: From Augustine to Nectarius" (A.D. 409)

June 25, 1933

D*ear Mama and Papa:*
Seven years ago today, I married William Macke Davis. We have had two children of our own, and he adopted my son as his own when little Will was just three. He has never raised his hand to do anything to me but make me happy. Perhaps you will think me a bit off, but I must say that I am often bored. I am really ashamed to admit that I think of S. H. more than I am comfortable with. (And I often wish things had been different with L. R. and me, too.) I remember how happy I was when S. H. was happy. Those joyful times make all the difference in my memories of him.

You <u>would</u> be proud to know that I am very kind to William. And he deserves it! He is a very hard working, brilliant man, who is always extremely sweet to me and to the children. I don't want for anything, even in these terrible Depression times. I have time not only to teach and look after my children, but even to take the children with me to the soup kitchens downtown to help feed people who are down on their luck. I have a good life.

But it has taken me this long to understand that on June 25, 1926, I entered a period of "abundant and reasonable joy" in my life . . . .

By June of 1925, Rainey Clark (Herndon) resembled the little urchin from Washington no more. During those months immediately after her return to Raleigh, Rainey lived with Martha Alice and Arthur in the triple-A vernacular house that Martha Alice's papa had built back in '08. It would have been a two story house when it was initially built, but Martha Alice's father lost the will to build any further. Martha Alice's mother refused to live in the house on Bloodworth Street, not because it wasn't pretty -- which it was -- but because in the days when the house was built, Bloodworth Street was in the country, on the outskirts of Raleigh. So the Chestnuts had continued to live on Martin Street in the heart of Raleigh's Negro district.

When Martha Alice married Arthur, her parents allowed them to take over the payments on the Bloodworth Street house. In the three years that they had been married, Martha Alice and Arthur had managed to build an ample upstairs to the house. Little Arthur, Jr. and Will slept in the third bedroom downstairs, and their cribs were just close enough together that they could clap each other's hands and sing their precious baby songs on their way to sleep each night.

Rainey followed the strict orders of Martha Alice, her sister-mother-best friend, eating all the thick meals that Martha Alice lovingly provided each day. Rainey mended all the clothes, and eventually let out all the ladies' clothes in the house as they enjoyed the benefits of those thick meals. (Rainey gained ten pounds; Martha Alice gained fifteen.)

It just so happened that Arthur cut the hair of the principal of Crosby-Garfield Elementary School, and it just so happened that Arthur mentioned to him that his wife's best friend was just back in town with a brand new Master's Degree in Music Education. Did the principal know anybody who needed a music teacher? Well, it turned out that the principal didn't need a full-time teacher of music, but part-time would do just fine. He promised to talk with the principals of Lucille Hunter and Washington elementary schools. Maybe they would all like to talk with Arthur's music teacher friend. In the meantime, Rainey wrote Mr. Belton and Mr. Willis at the Delicado High School in Washington, asking them to send letters of recommendation to the three principals. By July 28, Rainey was officially hired to teach music at all three schools, including the Washington Junior-Senior High School for the 1925-1926 school year.

Meanwhile, William gave her no opportunities to disappear from his life again. He endeared himself to her through baby Will. By August, little Will was taking his first tentative steps.

"Uh-oh," Martha Alice laughed when Rainey worried a little that he might be starting too soon. "He's just getting out of the way for the next one!" William was there for those first steps, standing behind Rainey as she cooed and fussed over her son's milestone. As Will squealed with delight, patting at his favorite big person's face, he couldn't help but see William smiling right next to his mother.

And when Will said his first breathless word, it was, as is with most babies, "Da-Da." He looked directly at William, holding out his dimpled arms to him from his crib.

Once again, William Davis found a sweet head on his shoulder on soothing Sunday afternoons as he and Rainey swung from a creaking porch swing. She looked up with her calm and lovely face into his own calm and lovely face, arched an eyebrow ever so slightly, and said, "Sweetheart, you've got a little sleep in your right eye." And they both collapsed into hysterical giggles, but his laughter was tinged with a generous dollop of gratitude and a taste of relief. For this beautiful woman was really paying attention to him. She wasn't preoccupied with other things or other people. And this beautiful woman wanted to make him happy and to make him feel special.

William would never know that it was Step Herndon's indifference to baby Will that sped Rainey into his own waiting arms. For every day of indifference or absence that Step Herndon tossed at Rainey and baby Will, William Davis had a matching act of loving kindness to bestow. So it was her personal obligation to make him feel happy and make him feel special; to Rainey's mind that was the least she could offer to this man who truly, sincerely cared enough about her son and her to wipe away every injustice that had been dealt them during their last days in Washington.

They were engaged to be married on Thanksgiving Day, 1925.

Nettie Ann Houser showed up at Martha Alice's house that Thanksgiving. She had trailed her brother to the Seaton house, lurking like a trembling shadow just behind him. When Eddie knocked, Rainey ran to the door with baby Will.

"Nettie Ann's out there," Eddie said simply. "I think she wants to come in."

Rainey's eyes, identical to Nettie Ann's, clouded for a second. She hadn't seen her "real" mother since Rufus's death.

And now Rainey supposed Nettie Ann wanted to be fed, this woman who had been an annual thorn in the Clark's sweet family life: usually drunk, sometimes weepy, mostly just silly, but abusive only once.

At dusk on a windy December night, at the dawn of Rainey's 16th year, the Thorn tried to stake a claim.

"Where Rainey at," she sneered at Evie, trying to burst past her daughter's mother.

"Wait a minute," Evie said, relieved that Rufus would be coming in from the back porch (where their brand new bathroom was) at any time.

"Wait a minute?! I wants to see my young'un! Is you plannin' to stop me from seein' my own young'un?" And on and on in like fashion Nettie Ann ranted, the seething liquor inside her urging her to the heights of rage.

Rainey cowered, out of Nettie Ann's sight, in a corner of the little parlor, wavering dangerously between fury and fear. Nettie Ann only tried to see her on the 14th of December each year, never mind that she had thrown her away on the 15th of December after her birth.

This year, Nettie Ann was very pregnant with her third (or fourth, or fifth) child. And so Rainey had grown accustomed to seeing her biological mother: either as thin as a bed slat or as round as a pumpkin. She sniffed her contempt now in the recesses of the parlor. Nettie often managed to give her children to somebody else for care, so Rainey wouldn't know any of her siblings unless they were walking with Nettie Ann. And since she never saw Nettie Ann (except on December 14th, each year), she wouldn't know any of these siblings until she had children of her own... and only then because her beloved Uncle Eddie believed in the unity of his family.

Now Nettie Ann Houser lunged toward Evie, trying to push past her into the house. Rainey saw Evie's shoulder twitch back and her wavering stopped. She felt herself running toward the front door, watched herself, amazed, as she gently moved her mother Evie aside and stood face to face with the woman who had given birth to her.

They stood amber eye to amber eye now, the striking, but ruined woman and the dazzling womanchild.

"You leave my Mama alone! If you want to see me, you ask her nice, you hear?"

"But, Rainey, I'M your Mama—"

"Did you name me? Did you ever change my diaper? Or kiss me when I was sick? Or tell me you were proud of me? Did you ever sing me to sleep? Did you EVER do anything but come see me once a year?"

Nettie Ann was reduced to tears now, and she struck out. Deeply hurt, she wanted to inflict that hurt upon someone else.

Nettie Ann's fist landed weakly on Evie's defenseless cheek, and Evie's eyes watered. By now, Rufus was finished in the bathroom and his baby girl's uplifted voice alerted him to rush to the front. He got to the front door just in time to see his sweet little daughter push her birth mother backwards, nudging Nettie Ann harshly until she was forced to turn away lest she fall backwards down the six wooden steps leading from the porch.

Nettie Ann stood at the foot of the steps, sniveling like a small child, her heavy skirts whipping around her swollen legs.

Rainey stood at the top of the steps, her fists planted firmly into her hips.

"The next time you come here, you better not be drunk and you better treat my Mama right!   Now go on 'bout your business!"

Rainey stomped back to the front door, tears of shame streaming down her face.   She could not believe that she had disrespected any adult, even Nettie Ann, so badly.

But nobody was going to hurt her mother's feelings. She draped her arms around Evie's neck.

"Mama, are you all right?"

"Yes, baby, Mama is all right."

Rufus stood by quietly, filled with pride and shaken with awe at his daughter's strength in dealing with Nettie Ann, and at the power of her love for his wife.

For the first time, Rufus Clark could see the woman that Rainey would become, and he was amazed.

On the next December 14th, Nettie Ann stood quietly, stone cold sober, outside the door of her oldest daughter's home, and finally knocked upon that door. With a quiet meekness, she asked the floor before Rufus's feet:

"Mind if I say 'happy birthday' to the baby?"

Rainey could see Nettie Ann over Eddie's shoulder now.

"Oh, I'm sorry, Uncle Eddie," she said absently, never taking her eyes off Nettie Ann's tiny unsteady form.   "Come on in here and make yourself comfortable!"

After an eternal five minutes, Nettie Ann made her way onto Martha Alice's front porch. She steadied herself on the banister and scuttled up to the front door, where Rainey stood, impassive and stony.

"Hey, there, Rainey."

"Hey."

"Eddie-boy told me you was back in town."

"I've been back. Since May."

"Yeah, I know. How you been?"

"Fine, thank you. And you?"

"Fair to middlin'. Look hear, can I see the baby?"

"Well. . . I . . . Yes, ma'am. That'll be fine," she said, as if trying to convince herself. "I'll get him. Be right back."

"Rainey --" Rainey turned to see Nettie Ann rubbing her arms. "Can I step inside? It's cold out here." Nettie Ann tried to give her child the conwoman's smile she gave to all her men, but the smile died in its infancy.

Rainey threw open the door and held it for Nettie Ann. "Come on in."

Nettie Ann came inside and stood timidly just over the threshold of the front door. She nodded to the three men, who stood when she and Rainey entered.

Inside, the boys were squealing on a blanket island in the middle of Martha Alice's parlor. William and Arthur watched them idly, laughing at their own tall tales. Eddie laughed with them, but said little. He was content just to be around folks.

"Come here, Mama's baby. Got somebody for you to meet." Will chirped, delighted to be picked up by his mother.

Eddie looked at her. "You all right, honey?"

"Oh, yessir."

Nettie Ann wiped her hands nervously against her dress. Her tongue darted nervously around her chapped lips and she looked miserable when her daughter offered baby Will to her.

"I...I better not." She laughed nervously. "I'm a little shaky." Still Nettie Ann leaned further into the door. "Hey there, little boy," she cooed. "How you?" Will gurgled and struggled in his mother's arms to go to this new friend.

"You can hold him if you want to. It's all right." Nettie Ann looked at Rainey as if she couldn't believe she would have such a privilege. She went to the wingback chair near the front door, arranged her skirts and lifted her puny arms to take the baby. Rainey set him carefully onto Nettie Ann's lap. And there they sat for a while, this strange sort of mother and her beautiful grandson with whom she would spend only snippets of time for the rest of her life. Nettie Ann saw no reproach in those little eyes, and the smile welcomed her as if she were a treasured friend. For a small moment, Nettie Ann felt that she really could make up for the 25 years she had ruined with her own little girl.

"Won't you stay to dinner?" Rainey had let Martha Alice ask. She had never in 25 years broken bread with this strange woman, and she wasn't all that sure she wanted to now.

"Why thank you. Don't mind if I do."

They dined as a family. It was not awkward at all that day and they all laughed and talked and couldn't get over how good Martha Alice's cooking was. Nettie Ann said that she had never had a better time eating, and she wished aloud that she could see more of Rainey and baby Will.

Later, as the babies slept and the grown ups drank coffee in the parlor, William walked slowly to Rainey, a nervous glint in his eye.

"What's the matter, William?"

"Er, Rainey?" He fumbled around in his jacket pocket and produced a small black velveteen box.

"Umm, here. Oh, I mean, um, yeah, okay...." He cleared his throat and sat down next to Rainey, so close that he sat on part of her dress.

"Raineywillyoumarryme?" Everyone laughed, startled at the swift ferocity of William's proposal.

Rainey's "yes" was nearly swallowed up in the tumult, and nobody saw Nettie Ann leave quietly in the joyful uproar that followed Rainey's acceptance.

JUNE 25, 1926

"Willie Otey, you are something! Ain't she, Rainey? Miss Mittie? This gown ... mm-mmm!" Martha Alice, matron of honor and best friend of the bride, stood back to examine her best friend in all her wedding finery. They were on the third floor of First Baptist Church, waiting for their summons from Mrs. Haywood, the wedding directress, in one of the tiny Sunday School rooms. Martha Alice was both pleased and awed. Mittie, rounder than ever, nodded her stern-faced approval. Willie Otey Kay, perhaps the best dressmaker in the state, had created this angelic dress. Recently widowed, Willie was known for creating dresses for governors' wives and daughters, yet she had taken time to make a gown that was just as beautiful for her childhood playmate, Rainey Elizabeth Clark (Herndon).

The basic gown was simple: straight skirts and a bodice of cream satin with a delicate overlay of organdy. The gown was made magnificent by its final covering of Queen Anne lace ("I had some extra from a bridal I did for the mayor's niece," Willie explained.) Rainey's bridal cap, which cascaded from the top of her head in elegantly scalloped folds, was also covered in the same lace. The total effect was breathtaking, and against Rainey's caramel skin, the cream ensemble was stunning.

Willie and Martha Alice stood now, along with Alouette Willis, Rainey's maid of honor, admiring the handiwork of God and of woman. Mrs. Haywood entered after a dainty knock upon the rickety classroom door. "Ready, Miss Rainey?"

And downstairs they went, to the foyer of the church, where Uncle Eddie stood waiting for her, his strong neck inflamed with a mild heat rash from his stiffly starched collar. He looked marvelous, Rainey thought, his magnificent hair cut close around his face. She smiled at him, and he responded with a sort of rumpling of his lips. He was miserably nervous, he would tell her later, and hoped that he would do nothing to embarrass his niece.

Inside the sanctuary, Emily Mae Morgan Kelly worked her magic with the pipe organ while Joe Reeves accompanied her in perfect sync on the church piano.

From that moment, all became as a sweet, misty dream for Rainey.

She was free!

There would be no bloodied specter hovering over her when she awakened each morning. And what a specter: what was left of the good looks that had trapped her glared balefully into her sleep swollen face. This specter did not emanate from any man who had ever slapped her face purple or kicked her baby-bloated stomach. This saintly specter couldn't be a representation of the man who had stolen her money. Nor could this specter ever have emanated from a man who had arranged to sell her baby to an elderly couple (she called them Elizabeth and Zachariah, because, like John the Baptist's parents, they were much too old to contemplate childbirth). The bloodied specter glaring at her each morning emanated from one who could not possibly have understood why she had abandoned him, nor why she had allowed him to become a specter. Surely, no laudanum or horsey had ever clouded the judgment and the wisdom of the man who projected this pathetic phantom. And of course no other man had known the owner of the specter in the ways that she had known him....

But the specter had not appeared this morning, and for the first time in more than a year, she was indeed free. Free to start her life -- and little Will's life -- with a man who loved her truly and really cared that she was safe and happy. No harm would come to them through William Davis.

There was a strange reassurance in William's back, she thought as she cascaded down the aisle of the sanctuary of First Baptist Church. Why it was his back that comforted her, she could not imagine, but she remembered that with Step she always felt afraid that if they were to leave the inner safety of Washington, of Georgetown, of Boney's After Hours Supper Club, they would be in a world of swirling danger and lethal encounters. She had always known, and feared, Step's cowardice.

Drifting elegantly down that aisle, accompanied by the jubilant organ of Emily Mae Morgan Kelly, Rainey shuddered to think of the life she might have had in constant flight with Step Herndon.

And relief burst upon her lovely, organdy covered face as a smile, brilliant and joyous, and so powerful that little Will, jubilant upon Uncle Mason's lap of honor (until, of course, Aunt Addie Rose, Claire Reeves or Helen Willis took hold of him), caught a glimpse of his mother and clapped his tiny hands and shouted as a testament to his mother's joy.

And so they were married, and through the years they enjoyed a relatively idyllic life together. William, his straight back ever a symbol of safety for Rainey, went out into his world each morning to deal with late paying insurance clients, law clients who paid in food and clothes and services rather than dollars and cents, and white folks who just couldn't believe that a colored boy, let alone a 36-year-old colored boy, could actually negotiate his way through the forests of fiduciary responsibilities, whole life, term life, and litigation. Yet he never brought home the concentrated bitterness and frustration he felt to Rainey or to Will. Oh, he would talk to Rainey about his day, but always in condensations and generalities. Instead he brought it home on his face; each day seemed to etch a tiny furrow more deeply into his brow, or to deepen, ever so slightly, those crow's feet around his eyes that Rainey loved to kiss as often as possible.

And he never brought it to their bed, where she knew that he was truly hers, totally committed to giving her his undivided attention. I never knew if Step was thinking of me or of some other woman. ... or of Cal Bertrand, Rainey thought on their wedding night just before her new husband convinced her with his tongue, his incredible tongue, that he would think only of her for the rest of their nights together. And again reassurance pushed a smile across that lovely caramel face, and those buoyant amber eyes clouded over for a while.

Wifehood: Married Again For The First Time

The first time she married, the union wasn't real in the eyes of the law. It was one man's insistence of his will upon her. And she had willingly complied, because she was certain that she was in love with him and that he had her best interests at heart. And he made her feel so happy, and so very much alive! There could have been no greater reality in the universe than Step Herndon, because he made her feel as if every fiber, every cell, every ounce of her was permanently enlivened by his presence. Even his cruelty was a lifeline and a link to her reality. Ultimately, Rainey had had to face the cold and ugly truth that he did not care about her. The only interests he had at his heart had been his own, along with a deep concern for his next opportunity to experience the full effects of his love affair with laudanum and heroin. (And Cal....)

The second time she married, it was real in everyone's eyes. This man adored her, and liked her, and was enlivened by her presence. He talked with her about all of their plans and all the decisions that had to be made. As often as he could, he shopped for groceries with her, but they rarely had a need for trips to the grocers, not as long as William was doing his job so well. They paid their bills together, though she paid the lion's share of them with her income. Her paltry salary (and Aunt Mittie and Aunt Addie Rose's generous endowments) went to payment of their utilities, but it was William's unique payment arrangements that kept them living a semblance of the high life.

When William's clients could not pay him with money, and after 1929, they were less and less likely to be able to, they always paid him on time with products: chickens, vegetables, fresh milk, handmade children's clothing, hairstyles, haircuts, and hand-cobbled shoes, tailor made dresses and suits, automobile repairs. On one remarkable occasion, one of William's grateful clients, both in insurance and in the law, carved eight beautiful

Adirondack chairs from heavy pine wood. He stained each chair with a redwood stain, and presented them to "Lawyer Davis" as payment in full for services rendered. Rainey was delighted, as usual, because even though she brought in the only steady cash flow, William's work always brought in more food, accessories, and other amenities than they needed. Together, William and Rainey arranged two of the Adirondacks on their tiny front porch. For a long while, those chairs, with their unusual, sloping shapes, were the talk of Cotton Place.

But "Lawyer Davis's" prize payment came to them in 1930. Jasper Killebrew had been severely injured in his line of work as a train mechanic's assistant. He would never walk again, and would need constant doctor's care. His salary stopped immediately, and his wife's meager earnings as a maid were totally inadequate alone to sustain the family. Their two daughters had to drop out of school and take sad, hopeless little jobs just to make ends draw closer together, for there was no making ends meet in the Killebrew household. Desperate, Mr. Killebrew turned to Lawyer Davis for help. He lamented that he had not purchased insurance to protect his family, but now he was about to lose his house, which had been in the Killebrew family since 1885, paid for since the turn of the century. The Killebrews had neglected to pay the taxes on the house for too long, and now the tax bill was coming due for the very last time before their beautiful home would be sold at auction.

First, William knew that Mrs. Killebrew had purchased insurance and saving bonds without her husband's knowledge. He helped her cash in the bonds and borrow against the insurance so that the family would be able to pay doctor's bills and keep food on the table. In his quiet, gently persuasive way, William made arrangements with Mr. Killebrew's former employer to have him earn a small pension each month. William induced the company to look beyond the fact that their former employer was a Negro; that was hardly as important as making themselves look good to the public. Why not make sure he has a small income, William reasoned, and even have a newspaper man come in and write a small human interest story about how Mr. Killebrew had been made to have a more comfortable life because of the kindness of his former company?

Next, William paid the back taxes on the home in the 1000 block of South Person Street, which was at that point of no return just before auction. Mr. Killebrew realized that he would only be burdened by the upkeep of the home, and he agreed that William should assume ownership. This move put them just around the corner from Martha Alice and Red Art, and William rented his smaller Cotton Place home to the Killebrews for a tiny monthly fee. Suddenly, William and Rainey owned two homes free and clear, and the newer home was a far cry from the modest, two-bedroom bungalow into which the Davis family, by 1930 about to be five strong, had to be crammed.

The former Killebrew home was a breathtaking jewel in a sea of shotgun and A-framed houses. Situated on a comically small lot, the new Davis home was a folk Victorian, built by Mr. Killebrew's father and uncles. It had a wrap around porch, seven bedrooms, all with fireplaces, four bathrooms, fully plumbed to at least 1920 standards, a parlor, a library, a sunny, cavernous kitchen with not only a hearth, but a back staircase, a full dining room, pantry, and a screened-in back porch. Throughout the home were such surprise features as the occasional high round windows, one lovely stained glass window, ornate banister knobs on the staircases, and elaborate latticework at several of the doorways. While it was uncommon for 19th-century Negroes to have had such "palatial" homes in Raleigh, the Killebrew brothers were known for their ability to build well, especially when they were building each other's homes.

The Davises hired the Killebrew girls to help Rainey around the house, which helped the Killebrew family to have a slightly higher income, and enabled the girls to return to high school. Eventually, one of the Killebrew girls enrolled at Shaw University and earned a teaching degree.

Though Rainey could have done without all the extra housework that was now her lot, she couldn't help but remember that just a few years earlier; she had had to juggle which bills she could put off paying for the month in favor of other, more pressing bills. Her "husband" in those days may have gone to work each day, but he never assisted her in keeping the household running efficiently.

William even cooked dinner for the family occasionally, and he turned himself into quite an adequate chef. This man sought her counsel in most aspects of his life, and he respected her ability to decide her own way in her own life. It took Rainey a couple of years to adjust herself to living with a man who actually respected her and her brain, who truly admired her ideas and her ways of navigating through life. Further, she was now living with a man for whom argument was never a form of in-home communication, and the only hitting he administered was the well-orchestrated, carefully metered spankings of their children. He was a disciplinarian who insisted that each child understand his or her offense, and why the spanking was necessary. He was a loving father who administered comforting hugs to the children after discipline. "I spanked you because I love you and I want you to do what's right. Do you understand?"

Rainey knew she had married a gem, and she loved William quite a bit, liked him infinitely, and was forever grateful to him. But she felt no thrill of illicit excitement when she talked about him, not after the drama her life had been with Step Herndon. It took Rainey at least two years to realize that she was free of guilt (had she killed Step, really?), and liberated from anxiety (before his death, she worried that he would attack her; after his death, she worried that he would haunt her). This new husband, the legal one, the real William in her life, did not make her feel frantically alive, nor did he orchestrate the positions of the sun, the moon, and the stars in her universe. But he did make her feel safe, and comfortable . . . and unfettered. After their sham marriage, Step Herndon had made her feel as if every burden known to woman was hers to bear.

Now, she found that she was not happy, exactly; it was as if she had entered some sort of sweet peace. It took her two more years still to realize that the undercurrent she was fighting beneath that sweet peace was a semblance of happiness, and she finally contented herself with her life in a state of joy that was a mild but reasonable substitute for ecstasy. She sighed. She could content herself with a reasonable joy that was free of danger, or violence or abject disappointment. Reasonable joy. Yes, she could live with that. She settled in for a predictable life as a beloved wife and mother. She closed off the Step Herndon part of her life and lived for the man who truly loved her. Sometimes, she chafed at her decision....

William, for all the incredible lovemaking he gave her, all the respect, all the adoration, all the friendship, didn't possess the edge that she had always sought, however unconsciously, in a man. Any edges he may have had as a younger man had long ago been softened by mega doses of reality.

William Macke Davis was never one to make a spur-of-the-moment decision. The logical and sensible Rainey felt great comfort in that reality, but the hell kitten in her missed, in a sick sort of way, the snap judgments or the unpredictable, helter-skelter reactions that she always got from Step Herndon. Each time Rainey and William had to make decisions together, Rainey had to put up a valiant fight against her compulsion to yell at William to "just make up your mind, for goodness sake!"

More often than not in those first years, Rainey sat on her hands to avoid showing her irrational frustration toward her husband. She understood that she was being damned foolish, and she wasn't about to lose this otherwise great relationship, or to go it alone, when she knew that William Davis was truly the best thing since ever to happen to her.

He was her one more chance; she would get no others, she believed.

Rainey made it her life's mission to be as kind to William as she could. She knew that his diligence and his methodical way of running his life was the best way.

So Rainey, ever one to listen to her sensible self, took out her mild frustrations in positive ways. She kept magnificent rose gardens in the back yard of their Cotton Place home, and later, in the surprisingly compact front and back yards of their huge Person Street home. She played hard with her children; William grew accustomed to seeing them playing tag or touch football or badminton in the back yard when he came home from work, and he made it his business, no matter how tired he was, to join in. Only rain and their weekly trips to help out at the soup kitchen kept them away from the games.

Sometimes, late at night, after William had shared portions of his day with her, asked her advice on how to handle certain clients, laughed and talked with and read to their children, and loved her to climax, Rainey was haunted by disturbing dreams of Step and his powerful passions, his unpredictable rages, and his painfully tender gestures of affection. She knew, when she awakened from those wild, lurid dreams, sometimes drenched with sweat, that no one except her children had ever made her feel more alive than Step Herndon.

She was never surprised to find that she awakened herself with the sound of her own weeping.

Still, life was good. William adopted baby Will, who would later request that he be called "Clark," so that his identity would be distinct from the only father he would ever know. Together, Rainey and William had two daughters, Willia Evelyn and Olivia Jane, who grew up to be rather stunning beauties -- both inside and out -- in their own rights. Willia was the smooth silky color of coffee and cream, while Olivia's satiny skin appeared warm and golden like a sugar cookie. Willia's eyes were black, while Olivia's eyes were a light brown, though not as light as Rainey's amber orbs.

While Willia tended to be almost skinny, Olivia enjoyed (endured) a slight roundness that would be a source of annoyance for her throughout her life.   And where Willia was bold and friendly, Olivia was quiet and courteous.   Willia stood out in a crowd, and even her audaciously elegant walk commanded attention from those around her.   Olivia sort of floated along sweetly in her beloved big sister's wake, a placid smile etched on her face, and she wore a detached expression that said she would gladly accept your friendliness, though she was a bit too preoccupied to initiate cordiality.

Rainey was a blessed woman, as she often told herself, free to be that sorority woman, that benefactor in a neighborhood where doctor lived next door to ditch digger, who lived next door to lawyer, who lived next door to Pullman porter.

In Negro neighborhoods, folks co-existed, and got along well. And so Rainey did in her own home, which she shared with "Lawyer Davis," who was infinitely kind, cordial, and passionate, but not her Prince Charming so much as he was her knight in dependable and functional armor.

She had eked out a palatable existence for herself in a world that would not afford her more than mere reasonable joy. She might never again know the heights of the foot-swinging joy she thought she had with Step Herndon, perhaps, but never again would she know fear, or the force of a hand slapping her face, or the pressure of that hand and its mate closing off her ability to breathe. A reasonable compromise, she concluded, one that she knew counted for something in the universe.

CHAPTER NINE

Adverse Possession

t was a simple case, really; insultingly simple. But it was one that had never, in the history of Raleigh, North Carolina, at least, been won by a Negro against a white man until that fateful day in 1934. And at its center was one "Lawyer Davis," who became a permanent folk hero throughout all the Negro neighborhoods in Raleigh.

An elderly white woman named Lillith Hanrahan lived in lavish squalor in a renowned neighborhood called Oakwood. She had been born in this house in which she had grown old. In fact, Lillith Hanrahan was nearly as old as the house, which had been built in a grand Victorian style. The mansion was replete with Mansard roofs that held onto the pride invested in the house even when the house was falling apart underneath. Its gables seemed to soar into the clouds when just the right light hit them; and its deep-seated bay windows encouraged the sun to bestow its essence upon Lillith Hanrahan's many lovingly waxed plants.

Lillith Hanrahan's father (who had insisted that his daughters remain Hanrahan women in public if not on paper, as they would always be his girls, not their husbands' wives) and husband (who despised his father-in-law for being such a curmudgeon) had left her a very comfortable fatherless widow, with property to be built upon or rented out all over Wake County. Lillith Hanrahan had but one child, and he was a wastrel of a drunken po-white-trash-acting cracker named Jesse Waldron. There was simply no other way to describe this sometimes noble woman's son; he was a waste of time and effort in so many ways, having done everything in his power to disabuse himself of his mother's valiant efforts at proper home training. He had diligently divested himself of every good table manner, every social grace, and every shred of human kindness that he could identify with anything positive or uplifting to humanity.

Confident that he was due to inherit every penny and every stick of furniture and every grain of sand his mother owned, Jesse never bothered to hold down a job. He lay about beneath his mother's mansard roofs by day and by night, shouting orders to her faithful and trusty servants. He drank only Southern Comfort with his oddly priggish assortment of crumpets, scones, and tangerines.

Jesse Waldron had been a thorn in Lillith Hanrahan's side for all but the first 18 months of his existence. She had only herself to blame, of course. Lillith Hanrahan was 42 years old when she gave birth to the manchild who was, by all rights, to be her pride and joy. She could not bring herself even to cut his flowing auburn curls until he was five years old.

"Mother, I want you to cut these cow turds off my head right now," he declared after he had torn away vital flesh from the lip of a boy who had dared call him "Little Boy Blue" to his face. Lillith Hanrahan complied immediately and joyously, calling upon Mr. Waldron's barber at the next corner to do the job.

Such was the pattern with Jesse Waldron: enroute to running to Mama, always concoct any tale plausible enough to win her sympathy and allegiance. That way, he could do any damn thing he pleased and not worry about consequences.

By the time he was a 44-year-old in 1934, his evil was fully crystallized into a poisonous art form.

One late morning in 1934, Lillith Hanrahan stood up on her increasingly wobbly legs and removed her weary body from the stately but relentlessly stiff mahogany chair at the gleaming mahogany table where she had just completed her breakfast.

"Thank you so much, Polly. That breakfast was simply delicious. The eggs were so nice and fluffy! You just outdid yourself!"

Lillith Hanrahan never failed to acknowledge her housekeeper, Polly Crowder, with deep and sincere appreciation for every duty she performed. It was no wonder that Polly had worked for Miss Lillith all those many years.   There weren't too many other white women in Raleigh who would even look at their maids, let alone talk with them like they were really human.

"You're certainly welcome, Miss Lillith," Polly smiled as she cleared away Lillith's breakfast dishes.   "You think Mr. Jesse is ready for his something to eat?"

"Well, now that you mention it, Polly, I haven't heard him stirring about this morning.   I reckon I'll go check on him."

Lillith dragged herself gracefully up the grand staircase, which seemed steeper to her each year, until she reached the landing of the second floor, a destination that she felt more grateful to reach each time she did.   Could she hear muffled sounds from the other side of Jesse's door?   Lillith's breath quickened as she tried to hasten her steps to the end of the hall, which was drowned in daylight from the half window facing the staircase.   When she finally arrived at her heir's door, Lillith distinctly heard laughter, Jesse's and what sounded like women's voices.   She hesitated a moment before knocking on Jesse's door. When she got no answer, she tried his doorknob.   It turned with great squeaky protest.   Later, she would wonder if the screeching of the doorknob hadn't been a warning for her.

Inside Jesse's room, which Polly could only clean hurriedly when he wandered into the bathroom, Lillith was alarmed by the fetid commingling of smells: whiskey, cigars, and --

Her beloved wastrel son lay on his back now, his hands behind his back.   His breath came in ragged intervals, and his eyes were closed.   His sunken chest was bare, except for straggles of gray hair, but from the waist down the quilt covered him. There was rhythmic movement beneath his quilts, and Lillith was sure she could make out the shapes of two heads there.   When she finally realized what was going on, Lillith yelped her son's name and fell against his doorjamb before she fell backward into the hallway.   Jesse sat up long enough to see where his mother had fallen. He lay back in his bed, lifting his hands only long enough to touch the covered heads to urge them to continue their work.

Lillith called weakly to Polly, who ran upstairs to help her "boss lady" to her bed.

Later that day, when Lillith felt stronger, she summoned her lawyer and his clerk to her home and, after conferring with the lawyer for about an hour, she commanded her son to come to her room. Lillith sat among her stunning white eyelet pillowcases and quilt, her hair dressed severely in a bun, her gown as white as her pillowcases. She was now almost fully recovered from the morning's shock.

Jesse had never seen the steel that glinted in her weak green eyes.

"I have been talking with Lawyer Tyler, Jesse, and I have made some changes that I think you need to know about. First, I have instructed Lawyer Tyler to rewrite my will. You are no longer in it, Jesse."

"Aw, Mother, you must be out of your --"

"You are also no longer welcome in my house. You have brought nothing but shame and disgrace upon me all your adult life. I have instructed Collins and Polly to pack your things and they will be moved to our little cottage on Tucker Street. You will be living there from now on."

Jesse Waldron was drawn out of his near-stupor.

"Mother! I ain't goin' nowhere . . ."

Raymond Tyler spoke. He was a tall cadaver of a man with thick snowy hair. His blue eyes were discs of ice in a solemn face. Lawyer Tyler had always scared Jesse Waldron silent.

"You are not going to upset your mother any further, Mr. Waldron. You are to leave now. There are some assistants downstairs waiting to move you and your belongings to the Tucker Street residence." There was no conciliation in Lawyer Tyler's voice, which was like frosty wind upon frigid glass. When he finished speaking, Jesse ceased to exist for him, and he turned his attention to his client, who was now weeping silently.

"The paperwork is already on file at the courthouse, Miss Hanrahan. You are not to worry about another thing."

Jesse choked back the cocktail of bile and stale whiskey and rage that rose suddenly from his empty stomach.

"Old man, you ain't gon' come up in my house and --"

Lawyer Tyler never looked away from Lillith Hanrahan. "Collins, tell the gentlemen to come up here and help Mr. Waldron to get to his new home." Walter Collins, Lillith's butler, and butler to Lillith's parents, detached himself from the shadows by the door and went downstairs. He returned to Lillith's room with two incredibly burly men whose biceps and triceps rippled through their work shirts.

"These gentlemen are going to escort Mr. Waldron to the Tucker Street house, Miss Hanrahan. This is Mr. Burton, and this is Mr. Dudley." The men shook Lillith's limply offered hand, and, like Lawyer Tyler, they never acknowledged Jesse Waldron. He and his meager belongings were escorted to Tucker Street without incident.

Lillith Hanrahan had the locks changed on every door in her home as soon as her son was out of her way.

Jesse Waldron retired to the Tucker Street cottage to stew over his vast misfortune, and to plot his revenge.

When Lillith Hanrahan wrote her only child out of her last will and testament, she divided her worldly goods among various relations scattered across the South. To Polly Crowder, she willed a lush parcel of land on South East Street in the all-Negro South Park community. Lillith Hanrahan instructed Polly to go ahead and do whatever she wanted to do with that land, and Polly decided to let her daughter Dovie and her husband, Billy "Buddy" Anderson, build a home there.

Jesse Waldron knew about the property on East Street, of course, and he set out to wreak havoc in his mother's life before anything of real worth to someone else could be constructed there. One spring morning, long before most people had to be up and on to their jobs, particularly early risers saw an elderly, wild-eyed white man on the East Street lot in the midst of cinderblocks and neatly stacked wood. He had his own small cadre of workers with him, and in a short time, they would begin to build something with those supplies.

One of the passersby was Polly Crowder's niece Lossie, on her way to begin cooking lunch at the Crosby-Garfield School cafeteria. She knew that those supplies and that land were now Dovie and Buddy's property. Of course, she knew better than to confront those white men herself, so she ran the short three blocks from East Street over to Aunt Polly's house on Bledsoe Avenue.

Polly was horrified though not surprised to learn that the "elderly" man would show up on her property. She told Lossie that the man was Jesse Waldron, and thanked her for telling her. Sending her on to work with a kiss and a hug, Polly finished dressing her hair and walked the twelve blocks to Lillith Hanrahan's home.

"Miss Lillith, I needs to talk wid you 'fore I get started on your breakfast."

"I'm mighty hungry this morning Polly, so why don't I come sit with you in the kitchen whilst you talk to me."

Polly related to Lillith what Lossie had reported to her. When she was finished, Lillith said quietly, "Polly, you got you a lawyer to call?"

Polly thought for a moment. "Why yes, ma'am, I do. I'll call Lawyer Davis."

"Good. Let's get him to work on this, because that land is yours now. I'll speak with Lawyer Tyler."

Polly Crowder and Rainey Davis had been friendly since Rainey had moved to Person Street with her precious children. Polly enjoyed welcoming new neighbors with some of her brownies, which everyone in the neighborhood seemed to love. The neighbor ladies were always asking for the recipe, as Rainey did. Polly, who was probably the most giving and unselfish woman most people knew, gave most of the recipe gladly, but held back two secret ingredients that made hers more moist and irresistible than any others. But from that first batch of brownies, which Rainey declared disappeared almost as soon as they arrived at her house, Polly could count on the occasional pleasant visit from Rainey or invitation to Rainey's house for tea.

Rainey Davis was a class act. She loved to cook and was always eager to improve her skills as a chef. No matter when Polly saw her, Rainey always had a pleasant word and a laugh for her. With Rainey, Polly felt like she was equal to anybody around. Rainey Davis treated Polly like folks, which is what Polly had loved about her adopted South Park neighborhood ever since she'd moved there from Lillington with her late husband and their children. It didn't matter who you were or what you did for a living (or, Polly shuddered, what your child did to others. Her furious son, once her beautiful prince full of hope, trudged through her weary mind, dressed in his military prison uniform). People were just nice in South Park.

Still, Polly felt intimidated by Rainey's husband, whom she could only bring herself to address as "Lawyer Davis." Polly knew that he was one of the nicest men around, but with his height and his solemn good looks, and his high position in the community, Polly got tongue-tied whenever he entered the room. She and Rainey could be laughing about children or sharing a recipe over a cup of tea in Rainey's kitchen. Lawyer Davis would walk in, just home from work, and give Rainey a kiss, and Polly would find herself suddenly silent, though Rainey's laughter would continue uninterrupted with her husband.

"Hello there, Miss Polly," he would say in his booming and jovial voice.

"Hey, there," Polly would say, suddenly a mouse squeaking a timid reply.

So it was without hesitation now that Polly called Rainey from her "boss lady's" house to ask if she could come by to ask a favor of her.

"Sure, Polly, come on over after you get off work. I've got some of that Earl Grey you like!"

"Oh, that'll be nice. See you then, hear?"

As Polly mounted the steps to the Davis home, she felt almost as awed by it as she did by Miss Lillith's house. Rainey had made the house beautiful again in the few years she had lived there. Like Miss Lillith's, the Davis house was a Victorian style house, but, unlike Miss Lillith's house, Rainey had allowed light into every room. There were places in the Hanrahan-Waldron house that were bleak and uninviting.

Rainey threw open the door to welcome Polly, and the smells of Earl Grey, freshly cut lemon wedges, cookies, and recently prepared dinner rushed out to invite her in. Rainey's little darling, Olivia Jane, a solemn three-year-old, stood at her mother's knee, leaning against her mother and holding loosely to her skirt.

"Olivia, say 'hello' to Miss Polly."

"Heyyo, Mish Powly."

"Okay, now run on to the library and finish looking at the book Mama had for you. Okay?"

"Yesh, ma'am." Olivia Jane turned away from the security of her mother's skirt, dragging her Raggedy Ann doll behind her.

When they were seated at Rainey's kitchen table, Polly cleared her throat and sipped at her Earl Grey.

"This is delicious, Rainey."

"You're mighty quiet this afternoon. What's the matter?" Rainey wondered what Polly's son had done this time. That Buck was big trouble, and everybody in the neighborhood knew it.

"Well, you remember I told you Miss -- my boss lady give me some property over on East Street? You know, she had put her son out of her house and she's done moved him over to their house on Tucker Street. Anyway, her son has done took over the property she give me. That boy is plain mean as a junkyard dog. And do you know she is still trying to find a girl to clean up his place once a week?

Everybody knows what a mean man he is. Anyways, I really need Lawyer Davis's help."

"Okay, but you really need to make an appointment with him --"

"Well, could you talk to him for me?"

Rainey looked at Polly for a moment, surprised. Then she understood. She had learned over the years of her marriage to William that many of the neighbors who were friendly with her became timid around her husband. On one level, Rainey was genuinely amused; William was probably not the intimidating one in their house. But Rainey also understood that it was William's position that made people feel small somehow. She would be reluctant to tell him, however, because he would be devastated. William was the kindest man she had ever known.

"Oh," she said now. "Well, when can you meet with him?"

"Any time after three-thirty through the week. My boss lady thinks that Lawyer Davis ought to meet with her lawyer."

"And who is that?"

"Lawyer Tyler."

"Oh, Lord." William had had a few encounters with Raymond Tyler, and had found him to be the most unpleasant, overtly prejudiced white lawyer he had ever met. Fortunately, they had only met on the most mundane matters, all of which had been simple to settle within the boundaries of standard law. Now, poor William would be forced to work with him.

"Well, I'll talk to William. Call me tomorrow from Lillith Hanrahan's house, and I'll let you know. Finish your tea! Tell me, how is Dovie doing with her new baby?"

The women chatted for a while longer, and then Polly had to go home. As she stood to leave Rainey marveled again at the older woman's beauty. She was tall and stately, and her perfect white teeth contrasted stunningly against her flawless ebony skin. Her hair, already thick, was beginning to whiten beautifully. Yet, her shoulders were stooped against the weight of her hard life: a son who couldn't seem to stay out of trouble, a husband who was probably lynched by some Klansmen on some back country road outside of Raleigh. Working anywhere near that worthless cracker Jesse Waldron had to be a cross to bear.

"Polly, you're just as pretty as you can be!"

Polly Crowder looked shocked. "Me? Hush your mouth, Rainey!" But Polly blushed and smiled as they strolled to the front door. At the library door, Olivia ran out to grab her mother's skirt and wave goodbye to Miss Polly.

"Thank you, Rainey. You've always been mighty sweet."

"Rainey, that man never even looked up at me." William and Rainey were lying in their bed one night two weeks later, their bodies and their minds still aglow from their usual intense lovemaking. They had grown quiet in each other's arms, and Rainey had nearly drifted off to sleep.

"Hmm?" she said now.

"That Tyler. He would not even acknowledge that I was in the room."

"So how did he talk to you?"

"Through his clerk. It was the clerk who asked me all the questions about my side, or Polly's side, and it was the clerk who acknowledged my presence at all. And you know I didn't get asked to sit down. So I just sat on down anyhow."

"Ummm, sugar, you're mighty bold, aren't you?" They laughed, and Rainey snuggled deeper against William's chest.

"Well, I had worked hard all day just like they had. I know for a fact I probably worked harder than that clerk. I'm writing up the agreement that we're going to try to get Waldron to sign. Tyler is going to enforce it. Still, I can't get over feeling like I was a ghost."

"Well, are you surprised? Why do you think some of them call us 'spooks'?" Their giggles were bittersweet. "You told me yourself that he was the coldest white man you'd ever had to deal with."

"But one thing I'm glad about this time. Even if he is pretending I don't exist, I'm still glad we're on the same side. He's the kind of man who'll cut his mother and say, 'Oh, excuse me, Mother. You seem to have a nick. Let me have the maid clean up the puddle you're making on the rug.' And go right on about his business as if nothing happened."

"I bet that'll work out fine for you and Polly, don't you? Somebody that cold will get you what you want."

"Well, I hope so."

Two weeks later, on a misty afternoon, while Eddie and his wife were visiting Rainey and the children, they were all alarmed when seven-year-old Willia came running into the parlor holding her arm and crying.

"What's the matter, Willia?" Rainey was truly alarmed. Willia, who didn't like to spend much time inside, was certainly not one to do a lot of crying.

"I burned my arm!"

"Oh, Lord. How? Where's Will -- I mean, Clark?"

Rainey's son had only recently announced to the family that from now on, he wanted to be called "Clark" rather than "Will" so that people would not confuse him with his "Papa."

"Here I am, Mama. It was the wall out there in the hallway."

"What?"

"It was the wall that burned Willia's arm." Clark, a very serious and responsible nine-year-old, seemed disappointed that he hadn't been able to protect his little sister.

"Okay, sugar. Calm down," Eddie said in his soothing bass voice. "Come to Uncle Eddie." Willia obeyed, still sniveling.

"Clark, go get Mama a little slice of butter. Don't get the Oleo, now, honey."

"Yes, ma'am." Clark went to the kitchen, as Olivia followed solemnly behind him, her Raggedy Ann doll bumping along on the floor as she walked.

"Rainey," Eddie said softly over Willia's well-groomed head. "Take the baby, and let me go see about this wall."

By the time Eddie came back into the parlor, Willia was cradled in Rainey's arms, her injured arm coated with soothing butter.

"Thelma, can you sit with Willia for just a minute?" Eddie's eyes never ceased to sparkle when he looked at his lovely bride.

"Sure, Eddie. Come to Auntie Thelma, Miss Willia."

When they were in the hall, Eddie showed his alarm for the first time.

"Rainey, I think you might have a problem. Call William and tell him he needs to call the fire department."

"Oh, Lord! What is it?"

"It looks like somebody tried to set a fire under your house."

First Rainey was genuinely frightened, and then, she grew furious. It was so obvious to her that if anybody had tried to set a fire, it had been that damned Jesse Waldron. Her fury went beyond the intrusion upon her property. It even went beyond the indignity of someone trying to disrupt her family's life. It was the sheer audacity that could spring forth from the heart and mind of any white person at any time, an arrogance and an assuredness that could inspire any one of them to act against any Negro, swathed in the confidence that they would probably not be prosecuted for their actions. And of all the absurdity, to strut about believing they were blessed of God to have dominion over colored folks just because their ancestors had stolen Negro ancestors to do their work for them and to build their nation for them!

As she steamed, Rainey had to admire her husband even more that he had the courage and the patience to deal with whites every day. And to think he can still come home to us and treat us like we're his prizes! What a man.

She squashed a memory of a slack-shouldered Step Herndon from her mind as he ducked his head away from a white couple on one of their rare strolls past the White House.

Within twenty minutes, which was probably a fairly quick turnaround time for a Raleigh Fire Department truck to be dispatched to a Negro's address, two firemen were searching the crawl space beneath Rainey's house. It only took them about five minutes to find the source of the warmth in the walls of the Davis's main hallway: deep underneath the house, a pile of rags had lain smoldering and was now beginning to blaze. The newborn flames were leaping upward to the floor of their hallway.

Rainey could barely contain her rage. That Waldron turd had come into her yard, and had gotten away with it! Let her or one of her people try to pull a trick like that in some young white woman's yard! The poor culprit probably wouldn't have lived to get out of that yard!

Later that day, after the dinner dishes had been cleaned and the children were bathed and settled into their rooms for an early rest, Rainey slipped some Earl Grey bags and wrapped lemon wedges into a paper bag and came into the library where William sat mulling over a case, his head swathed in smoke from his Camels.

"Honey, I believe I'll go around to Polly's and see how she's making out."

"Okay, sweetie. You want some company?"

"No, I'll be back in a little while."

"Hey, there, Polly. I was hoping I'd find you at home." Rainey held up her paper bag of treasures. "Earl Grey!"

Polly was, as always, delighted to see Rainey. They talked in Polly's tiny, sadly inadequate kitchen while Polly pumped water into a battered kettle for tea.

"Say, Polly, didn't you tell me Miss Hanrahan was looking for somebody to clean up behind her no-count son?"

"Yes, and I just don't understand it at all."

"Well, I think I know somebody who'll do it. I met a girl who was kind of down on her luck the other day. I bet she wouldn't mind cleaning that house just this once. I reckon she could use a few pennies where she could get them."

"Oh, okay. What's her name?"

"Jennie. Jennie Hankins."

"Oh, I don't believe I know that name."

"No, she's new in town. What's Miss Hanrahan's number? I'll have Jennie give her a call."

On the very next Saturday morning, "Jennie Hankins" stood at the door of Lillith Hanrahan's Tucker Street cottage at 6:45 AM. She was adorned in a painfully cheap wig, a faded apron, men's shoes, dark-rimmed glasses that obscured her face, and a dress that was much too big for her.

After a long time, Jesse Waldron yelled for her to come on in, and Jennie found the house in the kind of disarray that took normal sloppy folks about three months to concoct. Jesse Waldron had done it in just over a month.

"How-do, I'm here to clean up."

"Gal, fill my glass first."

"Why, sho', Mr. Waldron." Jennie had just gotten the cue she had been waiting for, and she prepared Jesse's drink with a little extra lemony zest.

"I'm-a clean the toilet first, Mr. Waldron sir." Cause I'll be damned if I go in there after a while, Jennie laughed to herself. The bathroom was an easy job; apparently, Waldron didn't bathe so often. The toilet was rather filthy, but, Jennie knew it wouldn't be long before she would come nowhere near it. She could hardly stop herself from laughing.

"This drank is good, gal. Fix me another one."

"Sho' thing, Mr. Waldron." This drink had an even zestier lemon flavor.

Jennie worked swiftly and efficiently to clean the two-bedroom cottage. She stood back to admire the cool sheen across all the surfaces, and the subtle scent of Spic-N-Span.

"I'm finished up, Mr. Waldron. You take care, hear?"

But Jesse Waldron was otherwise occupied in the sparkling bathroom. His face was nearly submerged in the wastebasket, where he deposited the contents of his stomach. His buttocks were engaged in the elimination of all the contents of his small and large intestines.

Later that day, Jesse Waldron was at a point of no return from dehydration, which would later leave him in a dangerously weakened state from which he would never fully recover.

Jennie Hankins was paid handsomely by Lillith Hanrahan, who knew that any person courageous enough to confront Jesse deserved to be paid very well.

Then, as Jennie Hankins walked down Person Street, she began to metamorphose. Her gray hair now rested in a garbage can, and was replaced by a neat bun of dark, thick hair. Jennie slowly and discreetly discarded her uniform in various garbage cans, until she was no more. In her stead was the neatly coifed, tastefully dressed, and ever refined Rainey Clark Davis, on her way to Soror Ruby McKinney's home for a meeting of the local chapter of the Zeta Phi Beta Sorority, a meeting for which she would only be a few minutes late.

The money from her stint as Jennie Hankins, the woman who had, so long ago, thought she would be able to buy Rainey's son, would help her buy her children and her husband a nice little frock or a new shirt and a few groceries for the family. And of course there would be a bit of Earl Grey for Polly for all her trouble.

"Hmmph! Mess with _my_ family and see what you get!"

The following Monday afternoon Lawyer Tyler's clerk came to Jesse Waldron's cottage to persuade him to sign an agreement drawn up by William Davis and sanctioned by Tyler. According to this agreement, Jesse Waldron would never again molest, confiscate, or alter any of Lillith Hanrahan's possessions, properties, or holdings. Further, he was never again to harass his mother, any of her employees or their associates, and he was to call his mother to ask her permission for a visit. If he violated the agreement, he would never again be welcome in or on any of Lillith Hanrahan's properties, and he could risk incarceration.

A foul smelling, unshaven, and noticeably emaciated Jesse Waldron met Lawyer Tyler's clerk at the door of the Tucker Street home. It took the clerk every inkling of his good breeding not to recoil from this monstrous sight. But he was not destined to stay with Mr. Waldron for long. The man was positively contrite, and agreed not only to sign the form, but to abide by every part of it. Further, he asked the clerk to please apologize to his mother and "that colored attorney" for any inconveniences he might have caused them. And then he excused himself, running with as much swiftness as his skinny body would allow him, to the bathroom. The last sound the clerk heard was what he thought was a bucket of water being emptied into the toilet.

Lawyer Davis was hailed as a hero throughout South Park, and his status as a champion of the Negro underdog was forever unchallenged throughout the various black neighborhoods. Rainey continued to cherish the scent of Spic-N-Span as a powerful cleaning agent, and she would ever adore the tart and lemony zest of magnesium citrate, along with a generous dollop of castor oil added in to give the concoction some real character. When applied in just the right dosages this concoction had the maximum effect.

Dovie and Buddy built a cute little house on the East Street lot, and promptly filled it up with children to join their firstborn, Billy, Junior.

Necrology

Mittie Clark Gaines, Rainey's beloved aunt, lived at the Q Street residence until shortly into the Great Depression. About 1932, Mittie saw her cherished neighborhood changing hands. Whites who had retained their wealth were quietly purchasing the homes of her neighbors who could no longer afford to maintain their brownstones, which were beginning to show signs of neglect. Mittie, ever the astute businesswoman, had quietly purchased a home in LeDroit Park, a fashionable Negro neighborhood near Howard University. She asked Addie to act as her proxy, and signed with a management company to rent her Georgetown treasure home to well-screened white tenants. During those first years, the tenants were a pot-bellied congressman from Michigan, his rotund wife, and their three egg-shaped children.

Mittie closed out her beauty shop, and moved it to the basement of the LeDroit Park home. There was no further need for a speakeasy. The Prohibition was repealed early in 1933. The Depression, that very trying time in American history, hardly made a true difference to Mittie or to Addie. David had taught Mittie what he had much earlier taught Addie: how to stash her money in foreign banks in order to protect it. "Those folks don't care what color you are, as long as your American money is green," David reminded her.

So Addie, Mittie, and Mason spent their increasing free time feeding the seemingly endless procession of hungry black folks, whose lines snaked around corners of buildings into the infinity of desperation. All three served, and more often than not, Mittie and Addie found themselves stirring vats of soup or chowder, singing to each other. Addie seemed enlivened in those last years, and Mittie and Mason were content.

Although she was devastated when Addie died in 1939, Mittie continued to thrive in a comparatively modest existence for the rest of her life. She kept in constant touch with her precious niece through letters, telephone calls, and visits. But, except for Alouette Willis's wedding in 1930, Rainey had never returned to Washington after her widowhood began. William and the children had driven to Aunt Mittie's any number of times over the years to retrieve their beloved kinswoman for extended visits, but all the adults understood that Rainey would not be ready for such a trip, no matter how brief, for quite some time.

Mittie often reminded Rainey that there was one letter waiting for her that could not be opened until her death. Rainey did not look forward to the day she could open that letter, which was locked away in a safe deposit box in Mittie's lawyer's office.

In 1945, 80-year-old Mittie was still thriving as a beautician. She was a "widow" by then. Mason had slipped away in his sleep in 1940. But Mittie continued to be a positive force in her new neighborhood until that cool spring morning when her heart ceased to function. She greeted one of her regular customers that morning, grabbed at her blouse, gasped, and collapsed over the chair that she had just directed the customer to sit in.

It was Alouette Willis Simmons's sad duty to call Rainey with the news that Aunt Mittie was dead. Now a wife and mother herself, Alouette had kept in touch with Rainey over the years. Her parents thrived still, having followed Mittie's lead and moved out of Georgetown while they could do so with little trouble. They had sold their Georgetown home and, like Mittie, had settled in LeDroit Park.

Rainey fought a battle against her qualms about returning to Washington, and she won -- with more than a few battle scars. She traveled alone to Washington to carry out the funeral arrangements that Mittie had already planned and paid for.   William and the children would follow a few days later.

How strange it was, after all those years, to step off the train into the teeming atmosphere of Union Station! Rainey half expected to see a well-dressed young man twirl before her, ending his dance step in a stylized bow. She made her way through the 20-year-old ghosts, along with their slightly moldy taints, to the front of the station, where Alouette and her husband Stuart waited for her.

Rainey could hardly breathe enroute to LeDroit Park. Having made a Herculean effort just to get on the train and return to this city, Rainey was grateful that she did not have to return to Georgetown. Such a prodigal excursion might prove too much for her after all that had happened to her. So much had changed in the city in the past 20 years; yet, its spirit was the same.   Only this time there was no monstrous, fear-mongering specter lurking just outside shadows, its fist clenched in anger, or hands outstretched in mortal pain.

Over the next days in Washington, Rainey met with Mittie's attorney, another black man who could have passed for white, Thomas Crenshaw. To her great surprise, Mittie had never sold the Georgetown property or Addie's mansion.   The attorney gave Rainey the address and telephone number of the management company that was unwitting caretaker for property owned by a colored woman.   Both houses, long paid in full, brought in respectable amounts of rental money each month.   The current tenant of the Arlington property had made a sizable offer to purchase. Rainey instructed the attorney to make the necessary arrangements to sell that house, but instructed him further never to entertain any offers on the Georgetown house.   After they had made the arrangements for Rainey to receive the proceeds of the house sale and the monthly rent, Crenshaw handed her a yellowed envelope.

Addressed to Rainey in Mittie's strong hand, Rainey knew immediately that this was Mittie's dreaded letter.

"It is addressed to you alone," Crenshaw told her.

Back at Mittie's charming LeDroit Park house, Rainey wept as she read the undated letter from her aunt, now gone from her forever.

Dear Rainey:

Well, since you're reading this, I reckon I'm dead.

You were the daughter I never had, and I am so proud to have known you and counted you among my kinfolks. You will never know the joy you've given me, and to Mason before he died. I'm mighty proud of the woman you turned out to be, and I will take any small credit I can for all the good you've done.

Folks really suffered during the Depression, Rainey. I never did, but I did what I could to help other people who were having a hard time. Cal Bertrand lost most of what he'd worked so hard for, if you remember, and it just about killed him. I'm pretty sure that losing all his precious possessions sent him to an early grave, but I'm just as sure that having Jeanne stick with him through those hard times kept him here as long as he was. But I mentioned Cal to tell you something else, and I'll get to it directly. Any how, while all the other folks, colored or otherwise, were out spending their money and carrying on back in the days they're now calling the Roaring Twenties, your uncle Mason and I saved our pennies. David showed us years ago how to put money aside in numbered accounts in a faraway place called Switzerland. Now that it's safe to do business with these American banks, I'm giving you all the necessary information to get my money, which is yours now, and put it in banks here in America. This money that I'm telling you about includes Aunt Addie's money that she left to me.

Rainey, I don't believe that you and your family will ever have to want for anything again! You've got a sweet husband who loves you so much. And your children have made my last years like paradise. Please use this money to do what you can to take care of them, and yourself, too, because I still feel mighty bad about all you went through with that Step Herndon.

I've never talked about this with a soul other than the ones who turned out to be my accomplices. Rainey, I pray you never find out just how bad that "husband" of yours really was. I still hate you found out about what was going on between Cal and Step, especially the way you found out. But when he tried to sell that precious Clark, I had had all I could take from him. I went to his rooms and was bound and determined to choke him to death with a rope. Then I realized that he was just a piece of horse doo on the bottom of my shoe. I enjoyed watching his eyes bug out, but then I came to my senses and made tracks out of that place.

Way after while, way after you went home to Raleigh, I was talking to Cal one evening at his place. He beat around the bush and finally told me how he had helped Step hurry on to his last stop. That's all he ever said, but I knew exactly what he meant. And then, when Joe Reeves and his family got ready to move overseas, he pulled me aside and told me that he had once sharpened his knives on some "Step meat." He said he felt real bad about that, and he intended to spend his life repenting, but that Step had asked for it over and over again.

Please forgive us, darling. We loved you so much we didn't want anybody hurting our baby Rainey. And you will always be our baby, Missy, no matter how grown you think you are.

Now. Do what you want to do with the LeDroit Park house and with Addie's house out in Virginia. But don't ever sell the house in Georgetown! The way those white folks were buying up our houses, I got a feeling the Georgetown house is like a gold mine. You keep renting that one out like I've got it set up right now. One of these days, maybe one of your grandchildren will want to live there. Keep it fixed up for the children to come.

I love you, Rainey, and I'm proud that you got to be like a child to me. I'll see you in the Rapture!

With love,
Aunt Mittie

Rainey was reeling from the shock of her aunt's confession. Rainey had always thought she alone had murdered Step, and had quivered with guilt for years over it. And now to find out that there were three other people involved, and all because of her, was a breath-taking shock. She knew she could never tell William the story of her life with Step. He respected her silence about her marriage, and she was grateful to him for that.

Rainey sighed as she re-read the letter. She later decided to rent the LeDroit Park house to a well-screened family through a reputable Negro management company. Rainey was stunned by the massive amount of money Aunt Mittie had left to her. In fact, she would perhaps never cease to be amazed. It was true that she and her family would never have to want for anything ever again.

Nettie Houser met with a bad end, as anyone who knew her would have expected. Still drinking and carousing like a teenager well into her fifties, Nettie was at a house party one night in 1935 when she was caught dancing with the wrong man. Mrs. Wrong Man cracked a beer bottle over Nettie's head, and Nettie, badly dazed by the blow, stumbled home to her bed. Her live-in lover of the moment discovered that she was dead the next morning after her scraggly younger children, hungry for their usual meager breakfast, could not awaken her. Rainey did not hear of Nettie's death until several days after she was quietly buried in a pauper's grave. Her passing was far less flamboyant than any aspect of her living days, and she was committed to the earth without even a ceremony (or her firstborn) to acknowledge her home going.

Eddie Houser married Thelma Lane, a fellow school teacher, in 1928 when he was 45 and she was 26. They built a modest home in a lovely section of colored Raleigh known as Gatling Heights. They reared their son, Edward, and their daughter, Leona, in that house. On summer Sundays, they would join forces with the Davis family for picnics at the all-colored Reedy Creek Park, or in one of their back yards. But the most meaningful trips for both families were those rare excursions they made down to Lumberton, near the site where Eddie and Nettie had grown into maturity. The house in which they had lived, and in which their mother had died of what they now knew was breast cancer, was long gone. The site was a lovely clearing now, and the creek running behind it was safe enough for wading and rock skipping. It was on this spot that the Davis and Houser children (and their parents) learned about life for Croatan Indians at the turn of the century: about the hardships they faced, and the prejudices they had to overcome. The children, including Rainey, came to understand and respect the particular traditions of the Croatan tribe of their heritage.

Eddie instructed them all that Negroes weren't the only people of color to suffer, literally, the slings and arrows of white hatred. For Eddie, the only kindness he had ever been shown outside of his own people had come from Negroes, which was why he went to the largest Negro church in Raleigh looking for work. In Lumberton, indeed all over Robeson County, the Croatans, who would be renamed the Lumbee tribe in the 1954, were respected, and, conversely, feared and hated. It was an atmosphere from which Eddie gladly removed himself, though he missed the solemn ways of his own people. As the years passed, Eddie took the families further into his old community to meet the remaining relatives and friends of his youth.

And so Eddie Houser was the consummate educator, always teaching his students, his children, and his nieces and nephews with great love, respect, and dignity. He was an elementary school teacher at various Negro schools in Raleigh from 1918 until he retired in 1950. But he never stopped working, taking care of the church, his home, and the homes of anyone else who would let him work. When he died in 1969, he was 87 years old, a great-grandfather, and a beloved gift to all his family and friends.

Joe Reeves continued to give the appearance of a man thriving in his various occupations. He continued to be a loyal Garveyite, even though his leader had been deported from the United States to London in 1927. As Marcus Garvey had promised, his "little cubs" still ran free, despite the tiger's travails. Joe was a loyal and tireless supporter of the idea of African unity and an advocate for the ultimate return of African people to the motherland. So it was no real surprise to him that he would be troubled by recurring bouts of guilt about his role in Step Herndon's death.

Joe watched his beloved children grow into straight-backed adulthood: no child of his would suffer the horror of being subservient to any other human being. He had trained them both that way, he reflected proudly, and he expected that they would train their own children to think the same way. Yet he was never surprised to look into his bathroom mirror and see staring mournfully back at him the specters of the people whose lives he had helped to end: Hezekiah Baldwin and his wife, and Step Herndon. Step Herndon would never see his own son, and even though Step had never made any efforts to see young Will (or his son who thrived in Delaware), Joe Reeves never felt free of the taint of murder upon his soul. His own self-labeling made him a deeply reflective man, a more solemn figure than he had ever planned to be. Though his butcher's business thrived, his soul ached. He expected at any moment to be forced into atonement for that ultimate sin.

Finally, in 1928, Joe Reeves, having saved his money carefully, persuaded his beloved wife to accompany him on an extended tour of the elusive and yearned-for Motherland. Irene Reeves eagerly agreed that Joe should sell his business to her brother, who was well trained as a butcher. Six months later, the Reeves family set sail for Liberia. Once there, they felt so welcome that they invited Irene's siblings to come over with their families. The onset of the Great Depression was motivation enough for the Thornhills and their spouses to give the Liberian life a chance. Despite the challenges of adjusting to a new culture, and of confronting and disabusing themselves of their own prejudices, the Reeves family settled into life in Monrovia, their new home. The grandchildren really thrived there, learning many dialects of English, and several of the many languages spoken there.

Joe Reeves continued to be an enterprising man, and along with his son and Irene's brother Nathaniel Thornhill, began their own business, a combination import-export company that specialized in marketing fresh fruits and vegetables through several black-owned produce companies in the northern states. He came to some sort of peace within himself about his role in the Maxers' deaths through his unobtrusive, philanthropic approach to his new countrymen. Though the business was never a raging success, the men were able to support their families comfortably.

When Joe Reeves died in 1974, he was a well-loved griot in his neighborhood. His stories about his life in the United States had grown to legendary proportions among his many admirers.

Rainey moved through her days surrounded by a loving gathering of ghosts.

Part Three: Progeny

1934 -- 1949

My Son, My Executioner

My son, my executioner,
I take you in my arms,
Quiet and small and just astir,
And whom my body warms.
Sweet death, small son, our instrument
Of immortality,
Your cries and hungers document
Our bodily decay.
We twenty-five and twenty-two,
Who seemed to live forever,
Observe enduring life in you
And start to die together.
-- Donald Hall ▲

▲ Hall, Donald. *White Apples And The Taste Of Stone: Selected Poems 1946-2006.* New York: Houghton Mifflin, 2006, Page 10.

1960

Her great joy, her true passion, and her fiercest loyalties were directed toward Clark, Willia, and Olivia. She often marveled, even now in this hour of hell, at how it was that she would be blessed with three such incredible people to call her own.

And though for the rest of her life her memories and thoughts would be drenched in sadness and regret, she did in fact have her memories.

She wept again silently. And gulls cried, and waves crashed, and the world continued to move on relentlessly, in spite of her, and for the moment, without her.

Her darlings, her precious ones.

The Lord giveth, and the Lord taketh away.

CHAPTER ELEVEN

A Most Serious Manchild

Surely a more serious manchild had never walked the earth before November 2, 1924. On that frightfully eventful day, Rainey Elizabeth Clark (Herndon) went into labor after being kicked in the belly by Step Herndon, her common-law husband. Three hours after her labor began, she brought forth a five-pound, six-ounce baby boy who uttered one startled cry and then stared into his mother's relieved face. She named him William Rufus Clark Herndon. The William was for the common-law husband who had hurt her, though surely this William would never hurt her or bring her any grief. She had to hope that naming this child William would in fact be a healing act for herself.

Step Herndon had hurt her badly, both physically and mentally. She would be damned if this manchild would grow up to hurt anyone as she had been hurt. She looked down on his serious countenance that first moment of his life and she felt hope that he would be an honorable man.

Rainey was unspeakably grateful to her second husband, William Macke Davis, when, nine months into their marriage and four months into her pregnancy with the child who would be Willia, he asked to adopt little Will. All papers were signed, and at the age of three, William Rufus Clark Herndon became, forevermore, William Clark Davis.

William Clark Davis became a manchild who felt everything deeply. He was not a humorless child, but the child in his family most likely to give deep thought to every issue. Consequently, people who didn't know him thought he might be a bit slow. On the contrary, the child was brilliant, effortlessly so. He was a constant source of pride for his deeply beloved mother and William Davis, the only father he had ever known.

When William Clark Davis was about nine, he decided to make a distinct identity from his adored father, William Davis. He announced, solemnly, one evening at dinner that he would greatly appreciate it if everyone would please call him "Clark" from now on. He went on to explain that it had nothing whatsoever to do with Papa; he just wanted to be known as Clark so that he could have his own special name.

He looked so very serious at that moment that Rainey's heart swelled with motherly pride and her amber eyes overflowed. She looked down quickly, wiping discreetly at her eyes with her napkin.

"Why, certainly, son," William agreed. "If that's what you want us to call you, we will."

And so it was settled. From that day, Clark signed his name as W. Clark Davis.

Rainey watched her sweet, serious manchild grow into lanky manhood. He never gave her a moment's anxiety, which was pretty miraculous considering his paternity.

Eventually, this serious young man went away to college at the Agricultural and Technical College at Greensboro, on a full scholarship, where he studied chemistry and earned high academic honors. Clark worked hard at his job at Nottingham's Grocery each summer back home in Raleigh, and saved up every penny he earned, despite his father's gentle teasing that he was "freeloading." Clark knew that William was pleased. He never cost his father a dime once he went away to school.

He joined Alpha Phi Alpha Fraternity while at A&T, and enjoyed his life as an over-achieving frat man. He hid behind that mantle for the rest of his time in college.

From A&T, he took a year off from the educational process to work with his father and to save even more money before going to Meharry Medical College at Nashville.

At Meharry, he studied medicine and majored, socially, in courting a fellow medical student named Anna Grace Carrington, who would be known as Grace only to Clark and his family. Clark wrote his mother weekly letters about nothing but Grace. He couldn't get over this woman's style and her elegance, particularly after he learned that she had been orphaned at age six when her parents were lynched, and the she had lived out her formative years at the Tennessee Home for Colored Orphans.

Because there were so many children at the orphanage, affection and teachings about refinement and social graces were scarce. The Anna Grace Carrington who would go on to become a physician would have about her a straightforwardness that was slightly unnerving to other Southerners. Rainey loved her instantly because she detected no subterfuge and no guile. Feminine wiles had always been annoying to Rainey, and she had often worried that her son might get tangled up with some secret shrew who pretended, during their courtship, that she was all sweetness and light. Anna Grace Carrington was as much a relief to Rainey as she was a joy to Clark.

Any good manners Anna Grace learned were standard stock teachings at the orphanage: end all requests with "please"; accept gifts, kindnesses, and compliments with "thank you"; chew with your mouth closed; hold your silverware with your fingers draped around the handle rather than wrapped around it, in fisted cavewoman style; sit with your legs crossed at all times; clear all food from your mouth before speaking; eat with a napkin in your lap rather than at your neck; and take care of all bodily functions, particularly "breaking wind," alone, thank you very much. With those basics, she fared well in the world, but there was no one to teach her the art of coquettishness or "feminine wiles."

An honors graduate of Tennessee State College, Anna Grace had devoted her study time to preparing for what would be a breeze of an admission to Meharry

Medical College. Socially, she had been actively involved in Delta Sigma Theta Sorority, though she had not had much luck with boyfriends. She did enhance her no-frills manners by reading the etiquette gospels according to Emily Post and Amy Vanderbilt.

During his first semester at Meharry, Clark noticed Anna Grace sitting alone at the front of their morning Procedures class, taking copious notes like the rest of their classmates. At the end of the class one morning, Clark, a tall, skinny Alpha, swathed in a seemingly cavernous black frat sweater with the fraternity's Greek letters in small gold letters over his heart, approached her as she prepared to walk out of the classroom.

"Hey," he said, and never cracked a smile. Anna Grace felt herself blush. He was, like so many of the men in the class, really cute!

"You on your way to grab some lunch?" He gazed into her eyes as if he had asked her a review question for a midterm exam. She nodded.

"Mind if I join you?"

Anna Grace shook her head to indicate that she didn't mind at all. The skinny Alpha stuck out his right hand toward Anna Grace's right hand. Mama would <u>kill</u> me if she saw me offering my hand to this young lady before she offered hers to me, he thought, amused.

Emily Post <u>and</u> Amy Vanderbilt say a lady should offer her hand to a gentleman <u>first</u>, she thought as she grasped his outstretched hand.

"I'm Clark Davis, Raleigh, North Carolina. A&T College, class of '47."

"I'm Anna Grace Carrington. . .Nashville. Tennessee State, class of '48. D.S.T., spring '46."

"Hmmm?"

"I'm a Delta," she said. "You are an Alpha, aren't you?" Anna Grace pointed at his sweater.

"Oh! Yes!" Clark pointed at his sweater, too. "A-Phi-A, fall of '44!"

Clark went on to discuss the challenges of the class they had just left, finally interrupting himself to ask her name again. After she'd told him for the third time, he looked very thoughtful before he said,

"Hmmm. You know why I can't keep your name in my head? You don't look like Anna. You look like Grace."

Anna Grace was truly surprised; she never thought she looked like a name. She knew she was short, with skin that was sometimes bumpy and always golden brown, with big round eyes behind rimless glasses. Her nose was sort of square in the middle and her nostrils flared when she was angry or amused or intensely involved in a discussion. She thought her full lips added character to her face in a way that a lot of Negro women tried to diminish. Her hair was thick and shoulder length, and she had to work extremely hard to keep from gaining weight. She thought she was pretty, but she accepted it as a state of being rather than a license to some mysterious privileges. But she had never thought of herself as looking like a name. Interesting.

"I do?"

"Yeah, you do. Mind if I call you Grace?"

"Well. . . no. . . ?"

"Yeah, you look graceful, like a dancer." He pressed his textbooks to his chest and executed a little foxtrot.

Anna Grace chuckled despite herself. She hadn't even mastered the waltz, let alone the jitterbug, so she was hardly a dancer.

"You're funny," she said, and meant it. It was good to laugh aloud with someone else. "What did you say your name was again?" Her mischief seemed to have slipped by him, unnoticed.

"Clark Davis. Don't forget it, now. You and I, we're going to be good friends. And don't think I didn't notice you trying to give me a taste of my own medicine with that name thing." They laughed.

Clark felt very pleased with himself. His Mama and Papa would be so shocked -- and Willia would tease him for days on end -- if they heard him being so lighthearted with a girl. He was the Serious One in the family. But he liked this Grace Carrington instantly. There was something really comfortable about her apparent serious nature and her seeming dedication to her medical school career.

He felt a twinge of disloyalty to Lorraine, his girlfriend, who was a junior at A&T. But, really, what was wrong with talking to Grace? He was just being friendly with a med school classmate. (And did he have a wife?)

But his friendship with Grace quickly progressed beyond the limits of his relationship with Lorraine, who masked her deep affection for Clark in sullenness and arguments. He never argued with Grace, and he only saw her sullen when she was frustrated about her school work. They became the best of friends, and before long, he fancied himself in love with her, in the vast span of two months.

He asked her to come home to Raleigh with him for Thanksgiving, but she declined, though she gave no information about her own plans. Somehow, Clark suspected that perhaps Grace didn't have anything to do over the holidays, since she didn't have any family. So he opted to work over the long weekend at his job at Maxine's Neighborhood Grocery and stayed in his tiny dormitory room. On the Wednesday before Thanksgiving, Clark used a great deal of his meager salary to purchase portable fixings for the dinner he planned to share with this young lady, whom he hoped would someday be his lady love. He felt great pride and hope when he looked at what he'd purchased, and the way he'd boxed it up so that it looked official, somehow.

That night he sat down to write his favorite confidante, his mother, to tell her about his hopes for a relationship with Grace. Several days into the next week, Rainey wrote him back, excited for him, and hopeful that Grace was as nice as she seemed to be on paper. She closed her letter to him as she always did: "Clark, words will never express how proud I am to call you my son!" But she added another sentence that stayed with Clark over the years: "No matter who you marry, make sure she is as proud to be your wife as I am to be your mother."

On Thursday afternoon at about 2:30, he sought Grace out at her own dormitory, and sure enough, there she was, seated on an ancient couch in the pitiful lobby, studying diligently. Later, he would write Rainey and tell her that Grace seemed to have a soft light above her, cascading down from the heavens. (It would be several years before he remembered that the light bulb in the floor lamp next to her seat burst during their visit. What he had seen was the light from the bulb at its brightest because its usefulness was at an end.)

His heart jumped for joy, though he felt oddly sad for her. Where were her people? Surely somebody in Texas or Tennessee knew who her surviving people were. Had they even sent her a food box from the orphanage? As he signed in at the lobby to visit (surprise) her, he wondered if she would be relieved to know she wasn't really alone in Nashville.

He walked on his tiptoes to the corner of the lobby where Grace sat, her mule-encased feet surrounded by open books, notebooks, and red pencils for highlighting. She had a book open like a shield against her Delta-sweltered chest, and another book was open in her lap. She was wearing black pedal pushers and she had her hair pulled back into a bun, which pleased Clark. His mother had passed on the tradition of the "busy bun" to his sisters; when they were working hard at something, they grabbed the nearest rubber band and pulled their hair back, pinning it into a perfect circle with bobby pins. Grace's hair was so designed now, her pens and pencils (did he see a compass there, too?) pushed carefully into her bun for easy access. The effect made her look regal and imperious, yet sweet and terribly smart.

Clark stood in front of her for a few minutes before he gently cleared his throat. She looked up slowly several seconds later when the sound registered.

Somebody is trying to break my stride, she thought at that moment, slightly annoyed. When she saw him, Grace's face relaxed into a dazzling smile.

"Hey, Grace. I thought I might find you here."

"Hey, Clark!" She began to move books to give him room to sit on the tattered couch. She pointed at the tightly packed box he had placed on the floor in front of them and grinned as she turned toward him.

"Did you stay in Nashville to see me?"

Clark was surprised by the directness of the question, much as he was often surprised by her honesty. Most of his girlfriends pretended to be unaware of his motives, but Grace (who was not his girlfriend, actually) seemed not to have been taught any such subterfuge.

"Well, yeah," he said as he sat down. "Yes, I did. I didn't think you'd notice."

"Well, nobody has ever been that nice to me, Clark Davis. Thank you. You did turn out to be a good friend."

On that Thanksgiving afternoon, they sat in the dank kitchen of her lonely dormitory, eating smoked turkey and canned string beans and cold sweet potato pie and Wonder bread. He found a poor, pitiful hot plate in the recesses of a rusty cabinet, and a battered coffee pot, and they drank brackish coffee with their meal. They talked and laughed and watched the wind swoop relentlessly through the trees outside the tiny window next to the rickety kitchen chairs and the lopsided table.

Later, they shared her books for study, taking a break only to dance to a tune that they hummed softly to each other.

"You didn't lie when you told me you can't dance," Clark teased, and they laughed together as if they had just heard the most splendid joke.

"Hey --"

"Hey, why you always sayin' 'hey' to me, Clark Davis?" Grace looked up at Clark and smiled slyly.

"Gets your attention, doesn't it?"

Grace giggled. "Yeah."

"Hey, come home to Raleigh with me for Christmas!"

"And stay in your house? Your Mama's house? Your Mama and Daddy's house? With your sisters? Your two sisters?" With each question, and each progressive emphasis that bespoke feigned shock, Clark and Grace became more and more giddy. Clark, not much of a laugher except in cases of extreme hilarity, was laughing in a high-pitched, silly giggle.

"And Mama's canary!"

"...And your Mama's canary?

"That's right, sister. Yeah. Yeah." He assumed his Edward G. Robinson persona, one he had shared only with his beloved little sisters.

Grace dropped her laughing, her face falling into a blank expression.

"Okay," she said simply, and they laughed again. Clark took a chance that the dorm mother wasn't being so diligent and sealed their agreement with a quick peck on Grace's lips.

"All right, there, young man. Watch yourself."

Clark whirled around to see crotchety old Miss Moore standing in the parlor doorway, hands on her massive house-dressed hips, one wide fat foot slamming impatiently at the floor through a fuzzy mule, chain-secured glasses quivering on her big face.

"You pull a trick like that again and you won't be allowed to set foot in this dormitory any more."

"But --

"Ah-ah-ah! Don't you open your mouth, especially on that gal's lips. Just sit down and be calm. You've only got ten more minutes to be in here anyhow."

"Yes, ma'am."

The dorm matron disappeared into the shadowy recesses of her little office, where, Clark and Grace guessed, she was watching them without being seen. They were on their best behavior, but they made their plans to make the long trip to Raleigh in December after their final examinations.

Clark wrote to Lorraine on the Tuesday after Thanksgiving to tell her that he didn't think their relationship was going to work out. There was the distance, of course, and then there was Grace. According to Lorraine's reply, she had been meaning to write him anyway; it turned out that a certain Kappa and she had taken a liking to each other. She was glad that his new flame was one of her Delta sisters, at least.

Perhaps it was her gentle humor, maybe her innate sense of family, or even her genuine interest in the stories of each member of the Davis and Seaton families. Whatever it was, over that Christmas and New Year's of 1948-49, the entire family fell in love with the idea of Grace Carrington being in Clark's life. By the time she left with Clark to take the long bus ride back to Tennessee, both Rainey and William were calling her "Daughter." Martha Alice insisted that she call her "Aunt Martha Alice."

"And you can call my husband 'Uncle Red', ain't that right, honey?"

"Darn tooting'," Big Arthur chimed in. Later, much to Grace's amusement, she found that "Uncle Red" was "darn tooting'" about a lot of things. Once, when she and Clark were newlyweds, Grace replied, "Well, hoity-toity!" to his rote exclamation. Everyone in the room grew quiet for a startled second. Then they all roared with laughter. Nobody had ever before thought twice about making any acknowledgment of this silly statement.

Grace Carrington was an instant hit with the only real family she would ever know. Perhaps it was Clark's family that pushed her headlong into love with this man, who was, without rival, her best friend. And so were his sisters, his mother, his father, his aunt, his uncle, and Darwin, his mother's canary.

Finally at this graduation, from medical school, she had a respectable contingent of family to applaud delicately for her when her name was called; announcing to the world that she was Dr. Anna Grace Carrington, and her best friend and great love was now Dr. William Clark Davis.

Clark and Grace were married in Raleigh at First Baptist Church in July of 1952. Rainey and William, sympathetic to her sad family background (or lack thereof) and pleased with her for being so genuine with them, not to mention damned glad their son had chosen such a nice girl to be friends with and marry, footed the bill for the wedding.

Two of Grace's favorite sorors and Willia and Olivia served as her bridesmaids. And will wonders never cease, her matron of honor was her mother-in-law to be Rainey Clark [Herndon] Davis. Uncle Red gave her away, and Aunt Martha Alice did Grace's hair <u>and</u> the catering for the reception in the Davis's cozy back yard. William was Clark's best man.

Dodging the salvos launched in a hail of rice, the young Drs. Davis headed off for their honeymoon weekend at the all-colored Atlantic Beach in South Carolina. They next headed for a new life together in romantic and inspiring Goldsboro, North Carolina. They had to do their respective residencies at the Cherry Hospital in Goldsboro, North Carolina, where, as they joked wickedly only to themselves, the "crazy coloreds" were sent. Raleigh's Dorothea Dix would only see black folk in its corridors as janitors until the '60s. Ironically, five years after they began their residencies, Dr. Charles Drew, one of the Davis's personal heroes, died on a rural North Carolina highway because he could not get to the Cherry Hospital or to Saint Agnes in Raleigh.

The Davises and the Seatons joked relentlessly that they never thought they'd ever know anybody who had to go to "Goldsboro," which was the code word for the "crazy house" there. On one of Clark and Grace's rare visits to Raleigh, Rainey, Willia, and Olivia pretended to cry in shame, and Martha Alice baked a delicious sheet cake decorated with a face that looked panicky, its tongue hanging out at a hilarious angle.

At the Cherry Hospital, Clark and Grace rarely saw each other. Because Cherry was a hospital especially for black people, the patient roster didn't only consist of mental patients. All manner of medical treatment was available there. Clark did his residency in family practice, while Grace fine-tuned her skills in pediatrics.

It was on one rare occasion when they found themselves at home together and reasonably alert that they conceived the child who would be Karen Grace Davis. Little Kakie was born at Cherry Hospital on June 23, 1954, a fabulous birthday gift for Grace, whose own birthday was June 26. Kakie joined four-year-old Olivia "Honey" Seaton as a joy in all the Davis's lives. In fact, there never would be a child born to that family (which always included Martha Alice and Arthur) who wasn't a delight to them.

When Kakie was two years old, and Grace was pregnant again with the child who would be Eric Clark Davis, Clark got a general practitioner position at the tiny Fort Monmouth, New Jersey family health center. The Davises found that they enjoyed the comparatively subdued racial climate of New Jersey and, in 1962, when Clark decided to go into joint private practice with another general practitioner; they bought a cute little three-bedroom home on Pear Street in New Shrewsbury. Grace worked part-time as the staff pediatrician in her husband's practice three afternoons a week, and soon they were able to buy a lovely home in nearby Red Bank.

Grace sat back one afternoon about mid-way through 1963 and realized she and Clark had this idyllic thing going.

Who'd have thought a "colored orphan" would make good?

Clark, still the Serious One in the family, even his own immediate family, was not the least bit surprised. Soon after he met Grace, he realized that she was a woman who would work hard to make a relationship work, which was exactly what he had seen his parents do in their marriage. Since he had planned to stay married to his first wife for the rest of his life, he had to make sure he married well that first time. He was always pleased with his choice, and mighty happy that he loved and liked her, too. So, for Clark, the idyll was a long-term event that was dressed for success

CHAPTER TWELVE

The Adventurer

Shining light and enticing mischief; pealing bells and dull thuds; lovely shimmering dresses and dungarees worn through at the knees; gleaming patent leathers and scuffed Buster Browns; Papa's little girl and the hero of all the neighborhood kids: she was Willia Evelyn Davis.

Rainey's first child with William was all girl and much trouble, a sheer delight and a challenge always. She was a constant joy and a major surprise; she was the light of her parents' lives.

For Rainey, this womanchild was a pistol ready to fire regardless of aim, and she saw her own wildness resurrected in this child. Rainey worked diligently to re-direct her daughter's energies to positive avenues.

William saw Rainey truly re-visited behind his face, softened by the essence of Rainey's features. He delighted in his Willia, because she was so much like Rainey. And though he would never admit it, Willia was his favorite child for that very reason.

Early on, a toddling Willia waddled her diaper-wearing hips into her parents' bedroom many a night to imitate, with puerile flawlessness, one of the neighborhood characters. By the time she was five years old, her parents and her brother could often be found, collapsed in tears, laughing at one of Willia's antics. Soon enough, Willia's very serious - minded baby sister Olivia would join the merriment.

For Willia Evelyn Davis, the world was a colorful pastiche of adventures. She was always the ringleader among her friends, the one to say, "Hey! I know what we

Reasonable Joy

can do now . . . ." And she was always the one to get the whole lot of them into seemingly hopeless amounts of trouble. Just when it seemed that all the neighborhood boys and girls in Willia's crowd (and that was all the boys and girls in the neighborhood, even the ones who, like her baby sister, were barely out of diapers) were about to get into trouble with their parents from which they might never recover, Willia Evelyn Davis would say something so indescribably sweet, so incredibly logical, and so genuinely complimentary to each child's parents that those poor, helpless grown-ups would promptly forget the children's offenses and feel the need to offer a huge hug not only to their birth children but to Willia Davis.

Willia quickly grew accustomed to hearing "That little ole Davis gal is the cutest, sweetest little thing! Bless her heart!" as she walked away from yet another victory in the tug of war that was childhood. Off she would venture again, blessed by the hosannas of the neighborhood parents, ready to plot the next adventure for her "tribe," as she called them.

And off they went, Willia's tribe, on a deep-sea adventure next to the Salter's Path Pond. Of course, they would understand as teenagers and adults that the pond was just a ditch, but in childhood, it was the mighty Atlantic. Or perhaps they would next go on a deep jungle expedition in that patch of woods that would someday become Chavis Park. The lions and the bears were ripe for the hunting any time Willia's tribe was on the prowl. Willia's personal favorite expedition was mountain climbing from the bottom of Bragg Street. It was a hilly dirt path back then, but it was a wide-open space, which meant that the little ones in her tribe felt safe because they could see the older children.

Willia Evelyn Davis was always on an adventure, but she was always a responsible leader for the babies in her tribe. Anytime a South Park child wanted to get out of the house to play, he or she had only to invoke the name of Willia Davis, and Mama and Daddy would always say "yes," or "well, sure, sugar, you can go play. And tell Willia to stop by to holler at me," which Willia always did, being careful to ask after Mrs. Harper's geraniums, or Mr. Lindsey's ditch-digging career.

At home, Willia was like a dream for Rainey -- in some ways. Where Clark was extremely indifferent to keeping his room clean, sending Rainey into annoyed tirades about the house catching on fire, Willia kept her room almost unnaturally neat. The truth was that Willia was compulsive about order. She had to have the white socks for her Buster Browns rolled together and placed neatly next to her white dress socks, and the pale blue and soft pink socks that went with her Sunday patent leather shoes in a neat collection. Meanwhile, her dainty little white slips had to be folded just so in her slip drawer, next to her precisely folded and stacked panties.

Inside, Willia Evelyn Davis was at constant war with a mysterious rage that threatened to overwhelm her at any moment. She was easily annoyed and vividly frustrated with inanimate objects. If a table dared to be in her way as she made her way through a room, she would fight the urge to kick viciously at its legs. She <u>had</u> kicked at the legs of one of Mama's wingbacks once, her voice muffled behind her clenched teeth as she told it to "move out of my way." On that day, Willia had heard a startled gasp, and she had looked up to see Rainey staring at her, shocked by the enraged five-year-old before her. And so Willia had taught herself to confine her outbursts to solitary moments. Since such moments were rare in the life of a little one, Willia decided to control her personal space so that she would not need to be annoyed, frustrated or enraged so often.

From a time shortly after her five-year-old rant, Willia kept everything about her in eerily perfect order. Rainey was thrilled at first, but soon she felt a bit unnerved. Even <u>she</u> wasn't as tidy as her own child. Meanwhile, Willia was quietly grateful that her unexplained rages were almost never directed at humans, only at things that stood in her way, wasted her time, or slowed her down.

As she grew, Willia Evelyn Davis felt germinating within her a wild streak that she would never know she inherited directly from her mother. Willia had to stifle her desire to simply scream at the top of her lungs and break into a wild and unbridled dance. She felt trapped somehow, as if she had been born too soon, or born in the wrong nation or state or body.

By the time Willia enrolled at the North Carolina College for Negroes in nearby Durham, she had taught herself just to accept the contradictions at war within her. She remained unnervingly neat, often cleaning both her own side of her dorm room and her roommate's twice to three times per week, so that she could keep all possible annoyances out of her personal space. Meanwhile, even as she did her work well, and consistently earned the highest grades in her classes, she was more likely than not to be the one of first people at the most anticipated drinking party, and among the last to leave.

Willia was known on campus as "that hell-raising Raleigh girl." She smoked heavily, and, when the occasion presented itself, she drank heavily, often carrying a glass of her favorite rotgut onto the dance floor at house parties.

Willia slept well. Her activities on the positive and negative ends of the burning candle that was her life kept her fully engaged in her waking hours. She would come to her room late at night after heavy studying or after heavy petting and heavier drinking, and her tiny body would simply collapse across her bed. She always just made it to her room before lights out. Her roommate, Rosetta Foster, a calm girl from Micro, North Carolina (a suburb of Kenly, which was a suburb of Wilson), would often awaken to find Willia, still clad in one of her cute little dresses with all that crinoline, snoring relentlessly and curled into the fetal position, in the middle of her bed.

To Rosetta Foster, Willia Davis epitomized the sophisticated city girl: she made really good grades, and she was so popular! And she still found time always to be nice to Rosetta. They had a standing breakfast appointment: anybody could join them for breakfast, but no matter how hung over Willia might be, she always spent her breakfast hour chatting pleasantly with Rosetta as they munched on overly fried sausage or bacon, and runny eggs, accompanied by scorched, brackish coffee and soggy toast.

Rosetta enjoyed spending time with Willia's family, too. She appreciated the quiet refinement that emanated from the Davis home, which to her, was some sort of mansion. She had never seen Negroes live so well and yet be so down to earth. The Davises, like her own family, laughed a lot, often conducted three or four conversations at once at the dinner table, welcomed family and friends into their home, got excited about issues of national import, and sometimes ran around in little circles -- of joy, or frustration, or boredom, or for whatever reason.

What separated the Davises from Rosetta's own family, in her mind, was their comparative wealth. Why, Willia and her sister and brother had their own private rooms, and those rooms were huge and airy! Yet, these folks didn't act all "high seditty" like the one or two "wealthy" Negro children in Micro or neighboring Kenly, or even in the comparatively big city of Wilson. Rosetta was fascinated by the fact that the Davises didn't seem to mind living next door to a Pullman porter and a ditch-digger. It seemed absolutely illogical to these people not to be friendly with their neighbors. Rosetta was amazed and awed by Willia and her family. In her eyes, they were so affluent, yet so "regular." In fact, when Rosetta had used that word to describe Willia's folks in Willia's presence, the "hell-raising Raleigh girl" had collapsed, laughing, onto her bed.

"Girl, how you sound? What you mean regular? 'Cause we ain't constipated or something?"

Willia and Rosetta had laughed until tears flowed from their eyes. When they settled down, Willia said, with hilarity still simmering behind her sincerity, "Girl, colored folks ain't got no reason to be acting all uppity around their own. When we leave Person Street, who are we to these white folks? Just some niggers, right?" Rosetta nodded solemnly, still too painfully aware of the extent to which she had been made to feel like "just some nigger" in the presence of her mother's "boss lady," who, though she was not much older than Rosetta, insisted upon calling Mrs. Foster "Mamie."

Rosetta had thought she would never want to introduce her mother to Willia's family, but when she met the Davises, Rosetta understood immediately that Mamie Foster, and her father, Job, and all the Foster children, would be welcomed warmly by Willia and her family. She resolved to settle in Raleigh, and wished that the Davises had another son so she could marry into the family. Rosetta, who would be Willia's roommate all through her college years, felt fortunate to have Willia for a roommate. They would always remain friends.

After college, when both Rosetta and Willia were living in Raleigh, Rosetta taught mathematics at Washington High School (and later at Ligon Junior-Senior High School), and Willia taught elementary school in Johnston County. Rosetta sought and found Albert Brown, a man with the familial qualities of William Davis and his son Clark. If she couldn't be a Davis, she reasoned, she would be like a Davis. The two women maintained their standing breakfast dates on each Saturday morning. Sometimes they met at Willia's aggressively tidy home on Cotton Place, or in Rosetta's often chaotic house, where they had to eke out a moment's serenity in the midst of the vibrancy of Rosetta's growing family. Their favorite breakfasts were at Rainey's or Martha Alice's, with Mrs. Davis as the chef, or better yet, with Mrs. Seaton setting out the victuals. Willia continued to raise hell, while Rosetta raised three boys -- and a husband, she joked.

Willia Evelyn Davis, anal retentive hellion, moved through her charmed life with the grace of a feather, the impact of a battering ram, and the memorability of the best and brightest day in the life of a child. She was an anthem to the youthful resilience of joie de vivre.

CHAPTER THIRTEEN

To Her Own Music

O h, Lord, Rainey often thought when she saw her baby girl. Here she comes. Bless her heart. What will she break, tear down, trip over or fall down on today?

Why, even the day of Olivia's birth -- February 27, 1931 -- seemed to be a day made just to be clumsy. William had slipped and slid across ice as he tried to move the car as close to the sidewalk of the Person Street house as he could. He had nearly fallen on a patch of black ice, his laboring wife in his arms and biting her lip to handle her pain. His near fall forced him to throw Rainey across the front seat of the car, apologizing profusely as he did so. The four and a half Davises had slipped and slid through icy shards of sleet that morning, while creeping along the roads of the blessedly short trip to Saint Agnes Hospital. Minutes later, as William helped Rainey into Saint Agnes's lobby, he did a hilarious version of a dance that would years later be recognized as "The James Brown." Rainey, despite her discomfort, laughed until tears came. William laughed with her once he got her and the children safely into the lobby.

Olivia nearly hit the floor when she was born three hours later. The doctor had stepped away from Rainey for perhaps two minutes. When he returned, Olivia's head was born so quickly that he had no time to sit; he could only squat and cup his hands like a baseball player, and hope he didn't miss. Luckily, mother and child were fine despite the comedy of errors.

That was the plight of Olivia Jane Davis. The poor girl was forever recovering from some fall, nursing some scar, or treating some bump. And she rarely cried; reacting to the injury beyond stoic acknowledgment took up too much of her time. With each new injury, Olivia went to her nearest elder and calmly announced her predicament, presenting the offended body part for perusal and repair. She always stood patiently while the necessary salve and bandage were applied, accepting the loving purrs, clucks, and kisses. She always thanked her current champion warmly, offering that savior a kiss back before promptly returning to her own world.

As Martha Alice said, "Olivia is the fallingest child I have ever seen in my life!"

Olivia didn't have much time to watch her step. In Olivia time, the world moved perhaps two seconds behind the "real" world. Olivia was a work-in-progress; her mind was forever creating, re-creating, inventing, and re-inventing. If she saw a blue balloon afloat in a bright spring sky, she had to consider what that balloon would look like as a red or purple balloon, or perhaps a flowered balloon, which would lead to a reverie about a gaggle of balloons afloat just above L. Frank Baum's poppy field just beyond the gates of the Emerald City. She had, of course, read all of Baum's works. Next, that original blue balloon would be magically transformed into a blue falcon, winging its way blithely to some distant, exotic land.

She most often liked to think of her falcon soaring along to Addis Ababa. She loved to hear Papa discuss Haile Selassie, a powerful, wonderful looking Negro man who was running his own country his own way despite a lot of problems from -- from -- what was it Papa had said? "Outside agitationers" or something? Or perhaps her blue falcon, which was by now a soft gray, was enroute to gaze upon the Great Sphinx at Giza, where she knew that some more of her ancestors had been at some point in endless time.

Now the falcon was a biplane, driven by a black woman pilot Mama liked to talk about named Bessie --

"Livy! Watch OUT!"

Plop!   There she was in that confounded ditch in front of Mrs. Mangum's house again.

"Oh, bore," she thought as she twisted herself out of the mine, her falcon now a flashlight attached to a metal cap that just barely stayed put atop her pigtails. "Down again."

As Olivia grew older, she came to understand that her dream world, though more fascinating and engaging than the world she had to inhabit with her physical self, was causing a bit of trouble down below, in the regimented and routine earth. She got tired of being yelled at (Olivia heard it as screaming) for keeping a careless room. She was tired of being accused of leaving tops off of mayonnaise or mustard jars, or of leaving the "last swallow" of milk in the bottle. She didn't want to hear all of that; she wanted to dwell peacefully in her magic world, where she was graceful, practically floating upon lush air as she went about the kingdom she ruled. It was a kingdom where beautiful things changed into precious and priceless things, and she traveled to places that the "real" world had never known. Olivia Jane couldn't take the stress of being chastised by folks in the outer world, so she trained herself to write about her magic world in her carefully kept journal, and to maintain the appearance of neatness that seemed to come so easily to Mama, Papa, Willia, and, with a little more difficulty, Clark.

When puberty kicked in for her, Olivia took a look at her sloppy outer self next to her beautiful sister's elegant, poised self, and made attempts to imitate Willia. Olivia, who had started to wear glasses when she was ten, now requested, with an insistence that was out of character for so dreamy-eyed and otherworldly a child, that her face be adorned with round rimless glasses. Such an attempt at stylishness was part of her rather lackadaisical efforts to "do it like Willia would," and reflect the flair for fashion that Willia seemed to wear with such ease. They placed the order with Dr. Debnam, who was one of several all-purpose doctors for Raleigh's Negro community.

At twelve, the sloppy, careless, dreamy Olivia Jane Davis thrived behind the façade of the serious, studious, elegant, and nearly sophisticated copy of her older sister.

Olivia had one great passion in her young life. He took up great globs of her thought processes, and he became a constant part of her thoughts beginning sometime shortly after her sixth birthday. Her great preoccupation was Arthur Seaton, Jr., and when she first locked her lovestruck eyes upon him, he was nearly 13. His reaction to Olivia at that time was to chuck her under her chin or punch at her arm and say, "Hey, Livy! You doin' all right? Good! Where's Clark? Okay, bye!" The awestruck first-grader would rub her chin absently for the rest of the day, formulating her grand and breathtaking wedding with Arthur. Meanwhile, Arthur and Clark were outside, running themselves ragged in silly circles of tag or basketball.

Over the years, Arthur's attentions toward her continued to be vague. For several agonizing months just before he joined the service, he had a hopeless crush on Willia. Both girls were miserable during those months: Willia would always think of Arthur as "Aunt Martha Alice's boy," and therefore, he qualified as a brother to her. She came to her pre-teen sister's room and threw her beautiful self across Olivia's squeaky bed.

"Livy! Why is that boy looking at me? I ain't thinking about him! He's too old, and he might as well be some kin to me! Oh, what am I asking you for? You don't even think about boys yet, do you, sweetie?"

No, Olivia didn't think about boys; she thought about Arthur Seaton, Jr.

Soon enough, Arthur Seaton went away to fight in World War II. Olivia, though she kept her feelings to herself, was inconsolable. He might never come back from the war, she worried, or, worse, he might come back with a wife. She sat in her room for many mournful hours, weeping silently over the one picture he had given her when he graduated from Washington High School.

"Class of 1942," she always murmured as she gazed at his picture, reciting a spell that conjured up pretty miracles in her head: Arthur Louis Seaton, Jr., born July 2, 1924, the eldest of the five sons of Martha Alice Chestnutt and Arthur Louis Seaton, Sr. Six feet one inch tall, 175 pounds, color of a caramel sweet, hair the color of darkened sand on the beach . . . .

And so they were married. It was the biggest social event in the history of Raleigh, and everybody who was anybody was packed into First Baptist. June the something-or-other, 19-whenever (she could never bring herself to predict a date) at three o'clock in the afternoon. There he stood, the man of her dreams, the husband she'd always deserved, looking breathtaking in his military dress uniform (she'd never actually seen a dress uniform at that point, but she put one together in her mind that had a high collar and gleaming white gloves, topped by a hat that was plumed and defined, much like the hat she'd seen dear Haile Selassie wearing. At his side, a dazzling sabre, and oh, he was beautiful!). She cascaded down the aisle, adorned in her mother's wedding gown -- they'd had so much fun getting it ready, after all those years, for Olivia's big day. And Arthur, Jr. was outdone by her beauty, and everyone in the church stood, gasping and clapping because she was the most beautiful and breathtaking bride the world had ever seen. . . .

She looked down at Arthur, Jr.'s picture and cried. He was going to die, or worse, he was going to marry some strillie he met overseas somewhere. Olivia smiled secretly; her Mama would have a conniption fit if she knew that Olivia used words like "strillie." That was one of those bad words, fit only for no-good cranks and fast-gals, like the ones that congregated down around Davie Street at Evans' Bottom or Duke's Corner. Well, there were no bad words (except "nigger") in her world. People just talked, that was all.

While Olivia Jane Davis pined away for Arthur Seaton, Jr., he was overseas learning some lessons that no school book author dared teach.   Arthur was a mistreated Negro soldier in a war that had not been declared upon him. He distinctly remembered reading that the Japanese emperor had declared war upon "the Anglo-Saxons." Arthur refused to call the enemy "Japs" because the term smacked of what he called a "niggerization." No matter what, Arthur discovered, white folks could always come up with some way to belittle other folks for being different from them. To Arthur and his best buddies Clark Davis and William "Buster" Perry, the term "Japs" could be interchanged much too easily with "nigger."

There was a chanteuse who had been displaced by the virulence of the war from the canteen she had built on the strength of her own sheer determination when she was in her early 20s.   At 35, Lili Vercruysse was a seasoned beauty. Her wheat-colored hair was now cropped short both as a tribute to Jeanne d'Arc and in protest of the ridiculous violation that the war had become. Even with so severe a style, Lili's face was lively and inviting. Her skin appeared slightly leathery, but was actually very moist and soft. Her eyebrows were thick, the color of dark honey, and close set in her heart shaped face. A hint of a moustache complimented her thin lips. The tiny crow's feet at her eyes and lips bore testimony to a life filled with laughter and a wealth of character-enhancing encounters. Lili Vercruysse was short of stature, and petite of build, but she entered a room and commanded most of its attention. She had lived expansively, loved deeply, hurt more deeply still, and mothered many more than the one son who had grown in her womb. Her life as a chanteuse was merely a convenient means by which Lili could live her life fully, and Lili Vercruysse was one who had lived her life fully and well, and who had brought her life's lessons along with her to all her new experiences. So her canteen had been destroyed by enemy fire; she now worked as a singer and hostess at a USO in ravaged Paris.

She took one look at Arthur Seaton as he sat huddled and isolated with his unit at that pathetic USO, relegated to a section behind the German prisoners of war, and decided he would be one of her new experiences. Lili decided she liked his coloring. It was like a cafe au lait, with subtle undertones of blush and pleasing, cinnamon sprinkles across the bridge of his broad nose. She saw in this 20-year-old Southern American Negro a new chance for adventure.

After her last performance of "La Vie En Rose," on the first night she saw Arthur, Lili approached him and began to talk offhandedly with him in her flawless British English.

"So you are just here from home, eh?" she asked him, looking up into his eyes from the deep pools of her own. She wore a fitted blue dress that evening that at its hem seemed to travel off into wispy directions.

Intrigued by her light brown eyes, Arthur had responded with suspicion at first. He saw a white woman, and white women meant death to American Negro men. But somehow, she had assured him of her sincerity and of her belief in the irrelevance of racial barriers.

"I read somewhere that race, like the feminine and the masculine, is a social construct. It has nothing to do with your biology, or your soul or how you look or how you conduct yourself when you are a man or a woman," Lili told him as she served him a tiny cup of the Turkish coffee she had managed to smuggle into her work place.

Fascinated, Arthur found himself letting his guard down with Lili Vercruysse. And soon, they became each other's adventure, though they kept their trysts under the thickest cloak of secrecy. He resisted, with great difficulty, falling in love with Lili Vercruysse, and she, fully aware of the fleeting nature of their affair, never let herself feel more than fondness for this manchild of the American South.

When the war ended, and his tour of duty with it, Arthur and Lili separated fondly, each knowing that they would never again talk or make love. Arthur returned to America laden with many lessons of love and lust. And though he never again thought of Lili in more than abstract terms, these lessons, coupled with his bitter experiences of racism in the World War II segregated military, fueled within him some passions that, if not directed to some goal or cause, could explode in impotent fury.

The jovial, carefree manchild who departed Raleigh in 1942 returned to his loved ones in 1945 a serious man who was on a mission to expose injustices done to his people in a quietly effective station in life. He would go to college, earn a degree in English, and write about those wrongs. It was on a wave of relieved rejuvenation that Arthur, Jr., veteran of the Second World War, enrolled as a freshman at Saint Augustine's College in the fall of 1945.

Meanwhile, the exuberant littlest Davis, overjoyed to have her light-o-love back in her line of vision, was 14, and a freshman at Washington High School. Once again, as Arthur embarked upon another treacherous journey fraught with eligible women, Olivia cried that he might marry some well-educated strillie and never know that he was loved right in his own neighborhood.

But Arthur, Jr. had very little on his mind besides getting his degree with the highest grades he could earn. He interned at The Carolinian, the local weekly newspaper that was black owned and black run. At first, his internship involved little besides acting as a gopher for Mr. Jervay, the sage publisher/owner. But Jervay saw potential in the young veteran, and soon gave him writing assignments that were immediately publishable. By Arthur's junior year, he was the paper's chief photographer. By the fall of 1947, when Arthur was not dodging the pranks planned by his big brothers in Omega Psi Phi Fraternity, he was out and about black Raleigh, photographing peers, acquaintances, family, and friends as Mr. Jervay commanded. Arthur, Jr. entered his senior year at St. Aug in 1948 wearing the purple and gold of Omega Psi Phi and bearing the mantle of trusted confidante within the black community.

During the Thanksgiving and Christmas holidays of his senior year, Arthur, Jr. spent a lot of time at the Davis house. At Thanksgiving, he had a duty there that was not at all unpleasant. Little Olivia, who was not so little any more, he noticed with growing interest, had asked him to be her escort in the Alpha Kappa Alpha Sorority's annual Debutante Ball, a big social event in Raleigh's Negro community. Every November, a select group of Negro girls in their senior year of high school donned white gowns and, armed with bouquets of red roses, made their curtsies before an audience of parents, relatives, and friends adorned in tuxedoes and formal gowns.

It was Arthur's job to take Olivia's arm when her father handed her over to him. Together, they promenaded around the swank floor of Raleigh's Memorial Auditorium. With the other debs and their beaux or brothers or friends, the participants built a simple ceiling of pink and green ribbons that was punctuated by each girl's bouquet. After the ribbon design, Arthur waltzed with Olivia.

All in all, it was a duty that had turned out to be a lot of fun in several ways. Some of Arthur's high school friends were escorting their little sisters or nieces that year. And it didn't hurt that Olivia looked exceptionally dazzling in her blinding white debutante gown. Arthur, Jr. was surprised to find that he and Olivia had quite a bit to talk about during that long, formal weekend. She had already read every classic that he had studied at St. Aug. She would attend St. Aug in the fall, also with a major in English, but her intention was to become a librarian in public school. They liked the same kind of music.

But perhaps most surprising to Arthur was Olivia's maturity. She had a wonderful sense of her purpose in this life, and he found he could discuss the horrors of his time in Europe with her, and she was genuinely interested, asking thoughtful, intelligent questions that prompted from him memories and insights that he had not previously given any credence to. Arthur liked this girl, who had always been a kid sister in his eyes, and he began to think of her in ways other than as some child. He was concerned that she was awfully young in years, though. After all, he was by then 24 years old.

At Christmas, his buddy Clark was home with his sweetheart Grace, and Arthur spent many hours in the Davis parlor along with Buster and his wife Elsie, both of whom were now teaching at Washington High School, and the rest of the Davis family. Olivia stood quietly on the periphery of the lively conversations, which were laced with the aromas of coffee and cigarette smoke that leapt out of that parlor. Elsie, who as a member of the Alpha Kappa Alpha sorority had been one of Olivia's chief sponsors, was now Olivia's French teacher, and it was so funny trying to remember not to call her "Elsie" when she entered the class.   Elsie had babysat her a couple of times when she was really young, and Elsie and Willia were what they called "giggling buddies." During that Christmas holiday, when Olivia sat quietly laughing with her older friends and relatives, Arthur motioned to her to come sit next to him on the couch. Olivia complied, and though she seemed composed outwardly, was jumping for joy inside.   She sat next to him for the rest of the evening, basking in the heady smells of his cigarettes and his cologne, thoroughly enjoying and contributing to the heavy talk that swept over the group later about being a Negro, and the ludicrous stresses attached to it.

When school resumed in January, Arthur returned to St. Aug to complete his senior year, but he spent a great deal of his free time visiting with Olivia. Rainey and Martha Alice were pleased that the two seemed to be hitting it off, though both were concerned about what seemed to be a vast age difference.

"Rainey, isn't William about nine years older than you?"

"Yeah, sugar, but I was a widow woman when we got married. Livy is just a baby. No tellin' what kind of French moves your boy is going to try to put on my baby." The two mothers laughed, but both still felt a bit nervous about the age differences.

Their apprehensions became reality on Olivia's graduation night. Arthur, out of college for all of two weeks, was the new managing editor of The Carolinian. Perhaps he was feeling the heady strength of the small measure of power his new job afforded him.   Perhaps Olivia was overjoyed to be a high school graduate. At any rate, on the evening of June 2, 1949, after Olivia's graduation and the attendant family celebration, Arthur asked Aunt Rainey and Uncle William if he could take Olivia for an evening ride. They wouldn't be gone very long, and he would, of course, take very good care of her.

Unbeknownst to everyone, Arthur brought along a bottle of champagne to congratulate Olivia, and, perhaps, to congratulate himself on his recent string of successes. It was a lovely evening as the last strains of glorious spring passed the torch to the velvety heat of summer. They rode out to what was then the country, but which is now an exclusive neighborhood in north Raleigh. There they sat talking easily, drinking the champagne from two coffee cups that Arthur had slipped from his mother's china cabinet. As usual, conversation flowed between them, and as they became more relaxed under the fondle of the champagne, their conversation took a silly, rather lascivious turn.

"Have you ever been kissed, Olivia Jane Davis?"

"No, Arthur Louis Seaton, Junior. I've been waiting to be kissed by you." She giggled, but her statement was totally true. She had rebuffed some really good-looking boys in order to hold out her hope of some attention from her ideal man.

"Well, here goes, Olivia Jane." And they kissed, awkwardly at first, because Olivia had never experienced a lover's kiss, and, perhaps, because Arthur was a little rusty at it. After all, he'd been a veritable bookworm since he'd come home from the war.

That first kiss opened a new line of talk and thought between them. Olivia was convinced she was in love with Arthur, as she had been since her childhood. Arthur certainly was attracted to Olivia.

"Arthur, may I tell you--"

"Olivia, I think you're --"

"Oh, go ahead."

"No, you."

"Oh, that's okay."

"All right, Olivia Jane. I think you're special.   Now you."

"Arthur, I really meant it when I said I was waiting for you to kiss me."

"Well, here goes another."

This time, their kiss didn't end until Olivia's panties were on the floor of the backseat of Arthur's jalopy and her glasses were wedged between the back door and the seat, while Arthur was plunging relentlessly into her.   Suddenly, very suddenly, his movements, which had been quite painful to her at first, increased in speed.   To her dismay, her beloved groaned loudly, and exhaled, dropping his head onto her chest as if he had been hit . . . or something.

"Are you okay, Arthur?"

"Huh? . . . Oh, yes."   He jumped up suddenly, rearranging his clothes and looking at Olivia frantically.

"Lord, what have I done?   I'm sorry, Olivia!   I didn't mean to get so carried away."

"Oh, I don't mind.   I just didn't expect it to happen until . . . ."

They stared at each other.   Olivia, suddenly self-conscious, closed her eyes and felt around the floor for her panties.   She demurely pulled them up and smoothed her dress.

"I better get you home.   Look how dark it is out here in this field."

They rode back to Olivia's house in silence, their eyes averted from each other.

Once back on Person Street,   Arthur promised to call Olivia the next day.

He kept his promise every day after that, visiting or calling faithfully.   They stayed in very open, public spaces, favoring rooms filled with family members.   They talked about their "backseat incident" a couple of times on Rainey or Martha Alice's front porch, and agreed they had made a mistake, but that someday, after Olivia finished college, perhaps they would think about getting married or something.

Then came the fateful day Olivia went to Dr. Nelson's office complaining of constant nausea, and of having an irregular menstrual cycle. (If irregular meant it hadn't come since May, then irregular it was.) It was late July by then, and Olivia was getting excited about going to St. Aug. Her life was going pretty much according to her plans: she had the attentions of the only man she'd ever thought about, and she was about to go to college, which she had always regarded as an adventure of sorts.

"Young lady," Dr. Nelson sang to Olivia when he returned from his tiny laboratory. He had the strangest look on his face, as if he had been told some bizarre secret.

"Yes, sir?" Olivia sat forward in her chair, nervous and apprehensive.

"You are in the family way. That's why you've been feeling so funny lately."

Olivia burst into shocked tears. Her one and only time doing that, and she got caught!

"Olivia, I am a little surprised at you. I didn't think you were that kind of girl."

"I'm not that kind of girl, Dr. Nelson. It was only one time, by accident. It hasn't happened since, we both made sure about that."

"What are you going to do?"

"I'm going to talk to . . . somebody. How much do I owe you? Mama sent a check for me to pay you with." As Olivia filled in the check, she felt numb and removed from herself. Anxious questions swirled about in her head. What will Arthur say? Lord, what will Mama and Papa say? I could just die, I just could!

Olivia walked down Person Street on feet made of lead. From a block away, she could see Arthur on the porch talking with her parents and Willia. Olivia pulled a tiny mirror from her purse, and arranged her face into a pleasant smile. Once on her porch, she chatted pleasantly with her family and Arthur.

"Did the doctor say you're gonna live, Livy?" Willia teased her.

"Oh, yes. I'm just fine. Just a little indigestion is all."

Soon, and an eternity later, Papa said he needed to get some insurance paperwork done, and Mama needed to get dinner started. Willia decided to go see Rosetta, and went inside to call to see if she was at home. That left Olivia alone, at last, with Arthur.

"Artie, I need to talk to you," she whispered intensely.

"Okay. What's the matter?"

"Come in the back yard with me for a minute." The couple went to their favorite spot in Rainey and William's back yard, a white wrought iron bench that wrapped around a pecan tree.

"Artie, I don't know any other way to say it. I'm going to have a baby."

Arthur leaned away from her as if he would fall to the ground.

"Huh?" was all he could say, finally, and Olivia cried in front of him for the first time. Arthur grasped Olivia by one shoulder and pulled her to him.

"Shhh. It's going to be all right. We'll be all right." Eventually, Olivia's tears died down, and she settled onto his shoulder as he made plans for them.

The couple set a lifelong pattern then. Arthur made the decisions, and Olivia abided by them, rarely asking any questions. She had decided long before her marriage to Arthur became a reality that she would have no arguments in her marriage. And she set about the business of keeping her home free of dissension by not providing any.

And so as Arthur decided, the two broke the news of the grandchild-to-be to their parents that evening, got married in the middle of August, and rented the Cotton Place house from the Davises while they hunted for a little house of their own.

On March 8, 1950, the consequence of "the backseat incident" became a very vocal reality with the birth of Olivia Rainey Martha Seaton. Her golden skin color and her sandy locks prompted her grandmother Martha Alice to name her "Honey," a name that stuck with her for life. In January of 1951, the young Seatons bought their first home, a three-bedroom ranch house in the growing Rochester Heights subdivision.

And, according to Arthur's plan, they would be very careful not to have any more accidents until they were ready to have another baby. He kept condoms in constant supply in their tiny master bedroom. They did not have another baby until Millicent Alice was born on September 5, 1958.

In 1952, Olivia entered Saint Augustine's College by day, while Arthur took courses toward his master's degree by night at North Carolina College for Negroes. Armed with a master's degree in English, Arthur taught evening classes at Shaw University to supplement his meager income at the newspaper. Olivia earned her bachelor's degree in English in 1956, and began teaching at Ligon High that September. As Arthur had planned for her, she began her master's in Library Science in the summer after she graduated from St. Aug, continuing her studies by night and through one more session of summer school, so that by 1957 she would have worked for a while as a librarian. Then, by 1958, she would be in a position to have another baby, which, he decided, would be their last.

Both Rainey and Martha Alice marveled at how passive Olivia was with "Little Arthur." But they both seemed to be happy with their own strange little system, so neither mother-in-law said anything to upset them.

Meanwhile, Arthur, Jr. had several affairs over the first years of the marriage. He loved Olivia, but her unquestioning devotion to him, and her compliance with all his demands, no matter how gently rendered, had begun to bore him. He sought challenges in these brief flings, some sort of resistance, perhaps some conquest.

Olivia always knew about these other women, who they were, where they worked, but she never confronted him or them. To her mind, he would always come home to her.   And he did.   He never stayed away from home overnight, nor did he do anything to embarrass his family. To Olivia, then, as long as she knew that he was her devoted husband, what was the harm?   Besides, she reasoned, nobody knew.

But of course, Rainey and Martha Alice knew. Martha Alice was not surprised; after all, Red Art "couldn't keep his pants buttoned when we first got married." She had nipped her husband's philandering in the bud early on. She told him with quiet fierceness that he would either unbutton his pants only to please her, or he wouldn't have a reason to unbutton them.   Red Art had never been a fool, and he knew his wife's temper and her ability to get any information she decided she needed. He chose to please only her.

It was with that soft ferocity that Martha Alice confronted her son in her kitchen one afternoon.

"Come here, sugar," she began, looking up at her firstborn as if she wanted to give him a kiss. When he bent down to her, smiling, she grabbed his earlobes. Whispering, she spat into his ear: "Look-a here, boy, I know what you've been doing! You are not slick! Now I'm gonna tell you like I told your daddy, you either do your husbandly duty only with Olivia or I'm going to make sure you don't have anything to do your duty with!" She loosened her grip on his earlobes long enough to push his face back gently.

Arthur, Jr. knew of his mother's temper, too. He didn't bother to deny his philandering; he knew that his parents (his mother) had ways of finding out things whether he wanted them (her) to or not.

After a brief reprieve, Martha Alice grabbed his lobes again and pulled his pain-etched face toward her. "Boy, you know I am not playing with you. You are NOT going to hurt Livy, do you understand? I'll hurt you myself."

Finally, Martha Alice let go of his ears, and hugged him at his waist. She looked up at her child with love and determination.

"And you know I will, don't you?"

Arthur swallowed hard. "Yes, ma'am."

"Give Mama a kiss then, and do the right thing."

Arthur chose to be a husband only Olivia from that moment, and taught her how to keep him happy. Looking back, Arthur silently thanked his mother. Playing around was much too complicated and tricky for him and trying to keep track of who liked what was too much trouble.

And so, Olivia had her man and her family, just as she'd dreamed, and though she had opted to be a submissive wife, the younger Seatons worked out a lifestyle that made them both content.

Contentment, Rainey's Interlude

It was in 1952, after 26 years of marriage, that Rainey Clark [Herndon] Davis became an adulterous woman.

When Miriam Ragland died in February of that year, of complications from the diabetes that had plagued her for years, Laurence Ragland was a man broken by guilt-threaded grief. His devoted wife was 56 years old when she breathed her last. Laurence Ragland knew that Miriam had been the very gracious victim of benign neglect.

Laurence knew that he was the source of any sadness Miriam had known during their marriage. He had thrown her morsels of kindness, and he had always provided well for her. But, as he always admitted to himself when he was alone with his demons, Rainey Elizabeth was his real passion. He was both horrified and validated by her constant presence in the hours immediately following Miriam's death. She was his angel and his guide through the steaming mists of his sometimes incoherent grief. He could hardly bear to face the fact that the source of his joy and passion stood before him as a beacon to his past memories of the life they never had together, as a bright reminder of the neglect he had dealt to Miriam, and as a beam of hope from a future he could not dare to expect.

Rainey took seriously her job as her "cousin's" caretaker in the weeks after Miriam's death. Now that all the children had gone on to their own homes, Rainey only had two other mouths to feed – William and Laurence. Laurence wasn't really up to coming over for dinner, so the three of them agreed that Rainey would take a plate to Laurence at his home in the afternoons, for a while, at least. Cousin Rainey made sure that Laurence had plenty of clean clothes, light foods for the evening and for lunch, and plenty of coffee and beer, especially beer. Laurence had adopted the drink as his personal potion since Miriam's death.

But all this nurturing was taking its toll, though Rainey chose not to share her weariness with either of the men in her immediate life. She was just at the point of telling Laurence that it was time for him to start coming over to Person Street for dinner when a bizarre thing happened: she found herself in her "cousin's" bed.

It had all happened in such a whirl of frantic passion that, looking back, Rainey still couldn't quite piece together how everything had led to that moment. She only knew that, though the encounter was not as physically satisfying as her lovemaking with William, she felt now that she was in the right place with the right man. It was never strange to her that she was now an adulteress: she was still passionate with and devoted to William, and she was at home with him every night. Laurence was a gift to herself; he was a faraway goal that she had thought she would never attain. She gave William candlelight and romance and quietly passionate evenings, but she received candlelight and romance and quietly passionate afternoons from Laurence.

And so, Rainey Elizabeth Clark [Herndon] Davis entered the late afternoon of her life with two lovers, her life otherwise ensconced in normalcy and mundanities. She was known to her peers and their children as a role model, a great lady, a diligent educator, and a devoted wife. In her world, she was all of that and she was also so much less.

Part Four:

'Til Love Has Nothing More To Ask

I want to die while you love me
While yet you hold me fair,
While laughter lives upon my lips
And lights are in my hair.

I want to die while you love me,
and bear to that still bed,
Your kisses -- turbulent, unspent,
To warm me when I'm dead.

I want to die while you love me,
Oh, who would care to live,
'Til love has nothing more to ask
And nothing more to give.

I want to die while you love me
And never, never see
The glory of this perfect day
Grow dim or cease to be.

-- Georgia Douglass Johnson (1877-1966) ▲

▲ *Johnson, Georgia Douglass. An Autumn Love Cycle. New York: Harold*   *Vinal,*

1928.

CHAPTER FOURTEEN

While Laughter Lives

When Rainey considered the adult Willia, she shuddered at the fulfilled prophecies echoing from her own young life. Rainey had yearned to paint Washington, DC red; the soles of Willia's feet were stained a permanent crimson. Willia was a flaming comet. Rainey had seen her beloved daughter out and about with her "night people" on more than one occasion, usually as she herself skulked away from some clandestine meeting with Laurence.

Rainey was worried. Willia was raising as much hell as she possibly could and seemed to Rainey to be a walking around the rim of a nervous breakdown. By day, she was a flawlessly perfect teacher. But her nights seemed consumed with partying as hard as she could.

Rainey prayed for her daughter's safekeeping and for forgiveness for her own adultery. She knew that they were both dancing with fire, and that neither of them could resist the flames.

* * * * * *

Since coming to Johnston County Consolidated School in 1949, Willia had been cordial with Frederick Douglass Baxter, who was about her age and who had been promoted from sixth-grade teacher to assistant principal. She found him attractive, and thought that he looked a little like her father, but had never thought much about him beyond that. She had noticed that his cordiality toward her was always tinged with some mysterious hopefulness, and she guessed that he found her attractive, too. Yet, he had never given her any concrete indication that he was interested in her until about 1951, when it became increasingly obvious that Doug had a "thing" for her. She enjoyed the way his eyes brightened each time he saw her coming. She could feel his admiration wash over her ravaged body like a spring breeze.

He had graduated from Fort Valley State College in Georgia in 1948. A native of Brunswick, Georgia, Doug had tried to make a living there, so that he could help his parents with expenses for his five younger brothers and sisters, but with little success. He loved his family with a ferocity that sometimes startled him, but he understood fully the origin of his devotion to them. Hadn't his parents done everything possible to see that "that boy" went to college? They had been his first and most ardent fans when he began to play football and basketball in the Brunswick colored schools. They had brought his siblings to every game, and they all looked up to him as their hero. Douglass Baxter was determined not to let them down; he made every touchdown pass for them and shot every basket for their eyes only.

At home, all of the Baxter children worked to please their parents, and love abided in that house. It was Doug and only Doug among the children who shared their parents' sorrows and disappointments as they sought to make a way for their family out of virtually no way. Neither of his parents had finished high school, so the jobs they had to resort to were menial at best. Food, adequate clothing, even properly enclosed housing were sometimes difficult to maintain. Doug felt, as his parents felt, deep anguish at his sisters' and brothers' hunger and their shame at their worn hand-me-downs. They deserved so much more in the world, from the world. They were five bright, beautiful, talented children. Doug knew, through his parents loving and gentle insistence, that he needed to do what he could to make their lives a little easier.

So it was with great sadness but unfailing determination that Douglass Baxter realized, soon after his graduation from Fort Valley State that he would have no choice but to find a decent job somewhere -- anywhere -- to help make life easier for his people.

There was not so much demand in Brunswick for a black man who wanted to teach elementary school. So he had contacted the tiny placement office at Fort Valley State for help. Johnston County Consolidated Schools in North Carolina was looking for a sixth - grade teacher. Other than that, the pickings were pretty slim. He wrote the Superintendent of Negro Education in North Carolina and expressed his interest in the job. He was accepted, sight unseen, with only two of the three required letters of recommendation.

In August of 1949, he set out for Raleigh, North Carolina, even though he had been told of the driving distance from Raleigh to Selma every day. He just had to live in a more cosmopolitan community than Smithfield or Selma or Clayton could offer him. He vowed to send one third of his money to his family each payday, which he did, and to stay in touch with his betrothed (Willia was touched by his reference to his fiancée as his betrothed), which he did but she did not -- she promptly married one of his cousins. Nevertheless, his life went smoothly in North Carolina.

Doug had lived in the tiny but progressive all-black community of Method since he had moved to Raleigh. He enjoyed his membership in Oak City Baptist Church out in Method, and he felt like a full-fledged part of that community. He was very active in his fraternity as a means of getting to know people in Raleigh. Willia was delighted to find that she knew most of the Omega Psi Phi fraternity brothers he mentioned, most notably her brother-in-law, Arthur Seaton.

It was a good life but a lonely one. He had dated several lovely young ladies, and had admired Willia from afar ever since they had both started at Johnston County Consolidated together.

He couldn't know that the woman he admired so was living a double life.

Willia managed, during those years after her graduation from North Carolina College, to keep her personal life separate from her lives as educator, daughter, and sister. She took care to nurture her eight- and nine-year-old charges, to instill in them a joy for learning, and to urge them to embrace moral credos that she herself had long ago abandoned. Further, she never appeared at work late or disheveled, but always brightly attired and overly prepared for work.

Douglass Baxter was dating, when she allowed it, Willia-as-educator. She never let her guard down around him, which was why they only dated, at most, once a month. Willia wasn't about to give up her nightlife. By day, she was the sterling educator and by night, she was all hell-raiser. She wasn't ready for Douglass Baxter to be a bridge between the two worlds too often. She was holding the two worlds at bay all by herself, thank you very much.

Enter James "Buck" Crowder, and while her steady, promising career continued on course, her personal life took a smoky nosedive.

Buck Crowder, fourteen years Willia's senior, was a powerfully built, fiery-eyed man whose demonic temper had landed him in Central Prison for three short visits. His square-jawed good looks, his silky chocolate skin, and his tightly roped, powerful build were obscured beneath a steaming veneer of concentrated violence. All of South Park knew him to be a dangerous man whose own white-haired mother was not spared from his wrath. His mother, however, was the only woman he never hit.

More than once, Rainey had seen Polly Crowder Butler, Buck's mother, lift her skirt elegantly as she fled her enraged child, her long legs engaged in the flight of the gazelle, while that bull called Buck charged at her from behind. Perhaps she had burned one biscuit too many after a long night as a licensed practical nurse for old man Nowell, the Fayetteville Street haberdasher. Of course, she still cooked for her only son even though he lived in his own house and had a stream of willing women at his enforced beck and call. Was it really important that she had worked all day long at Earp's Seafood in the back kitchen beheading, deveining, and eviscerating all manner of seafood? Perhaps she had not told him that Bessie Lou had come by with some money for him; never mind that the girl had come by, drunk as Cootie Brown, knocking on Mrs. Polly's rickety front door at the very moment she had removed her bandanna scarf from her magnificent, powder white hair in search of a few moments' peace.

Buck meant his mother no real harm, even though he was the only one who knew this to be true. He just wanted to put the fear in her so she wouldn't be so damn slack. (Although he never really knew, he was certain that it was her slackness that had driven her second husband, Willie Butler, to an early grave. Of course it had nothing to do with his own intimidating presence in and out of the man's little house, or the threats, wrapped as they were in raggedy veils, of what Buck would do to him if he EVER hurt HIS mama. No. His mama had eventually worried the man to death.)

After all he was THE Buck Crowder, wasn't he, the one who had stabbed Boo Sharper -- the second baddest cat in South

Park -- in the middle of Bragg Street for short-changing him in an unofficial card game. Buck Crowder gladly went to jail for that manslaughter rap. Wasn't he the Buck Crowder who had left his wife broken and bloody in a gutter at the corner of Person and Smithfield Streets after she had had the nerve to back talk him at all, let alone in front of folks? He taught her a thing or two about asking him for some milk money for some damn kids! He didn't give a damn to this day, if she was pregnant with those retarded-ass twins of hers at the time. Wasn't his fault anyway.

Women didn't mess over him because they knew he didn't have a problem with knocking them around when he felt they needed some training. Two of his visits to Central Prison had been behind some silly women going to the police (or the police coming to him) over a little falling out. Never mind that the reality of those fallings out was the accumulation of dozens of lacerations, broken bones, and several daughters and sisters missing from the lives and homes of community residents too timid to confront him or go to the police about him ....

The only person who dared challenge Buck Crowder was his sister, Estella, who was known to everyone as "Stell." In another era, given more advantageous circumstances, Stell would have been an Olympic contender on a par with any great female runner of the twentieth century. Her sideline occupation, had she been that contender, would have been fashion model. Martha Alice Seaton described the Crowders as some of the prettiest black folk she had ever seen. Beauty and speed and violent tempers were all Crowder family traits. But once the liquor took Stell over, it was hard to see her beauty beneath the ravages of Johnny Walker Red's caress. Stell's stride, when she taunted Buck or a current lover, was an improvement on her mother's. Stell moved as if through silken air, and Buck could neither catch her nor better her in any competition. She taunted Buck relentlessly for being a punk or a faggot, inviting him to "kiss my ass to the bone," and she didn't back down even when a silently enraged Buck chased her through South Park with an ax uplifted on the power of his anger, his legs propelled by the fierceness of his previously uttered promise that he would slice her open and feed her to Mrs. Vincent's German shepherds. Buck couldn't make good on that promise because Stell had sense enough to run to the haven of Maggie Jones's front porch. (All of South Park knew

Mrs. Maggie took no garbage from anyone, and she was rumored to have the fire power to back herself up.). Mrs. Maggie stopped Buck just short of her front porch with a simple declaration: "I don't give a snap ginny what she done to you. Don't you come in here!"

Willia had seen Buck in action, had heard about his brutal beatings of woman after woman. Yet when she practically bumped into him downtown on Hargett Street one fateful Saturday afternoon in February 1958, Willia found herself drawn to this six-foot tall linebacker of a man.

On that afternoon, Willia and Olivia were downtown enjoying the bleak sunshine. Olivia's daughter "Honey" was about to turn eight, and Olivia called herself just barely pregnant with the child who would be her youngest daughter, Millicent. The ladies strolled along fondly together, and Honey skipped along beside them, occasionally blowing kisses to her mother, her aunt, or the air.

Willia considered her baby sister to be her best friend and closest confidante -- up to a point. There were things about herself that nobody could know except for the people involved, and usually they didn't want anybody to know they were there, either. However, no matter how outlandish her behavior became, Willia knew that if Olivia ever found her out, no reproach or judgment would come from her, only quiet and loving concern. Willia also knew that there would be the slightest tinge of vicarious joy or even wistfulness from this perfect lady.

Willia often laughed to herself that Olivia's only indiscretion had been what the family now laughingly referred to as "that backseat incident " back in '49 with the man who would be her husband. Well, we got Olivia Junior out of the deal, Willia thought as she smiled down at her serious niece.

At this point in their stroll, the sisters laughed easily about their experiences as elementary school educators. Olivia was the no-nonsense but nurturing librarian at Crosby-Garfield School. Willia shared several anecdotes about her own students. They were just in front of Hamlin Drugs when, as Willia stopped to imitate a particularly goofy boy, she backed directly into Buck Crowder as he emerged from Hamlin. She turned quickly, an apology on her lips, and stopped in the middle of her sentence, stunned. She had unwittingly assaulted one of the most dangerous men of her time.

"Oh, God, Buck! I'm so sorry; I didn't mean to step on your foot."

Olivia instinctively moved closer to her sister, ready to offer support, she knew not how. Honey stood slightly behind her mother.

"'S all right, baby. No harm done." With a tip of his fedora, Buck sauntered away from them toward his late model Buick. When he was in his car, he rolled down his window and said, "Y'all need a lift anywhere?" To the women's demure refusal of his offer, he tipped his hat again. "I'll be in touch, Willia." He sped away up Hargett Street.

Several seconds passed before Willia found her voice. "What did he mean by that, Liv?"

"Who you askin', Will? All I know is that's a mighty dangerous man. If he knows how to get in touch with you, you better get a private line."

"I know that's right!" She had conveniently forgotten her own brief encounter with Buck at a local den of iniquity 'way back in '57.

CHAPTER FIFTEEN

Turbulence

The Cave was the prime hangout for South Raleigh's wild crowd in the '50s and '60s. With its entrance a steel door cut into the Cabarrus Street wall of Cottingham's Grocery Store on Bloodworth Street, it was a fifteen-hundred-square-foot bunker of moist, throbbing heat beneath a thriving food store that prided itself on being a fair place for community families to do all their shopping. The club's low ceilings and lone doorway forced some of the taller patrons to stoop upon entering and to remain stooped throughout their visits. The bar sat off to the left side of the room, illuminated by a lurid red light that shimmered against spotted shot glasses. The middle of the concrete floor was covered with black linoleum and served as the dance floor. Metal and green vinyl kitchen chairs adorned Formica kitchen tables nestled between five-foot high slabs of wood to serve as candlelit booths on the right side of the club. A reprint of a Rembrandt or a Reubens hung on the wall of each makeshift booth. It was an oddly dainty touch in a sea of decadence.

A strange fat woman wearing a dusty blonde wig and too many clothes sat smoking Newports and drinking Tangerray on the rocks, wiping beads of sweat from her forehead as she read Baldwin or Wright or Petry inside a cramped glass booth next to the front door. She never changed her blank expression as she collected the dollar-fifty admission fee and stamped hands through a square opening in her little three-sided evening home. Nor did she so much as blink faster on those occasions when she made silent deals for tacit club features: blowjobs, or other such services some of the patrons felt they needed to make their Cave experience complete.

This strange fat woman was by day neither fat, blonde, nor particularly strange. She was a fixture at The Cave from its beginning to its abrupt end on the night its owner was beaten to death by Raleigh police officers, and she had been known to make herself available to provide the "optional" services if no other staff member were readily available. She would lock the front door until she had rendered those services, either in the darkened bathroom, or in the tiny storage room with its ever-ready rollaway bed.

At The Cave in its heyday, the only patron who knew who she really was never acknowledged their family relationship except through an occasional conspiratorial smile or a Newport slipped through the hole in the booth. Aurelia, the strange fat woman, was a granddaughter of Nettie Ann Houser.

The Cave was the scene of some mighty nasty goings-on: Buck Crowder himself had beaten one of his errant girlfriends nearly to death behind the rickety bar one night because she had gone out for a night on the town with her sisters without his permission. From that day, a stain remained on the frayed white piece of carpet behind the bar where the hapless woman vomited blood and hunks of her pork chop and collard dinner as Buck wailed on her back with his massive, callused fists. No amount of Clorox, Tide, or white dye ever quite removed the shadow of that grisly night from the carpet. Finally, Nat Burton (the man Aurelia shared with his wife) threw the thing out and stood on the bare concrete as he doled out beer and whiskey.

The bathroom was another sordid spot: many a baby had been made on top of the shaky commode in the six by eight cell, and many a baby had been flushed away down that plumbing.

The Cave's concrete slab floors never quite lost the ruby tinge of blood spilled in drunken rages over men and women and small change. Some of the patrons of The Cave were more efficient butchers than those skilled artisans upstairs at Cottingham's could ever hope to be. From its patched and re-patched vinyl barstools to its one dank, mildewy bathroom, with its single swinging 40-watt light bulb, The Cave reeked of Schlitz and Richard's Wild Irish Rose and Kool Filter Kings. Not too far into the '50s, a new conglomeration of smells insinuated themselves into the molten confines of the club -- Acapulco Gold, Colombian -- MaryJane aromas that made the eyelids ease up on their attentive duty and the stomach and the libido growl in time to the sultry blues and pulsating rock and roll pouring from the piccolo. As the prominence of the ganja smells grew, Nat Burton added incense burners and a little grill to the back end of the bar to slake the intensity of what would later be called the "munchies" by the children and grandchildren of those patrons.

Into such an environment did Willia Evelyn Davis regularly inject herself. She was usually the life of the party at The Cave: early to arrive, she would be among the last to stumble out of its cloudy atmosphere. She was among the first to try the ganja, and would occasionally take a nickel bag home with her to the tidy bungalow on Cotton Place. She rarely entered the club alone; she traveled with her night people. She met up with them at a common place: somebody's card party, or the front door of The Cave. Sometimes they even got together in front of Raleigh Funeral Home, which was diagonal to The Cave. She never saw these folks in daylight. Simply stated, their paths never crossed in the sun.

Buck Crowder's desire for her had been whetted at the very bar that had been the scene of his championship bout some years earlier. As the drunken Willia, adorned in her usual form-fitting sleeveless dress, black tonight, had slumped against the wooden counter of the bar, fumbling with the plastic wrapper of a lemon drop, Buck offered to buy her a beer. She had accepted, her black eyes dulled by large quantities of Jack Daniels. She thanked him clumsily for his kindness and offered herself to him for a single dance, popping yet another lemon drop into her mouth as they made their way to the floor. As he slow dragged with her, he stiffened against her.

"Now, Buck," Willia slurred, throwing her head carelessly back to reveal a luscious long neck, "'Taint while for you to get no ideas like that! The only things I'm openin' up tonight are my two lips to have another drink!" She winked drowsily at him, moving against his erection with such slow, deliberate lewdness that he had to hold himself back from taking her to the storeroom right then. He made a silent vow to himself, his only god, that he would someday have Willia Davis. He knew she was an educated woman acting out her wild streak; therefore, he knew he was probably going to have to court her ladylike side to get anywhere with her. After the music ended that night, Willia had pulled abruptly away from Buck Crowder, weaving her way over to a booth full of some of her high school classmates. She never again acknowledged his presence in the club that night, and she had left with Sammy Hinton. Later, whenever Buck Crowder saw her around town, Willia always spoke to him cordially, but gave no indication that she remembered their brief encounter at The Cave.

At about six o'clock on the evening of the Hamlin Drug Store encounter, a green Buick pulled up in front of Willia's neat little house on Cotton Place. Buck Crowder, well dressed and drowned in cologne, stepped from that Buick, a cigarette dangling carelessly from his thick, brutal lips. He rang Willia's doorbell, but he couldn't know that she had decided to engage in her practice of spending a night at her parents' home, just around the corner from his own. Clark Davis and his family were down from New Jersey to spend a few days there at Rainey's house. Willia and Olivia were great friends with their sister-in-law Grace, and Willia couldn't get enough of seeing her nieces and nephew interact with each other. They were the cutest little honey-eyed kids. So Willia was excited about this night. She had rushed through her tidy little house, puffing frenetically on a Newport as she packed her overnight case. Within ten minutes, Willia sped away in her little Renault. She had probably passed Buck Crowder enroute in the deepening dusk.

Willia returned home after church the next day just long enough to change clothes so that she could head back to Mama's to help with dinner. She was pleased that Doug Baxter had joined her family at church. She didn't quite want to admit to herself that his presence among them had seemed, well, as if he just plain belonged there. Now he was going to join them for dinner. Still, Willia stifled a yawn. Doug Baxter was damned nice, but he was just too calm. She still longed for excitement, and she still knew just where to find it.

She had not known such utter contentment in ages: just being with her whole family (and Doug) had been like a soothing balm for her. Last night, Olivia had pulled her aside to comment on her relaxed and happy demeanor. Then Grace had mentioned to her in passing that she hadn't seen her look so rested in a long time. Willia frankly had to admit to herself to that maybe she needed an extended rest from the edge she'd been living on for the past eleven years. No, she shushed her sensible side, Doug Baxter is <u>still </u>too sedate for me right now. Maybe when I retire.

So when she opened the storm door, and a rough piece of paper fluttered to her porch, right next to a bag of Brach's lemon drops no less, she was annoyed and disgusted by the crude handwriting, yet mystified and somehow touched by the gesture of the lemon drops. Who sent these, she wondered vaguely. The note seemed to burst into her peace and grab at her temporarily arrested wild self. She felt a deep chill course down her spine as she read:

"Willia, I cam by to call own you. James Buck Crowder."

Willia gasped and hurried into her house as if she didn't want the neighbors to know that Buck had shown up at her door. Still, she could not deny that tinge of fear and excitement, and not a little titillation at the prospect of being pursued by the most dangerous man in South Park, if not Raleigh. Her breath shortened in apprehension, but her body tingled, too. She'd heard through the grapevine that survivors of relationships with Buck Crowder declared he provided the best sex they had ever had.

"But damn. He can't even spell," she muttered as she pulled on slacks and a pullover sweater and tried to ignore the tingling stiffness in her nipples. "What would I want with something like him anyway?"

It was a question she would ignore shamefacedly over these next few months.

The note he left her on that February Saturday was Buck Crowder's way of courting Willia's ladylike side. His approach worked with extreme speed, but not for the reason he assumed. Willia could not resist the ignorant brute that she perceived him to be, and she suspected that his lovemaking would be as fierce and lowdown as his writing was hopelessly inept.

So they began to "date" shortly after she found the note on her door, but on her own double-minded terms. She had an infinite supply of excuses to keep her from being seen with him in public. She was always just finishing up this meeting or that parent-teacher conference, so she would meet him at The Cave, or at The Lady In Red Supper Club on Old Garner Road, or at The Renegade Club out in Oberlin.

She became secretive toward her family. No daughter of William Davis would dare be seen in public with a rogue and woman hater like Buck Crowder. During those months, the Davises grew frantic about Willia. She had never stayed away from them, no matter how wild her other life might be. She had always seemed to find solace in their stability and consistency. Now ten days might pass between her visits. Those visits were always furtive, antsy times. She never stayed for dinner any more. Neither Rainey nor Olivia could remember the last time she had called just to chat or called to see what they were doing.

They could not know that she was addicted to Buck Crowder's sexual prowess -- and her own proficiency which he had by now fine-tuned -- just as surely as Billie Holiday was addicted to the white horse. She wanted desperately to break away from him, and she tried in so many ways, most of them obscure, to withdraw from him. But once he got his foot in the door, Lordy Lord, she had no more will power! One suck of her willowy neck, and she was limp and so overcome with passion that she could hardly breathe.

But when he wasn't with her, she felt like a very sick woman, someone who desperately needed treatment for a chronic disease. It was difficult for her to concentrate on teaching when she was there at school with her beloved third graders. Why? It was just sex. She always shook her head against the onslaught of pungent, tingling, pulsating memory. Willia was a prisoner of contaminating lust and she just couldn't understand what was happening to her. She had enjoyed wonderful sexual encounters before, but they had never rendered her incapable of functioning fully in her other life. Was it the ever-present threat of violence that added the irresistible edge to her relations with Buck? Was she courting that edge? After all, she could barely hide her contempt for him when they were together He had to know she thought he was pretty stupid. Still, it was difficult for Willia to push their last steamy sexual episode from her mind. She suffered from uncomfortably frequent flashbacks of the relentless pull of his lips against her often swollen nipples, at the brutal force with which he pushed himself into her as he muttered filthy words into her burning ears or the way he snorted into her tousled hair when he climaxed.

She cut back on her night drinking in those days with Buck. He made it clear to her that no woman of his was going to be stinking of liquor when he was making love to her, and she knew that if she tried him, he would show her his displeasure in a way that would leave long-standing bruises. She only smoked cigarettes to and from work on the days she knew he would be coming to her house. He made sure she understood that no woman of his was going to be stinking of cigarettes when he put his tongue in her mouth. And to prove his point, he kissed her deeply, biting down on her tongue just enough for her to taste the salt of her own blood. Later, she looked at that bluish spot on her tongue and felt a shiver of carnal delight as she reminisced about the brutal lovemaking that had followed.

They had been lovers for two months before she sat in his car, and only then because he insisted that she hear Dakota Staton's latest song, "Trust In Me," on his failing radio. Her time spent in that seat left it as cold as when she had sat down. She raced back into the house, waving almost dismissively at him as he drove away.

It didn't hurt Buck Crowder's position in her life that he always managed to leave a $20 lying around on the floor near her bed. The first time he did it, she felt -- silently -- offended. He must think I'm some kind of whore, she fumed as she stuffed the aged bill into her billfold and placed the fattened billfold into her pristine "school-marm" purse. But she said nothing; she always kept his violent nature just on the outskirts of all her dealings with him. Soon it became a ritual for Buck Crowder to pay her telephone bill along with his own. She noticed one day soon after they began their sexual odyssey that, among her pile of neatly stacked bills to be paid, she could not find her Southern Bell notice. When Buck came over that evening, she expressed her concern about it to him as they undressed each other. She knew she couldn't have misplaced it because she kept all her bills in one place. Buck laughed his nasty gangster laugh as he licked her neck.

"It's all took care of, baby."

"Hmm?" She was sliding down a slope into what she secretly called her "good-to-me stool." She felt shitty afterward, like she had just floated, turd-like, in a toilet. But while she was in that toilet, she couldn't deny how incredibly good she felt in that place.

"I say, it's done been paid. Now don't even worry about it no mo'. Now come here . . . ."

It became a ritual for them, this tacit pay-and-play game they engaged in. Willia didn't really mind the set up -- for a while, at least. His quiet removal of her phone, light, and water bills to the payment offices, with payments, certainly helped her budget.

But it wasn't very long before she began to feel the slimy water from the "good-to-me toilet" puddling up around her knees, and climbing.

"Buck," she moaned into his neck one steamy evening, "I really appreciate you helping me out with my bills --"

"Yeah, bitch, and as long as you keep putting it to me like you doin' right now, you and me, we gon' be all right."

Willia was stunned; Buck had only ever called her "baby" and "Willia." So she was property now. The slimy water grew even more chilled as it inched upward to her thighs.

She could envision herself drowning in that water some day.

Slowly, hoping that he wouldn't notice, she began to put her utility bills in another space. She tried to fend off his questions by saying that her Papa had found it convenient just to go ahead and pay her utilities at the same time he paid his own. Buck grudgingly accepted her explanation, but Willia could also tell that he felt competitive with her Papa.

Soon she hit upon the perfect reason not to have him park his Buick in front of her little house: suppose Mama or one of her friends comes by while your car is out front? Everybody knows your car, and you know what a scandal that could cause. I have my reputation -- as a schoolteacher -- to think of, you know ... Baby.

Buck complied, mainly because after her request she had sexed him nearly out of his mind, almost wrenching a scream from him. From that time on he parked over on Hargett Street, cutting through Willia's back yard, which faced Hargett, and knocking quietly on Willia's back door. He was rocking Willia's sensual world, and she, too, made him see stars and feel the earth move. Slowly, even though she would not be seen in public with him, he was encroaching upon every aspect of her life.

She knew, and was worried sick about it, that he had made a permanent impact upon her when she stopped going to clubs without his permission and presence. He had often mentioned, with subtle menace, that no woman of his was going out partying without his protection. That was why he had had to punish Deborah Banks that night at The Cave: she had no business out by herself since she didn't know what could have happened to her.

She felt a thrill of fear course through her. At last her rational mind prevailed. She felt suddenly that she must get away from this man. She had played with these flames for far too long, and now she could feel them scalding her. She felt like a tiny prisoner in some sort of glass bottle: she was screaming for help but nobody could hear her. It took every ounce of will within her to try to stand up straight as her own woman and try to walk on her own again. She felt that the old Willia was being held hostage in some dangerous extortion game. Willia set out in search of that woman of yesterday, and she was determined to have her back without paying any ransom.

Willia made a valiant effort to pull away from Buck. She suddenly had extra parent-teacher conferences; she had to baby-sit Olivia's girls; Mama needed some help with her housework; Papa needed somebody to type some extra paperwork at his office. Yet she could still melt like chilled butter on a steaming cob of corn whenever he caught her at home. She felt as if she were struggling for wakefulness through the crippling fog of a nightmare, and more often than not, it seemed, the nightmare was winning her over. Gradually, though, Willia could see real daylight before her through this dark time, and she made it her business to be at home less frequently so that she would be less accessible to Buck Crowder.

She made what she thought was a final break from Buck Crowder in the spring of 1959, pulling herself up to freedom from the lurid fog with some potent help from an old and long neglected friend.

Toward the end of the 1958-1959 school year, on a Friday afternoon, Douglass Baxter sent Willia an official looking missive by a very serious fifth grader. He wrote to her with great respect and deference that he missed her. Could they please get together after the faculty meeting that was scheduled for the following Monday afternoon? He went on to explain that he was going to a tournament with the baseball team at the high school, otherwise, he would love to have seen her that day or over the weekend. Willia was touched by his needless explanation. He cared enough to want her to know about his life. She knew she could never have said the same of Buck Crowder.

Willia glanced, amused, at the fifth-grader, who had been instructed to wait for her written reply. She wrote in her neatest hand, "Certainly, Mr. Baxter. I will see you then. Miss Davis." She drew a smile beside her name, and stifled a giggle at her silliness. She started to hand the refolded note to the child, but had then held up a finger to him to wait just one minute. She unlocked the drawer in which she kept her purse, took out her little jar of sweet sachet hand cream, and rubbed her hands hurriedly with it. Then she re-opened the note as if she had forgotten to write something, smoothing its creases with the flat of her moisturized hand, and wrote a postcript: "And I kind of miss you, too." Then she carefully re-folded the note and made sure to smooth the creases again before handing it over to the child.

The truth was, Doug had stopped by to see Rainey and William the previous evening, asking about Willia, and acknowledged to them that he was reluctant just to drop by her house. Willia's parents had urged him to ask her out again; what could be the harm? They knew she liked him, although she may have seemed a bit aloof. She always spoke highly of him. Heartened by his visit, Doug had opted to write this note, wondering to himself why he had been so nervous about approaching Willia again. Was it because she seemed to be spoken for, preoccupied?

As for Willia, even though she had had the best sex of her life with Buck Crowder, she never lost the feeling that she was dirtied now, a tainted and unworthy product of a smoky relationship that had somehow singed her self-esteem and had sullied her outer reputation as a well-educated woman of substance. Doug Baxter could well offer her a plausible way out of this sensual sewer. Again she shushed her sensible self when it told her, It's about time you came to your senses!

On that Monday, she taught her dear little third-graders with added enthusiasm, and she glanced constantly at the wall clock to see how close she was to the end of the school day.

The faculty meeting dragged on like molasses uphill. Willia sat with an attentive posture, her face a waxen mask of absorption, as Principal Melton droned on about sundries: the lavatories have too many wads of toilet paper on the ceilings; I'm appalled at the misspelled obscenities on the walls in the lavatories; we need to teach these children how to spell ("Now children," Willia imagined herself saying. "It should be "Larry Daniels a-i-n- apostrophe-t s-h-i-t, not Larry Daniels a-n-i-t s-h-i-t-e. And "pussy" has two S's, not one, just as doo-doo has two O's in each doo."). Willia covered her mouth and stifled, with great effort, the upward motion of her black almond eyes; this man must spend all his free time, when he isn't picking his nose, in the 'lah-vah-toe-rees!" She snorted at her own sarcasm and cleared her throat as if she were recovering from a cough. She popped a lemon drop into her dry mouth and waited out the onslaught. Finally, Principal Melton ran out of sundries to summarize and the meeting was adjourned. Willia's eyes glittered.

"Hi," Doug Baxter said as he walked toward her. She stood at the back of the rapidly emptying room, glad she had worn her favorite royal blue shirtwaist dress today. The blue contrasted beautifully with her coffee brown skin and complemented her thick hair, which cascaded to just above her shoulder blades. Doug Baxter was taller and thinner than -- her eyes cast downward in shame as a naked Buck Crowder swaggered boldly through her mind – and Doug was powerfully built. Looked like he might enjoy tennis and golf. Today, he wore a seersucker suit that looked chic on him. His hair, lightly powdered with gray, was carefully cut and waved. She felt reassured by his smooth rich brown skin; she felt comforted somehow that he looked just a little like her father.

"Hi," she replied, suddenly nervous. "Long time no see. Where are we going for coffee?"

"Well, actually, I was wondering if you might like to go to dinner tonight?" Willia's heart jumped for joy.

"Why, sure. Wanna go to Payton's?"

Doug laughed. "Well, there's a new place I've tried over on South Saunders Street. Have you heard of Mama Trinie's? You're talking about some good cooking and a nice place to eat. What do you say?"

Willia actually felt herself blush. "Okay. Do you want me to follow you there?"

"Why don't I follow you home and then we'll go there together?"

Willia ignored a moment of clutching fear.

"Okay," she said, stifling a gulp.

All the way back to Raleigh, Willia prayed that Buck Crowder wouldn't just happen by her way. She figured he wouldn't know about any nice places that Doug Baxter would know about, so if she could just get to her house without incident, the coast would be clear.

Buck Crowder had gotten off work early on this day, wouldn't you know. He was at home bathing and shaving as Doug and Willia made their plans. He knew Willia would be at home after her faculty meeting. Even though she seemed to be extra busy these days, she always welcomed him when he could catch her at home, eager for him to take her over the edge. He lotioned himself with Jergen's until his entire body glistened -- he liked the way she liked to lick him all over -- and put on a new pair of dungarees, sans underwear, careful to tuck himself in so that he could surprise her with his instant nudity. He completed his dressing and left his tidy house, humming in confident anticipation....

... And cut through HIS woman's back yard just in time to see HIS woman get into some nigger's car and go driving off somewhere. Rage exploded inside him like Independence Day Fireworks at the Fairgrounds. He ran back to his car and slammed his fist against the steering wheel until his palm was tender and red. His jaw was set in an angry line. He was going to fix that whore. She must have been playing him for quite some time to go speeding off with this seditty - looking nigger. He'd been mighty nice to this bitch for a mighty long time. She needed some lessons, yessir, she needed a little more education than she thought she had. Buck Crowder sped off home. It was time to bring Minnie out of retirement.

Buck Crowder had managed to purchase Minnie, his hunting rifle, even though he had a prison record. He just bought it hot and went on about his business. He had never hunted anything but women with Minnie, and although he had never shot anyone with it, he had managed to intimidate the hell out of every deserving woman who had dared to cross him. He pulled Minnie from the back of his closet, caressed her like an old lover just back in town, and headed back to Hargett Street where he waited until Willia and that high-seditty nigger came back from wherever the hell they had gone. Yeah, he worked himself up to a throbbing fury, Bitch can't be SEEN with ME, but the first educated dicty nigger come along, she hops right in his car. Uh-huh, I'm gon' fix both they asses!

Buck would neither have recognized nor acknowledged that his fury was borne of hurt and jealousy, that he felt far more deeply for Willia than his next orgasm or his ability to overpower her. She was a class act, he knew, but he couldn't help feeling that she must have some real problems if she dealt with him on any level. He understood, deep in his uncharted subconscious, why she didn't want to be seen with him. He knew that he was bad news. Still, no bitch was gonna treat HIM like a dog. He waited, hoping to catch them doing some of what he had been doing with her all these months. Then he knew he would have every right to fire Minnie for the first time. He checked for ammunition, found it at the ready, and sat rubbing Minnie absently, enjoying the feel of his partially erect penis between his legs.

CHAPTER SIXTEEN

And Life Is Like a Song

Willia had forgotten how much she enjoyed talking academics and ideas with this man! She lingered over her heavenly trout dinner, sipping gingerly at her coffee, playing occasionally with a lock of her hair, thoroughly enjoying her date with Doug Baxter. He was such a gentleman, and so attentive, and she had forgotten just how good and secure she felt with him.

He seemed, as always, so proud to be in her company, and he respected her vast intellectual capacity. She sighed; how nice not to have to hide that side of herself from a man for a change. She was also amazed at the extent to which she had never bothered to get to know Doug on their infrequent dates together. She had dismissed him as something of a dufus, albeit a very handsome one, and, try as she might now, she could not quite remember why.

"So, Willia, what have you been up to?"

Willia took a deep breath. If he knew what she had really been up to with Buck Crowder, he would probably leave her sitting right there in Mama Trinie's all by herself.

"Oh, nothing. Just working, going to church, and being a good girl." She laughed nervously.

"Oh, come on now, a beautiful girl like you can't have that much of a dull life. I still don't feel like we know each other very well, even after all these years. I want to know what makes you tick."

Willia laughed a tight chuckle. "Even after all these years, I still don't know what makes Doug Baxter tick, so I guess we're even, eh? Maybe we'll get to the ticking later." They laughed easily. But Doug persisted.

"Are you dating anyone?"

Willia stifled a gulp. "No, not really. I don't have time. I told you I've been working and going to church." They laughed at her evasions, but Willia could have choked with shame.

"Have you really missed me?"

"Well, yes. Yes, I have."

And she realized at that moment that she had missed him and his calm steadfastness, his reserved earnestness, and his deep intelligence. She wondered now how she could have taken him for granted all these years. He finally seemed as attractive to her inside as he had always seemed outside.

"Hey, you want to go by and see Mama and Papa?"

"Sure, but I gotta know. Do you really call him 'Papa'?"

"Yeah," Willia laughed. "I always do. Wanna make something of it?" They left Mama Trinie's laughing. As they stepped onto the sidewalk, Doug grabbed Willia's hand.

"It's about time you went out with me again." He leaned down and kissed her on her lips before he turned and opened her door for her.

Olivia, Arthur, and their daughters were visiting Rainey and William when Willia and Doug arrived. The adults laughed and talked with great ease over many cups of coffee. After all, Doug had been a part of their lives for years now.

Olivia and her family left at about 8:00 to get the girls to bed. As they left, William and Arthur invited Doug to come fishing with them and "Big Arthur" soon. Doug allowed as how he loved the serenity of fishing, and Arthur said, "Man, now you know from the last time you went fishing with our crowd that we make a lotta noise."

"Oh, yeah," Doug laughed. "That was most of the fun right there. The noise factor!"

Willia and Doug finally left Rainey's at about 9:30 that night. Back on Cotton Place, Doug and Willia sat in contented silence in his '57 Chevy.

"Doug, I really had a good time tonight. What took you so long to ask me again?"

"Oh, I don't know. You seemed ... spoken for, or something. So I finally asked Sarah Fletcher about you. You two seem to be pretty good friends."

"Yeah, that's my buddy. What did Miss Sarah say about me?"

"That's Mrs. Sarah to you and me." They laughed.

"Yeah, she is pretty taken with being a wife, isn't she? So? What did she tell you?"

"She said she never heard you talk about anybody at all. So, I figured that was my big chance. So here we are."

"Here we are," Willia agreed, and settled back in his big front seat. "I know it's late, but why don't you come in for a little while?"

"Hey, why not," Doug laughed as he came around to her side of the car to open her door for her.

As they walked down her petunia - bedecked walk to her front door, they heard a frenzied rustling of the bushes that led around to the back of her house. Willia's heart hardly had time to jump. Buck Crowder, wielding a rifle, blocked their entrance to Willia's door. Willia screamed, and house lights went off up and down Cotton Place. Neighbors got quiet to see what was going on.

At that point, everything happened so quickly that it was only later that Willia understood that Doug, who was only surprised, moved with more speed than Buck Crowder, who was enraged. So when Buck charged at Doug with the rifle raised ax-like above his head, his mouth filled with foul curses and oaths, Doug simply lowered his head and charged at Buck's stomach, knocking the wind out of him, and then rose into a tight boxer's stance. He had sent Buck sprawling backward across Willia's steps. Buck saw stars of a different twinkle when the back of his head met with stiff opposition from Willia's bottom step.

Down Cotton Place, Mrs. Rosa Jones looked anxiously at her husband Henry snoring in his reclining chair, and called the police and then Rainey. Up Cotton Place, Mrs. Evelyn Hunter shushed her toddlers, called the police, and then got a busy signal at Rainey's. Across Cotton Place, Miss Vivian Malone called the police and then called her distant cousin Arthur Seaton, the younger. By the time Buck Crowder recovered his wind, still clutching Minnie, at least three representatives of Raleigh's finest stood over him, guns drawn and aimed at his throbbing head. Buck dropped his rifle and raised his hands in a gesture of reluctant surrender. Only then did Douglass Baxter relax his boxer's stance.

As Buck was led away in handcuffs, loudly vowing to get even, Doug's only concern was for Willia, who was silent now, but who seemed deathly afraid. And beneath that, she seemed resigned. Her parents and her brother-in-law got to her house in record time and joined Doug, whom they thanked profusely, in escorting Willia into her living room. Mrs. Rosa, Mrs. Evelyn, and Miss Vivian, all in various colorful housedresses, followed the family into the house. While William, Rosa, and Evelyn fussed over her and made sure she was all right, Miss Vivian fussed over Doug. After all, she hadn't seen too many men come calling to Willia Davis's house, and she hadn't seen this one in quite a while. She had to size this one up.

Rainey slipped away, with a stony face and tears welling in her amber eyes, to Willia's bedroom to pack underwear, slacks, toiletries, and dresses enough to last for at least a week. Arthur simply fumed, walking up and down, smoking Camels. He had written enough "Crime Beat" articles on Buck Crowder during his years at The Carolinian to know that this cat was more trouble than he was worth. He was not puzzled about Buck's obsession with Willia; after all, he had been known to become fixed on certain women before, with or without their willing participation in the games. He finally remembered to call Olivia to let her know that her big sister was just fine, he would explain it all when he got home.

William went to the phone after Arthur and put in a call to Millard Peebles, the masonry and construction man who did much of the home improvements for Raleigh's black residents. Within five minutes, William had made arrangements for Peebles's men to erect a seven-foot barbed wire fence around Willia's house. When he explained that this was an emergency, Peebles immediately made arrangements to have the fence in place within the next three days. When he hung up the phone, he said to Rainey: "Do you need me to help you get her packed?"

But by that time Rainey was finished with both a suitcase and a dress bag that she had found easily in Willia's tidy closet.

"All ready, sweetheart," she said, and winked gently at William. Rainey then went to sit on the arm of the chair where Willia slouched, dazed.

"Willia, what in the world was a Buck Crowder doing runnin' up on y'all," Mrs. Rosa asked with her gentle bluntness.

Willia, still in shock, muttered only, " I reckon he thought he had the right," The women were silent, and over the heads of Doug and Willia and Rainey, they looked at each other with raised and puzzled eyebrows.

Ultimately Willia told Doug   and her family a highly doctored version of the true   story: Buck Crowder had been pursuing her for   months, but she had rebuffed his advances. Buck, as her family well knew,   was not one to take no for an answer, and as his advances were more likely to be denied, he was more likely to get meaner.   They all figured he had finally snapped when he had seen her with   a man.

"Well, you come on go home   with us, and you   stay just as long as you need to,"   William said as he and Arthur gently helped her to her feet. The   Cotton Place neighbors promised to keep their eyes peeled on Willia's house. Rainey drove Willia's car and Doug followed Willia's family over to the Davis home

That night in the big white house on Person Street, no one slept and coffee was abundant. And no one thought it out of the ordinary that Douglass Baxter kept vigil with them.

The summer of 1959 was glorious if for no other reason than that the heat was less laden with humidity than usual for a North Carolina summer.   During the summer of 1958, heat lay upon their sweltering bodies like dusty, woolen cloaks, and for Olivia the pointlessness of that heat was belabored by her own internal roaster, as Millicent was not born until September 5 that year.   Willia quietly remembered that during that smoky summer of '58, she had engaged in some acts with Buck Crowder that were still illegal on the pages of North Carolina law books. She blushed as she pushed those memories away, and was grateful for Doug Baxter's full presence in her life.

The summer of 1959 was one that allowed the Davis women the luxury of sitting on the   rambling porch on South Person Street, rocking languorously in black wrought iron chairs with huge tulip designs. The best times for languorous rocking came   during   the   hour   before   those   glorious   afternoon thunderstorms.   First, the too-bright sun slid behind some dark clouds. If the slide was quick enough, unsuspecting street lights went to work. The sky darkened to a luminous charcoal gray as the wind picked up.   Then the dust from that unpaved part of Lee Street (the only block of Lee that was paved was Buck Crowder's block -- perhaps for easy police access to Crowder?) lifted up from the rock strewn surface in a jingly little dance, finally raising itself to a stylized maelstrom, right in the middle of that block of Lee between Person and Blount Streets.

Then the leaves turned bottoms up all over Person Street, shaking themselves in frantic anticipation and sounding like pom-poms. Empty porch chairs rocked crazily with no weight to anchor them, and gradually the thunder timpanied to a wondrous crescendo. Lightning cracked. And through it all, the Davis women sat, rocking their tulip chairs as if a children's parade were passing by, talking easily about their sundries: teaching, clothes, church, their men, children, and gossip in just enough installments to keep talk spicy.

For Rainey, Willia's return home meant that her lively child had made a full recovery from her time in whatever hell she had placed herself in. One porch-sitting afternoon, Rainey smiled at Willia and said: "Glad you're back with us, baby."

Willia looked surprised. "Mama, I never left."

Olivia cleared her throat. "Yeah, you did. I'm glad you're back too."

Willia blushed. Had Buck Crowder's violent sexual hold over her been so obvious?

They grew silent for a moment, each given over to her own thoughts.

Rainey still felt fury at a low boil each time she thought about that Crowder monster trying to hurt Willia. She didn't much care what kind of relationship, if any, Willia had had with Buck; he still had no right to try to hurt her.

Olivia was relieved that whatever had been going on between Buck and Willia had ended without her sister getting hurt. She felt a little ashamed that she was curious about what Buck was like in bed -- and if Willia had found out. She felt sheltered, as if she had gone from the protection of one man, her father, to the care of another man, her husband, and there had been little life for herself in between the two havens. Olivia worried about Willia, but she envied her more than a little.

Willia worked very hard to push all memories of Buck Crowder from her mind. She was horrified that she had changed so much in those months with him that her family had noticed the change and thought it drastic. She slammed the door on her memories of Buck and started a new line of conversation.

"Did y'all hear about Macey Crowder other day?" Willia sat straighter in her chair in anticipation of telling this tale. She had changed the subject, but she had kept it in Buck's family for now. She felt that was a good way to move away from him completely.

"Nah. What she done done now?" Olivia was now browsing through the Ebony magazine that had earlier served as a fan.

"Uh-uh. Tell it, child." Rainey sipped her iced tea and pushed her hated bifocals up her nose.

"They tell me she was --" with exaggerated airs "-- incarcerated downtown."

"Aw, that ain't news."

"They tell me she looked out her --" clearing of the throat "-- suite window and saw her sister Dovie's boy Billy Junior walking down Wilmington Street with some of his friends."

In unison. "Um-hmm?"

"I heard she leaned all out the way out the window, yelling 'Billy! Billy Junior!' Billy Junior tried his best to ignore her, but, naw, she kept on, 'til finally he did look up. Well, by this time, all Billy Junior's friends were just about dead laughing at him. He was so embarrassed, he didn't know what to say to her. So he said, 'Ma'am?' kinda like he was mad but respectful at the same time. 'Looky here, Billy Junior, tell yo' mama where I'm is. Tell 'er I'm-a be home in 'bout two-three days.' Those boys just about laid out in the sidewalk laughing."

Rainey and Olivia threw back their heads, laughing in perfect harmony.

"What'd he say then, Will?"

Willia bowed her head and stuck out her bottom jaw. "'Yes, ma'am, I will.'"

The women laughed together, embellishing Willia's story with their own anecdotes about the Crowder family, carefully avoiding any mention of Buck.

"I'll never forget the time old Jo-Jo "Drunken" Walser, Macey's old sorry husband, got so drunk he couldn't even walk forward."

Olivia, who like Willia had heard the story before, egged her mother on. "What did he do, Ma?"

"What you think? Walked backwards!" Rainey sat, looking delighted, as her daughters laughed together. Willia got up and imitated JoJo "Drunken" Walser's three steps up, half step back progression down the streets of South Park with such skill that even little Honey looked up from Caddie Woodlawn to giggle at her aunt's antics. This expert imitation confirmed for Honey her dearest ambition: she wanted to be just like Aunt Willia when she grew up.

Little Millicent, almost a year old now, stood close by them in her well-padded playpen, rocking determinedly from side to side, singing her baby songs. She joined in with their raucous laughter with a cackle all her own. Her contribution to the gaiety made the women laugh harder as they hastened into a marathon of Jo-Jo "Drunken" Walser recollections.

"Well, Mama, what IS Jo-Jo "Drunken" Walser 's real name?"

"Um." Rainey stopped to consider this question for a moment. "I think it's Walter ... or is it George? I can't remember 'cause all we ever called him was "Breezy" when he was little fella."

Willia and Olivia sang in unison. "'Breezy'?! Why?"

"'Cause he was always breaking wind! Have you ever known Negroes to name their folk off the mark? We used to call Macy 'Miss T' when they had their first baby, and later it got shortened to 'Misty.' The 'T' stood for 'Tits' as long as I knew her 'cause she had a baby by him when she was about fourteen or fifteen and she'd sit out on Polly's front porch and nurse that baby for the world and all to see."

Olivia chimed in, "Well, we used to call his brother 'Jack Daniels.' I never did know his real name, either."

And so their conversations continued until the wind picked up to a fierceness that knocked over one of the black chairs. Then the women and Honey leaned the chairs forward against the white wood walls of the porch, someone picked up sweet Millicent and folded down her playpen, gathered up Rainey's beautiful potted plants, and headed inside.

During that summer, Willia never stayed at her Cotton Place home, even after Millard Peebles's men constructed the barbed wire fence. She knew that Buck had been found guilty of trespassing, illegal possession of a firearm, malicious mischief, and communicating a threat. She knew that he was probably going to be in jail until the middle of August. She also knew that he was ordered to stay at least five hundred yards from both Doug and her at all times. But she could not shake the fear that somehow he would break out of the Wake County Jail and make good those threats he had communicated to them....

Buck Crowder could not remember ever having been so committed to anything as the passion that had rendered him a brooding and quiet man. He had lived his life for 45 years on sheer animal instinct. When he was hungry, he ate, when he was horny, he screwed, when he was angry, he hit. The only planning that he had known in his life was the guards' harsh orders to him during his stays in prison. Now he was a man transformed by his commitment to get Willia Davis.

He had begun his planning while he was in the county jail. He decided that he would follow her any chance he got. He would figure out her routes to and from everywhere she went. He would get to recognize all of her friends, those friends that she was always too ashamed for him to meet, so that he would be able to follow them to Willia. And he knew that sooner or later he was going to follow her to a place where she was completely alone. Okay, he then considered, what would he do with her once he followed her to that lonely place?

He thought about that while he was being transferred from the Wake County Jail to what folks in South Park called the State Hotel over on Morgan Street. It was enroute to Central Prison that Buck Crowder decided to police-proof his home. He had to make sure that he only beat her ass in a room that had been made as close to sound proof as possible. He thought about the worthless little hi-fi he had to play his record albums on. That piece of shit couldn't possibly cover up any leftover noises. He wondered if he could con his mother out of the floor model hi-fi that his kiss-ass sister Macey had given her for Christmas. Naw, forget that. He would get his own damn stereo. He knew his partner Dolby would be out to Central to see him. Dolby could get anything, so Dolby would be the one to help him with the soundproofing of the kick-ass room.....

Then he remembered that his attic was big enough to be a room. Sure, no adult could stand straight up there, but he could pad that place up and steel it up and make himself a right nice little kick-ass room. So. It was gonna be the attic, then. And he decided that he damn sure wasn't going to tell Dolby everything he was going to be up to when he got out. He would just tell Dolby to get the supplies he needed from Willoughby's Building Supply, where they both worked -- when they were both out of jail. Dolby had a key to his house; he could just ease the stuff into the house as he got it....

Neither her parents nor her sister made any comment at all about Willia's quiet move back into her old bedroom. Without ever discussing it, one (or all) of them always escorted her to the house when she went to check her mail or went to get more clothes. Not a word was uttered by anyone as she gradually moved her potted plants and her jazz albums back into her old room, which was as large as the living room and dining room on Cotton Place.

For Rainey, the most important aspect in Willia's move back home was that Willia was truly back: her effervescent, comical child had made a full recovery from whatever trouble had been chasing her down. Rainey was more than grateful. The change in Willia had been so intense that it was becoming difficult for her to remember those great sayings and mannerisms of her favorite comic.

Willia had been so distant from her family during the previous summer that she had barely been present at their annual all-family weekend at Tesima. Rainey and William had owned a little house there since 1950. The house had been a dream realized for Rainey and William, who were passionate about taking beach vacations. How wonderful, how pleasurable it would be, they had often mused wistfully, to go to the beach and stay as long as they wanted, without having to worry about trying to get back to Raleigh before sundown because there was really nowhere for Negroes to spend the night! When they had heard about Tesima, they had tapped into their carefully lined nest egg to build their own little paradise house right on the oceanfront. The house had been designed by the elder Davises, in consultation with their builder.

With Rainey's fine eye for style and economy, the Davises built a house that was cinderblock at the bottom and green masonite siding at the top. To the left of their modest one-car garage, the Davises had a chimney/grill built for summer gatherings. On the ground floor of the house were two bedrooms, a den/playroom, a small bathroom with a shower, and a well room; in those days, all the Tesima houses relied on wells for their water supplies. Upstairs, all the walls and ceilings were of shellacked knotty pine. In the living room, William designed recessed lights at the top of each wall. The living room's back door led directly onto their old-fashioned screened porch, and a side door from that porch led to a ramp and staircase directly down onto the sands of Topsail Island. The living room flowed directly into their modest kitchen, the window of which faced Ocean Drive. To the left of the living room/kitchen stretched a long hallway. The first room on the right was Rainey's music room, William's special present to his beloved wife. He had the carpenter install special acoustic panels in the ceiling to give her piano playing an extra beauty. The rest of the upstairs was composed of a master bedroom, two smaller bedrooms, and a full bathroom. Though modest on the outside, with its flower boxed azaleas and simple landscaping, the Davis's beach home was as comfortable as any year-round home. It was one of the first homes in the Surf City community of Tesima.

Rainey still felt bewildered when she remembered the usually sociable Willia's solitary walks along the shore during the summer of 1958, her frenetic chain-smoking, and her nervousness, none of which had desisted until about two hours before they were to return home.

Where is Mama's Willia, Rainey had teased gently during that long weekend. As usual, the trip was a 72-hour frolic for the Davises, who were, during that muggy summer, nine-and-a-half strong, much to the discomfort of the waddling Olivia.

Oh, Mama, I'm just tired, that's all, Willia had said somewhat dismissively, searching in her purse for a fresh pack of Newports to chain smoke.

Well, do you mind if I walk with you? You haven't talked with me in ages!

Rainey and Willia had walked along the shore for a brief time, their arms intertwined, each silently staring at the majesty of the ocean, neither saying a word to the other. Rainey squeezed her daughter's arm several times, partly as reassurance, mostly as a prompt. Talk to me, girl, the squeeze insisted. And if Rainey added a little nudge to that squeeze, both she and Willia knew that she meant to say, What is your problem, daughter? Where have you gone? And, in the cloak-heavy heat of that summer of 1958, Willia Evelyn Davis never arose from her brooding to respond to her mother.

But in that glorious summer of 1959, Willia was fully back.

"Mama!" Willia bound into the music room on the Friday afternoon of their 1959 visit, where Rainey sat placidly at her "old beat-up piano," playing a Gershwin-Ellington conglomeration of her own concocting. All the Davises were outside playing in or near the water. Rainey, who had heard her daughter's forceful stomping in from the screened back porch, pretended to be startled.

"What!"

"Come walk with me and Doug!"

"But, I'm --"

"Please?"

"Okay, sweetheart."

The three of them walked along the shore, their feet sinking into the sand as they strolled. They were the calm in the midst of a maelstrom of squealing children and water-splashing adults.

"Miss Rainey," Doug said, and Rainey was reminded for a chilling second of Step's term of endearment for her. "Willia tells me that Tesima has a history. Would you tell me about it?"

"Well, I'll tell you what I've heard over the years. But I don't know where the real story ends and the legend begins. I call it the 'gospel according to John Amos'."

In 1949, just as the beach town of Surf City, North Carolina on the island of Topsail was being incorporated, a gorgeous lady lay dying and heir-less in Wilmington. She was heir-less through an act of her own dominant impatience, having written all of her ostensibly errant children our of her massive will. She lay on her king-sized four-poster bed, her thick locks of white hair spread out around her striking, square-jawed face. She had lived 68 years, and, having come from only near-wealth, she had possessed the good common sense to marry into extreme wealth. And the source of that extreme wealth had the common courtesy to precede her in death.

She was Josephine Austin Little, of the Wilmington Littles and the Ahoskie Austins. In attendance upon her was her one great love, John Amos Sutton, a 65-year-old butler and loyal lodge brother in the Kabala Temple, a national brotherhood of Negro masons. Sutton, a native of Charlotte, North Carolina, had worked for the Austin Littles for 33 years at the time of Mrs. Austin Little's final illness, and they had grown old together. Both had maintained normal family lives outside of their relationship; however, on Thursday and Saturday afternoons for 29 of those 33 years, Sutton drove Mrs. Austin Little to her beach manse one hour away on Topsail Island where they danced in the ballroom and made exquisite love beneath the chandeliers or the classic ceiling fans as the fancy took them.

They never worried much that they would be found out, apparently. Mrs. Austin Little's spouse was about as interested in her as he was in their Afghan Hound, Cherish. She had only to remain slim and beautiful and cultured so that she would not embarrass her husband at the many parties they were required to attend as part of North Carolina society. And so, until John Amos Sutton entered their employ, she had only to give birth to children for the nannies to rear, and choose fashions for her seamstress to create. Even the family menu was left to the chef.

John Amos Sutton was good, really good, in every way to Josephine, and his goodness paid off. In the end, it was John and only John who bathed Josephine's withered body, that body which was once so fabulous and completely submissive to his own. He spoon-fed her the clear broth she hated so fiercely, and he cleaned her and her bed when that broth invariably returned a few minutes later. He read novels and sang to her. Meanwhile, her children sort of breezed in and out to check on her. The only lengthy visits she had now were from her doctors. John Amos Sutton told his wife Mary to be patient; he was being paid handsomely for his dedicated service. He knew that he was in Josephine Austin Little's will, he even knew what he was due to receive; however, he never mentioned these facts to his wife.

When Josephine Austin Little wrote her children out of her will, she left her fortune, minus $75,000, to charities that she had either supported or admired during her life. For example, she would never dare openly support the efforts of the United Negro College Fund or the National Association for the Advancement of

Colored People in her socialite's life; however, both agencies received well over $40,000 each from her estate. As for her mansion in Wilmington, it was sold after her death and the proceeds divided among the errant three, who were guilty only of inattention to their mother. The mansion and six acres surrounding it at Topsail, in what was becoming Surf City, were willed to John Amos Sutton to do with as he wished. The remaining $75,000 Sutton received also, and with that money he saw to it that his six children and wife Mary were comfortable before he disappeared from their lives forever into an idyllic life at Topsail Island.

John Amos Sutton never loved Josephine Austin Little. Indeed, he had never loved his wife Mary, and as for his children, well, they were his responsibility, and he was never one to forsake responsibility. There was only one woman, one person, John Amos Sutton had ever loved: his baby sister Tessie Mae Sutton. He was deeply and desperately hurt and embarrassed about his feelings toward her. He felt cursed that his own sister could make him wish for intimate relations, as he modestly called his feelings. Rather than act on these incestuous feelings, John Amos Sutton slipped away from Charlotte as soon as he could, joining the Navy and traveling around various ports on the East Coast. In Norfolk, he finally met Mary, a woman who looked enough like Tessie Mae, but whose disposition was dissimilar from Tessie's sweet, laughing personality. He married Mary about four months after they met, and he never mentioned that he had a sister named Tessie Mae.

So when Josephine Austin Little died leaving him all of that glorious property, he sold the mansion to an enterprising, and he thought, insane white man who had it moved off the land by six huge trucks and an infinity of pulleys and ropes down to the south end of the island. The man had been searching for a mansion, but had been unable to find one until he happened upon John looking up in wonder at his. Both parties were satisfied; John had told this man that he hated to tear the house down, but what could a colored man do with a big old house down on a beach in the South? With the house out of the way, John built himself a six-bedroom house on the spot, even though he still did not contact his family to tell them where or how he was. He divided the remaining acreage into 30 plots, contacted 30 of his lodge brothers whom he knew had the means to buy the property, advertising the property as "The New and Exciting Development of Tesima." He sold the land for $900 per lot, and, with the combined proceeds of his sale of the mansion and his rapid sales of the lots, John Amos Sutton became a wealthy man by the standards of the day. He next contracted with several masonry contractors, including Millard Peebles and Raymond Smith of Raleigh, to have houses built on the lots.

Among the first lodge brothers to buy property was William Davis of Raleigh.

John Amos Sutton would still be very active in the community he had developed as late as 1965, and he was largely responsible for the legendary annual July family pig pickin' and seafood festival, an event that is still enormously popular among Tesima families even now.

And so it was to this July gathering that all of the Davis children and their families went in that glorious summer of 1959, that final summer of idyllic happiness among them. It was there in the dining room of the oceanfront summer home of William and Rainey Davis that Douglass Baxter asked Willia Davis to marry him and she turned him down; after all they had only been dating seriously for a few months. But she urged him to ask her again in oh, say, three months or so, and she was sure the answer would be different. But it was also there in that dining room that Willia Davis knew she was in love, gratefully in love, with Douglass Baxter. She would always appreciate him for the kind and loving man he was, but more importantly she would always be thankful to him and to the God in whom she had regained faith for rescuing her from a deadly situation.

But there were times, late at night, when seagulls cried and waves washed desolately across the shore and the earth seemed to wipe away the smudges and slights of the day to rest itself for the bright day to come, that Willia remembered: a biting and sucking mouth all over her body, a body that was caught up in relentless rhythms that mothers who were ladies never told you about, guttural screams from the dregs of an unexplored id.

She looked out into the black sweet breeze of those late beach nights and recalled palpable fear and loathing ... deep fear, utter loathing... Memories flooded over her; powerful, skin-tingling memories that caused her nearly to swoon before their potency. Who had she become in that time with ... him? A sex machine? An addict? Why had the sex been so intoxicating for her? She shook her head in confusion each time she was forced to recall.   And she would never forget that a deep part of her innermost self had been brought out like a raging hemorrhoid (she snickered bitterly) and she would never forget to hate (fear) the man who had forced it out of her.

As they walked along the shore during that long July weekend, holding hands, Willia searched for her beloved moonstones while Doug gazed at her, awestruck, as she did so. She squeezed his hand often to remind herself that he was really in her life and that she was truly free again to be the Willia Davis she had nearly ceased to be.

At nightfall, they danced on the beach and sang to each other:

Trust in me in all you do,
Have the faith I have in you.
Love will see us through,
if only you trust in me.

And when he asked her to marry her again exactly three months later, armed with a diamond solitaire, Douglass Baxter was both joyful and relieved to hear her say yes. It was that night and no night before that they made love in his Method home. They both felt it was worth the wait, but afterward, in the midst of all her bliss and their ecstatic finish, Willia cried herself to sleep on Doug's strong shoulder. Having put the late beach nights behind her, she would never understand why she was so overcome. She could only tell Doug, "It's not you. I have never been happier. Maybe that's why I'm crying. I just don't know."

She was a hit with Douglass's family, as he had been with hers, when they took the long train ride to Brunswick, Georgia that Thanksgiving of 1959. It was in Brunswick that they set their wedding date for May 21, 1960. It was in Brunswick that Willia, in a giddy state of mind, began to write her name as "Willia Davis Baxter." They returned to Raleigh in a glow, ready to plan their life together.

In the weeks after he was released from prison, Buck Crowder bided his time. He went back to work at Willoughby's Carpentry Works, where he was greeted with decidedly mixed reactions. As the company bully, he governed the kind of day the workers would have. If Buck was unhappy, everybody was unhappy. He was likely to pick an argument with anyone -- except the boss -- when he was in a foul mood. After this stay in prison, Buck Crowder had been a little sullen, but much more withdrawn than anyone could remember him being. He seemed always to have something on his mind. He had stopped bragging about his educated woman; after all, everyone on the job knew that his incarceration had some connection to his relationship with her. Nobody really wondered if his brooding mood and his silence about Willia had any connection. They were all so relieved just not to be bullied....

He had driven by her house on Cotton Place at least three times each week since his release. He'd only seen her there once, and that high seditty sonofabitch had been there with her. He knew that she seemed to be staying at her parents' house, even though there was now a seven-foot high fence around her little Cotton Place house with ivy draped across the barbed wire. The sight of that ivy infuriated him almost to the point of apoplexy; this bitch was really off her rocker if she thought she needed to -- that she **could** hide from him. His plan was much too airtight for him not to catch her and make her pay.

Rainey called Willie Otey Kay as soon as Willia told her the wedding date. "My baby is getting married at last, Willie. I need you to do the wedding gown. When can we come see you?" Willie scheduled the time and then reminded Rainey that her nephew Jimmy Taylor's wife Bessie made some mighty good wedding cakes, but she was busy with her young daughters, Camille and Carmen, so the sooner Rainey called her, the better.

The Davis household was in a pleasant uproar as November melted away into December. Willia had by now moved out of the Cotton Place house altogether, and was devoting herself to this role as fiancée, devoted daughter, and renewed teacher. So when Arthur mentioned to her carefully right after her Thanksgiving trip that Buck Crowder was out of jail, she shrugged and tried to hide the sudden tremor in her hands.

"He still has to stay away from me, right?"

"Yeah, and you should be okay, because I heard he met his match in the joint this time. Seems he tried to break bad with the wrong cat and got cut up pretty badly."

"Good. I just feel safer here with Mama and Papa. I'm glad I moved out of the other house because he might try to get in -- " Her sudden silence was more telling to Arthur than if she had kept talking. He looked at his sister-in-law sharply, his journalist's mind clicking and his photographic memory whirring alive, but he said only: "Just be glad you didn't get hurt."

As the fifties faded into the sixties, Willia Evelyn Davis's life became all the more regulated and hopeful. She and Doug were only separated at Christmas, when he went home to be with his family. But he brought his younger sister back to Raleigh with him and accompanied all the Davises to the Omega Psi Phi New Year's Eve cabaret at the Arcade Hotel. Arthur Seaton, emcee for the evening, announced his sister-in-law's May wedding to Brother Douglass Baxter. The entire room cheered.

And in the kitchen of the Arcade Hotel, one of the dishwashers considered how he could send poisoned lemon drops to the Davis party.

Life was now better -- and saner -- than it had ever been for Willia Davis as an adult. She looked ahead now to a life with Doug that was infinitely less exciting than her Cave days (and her Buck nights) and breathed a sigh. Sometimes excitement was not a good thing.

As winter mellowed into spring, all of Willia's wedding plans were complete. Rainey relaxed back into her own life as the mother of three reasonably normal children and stopped worrying about Buck Crowder's role in Willia's life.

Rainey signed on with the NAACP to campaign for the 1960 presidential campaign. Although it was merely primary time, most everyone felt that John F. Kennedy would be the likely Democratic nominee for president that year. Negroes felt so hopeful in Raleigh during that time. It was like that lull you feel just before a long awaited loved one returns home after many years. Maybe this time Negroes would get their richly deserved rights as first-class citizens. Although Rainey didn't want to do a lot of mixing with whites, she did want to feel that when she went downtown to shop or take care of business like other citizens of Raleigh, she was going to be treated with respect beyond mere tolerance.

Spring dawned upon the Davis household like a genesis: Willia was truly back home, and life as a Negro could possibly acquire more equitable terms.

Willia sighed in her contentment often during those sweet spring days; in just over two weeks, she and Douglass would be married. Life was good.

CHAPTER SEVENTEEN

Turmoil

May was usually a good time for Willia. As much as she enjoyed her students, it was a pleasure just to look forward to the imminent end of another school year. She expected as much this year. But there was so much to do to get ready for the wedding. By May first, Willia often found herself downtown or in the quaint Cameron Village shopping center, looking for just the right napkins, or the perfect earrings.

Wednesday, May 4 was no different. She arrived home from work at about 3:45 that afternoon, with Douglass in tow. While Doug and William sat in the living room, talking over some "man stuff" as the women liked to scoff, Willia cooked alongside her mother and her sister in Rainey's rambling kitchen. They sang spirituals, in perfect harmony, as they cut and chopped and peeled and basted together. Honey joined them, and Millicent squealed along with them, too. The younger women even almost had a food fight, but Rainey stopped them, concerned as always about the aftermath of their giddiness. After dinner, Willia sat between her Papa and Doug on the huge old couch just like old times, holding Papa's hand and talking with both men about everything and nothing. In such a happy environment, it was easy to forget that the man who had come after her with a gun lived just around the corner. She hardly gave Buck Crowder a thought anymore, didn't wonder why she hadn't seen him anywhere around Raleigh since his release from jail.

So when Annie "Pixie" Wilson called at about 6:00 to say that she was in town from Charlotte for a long weekend, Willia felt comfortable enough with the sweet, still peace of her life to suggest that they "grab a quick movie." Pixie was fond of Willia's college chum, Rosetta Foster Brown, so Willia called Rosetta and told her that she had been such a devoted wife and mother, there would be no harm in her going to the movies, even on a week night. Rosetta agreed, anxious for a short break from her man and her menchildren. Pixie and Rosetta arrived at the Davis home about half an hour later. After a few minutes of giggles and teases, Willia and her friends left Doug and the rest of the Davises to watch the Huntley-Brinkley Report while they headed downtown to the Lincoln Theatre. It was only when Willia got into Rosetta's little Plymouth that she thought about Buck Crowder, and hoped he would not see her while she was out.

As they left, Willia hugged her fiancé and kissed her father's forehead, commenting, "Hmmm, Papa. That hairline is taking on a new shape, I do believe." William laughed and squeezed her hand. Rainey stood up to receive Willia's kiss, and her eyes glistened as she removed her bifocals. She smiled at Willia.

"Now you be a good girl, hear?" Rainey grabbed Willia's shoulders to give her a playful hug, and suddenly, inexplicably, she hugged her daughter fiercely. The glistening in her eyes overflowed as she kissed her child on the cheek.

"Mama!" Willia pulled back, shocked and concerned. "What is it," she asked quietly.

Rainey had no idea what "it" was, only that it shook her so strongly when she touched Willia's shoulders that she grabbed at Willia in that instant to hold onto the reality of her daughter.

"I'm just so glad you're back here with us, baby. I know you want to go out with your friends ..., so you go on. Mama loves you."

Willia looked at her mother curiously for a moment and then said, "And Willia loves Mama." Willia smiled down at her mother. "You're really all right?"

"Yes, ma'am." They laughed softly, and Willia turned to her friends.

"Okay, now. All right y'all. I'm ready." And with a mischievous smile, Willia straightened her jacket and left with her friends.

Rainey hurried upstairs to her bathroom, her eyes streaming. She felt a slight chill, but she shook it away from her like dust from an old blanket. She stared at herself in the mirror for a long, puzzled time. Then she headed over to Laurence's for a few hours of solace, Ragland style.

From his tiny bathroom window, Buck Crowder watched the women leave Lawyer Davis's house. He noted the direction in which they traveled up Person Street, and during the two-minute headstart he gave them, he checked the bolts that held the back door and windows slammed shut. Satisfied that the blinds against all his windows were tightly secured, he went outside to fire up the little Ford. He missed his Buick, but this car wasn't known to anyone (Willia).

He trailed them and entered the Lincoln about five minutes after they did. As he strode through the lobby of the theater, he looked at the layout of it. The concession stand was separated from the main lobby by a partition so that the attendant there would not be able to see things going on near the bathrooms or the door leading to the street. The floor was carpeted with cheap carpet on top of plush padding, so footsteps were muffled. I might just get my chance in here, he smiled to himself.

He sat through Anna Lucasta (This ain't nothin' but some bullshit! That's what niggers get for running around with whores.) The women sat motionless, second row center, through the entire movie. But during the break before Carmen Jones (Just one mo' whore!), they all walked to the back of the theater, laughing softly, apparently headed for the bathroom. They walked out during the credits, so they didn't know who was in the darkened room with them.

Buck Crowder smiled wickedly to himself. I'm gonna fix her ass tonight.

His chance came about halfway through Carmen Jones, when Willia and Pixie rushed out into the lobby. Buck followed them out, hanging back in the shadows. Both women went into the bathroom (a-damn-gain?! What the hell do women do in the john?), but, as they came back out into the lobby, unbeknownst to Willia, Pixie turned back into the bathroom. Pixie would later tell Rainey and William that she had forgotten her lipstick. Unaware of her solitude, Willia stepped into the deserted lobby. Buck acted swiftly; he was sure the other girl would be out any second. He rushed up to Willia, one hand thrust with easy menace into his pocket.

"How ya doin', Willia," he slurred, enjoying the sheer horror that leapt into her lovely face.

"Oh, hi, Buck. How are you?" Willia's voice cracked as she turned to look at Pixie. She entered into hysteria when she found herself alone with Buck.   His grasp was deadly firm, but not painful.

"Let me talk to you for a minute."   Before Willia could protest or struggle away from him, he put one massive hand across her face and dragged her across the cheap floral carpeting and out the front door of the Lincoln into the still, closed night. All that Pixie saw of any of this was a slim section of the back of Buck Crowder's head. She looked around for Willia for a moment, and then, assuming that she had gone back into the theater, headed back in. To her confusion, she found only Rosetta second row center.

"What happened to Willia?"

"I thought she was with you."

"Maybe she went back into the bathroom?'   But neither woman was convinced of this possibility.

They searched the darkened theatre, the lobby, and the bathroom frantically, calling for Willia. They looked at each other, and said together: "Let's go."

They went back into the darkened theatre, and got their coats, searching each row once more for a familiar silhouette. Dorothy Dandridge, Harry Belafonte, and company were now completely forgotten.

Maybe she was hiding? That would be too silly; 32-year-olds didn't hide! Rosetta and Pixie stared at each other and headed for the street.   Neither had any notion of Buck Crowder's existence in Willia's life.   After ten minutes of searching every storefront, every parking lot in the two square block area, they hurried to alert Willia's family.

CHAPTER EIGHTEEN

Intersections

Y ou need to wait at least 48 hours after she was last seen," the police officer growled to William, his voice only barely tempered with tolerance because William Davis was highly regarded by some of the powers that were in Raleigh at the time. Rainey listened on the living room extension, hardly able to contain her rage at this cracker boy's indifference toward the endangerment of another human being's life.

"But she disappeared. She was on her way back from the bathroom at the movies, and all of a sudden she wasn't there. And besides, I'm pretty sure I know where she is."

"Where?" The police officer sounded almost bored.

"Buck Crowder's place, 3-- East Lee Street."

"Why do you think that?"

"Because he tried to kill her a few months ago and he went to jail because of it."

"All right. We'll send a man over there to check. But only because we know Crowder so good. We ain't supposed to consider nobody as missin' 'fore two days have passed."

Rainey sat down heavily in her wingback chair. William stared at her anxiously, still unable to speak. Olivia and Arthur and Doug paced up and down in the living room, which was now alive with William, Laurence, and Arthur's cigarette smoke.

It was 12:30 the next morning.

Rainey paced the floor, rubbing her palms against seemingly permanent goose bumps. She couldn't believe the nightmare her family had sunk into. Her little girl had been stolen, and she hadn't even been at home to see about her. Rainey had been out doing with another man what she should only have been doing with her husband, and she had apparently sacrificed her daughter in the process. She looked at Laurence balefully from behind her bifocals, and then looked away, her eyes overflowing with hot tears of shame and anguish. Laurence dropped his head down against his chest, his own shoulders heaving in misery.

They had just sent Rosetta and Pixie home, and after having talked with three policemen, they had finally spoken with the one who'd agreed to send a man over to get the facts as the Davises, Rosetta, and Pixie knew them.

"Bitch! You BITCH! Who the hell you thought you was messin' with? You thought you could screw me, take my damn money, and just drop me when you had enough?!"

In an attic room with a swinging light and deadly shadows playing against their glistening nakedness, Willia Evelyn Davis was being raped by her former lover. With each brutal, bloodying stroke of his relentless penis, he spat his hate at her, and after each stroke, he slapped her or punched her or, once, bit away at the delicate lobe of her right ear.

In a padded attic room, just around the corner from her parents' home, and so many miles away, Willia Evelyn Davis felt her eyes slam shut, a few of her ribs crack, her right arm snap, and her will to survive ebb away from her. Buck Crowder beat her for hours and raped her over and over and over. She thought she was paralyzed.

In a padded attic room, so long and far away from the Willia she once was, she felt her womanhood betray her. After one of his slaps or one of his punches, she would never know which, Willia Evelyn Davis felt her clitoris give in to the once delicious sensations of orgasm. She screamed hysterically through her swollen lips as her hips moved against Buck's feverish pelvis, and her rhythms matched his own. And her throat betrayed her too, crying out in agony, shouting forth in obscene passion, before she relaxed, in total release, in the quagmire of throbbing humiliation.

"Uh-huh, I knew you missed this good dick. That sedity nigger probably can't even get it up. Can he?" Slap on the left cheek. "Can he?" Punch on the right cheek. "Can he?" Punch in the stomach, followed by a hot load of saliva aimed successfully at her distended nostrils.

Soon, heavy rope bound her, hand and foot. Buck grabbed Willia by her sweaty hair and pulled her head toward his steaming crotch.

"Now. If you put one tooth mark on me, I will kill you, bitch."

She wept through throbbing eyelids, saliva and snot cascading from her once lovely face as she bent to do his bidding.

"Open this door, Buck Crowder."

Behind her in the misty, warm darkness 2:35 AM, Rainey could hear footsteps rushing toward her. Before her, she could hear muffled footsteps advancing. She stood, arms folded, face grim, ready to stand down this piece of shit who had her baby against her will. She would use language she had not used since she gave birth to that baby.

Finally, Buck Crowder made it to the front door, and stood looking at Rainey, rubbing at his eyes as if he had been aroused out of a deep sleep. By this time, Douglass Baxter stood next to her. Buck Crowder stared at Rainey Davis, his eyes frozen in a bizarre mixture of fake surprise and deadly amusement.

"Give me back my child." For a long moment, their eyes intertwined; surely, if those looks could have killed, there would have been two funerals within the next few days.

"Excuse me, Miz Davis, but I ain't got no idea what you are talking about. The po-lice done already been here this evenin'. They ain't found nothin' either."

"Don't give me that bullshit, Buck Crowder." Later, much later, perhaps, Rainey might look back in amusement at the genuine gasps of shock that she heard forced out of the throats of both Buck and Douglass. But right now, she meant to get her baby back.

"There is not one damn thing my daughter ever did to you that gives you the right to steal her from me."

"Listen lady --"

Rainey nearly made it past Buck Crowder into his tidy, air-freshened room.

"Whoa, now. Is you got you one of them search warrants? 'Specially this time of night. Like I said, the po-lice came up in here with a search warrant and they didn't find Willia Davis or nobody else -- "

"Look," Doug interjected. "What have you done with Willia?"

"I absolutely do not know what the hell you all are talking about."

"Look, Buck Crowder, I don't mind killing you to get my baby back." Buck Crowder looked down at this skinny old lady (old stick bitch) and laughed quietly.

"Ain't no need for that kind of attitude, Miss Lady. I ain't got your daughter. Don't you know I knows when to move on? Why would I waste my time with your daughter? She don't want me. I tell you what, Miz Davis. You come on in and take a look around. You too, Mr. what's-your-name. Y'all look all around the house if you want to. You ain't gonna find nothing."

Buck stood back to let Rainey and Douglass enter, careful to keep his bloodied hands in his pockets. He stood nonchalantly in the living room while they searched. Together, they went through every room in Buck Crowder's house, checking underneath furniture and in closets, pulling furniture away from the wall, knocking on walls. Finally, having found nothing, Rainey and Doug returned to Buck Crowder.

Upstairs in the kick-ass room, Willia Evelyn Davis, bound and gagged, lay naked, bleeding, and unconscious on the dusty floor. Bruises bloomed over her ravaged body.

"I don't know where you got her, but I know you got something to do with my baby being gone. So let me tell you something. Let me find out you got something to do with it, which I know you do, and let my baby get hurt. The next time you hear anything about some lemon drops, they gonna be poisoning your ass."

Rainey slapped at Buck Crowder's shoulder, knocking him back a bit as she walked past him. "Now get the hell out of my way. I will be back." Rainey walked purposefully out of the front door.

Behind her, Douglass Baxter, thinner than Buck Crowder, but several inches taller, walked up close to Buck.

"Listen, man." He, too, was deadly serious. "I know you've got my lady somewhere around here." Doug watched the confirmation leap onto Buck's face as the bare flicker of a wild, jealous look flitted across his features. "You better make sure she's all right next time we see her, or I promise you I will mess you completely up. I, too, will be back."

"Oh, nigger, please. You don't scare no damn body. Get the hell out my house 'fore you stink it up."

"Oh, we can stink it all the way up right now. You want to?"

"Come on, man." Buck Crowder always was a coward when it came to mere hand-to-hand combat with another man, particularly one who had already bested him – and in front of a woman, no less.

"I ain't got no quarrel with you. Now I done told y'all I know Willia Davis did not want me. I understand that. Now why can't y'all understand that I ain't got nothing to do with whatever happened to her?"

"Look, just know that we'd better not find out that you hurt her in any way. I believe you've messed with the wrong girl this time."

Douglass Baxter pushed Buck Crowder across his own living room floor and turned and walked outside with the same resolution as his beloved's mother.

CHAPTER NINETEEN

And Nothing More To Give

Since the first of May, a representative of the Census Bureau had made her way through South Park to conduct interviews for the 1960 census.

Jenna Walton was a Texas-born, self-professed cracker woman who needed a job in mid-1959. She had sort of ended up in Raleigh, partially on the run from an irate lover, partially on the run from a rather nasty past life that was beginning to encroach on her in her 40-plus-year-old settled state.

Jenna had enjoyed immensely her journeys to the little shotguns and ranch-style houses in South Park, with its occasional elegant, two-story home, or to the neat brand new brick homes in Rochester Heights and Biltmore Hills, or even to the hopelessly identical tenements in Chavis Heights or Walnut Terrace. It was in these places that she had experienced her most pleasant, amusing, and edifying times as a "census taker." She had found the ladies of the house she visited to be cordial and oh so ready to talk.

A favorite stop for Jenna some days earlier had been at Mrs. Rainey Davis's house over on Person Street near the intersection of Lee and Person. Mrs. Rainey had just retired from teaching and had plenty of time to chat. Oh, what a life she'd had, too! Jenna knew (almost) all about Step Herndon, Aunt Mittie's beauty parlor and speakeasy, and Rainey Clark's little piece of Washington from 1922 to 1925. Mrs. Rainey was now bursting with excitement about her eldest daughter's upcoming marriage.

By the end of the first week in May, Jenna Walton finally worked her way around to a little green pasteboard shotgun house over on the Bloodworth end of Lee Street. She was startled by two things at this little house: she was not allowed inside, and, in the middle of the day, the man of the house was at home to answer her questions. He'd remodeled it back into a house from a rooming house with his own two hands, he boasted. He stood out on his porch with Jenna, and she noticed that he was careful not to allow her to see into his house. He wasn't rude to her; he just seemed in an awful hurry for her to ask her questions and leave.

She needed to use the bathroom again, and was grateful that Buck had unbound her after his first morning assault upon her damaged body. She could not bear to use the slop jar again; it was full, and the stench from just these few hours of usage was about to knock her out. She knocked and knocked on the little door that led downstairs. Buck must be ignoring her. Or maybe he was gone. She couldn't stand it anymore and tried to pull the little door open, expecting it to be latched from outside. She couldn't believe it. He had forgotten to lock it from this morning. Afraid to waste any more time, Willia unfolded the tiny staircase and scuttled down its creaking stairs. She stopped for a moment to look around. Where was he? Was he hiding from her so he could beat her again? He had already slapped her across the attic floor twice this morning. The second time she had almost sailed again into blessed unconsciousness. She saw that the front door was open and she hurried into the bathroom, bumping her broken arm against the doorjamb. The urine stream was weak and bloody, and wiping herself was extremely painful. She caught a glimpse of herself in the mirror as she hurried out, and she nearly stopped, overcome with tears. Was it just two days ago that her skin was flawless, her hair was full and neatly coifed? Now she looked as if she had been beaten for years -- and all in one night. She finished in the bathroom and hurried out so that she could climb the stairs before he saw her. She took a fateful second to look out the front door.

But Jenna Walton did see into the house, and it was only her years of cool learned in the harsh underbellies of several cities, plus the shades that she wore to shield her now-sensitive eyes from the early May sun that kept Buck Crowder from knowing that she had seen. She gave no visible signs of just how shaken she was by the sight of the young (?) woman inside, but later that night, after everything was said and done, Jenna Walton tied on the biggest, most tearful drunk of her life.

"How many years have you been a carpenter down to Willoughby's, Mr., uh -- Crowder -- sorry I forgot you name there for a minute; I see so many folks in the course of the day."

"Oh, I reckon I been there now off and on 'round-bout 14 years," Buck Crowder was saying as Willia Davis stood weakly at the back of the living room, shivering like an abandoned animal in what was left of a filthy, bloody slip. Jenna could not possibly guess the woman's age. That once proud posture was now a concave stance on a too-skinny, much abused body. Willia's once luminous and exotic eyes now looked like crusted-over sores with a slight oozing of pus in the left eye. Her right arm hung useless at her side. Willia waved hopelessly at Jenna, who nodded slowly as if to indicate that she understood something that Buck Crowder was saying.

"Matter of fact, there, Miss Walton, you caught me on my way to work. I better get a move on if I want to see 15 years on the job."

"I know how that is, Mr. Crowder. Listen, thank you for all your information -- oh, I forgot to ask you one more question. You're living here alone, right?" Jenna hoped that he didn't hear the uncontrolled gulp at the end of her question.

"Yes, ma'am, sho' am. I'm what you'd call a eligible bachelor." Buck Crowder burst into overly loud laughter; behind him, Jenna could see the woman shuffle up a tiny attic staircase at the back the house as fast her infected and swollen legs could carry her. She seemed to have a piece of paper clutched in her good hand. Buck Crowder leaned deftly into the doorway of his house and grabbed a hat and a set of keys with one hand, while swiftly locking the door with the other hand.

"Thanks again, Mr. Crowder. You have a good day now." Jenna cut a quick right off of Buck Crowder's porch and got to Bloodworth Street in record time; she was afraid she would faint from the shock of what she'd seen. She nodded at Buck Crowder as he passed by in his little foreign car. He tooted his horn gaily and sped away.

The next five minutes seemed to pass as months for Jenna Walton. She stood at the corner of Lee and Bloodworth Streets, pretending to contemplate where she should go next. Finally, she looked at her watch and nearly ran back to Buck Crowder's house.

In the attic, Willia wrote a note to her mother as quickly as she could. The woman may not ever come back here but she had to be ready. She struggled down the tiny staircase again and scuttled back and forth until she could see out of the living room window, peering out with the feral curiosity of a sick animal. She saw the little white woman coming toward the house looking nervously left and right. Willia struggled to the front door. By the time she got to the door, the woman had knocked several times.

At her urgent knock, Jenna heard the desperate shuffling of the woman as she approached the front door. A light flutter of the curtains to the left of the door told Jenna that the woman had seen her. Willia Davis finally opened the door a crack and handed Jenna a note.

"Honey, what in the world are you doing in there? Come on, I'll take you home. You live 'round here?" Willia nodded, a first glimmering of hope dawning in her eyes.

"Please take this note to my mother, Rainey Davis. She lives on Person Street."

"Lord, Mrs. Rainey! Let me call the police now!"

"No, there's no phone here!"

"Well, come on go with me, darling -- "

"NO! Look at me! Just please take the note to my mother as quick as you can. It wasn't time for him to go to work yet. I swear he'd kill me right in the street if he saw me out there. Please." Willia slammed the door shut and scuttled back to the attic stairs.

Surely Jenna Walton broke some track record somewhere in the world that afternoon. But, what good would it have done her to look back towards that little sherwood green shotgun house?

Maybe it was the excitement of possible freedom, but her bladder was throbbing for relief again. She sighed and backed down the attic stairs, her damaged body crying out against every move she made.

Not thirty-five seconds after Jenna Walton turned the corner from Lee Street onto Person Street, James "Buck" Crowder returned to his home. His fist throbbed, both from the previous fisticuffing he had lain upon Willia Davis and from the thrill of anticipation he felt from the next beating she would endure. He found her in the bathroom, on the commode, wiping blood and urine from between her legs. She jumped, terrified, and pulled up her panties (which were nearly off the elastic from Buck Crowder's brutal hand). Buck Crowder said nothing to Willia, did not even look her way. He quietly went to the bathtub, placed the stopper in the drain, and allowed hot water to drain sluggishly into the tub. With his back to her, she crept slowly away from him, and then she dashed toward the bathroom door, screaming for help. Buck Crowder took one firm step toward her and yanked her toward him by her broken arm. She yelped pitifully and began to weep.

When he spoke to Willia, she could feel the heat of his words. They assaulted her like cyanide-dipped lemon drops. "Bitch. What I tell you 'bout spreadin' my business in the street?"

In her parlor, Rainey, despite herself, nodded in a light valley sleep, as Martha Alice called it. She was startled by a calm voice that she thought she might never hear again. "Mama." She looked up to see Willia standing in the parlor doorway, her face placid and resigned and ragged. Rainey jumped up to face her child, not realizing until she tried to stand that she had not left that valley of near sleep.

She was utterly alone in that living room: William was in his study pretending to work, and Douglass, Olivia, and Arthur were in the kitchen trying to calm themselves with endless cups of Maxwell House. Little Honey was at school despite the calamity that had been visited upon her aunt, and Millicent was asleep in an upstairs bedroom. Rainey had taken Laurence aside several hours earlier to tell him that the "intimate aspects" of their life would have to end. He had been sad, but had understood fully. She had welcomed him to stay with the family as they waited to hear news of Willia. She would miss their intimacy like a much-needed balm in some slightly lewd Gilead, but she knew that, finally, she was doing the right thing. Perhaps her decision would calm some angry muse and her precious Willia would come home safe and healthy.

The harsh rapping of the knocker caused her to jump and scream. Rainey hurried to the door.

Jenna Walton was nearly jumping by the time Rainey got to the front door.

Rainey swallowed the bitter gall of her disappointment as she opened the door to Jenna.

"Oh, hello, Miss --"

"Mrs. Rainey, call the police. It's your daughter. You gotta read this note." Jenna followed Rainey Davis back to the kitchen, and then back up to the parlor. During the first leg of her roundtrip, Rainey yelled to William and to the brood awaiting her in the kitchen that she needed to talk to them right away. Everyone rushed forward into the parlor, where Rainey picked up the phone to call the police. Suddenly Rainey's hand went weak, and she dropped the phone. Jenna Walton grabbed the receiver and dialed "0." Quickly, but in the broadest drawl she could manage, Jenna told the operator the situation, and then repeated her synopsis to the police operator.

"They on the way, ma'am."

"Well, thank you, Miss, but I cannot stay here and wait. I'm going 'round there."

Rainey Davis stood up from her wingback chair, thanked Jenna Walton for all that she had done, got Jenna's phone number and address and walked her to the front door. Jenna and Rainey, with the rest of the Davis family in anxious tow, went in opposite directions at the bottoms of Rainey's steps: Jenna hurried away to the right to her car over on Bledsoe Avenue (in front of Buck's mother's house). Rainey and family walked away to the left with hurried dignity to the corner of Person and Lee Streets. Rainey was totally unaware of her family behind her; she was in a vacuum. Nothing mattered to her in those moments except getting to Buck Crowder's house. Sirens screamed closer and closer to her. As she got closer to Buck Crowder's house, she was certain she could hear Willia screaming, and she wished she had gone back for her pistol. Rainey broke into a run, but she could outrun neither the police nor whatever it was that transformed Willia's screams into clotted, muffled growls.

A final, faint groan unleashed all the pent-up hysteria that Rainey had suppressed over the agonizing hours since Willia had disappeared. She got to Buck Crowder's front porch just as two police officers broke down the front door. A third police officer stood on the porch, gun ready. Rainey heard someone screaming, "Let me in there ... Let me in there.... That's my baby in there!" Only later did she realize that she had done the screaming. She felt, vaguely, restraining hands at her upper arms, and a large body trying to block her view. She heard someone at the back of the house gasp and comment, horrified, at the amount of blood in the bathtub, and the world for Rainey Davis went from red to gray to white.

In a tiny duplex on the Fort Monmouth campus, a woman named Anna Grace Carrington, a Davis by marriage, screamed, dropped the telephone receiver from her right hand and nearly dropped her squirming three-year-old son from her left arm.

Next door, through the paper-thin wall separating their homes, Freida Lupton heard her neighbor's screams and snapped off the TV, killing the images of her beloved weekday friends on "As The World Turns." Hoping that her children would remain asleep, Freida hurried to Grace Carrington Davis's aid. After at least a minute of Frieda's frantic knocking, Grace finally answered the door, a damp, unlit cigarette dangling from her lips. Tears flowed generously from her swollen eyes.

"Frieda...Frieda . . .Frieda!" And the last utterance was more scream than declaration. Grace sobbed loudly, dropping the cigarette and holding out her arms to her neighbor. "My Willia's dead."

Grace collapsed against Frieda's shoulder, screaming again. Frieda cried, too, for she understood that the Davises were, for Grace, the only family she would ever know.

OFFICIAL POLICE REPORT: Willia Evelyn Davis, 32, deceased as of Friday, May 6, 1960 at approximately 1:30 in the afternoon. Last known address: 1--- South Person Street. Probable homicide. Prime Suspect: James "Buck" Crowder, 45, of 3-- East Lee Street, Crowder was found at the scene with blood and water all over his clothing. Crowder was caught in the act of trying to drown the decedent when police entered the bathroom of the residence. Victim was already dead at the time of the drowning.

The decedent had been reported missing on the evening of May 5, 1960, having disappeared during a trip to the Lincoln movie theater with two friends. Crowder apparently held Miss Davis hostage in his home from that time until her death.

Other remarkable aspects of this death: Miss Davis had a broken right arm. Both eyes were badly lacerated, infected, and swollen shut; decedent probably could barely see through the lids. Multiple lacerations and concussion sites throughout the body. Earlobes had been partially bitten off. Freshness of wounds indicates one of the lobes was mutilated during final beating. Autopsy must be performed to determine additional factors.

Condition of the house: Blood stains in only one room of the house: the bathroom. The entire bathroom was striped with blood, apparently from the violent and repeated blows to Miss Davis's body during final beating.

Bathtub was full of hot bloody water. No water was found in decedent's lungs.

The kitchen, livingroom, and two bedrooms were immaculate.

Suspect was booked on suspicion of first-degree murder, held without bond in Wake County Jail.

Arraignment set for Monday, May 9, 1960.

OBITUARY

Miss Willia Evelyn Davis

Miss Willia Evelyn Davis, 32, of 1--- South Person Street, died on Friday, May 6. Miss Davis, an elementary school teacher in Johnston County Consolidated Schools, was the daughter of attorney William Davis and his wife, Mrs. Rainey Clark Davis, a retired music teacher in the Raleigh Public Schools.

Survivors, in addition to the parents: brother, Dr. W. Clark Davis, of Red Bank, New Jersey; sister, Mrs. Olivia D. Seaton, of Raleigh; sister-in-law, Dr. Grace C. Davis, of Red Bank, New Jersey; brother-in-law, Mr. Arthur Seaton of Raleigh; three nieces: Karen Davis of Red Bank, New Jersey; Olivia Seaton and Millicent Seaton of Raleigh; one nephew, Eric Davis of Red Bank, New Jersey; fiancé, F. Douglass Baxter of Raleigh.

The family will receive visitors from 7-9 p.m., Friday, May 13, at First Baptist Church, Morgan and Wilmington Streets. Other times at 1--- S. Person Street. Funeral service, Saturday, May 14, 12 noon, First Baptist Church, Rev. Charles Ward officiating. Burial, Mount Hope Cemetery. Raleigh Funeral Home in charge.

Rainey insisted on an open casket at the wake because she wanted everybody to see what a monster like Buck Crowder could do to another human being. She spent that hideous time after Willia's death in a state of coherent hysteria: everything she said, everything she did made total, ice-cold sense. But there was a scary, bitter, frantic edge to it all. During those days, Rainey's amber eyes glittered like the diamond William gave her for their twenty-fifth wedding anniversary. Each time she stopped for a moment, to take a breath, perhaps, or just to hug Clark, Grace, Arthur, or Olivia, they all looked at each other over her head; she was feverish, and on as cool a May day as the Saturday after Willia's death turned out to be, Rainey sweated furiously all day. Clark finally convinced her to let him take her temperature. She fussed, but agreed to it. The thermometer read 102. Alarmed, Clark gave her some Bayer aspirin and insisted on sitting by her bed while she took a nap.

At any point in the night, Rainey was awake, pacing the floor, her arms folded, and her eyebrows furrowed into each other. It didn't help that the funeral had to be delayed a week because of the autopsy. That fact only made Rainey more coherent, and more on the brink of some chilling abyss. William couldn't comfort her, though she accepted his efforts lovingly. In fact, she only seemed to find a measure of solace when her grandchildren sat around her. It seemed that the only adult who could force a glimmer of true calm from Rainey was Martha Alice. For the Davis children, despite all their own pain and sorrow, seeing Rainey suffer through it was just more than any of them could bear.

William was too distraught for full sentences. He sat in his study and smoked Camel after Camel, shaking his head as tears funneled down his face. Every once in a while, he would reach out to his children, but for the most part, the person to whom he was drawn, moth-like, was flame-hot Rainey. Olivia had to give her mother credit: she didn't know if she would have been as kind to Arthur, had they lost a child, as her parents were to each other. Rainey continued to pamper William, and William continued to lavish a form of his adoration upon Rainey. They seemed to cling as hard as they could to some form of normalcy.

ju au de
vee vra

enjoyment in life

Olivia knew that having lost Willia, her very best friend in the world, had jarred every sensibility she possessed. It was through Willia that she got her joie de vivre. Willia always told Olivia to "lighten up" and to stop being so stuffy. Olivia smiled desolately, remembering that Willia had, of course, been right about that. Olivia believed that she and her father were cut from the same cloth in that regard, taking life so seriously. From her beloved sister, Olivia developed her sense of style. Although Willia was much more flamboyant in all her ways than Olivia, somehow Olivia managed to pattern herself into a bland carbon copy of the bright star that Willia was. Olivia was certain she would not be able to endure the pain she felt. Willia's murder was a brutal, unnecessary loss that had cut her to the core. Too few people, not even her parents, understood the depth of the cut.

Olivia felt a deep gash of grief for Grace, who adored Willia, too. For Grace, the Davis sister had become the sisters she would never have. Over the days, Olivia had wept with and for Clark, who felt like a failure for having not lived up to his job as protector to his sisters.

On Monday, May 9 at just twelve minutes past nine o'clock, James Crowder, shackled at hands and feet, was escorted into the courtroom of the Honorable Philip Weston. Judge Weston, a rather young man who would in just a few months be characterized by The News and Observer as a Kennedy Democrat, could not remember feeling such disgust and personal involvement with a case he had judged. He was a native of Raleigh, so the name of James Crowder, though he was a Negro, was in no way unfamiliar to him. Crowder had gained some semblance of notoriety in Raleigh's legal community as a volatile criminal who never regretted his inhumanity to his fellow man and who seemed to revel in his power to intimidate his peers both inside and outside prison communities. Seated in his chambers now, Weston knew that Crowder had not only done severe bodily harm in his community but that, during World War II, he had nearly killed a fellow Negro sailor in Norfolk's rough and tumble shipyard area. He had shown no remorse that this sailor would never again have the use of his eyes or his right arm because Crowder had taken violent issue with his defense of a favorite team in the Negro Baseball League. Crowder's record showed that he had simply stated, with a languorous shrug: "I didn't like the way he said what he had to say to me." Three months in the navy brig for that one.

Weston remembered now that Crowder's offenses against the women of his race had been many and in all cases, heinous. This man had left a trail of broken bones, missing body parts, damaged brains, and lost children for which he could never hope to atone in this world or the next.

But now to this case. At one point in his review of it, Judge Weston had experienced a great deal of difficulty in keeping the contents of his stomach in their rightful place. Of course he knew and greatly respected Attorney William Davis. He was a gentleman and an extremely skilled lawyer who defended his clients with grace and awesome preparation.

Judge Weston had seen pictures of Attorney Davis's family. He remembered the exotic looks of Willia Davis. Now before him were final pictures of Willia Evelyn Davis, her arms and legs dangling out of a tub full of steaming and bloody water, her eyes stretched open, despite their swollen state, in one last look of abject horror, her mouth, what was left of it, in an attitude of supplication. Weston grimly viewed the close-up photographs of her legion of scars, contusions, cuts, breaks, rips, and bruises. He read the report of the scene of the crime and the probable circumstances of her captivity there. Judge Philip Weston could only conclude from the evidence before him that he would soon have standing before him a monster disguised as a human being. With great effort, Judge Weston donned his robe and entered the courtroom.

When that monster was brought before him, Judge Weston fought to retain his composure.

The district attorney, who was usually inclined to send his assistants to try cases involving Negroes against Negroes, took this case himself.

"The state has evidence of probable cause to charge James Earl Crowder with the following: one count each of kidnapping, unlawful imprisonment, assault with an unknown deadly weapon, and first degree murder."

"Does the defendant have legal representation?"

"Yes, your Honor," said a scrawny young attorney who looked none too pleased to be in the company of his client. "I represent the defendant."

"How does defendant plead to these charges, Counsellor?"

"Not guilty, your Honor." Judge Weston sat back in his chair for just a moment. This would be an open and shut case, he knew; Buck Crowder's bloody fingerprints were easily identifiable around the decedent's neck, on the walls of the bathroom, even on the floor of the bathroom. But this was one open-and-shut case that could not be tried in Wake County. Weston realized that at the end of this arraignment he would have to make arrangements for a change of venue. He almost felt too strongly about this case to give an impartial ruling even at this early stage. He knew that no judge in this county could be objective about this case, no Public Defender would willingly represent him. Like him, they all knew and respected Attorney Davis as an outstanding Negro lawyer of spotless integrity.

"James Earl Crowder, you have heard the charges against you and, through your attorney have pleaded not guilty to them. You are to be held without bail in the Wake County Jail until such time as your trial should begin at a venue other than Wake County. Next case."

Willia Evelyn Davis lay in state before the oak altar of First Baptist Church. She was clad for all time in a lovely royal blue shirtwaist dress, faux pearl earrings glued inconspicuously to the sides of her head where her earlobes should have been, some putty, dyed a mild red, in the place where her upper lip had once been, her mangled right arm, now wired into a semblance of straightness, folded gently beneath her intact left arm. Her once lovely hair, now darkened by blood and water, was pulled tightly away from her face in an uncharacteristic, school-marmish bun. The scars on her face seemed somehow less prominent with this style. The Raleigh Funeral Home technicians had done a remarkable job of making her blackened and swollen eyelids look elegantly made up. But anyone who had ever seen Willia Evelyn Davis knew that the body in that steel-blue casket was the final remnant of a woman who had suffered unspeakable abuse. Most of Willia's high school and college classmates, and her Johnston County co-workers had turned away in horror or had even left the church to regain a façade of composure; the body of the woman in the casket was now a hideously malformed representation of the Willia they had known.

A heavily sedated Rosetta Foster Brown sat between her husband and her mother, her hands grasping theirs. Her only outward signs of grief were the whitened state of her knuckles and the constant change of expression upon her face. Her eyes were dulled by Valium and desolation: her best friend had been wrenched from her life by a man whose existence had been a hint, a footnote in her knowledge of Willia's life. How had Willia known this man? Why had his name never come up in their whispered conversations about their sex lives? At one point, Rosetta knew that Willia had a really satisfying lover, but his identity had remained cloaked in omission. Rosetta supposed Buck Crowder was the mystery lover. From behind Rosetta's Valium-fortified façade of calm, walls crumbled, floors shook, and enemies retreated from the force of her rage. There was no justice, none at all, if a wonderful girl like Willia, for whom the world had been a golden adventure, could be killed practically in her own backyard.

Rosetta's lovely face had become a spasm of twitches since Willia's disappearance. Why couldn't she and Pixie have saved her? Why did Willia have to leave the bathroom first? What could Rosetta have done to stop the abduction? She looked across the pew at Pixie Wilson. Their eyes met and they slowly rose and approached each other. They embraced in the aisle, each a sedated mess, racked with guilt, fury, and just plain hurt. They had both viewed the remains of their friend, and now they locked hands and turned toward the door of the church. Rosetta pressed her husband's shoulder to let him know that she'd be back. The women went outside into the midst of the milling crowd of stunned mourners. They sat unceremoniously on the steps of the church and stared upward, perhaps for answers, into the darkening sky.

Mr. "Doll" Haywood, the owner of the funeral home and a dear friend of the Davises, had finally convinced Rainey that if she wouldn't allow the casket to be closed, she must agree that the extent of her daughter's injuries was so great that they should at least drape white netting from the lid of the casket down to its side to soften the blow for those who would be seeing her body for the first time. Rainey, her eyes still glittering, finally concurred. She knew that no amount of make up or the thickest netting could obscure the ways that Buck Crowder had ravaged her child.

Rainey wore a pleated white dress, Olivia was dressed in solemn black, and Grace, adorned in a steel gray suit, stood limply with them in front of Willia's ice blue casket, with candle light reflecting mournfully off of its surface. Martha Alice sat directly behind her beloved friend and her daughters -- all three of them -- her face a mask of stunned resignation, and her posture one of steely resolution to do whatever needed to be done to assist and comfort Rainey and her girls.

Those in attendance would always have a vivid memory of the three Davis women, arms around each other's shoulders, standing before the open casket, finally given over to the reality of their loss, the infinite nature of their grief. They talked to Willia's remains.

"You know we love you, honey."

"Mama wants you to be at peace now!"

"No more suffering, Lord! No more!"

"Did you know we tried to get you back? Lord knows we tried!"

"Oh, God, oh God, oh GOD . . . !" (A protracted moan.)

"You know he's not going to get away with this." (In a whisper.)

"Jesus!"

They wailed and blubbered, their lovely faces turned upwards to heaven, their tears rushing downward to dampen the netting covering the coffin. And through those tiny circles of salty wet, the ravages of Willia's last days revealed themselves with horrifying clarity.

Their husbands gently helped them back to their seats.

Douglass Baxter, stunned into stillness, sat through the entire service, staring at Willia's body beneath the white netting. His eyes were red-rimmed and glazed. Tonight he was a broken man who could see only the remains of the woman he was to marry in just over a week. His family seemed incapable of comforting him, and even his mother could not rouse him from his stupor.

At about 8:30, with about a half-hour to go before the end of the wake, Rainey stood slowly from her seat. Her family looked at her cautiously; they had no idea what to expect. She spoke calmly with Reverend Ward, and approached the microphone that she had used so many Sundays to sing to the congregation or to welcome visitors. When she spoke, her voice was low, nearly monotonous, and most admirably calm. And yet, her words seemed to have been memorized, giving her speech a strange, automatic quality.

"I want to say something to you all. Let's not pretty up this situation by avoiding the reality of it. Our child was murdered. I wanted you to see what a monster can do in real life. Mr. Haywood made me see the wisdom of covering the harsh truth of what was done to my baby. I guarantee that if you could have seen what I saw, how she really looked, you would be physically ill right now. I want you all to know that our child was murdered before she was actually dead because she was forced to be a hostage for almost twenty-four hours before she passed. Well, thank you for all your kindness during this time. We won't ever forget it."

With that, Rainey sank slowly to the floor, still conscious somehow, but unable to move another step; all her strength had gone into that speech. Her son and son-in-law (and poor Doug) rushed to scoop her up and carry her out to the waiting limousine.

I'll fly away, oh Glory! I'll fly away!
When I die, Hallelujah, by and by,
I will fly away!

On that glistening Saturday afternoon, Willia Evelyn Davis should have been a week away from her wedding to Doug Baxter. She should have been making last-minute arrangements or perhaps she should have been downtown shopping with her mother and sister. She should have been grading papers, with pink foam rollers in her hair and a Newport dangling dangerously close to the point of incinerating those papers. Or she should have been babysitting (spoiling) her nieces. Perhaps she should even have been planning -- or recovering from -- her evening's activities. Instead, Willia Evelyn Davis was laid to rest beneath the first symptoms of summer on that remarkably bright Saturday afternoon. For just a startling moment, the world seemed to stand still and take note of the passing of what could have and should have been: hardly a bird could be heard to twitter or a car heard to pass the cemetery; no children lifted voices to the heavens in the throes of all-consuming play as Reverend Ward's final prayers intertwined with the wails and moans from her mourners. In place of the usual simple marker of beginning and end that had become a tradition at Mount Hope Cemetery, the Davises had hurriedly commissioned another, more fitting marker:

Starlight burned bright,
extinguished by hatred made manifest.
WILLIA EVELYN DAVIS
August 14, 1927 - May 6, 1960

CHAPTER TWENTY

Reflections and Retribution

R ainey, I cain't even start to tell you how sorry and ashamed I am about this," Mrs. Polly Butler was saying to her neighbor.

"Polly, I know you are," Rainey replied into the telephone as she reclined among her pillows in bed. It was 1:00 o'clock Wednesday afternoon, but Rainey had only been able to pull herself out of bed long enough to sit in a hot bathtub and imagine the horror of her daughter's last moments. When the intense horror had grown too stark, she had washed vigorously and hurriedly, drying and lotioning herself frantically before putting on a clean gown and underwear and dragging herself back to bed. Here Rainey had lain, unable to eat or sleep, only halfheartedly answering the telephone, sitting up to finish writing out the many personal thank-you notes that had to be sent to friends and family.

She couldn't tell anyone that what weighed her down more than grief, far more than desolation, was a fury that fallen upon her traumatized soul with the force of bricks from a skyscraper. It just wasn't right for Buck Crowder to get away with this. And now his mother, God bless her, was calling. Rainey admired Polly Butler's courage, loathed her gall.

"This has got nothing to do with you. It's not your fault," Rainey was saying now. But at the same time it has everything to do with you, she heard her inner voice scream. And it is your fault. You gave birth to him, to it. You allowed it to grow into a monster. That monster killed my baby. Rainey slammed her left hand over her left ear to stop the feverish whispers rattling in her head.

"Me and Stell just don't know how to let you know how sorry we is," Polly was saying now. "Can we do anything for you?"

"No, just pray for us. It's going to be a long process ... you know, trying to deal with this.... Polly, thank you so much for calling, hear?"

"You know you and I have always got on just wonderful, and I'm just so ashamed and sad that this had to happen...."

Had to happen?! Rainey felt the sharp pressure of her teeth on her tongue as she fought back these words.

"... and this is gon' be my first night back on the night job," Polly said. "I ain't got to go back to my boss lady's until sometime next week. So during the day, if you needs anything, please let me know. Well, you take care, hear? I'm so sorry."

Rainey sat up straight in her bed, and the feverish glitter returned to her amber eyes. She beat her pillows into shape and, cradling the phone between her chin and her shoulder, she got up to make the bed. She sat down on it long enough to slide her feet into her slippers.

"Thank you, Polly, and God bless you for calling." Rainey slammed the receiver down and hurried downstairs.

On Bledsoe Avenue, Polly Crowder Butler placed her phone's receiver in its cradle and wept hot and bitter tears of shame. Her son had been a curse on just about every good thing in her wretched life.

Brownies To Comfort Him

At about 3:15 on the afternoon of Wednesday, May 18, the Wake County jailer noted in writing that Buck Crowder's mother brought a small gift to her son. She seemed shorter somehow, stooped and weighted down perhaps by the horror of her son's inhumanity. Her magnificent white hair had lost its luster and was flattened to her head. The jailer had only seen Crowder's mother once before, but today she seemed paler. He had only recently heard the graphic details of what Crowder had done to the Davis girl. Every time he had to deal with Crowder now, he felt slightly ill, his appetite destroyed until several hours after he got home. So he understood why Crowder's mother would seem so withdrawn and defeated. Her eyes were different somehow, he noticed, but he shrugged it off. Maybe she had on some different glasses. She was dressed in a heavy tattered man's overcoat and some strangely dainty white gloves. Again the jailer shrugged; he knew it often seemed colder to older people than to others. This jailer, like all the jailers there, had no real knowledge of anyone or anything in Raleigh's black community. So ultimately, nothing seemed overly unusual about the changes in Crowder's mother's appearance.

"Evenin'" she said as she shuffled up to his desk, carrying a small blue cookie tin. "Can I leave these four brownies for my son, James Earl Crowder? I had some left over from when I was cookin' at my boss lady's house yestiddy."

"Why, yes ma'am, you sure can. It's gon' be a while 'fore you can visit with him, though. He's been pretty ... upset here lately."

"Well, tell him his Mama is prayin' for him, hear? And please make sure he gets all four of them brownies. Brownies always did comfort him, you know."

The jailer laughed uneasily. He hoped fleetingly that Crowder's mother had put a little something extra (sleeping pills, maybe) in these brownies to put all of them out of Crowder's misery.

"Okay, ma'am. I promise not to eat any. I'll get to him tonight, right before I go off duty." He leaned toward her conspiratorially. "That way, nobody'll know he has 'em. Okay?"

"That's just fine, son." She started away, and turned back to the jailer. "Oh, yeah, and one more thing ...."

"Yes, ma'am?" The jailer turned to her, wondering how somebody as nice as she was could have a monster for a son.

William arrived home at 5:30 that afternoon. Downstairs a small fire burned in the living room fireplace. A book was face down next to Rainey's chair. William was encouraged; Rainey had tried to sit up for a while and read. He smiled a little and went upstairs. Their bedroom door was slightly ajar. He entered quietly so as not to disturb poor Rainey. She was just awakening from a nap as he walked in. Her hair was matted her head from hours of sleep. William guessed that his beloved must have slept soundly in one place; her hair was usually all over her head when she slept for any length of time. She sat up slowly, and when she saw him, she held out her arms to him. He rushed to her, ignoring the dull throb in his upper right thigh. They embraced, as if their lives depended on it, for an infinite, warm time, rocking slowly back and forth.

Finally, she spoke into his neck. "Are you hungry, baby? I made us a meatloaf."

William pulled back from his wife, amazed.

"You did?" His face beamed.

Rainey nodded, childlike. "Uh-huh, and some cream potatoes and some string beans."

William kissed her deeply. "You are so strong, Rainey! To get up and cook after all you've been through!"

Rainey laughed softly. "After all we've been through. Come on, Sweets, you have to eat!"

William's face lit up with the hope of a child. "Will you have dinner with me?"

She kissed her husband. "Of course, Sweets."

At 10:55 that night, just before he went off duty, the jailer who had talked with Crowder's mother put The Raleigh Times under his arm and brought the little blue tin of brownies to the prisoner's isolation cell.

"Here, Crowder. These are from your mother."

"Oh yeah?" Crowder sneered, a venomous chuckle curdling up from his throat. "I can't get her to stay away from me for nothin', can I?"

"You know what they say. Mother's love." The jailer shrugged. "I checked 'em already, so don't think she put any tools in there or nothin' like that. They look pretty good." The jailer lowered his voice. "Now you know you not s'posed to have nothin' extra, so be cool, Crowder. I'm only givin' 'em to you because your mama is one sweet lady. Look, put them brownies in this newspaper, and gimmee the can. I'll give it to your mother next time she comes around."

The jailer locked Crowder's cell door, and went back to do some final paperwork.

Buck Crowder tore into the brownies. His mother could cook her ass off, and he hadn't had anything but slop in here. When he finished the last brownie he sat licking his fingers. He ignored the sharp cramps in his stomach. He'd probably eaten too fast.

The jailer came back by, zipping his jacket. He noticed that The Raleigh Times lay in a wasted heap on the floor next to Crowder's cot.

He musta swallowed them brownies whole, the jailer thought.

"Crowder, you mother said next time she'd bring you some, uh, lemon drops, I think it was. See ya." The jailer hurried away.

Buck Crowder tried to call after him, but he could only fall weakly to his cot, a debilitating wave of dizzy nausea rendering him incapable of speech or any other voluntary movement.

At 11:35, the graveyard shift jailer made his rounds to check on all the cells in the tiny Wake County jailhouse. He could see that Buck Crowder was asleep, and he breathed a sigh of relief: Buck Crowder had raised so much hell that he had just about caused an uprising in the little jailhouse. He and two of the guards had nearly had to knock him out to drag him into the isolation cell. The jailer walked away from Crowder's cell, shaking his head. He ought to be tired, he thought. Holding somebody hostage all night long and beating her to death ought to wear a guy out. Hope he's out for the night.

The graveyard shift jailer handed his massive keyring over to the morning jailer with a weary flip of his wrist. "Good news. Crowder has been quiet as a church mouse all night long."

"Well that's a miracle ain't it?"

"Yeah, see for yourself. See you in the morning."

The morning jailer had his stretch, half a cup of coffee, and a glance at the morning News and Observer before he declared himself awake enough to do his usual morning check of the prisoners. Crowder had obviously finally worn himself out. He was still sleeping like a log. Good, this jailer mused, 'cause he was in for a clubbing today. I wasn't gonna put up with that shit again. Satisfied that he was in for a relatively quiet shift, the morning jailer went back to reading his paper until 9:00 when the prisoners' breakfast trays were brought in.

By 9:30, Crowder hadn't sat up to complain about the slop on his tray. The morning jailer wrapped his right hand around his billy club before entering Crowder's cell to rouse him. The jailer withdrew his hand from Crowder's shoulder, alarmed. Crowder's arm was cold and stiff. Cautiously, the jailer felt for a pulse. Crowder's skin felt like a cinder block. No pulse.

"Oh, shit!" The jailer rolled Crowder's body onto its back. He had to pull Crowder's face around separately from the rest of his body because the left side of his face was mired in a pool of dried, bloody vomit. The jailer ran from the cell, still careful to lock the door behind him, and called for the sheriff's office to send deputies.

William and Rainey sat at their kitchen table drinking coffee and trying to make small talk. It was a sunny Thursday morning, and Rainey seemed to feel a little better, William noticed. She was still in pretty shabby shape, but she was really trying to make a positive recovery. She was fully showered and dressed when he awakened, ready to cook breakfast for him. He declined; why didn't they just eat some buttered toast and drink coffee? And so they had, sort of gazing at each other over the paper, grasping each other's hands, avoiding the pain at their core.

The phone rang, and William got up to answer it. Rainey was thinking that they really should go ahead and get a phone put in the kitchen. She noticed with a detached anxiety that her husband was beginning to shuffle when he walked, that he relied more heavily than ever on his cane. She would offer to massage his legs this morning before he went to the office. She wished, in an abstract way, that he wouldn't go in today.

When he came back from the living room, William's face looked bleached and he was more stooped as he dropped himself into his chair.

Alarm flooded Rainey. "What is it, William?" She jumped up and rushed to him, wrapping her arms tightly around his shoulders.

"Just got a call from Phil Weston. Buck Crowder is dead."

Rainey froze for what seemed an endless time.

"What happened?"

"He says it looks like he choked on his own vomit during the night."

"What?" Slowly she walked back to her chair, now dropping herself into it. William and Rainey just stared blankly at each other.

And that was how Olivia found them that morning when she came by to check on them on her way to work. When they told her, she, too, sat and stared for a while.

The afternoon jailer never made a connection between Crowder's mother's brownies and Crowder's sudden death. In fact, he thought that the world was perhaps a better place because Crowder was not in it. No one suggested an autopsy as a necessary procedure in this case, and Buck Crowder was pushed away from the stung memory of the legal system of Wake County as rapidly as possible. He was buried swiftly in a pauper's grave; none of the Crowders had any willingness or money to bury him. No wake, no funeral, no mourners.

The case of the State versus James Earl Crowder was closed irrevocably and for all time.

When William came home from work that Thursday afternoon, he found a note from Rainey that read simply: "Gone to Tesima. I need some time."

CHAPTER TWENTY-ONE

Shadows In Fog

She sank her slim feet into the warm heavy sand along the shoreline in back of their house. She stopped at each moonstone, inching it out of the wet sand with her toes.

Moonstones.

She stopped and looked up at the bright sky. Sea gulls circled and flew over her. Their cry, once a source of joy for her and a confirmation of Tesima's natural beauty, was now a plaintive lament. The sun had burned off the morning clouds, and the breeze that wafted past her was like so many silk scarves wrapping themselves around her thin frame. The waves, at low ebb, washed over her feet like chilling but soothing memories. And she remembered.....

It is 1930.

Willia is almost three and Rainey is pregnant with the baby who will be Olivia. They are at the shore on the all-colored Carolina Beach. Rainey feels ill all the time now and is grateful that little Will likes to run behind William. She can see them far ahead, in silhouette. One is jumping around the other, gleefully asking questions and pointing. The taller silhouette looks down lovingly at the tiny one, and takes his hand. Soon the taller silhouette pulls the tiny silhouette up to give him a great big hug. Rainey sighs.

It is a good life. Has it been only five years since she fled hell for this life?

"Mama, can I have a lemon drop?"

"May I what?"

"May-can I have a lemon drop?"

Rainey laughs and fishes in one huge pocket of her pink summer duster for yet another of the many lemon drops she keeps in supply for her baby girl. She looks down at the little doll walking beside her. Willia is so pretty she can hardly believe she produced her. Willia is all William's child with her coffee brown complexion, her almond-shaped black eyes, and her thick (unruly) black hair. Willia keeps up with Rainey, her sturdy little thighs pumping her along, and her muscular little arms swinging in short babyish strokes. She sucks contentedly on her beloved lemon drop. Rainey notices that Willia is outgrowing her little bathing suit.

"MaMA?"

"Hmmm?"

"You know what I like?"

"What, sweet baby?

"I like picking up these rocks! See?"

Willia is holding up a moonstone, its texture broken only subtly by stripes lighter than its taupe surface.

"That is pretty, baby. That's called a moonstone. Here, I'll keep it in my other pocket for you in case you find some more, okay?"

"Okay, Mama. Moonstone. Can you make a wish on these?"

"If you want to. What are you going to wish for?"

"Hmm. One day I want to grow up and marry the prince."

Rainey laughs. "Who is the prince, baby?"

"I think he ridin' on a white horsey. But I don't know what he look like yet."

"Well, that's okay, sweet baby. You'll know when he comes."

"Okay. And I bet I'll have all the lemon drops I want. . . . . MaMA?"

"Hmm?"

"May-can I have another lemon drop?"

William and Will run up to them now.

"How's it going, girls?"

"Just fine. When y'all goin fishin, Hubby?"

"Oh, girl, you know I thought we'd go over to Kilroy's Kitchen tonight."

"I was hoping you'd say that, because I do not feel up to cooking tonight."

He pats her still flat stomach.

"We've got a good thing going here, eh?"

"Eh."

And they walk along the beach together, all four and a half of them: a family intact, a family unmolested by the ravages of time and outside forces.

It will never end.

Rainey walked slowly up the back stairs of their beach house, slamming the door behind her. She collapsed on one of their prized Adirondacks, all the strength drained from her. She sat, breathing heavily, until she could handle the intensity of the beach memory. She had to force out other more poignant memories. They would have to wait for another time. She could feel them, and all her grief, jockeying for position inside her damaged psyche: there was anger, there was despair, and there were so very many questions. She had held so much of her emotion back for so long, trying to be strong for her husband and for her children. She had not yet screamed the scream that was tearing at her insides. She had worked off some of the anger when she .... when she .....

She jumped up from the chair and rushed to the bathroom, where she drew herself a hot bath. Perhaps she could sweat out this grief, this hopelessness. But it was sitting in this bath water that seemed to bring all the pain to her surface. She had sat and thought and cried and raged.

She drew her breath in one quick gulp, almost a belch. She sank and slid downward. The water, recently warmed, soothed her intimately as she descended. As it rose to meet her shoulders, and her shoulders moved downward to meet it, the warmth of the water lulled her. Startled, she drew in another huge, quick breath and continued. She soon felt the water tug against the middle of her bun She would not stop now; she would proceed.

When her lungs felt full to bursting, and the water had moved up to the middle of her forehead, she sat up swiftly, opened her eyes slowly. Smiling now, eyes filled with tears.

She stood up quickly, shivering against the sudden chill. She had things to do. She dried her hair and dressed quickly; she was anxious to return to her family.

But her heart had still more work for her soul to process, and she found herself drawn back to the prized Adirondack chair on their screened porch ....

Reasonable Joy

Autumn.

It is November, Willia's last November. Color dazzles in the trees against the stark gray sky and the dull brown bark of ancient trees. They take one last afternoon to porch sit, Rainey and her girls. It is an odd occasion that ALL of her girls are there with her: Willia, Olivia, Grace, Martha Alice, Honey, and Kakie. Inside, babies Eric, two years old, and Millicent, fourteen months, are fast asleep, having worn themselves out, playing and squealing and jumping up and down.

The men are smoking zombies, their eyes and ears glued to some football game or other, and their lips wrapped around cigarettes or food. She'd only hear from them if they felt like they needed some more turkey sandwiches. Turkey sandwiches, Lord, do they have turkey sandwiches! And Thanksgiving was one week ago! Rainey's hands still throb from preparing that 29-pound monster of a bird last week. She resigns herself to the reality that it's going to be turkey for quite some time . . . turkey a la king. . . creamed turkey on toast. . . turkey noodle soup. . . turkey pot pie. . . . turkey on the brain. . . .

Rainey is happy; no, ecstatic is a better word. All of her beloveds are there with her; there's simply no one to miss. It feels so good to be in the midst of all her folks. It is a Saturday, and, despite the chill running through the afternoon breeze, the women and the womenchildren have bundled up to come and sit and chat and laugh. Oh, there is so much laughter when Willia and Grace are in their midst. And on this afternoon, the women are hysterical from the time they come out to the porch until the cold and the dark force them back inside.

Rainey tells Willia and Grace they should go into business together; give Moms Mabley a run for her money.

"At least we won't have to worry about taking out our teeth," Grace laughs. "That'll cut down on the overhead."

Willia launches into a perfect, seemingly toothless imitation of the comedienne. "Moms says 'the only thing an old man can do for her is hold the door for a young man!'"

"Yeah, or introduce her to his young son! That woman is crazy!"

"Jackie "Moms" Mabley," *Grace and Willia say in unplanned unison, and the laughter peals up again.*

Honey is nine, and five-year-old Kakie is so taken with her big cousin that she nearly falls on her as they walk back and forth across the porch.   Honey is gracious; after all, she must set a good example for the little girl.

"Hey, Grace," Willia calls across the vast expanse of porch after a bout of hysteria.

"Y'all are the 'hey' sayingest folks I have ever seen.   Where IS that stable?"

"Shut up, Grace."

"Okay."

"Love ya.   Now here's what I want to say to you, baby." Willia walks across the porch, her pink cardigan sweater trailing off her thin shoulders as she steps conspiratorially toward her sister-in-law.   Rainey notices how elegant Willia is in her gray pedal pushers and her pale pink mules. Even with the strange addition of white bobby socks, her oldest baby looks chic.

Grace looks up at Willia now, expectantly. And neither Rainey, nor Martha Alice, nor Grace, nor Olivia, nor even little Honey will ever forget what Willia says next.

"Listen here.   If I drop dead, nobody has to perform an autopsy 'cause I'm going to die laughing."

It is strange how none of them laugh for a suspended second or two: Grace continues to gaze at Willia's face as if she is still waiting for her to speak.   Rainey and Olivia and Martha Alice continue to rock in their tulip chairs, their faces still framed in slight attitudes of expectant half-listening.   Does Willia's voice crack ever so slightly when she makes this pronouncement? Does the wind pick up a howl for just that moment? It is as if time has stood still and even the leaves cease to shake for a moment.

And just as suddenly as the suspension begins, it is over. All the women and both the womenchildren are laughing, for Willia will surely send them to an early grave, hysterical, rather than seeing her own end in such a way.

It is November.   Willia's last November.   After this day, she will never sit on the porch again. . . .

Rainey took a deep breath and pressed her hands against her thighs as she sat up straighter in the Adirondack.   She had to admit her deed to herself if to no one else.

Yes, she had worked off some of her anger when she had done all that baking that afternoon.   One pinch for every person whose heart was broken by Willia's ... departure. One more pinch for every day the funeral was delayed by autopsy. Two large pinches for the wedding that would never be. By the time she had finished pinching off her secret ingredient and adding it to Polly Crowder Butler's brownie recipe, every rat in her neighborhood could find safe haven at Rainey's house. And thank you, Negro attorneys, for having a costume ball to bring in the year 1958. She had gone as Mother Goose and William had gone as Jack Sprat. Martha Alice was so incredibly talented that she had made a human hair wig for Rainey's costume and dyed it silver. And she guessed that perhaps the most ironic item of the ensemble for her jailhouse trek was that Polly Butler had made her some cookies for her 60th birthday. Rainey's thanks to her that day had been sincere; she couldn't fathom that any of Buck Crowder's heinous actions could be attributed to his mother. Rainey had saved the blue tin, along with all the other tins she had received over the years, on the top shelf in the pantry off the kitchen. Perhaps it was because it was the last tin to be stored that it practically fell into her hands when she stood on her step bench to get one. Maybe it was all just meant to come off that way.

It was enough to know now that he would not live in this world when he had taken her beloved child out of it.

It was an era when colored ladies of a certain age, when they were not invisible to the whites, looked enough alike to them that it was hardly worth the bother. So the jailer hadn't bothered: to see if she was really Polly Butler -- he had called her "Mrs. Crowder"; to see if she had any identification, or to see if there was anything out of the ordinary about her blue tin beyond the absence of sharp objects. Still, when she had asked him not to tell Crowder about the lemon drops until he had started to eat the brownies, Rainey could tell the jailer had home training; she knew that he would wait to tell Crowder just before his shift ended. And she had told him just what to say: "Now, don't give them brownies to him 'til tonight. I'm gon have somethin' else for him pretty soon. I don't want him to get too excited, so don't tell him this part until you're 'bout ready to go home, hear? He loves lemon drops, so when you 'bout ready to leave, say "Your mama's gon' have some lemon drops for you next time."

Rainey's laugh was bitter and humorless as she remembered her cleverness. He had to know that Willia loved lemon drops, and if not, she had promised him some poisoned lemon drops if anything happened to her child. But she stopped In the middle of the first half-hearted chuckle. This was no repayment for disservice. This was a deadly game, and she was pretty sure she had played it for the first time many years earlier. It didn't feel good to be a murderer; she wasn't proud. She had simply done what she had to do, and given the same circumstances, she would gladly do it again. No. Not gladly. There could be no joy in this. Because there was no bringing back her baby.

In 1947, girls don't fight back when boys try to hurt them. They tell Papa and let Papa handle those punk boys.

But when that fool tries to hurt her baby, Rainey and Papa don't find out about the way Willia stabs him with a pencil until after Louise Latham brings their daughter home, telling them that maybe Willia needs to take a little break from school.

'Why, Willia? What did the boy do to you?" Rainey and William are worried; they both know the potential for damage that Willia's temper wields.

"He had no business trying to sneak up in my room in the first place," she sniffs.

"He snuck up in your room. That's why you stabbed him, baby?"

"No, ma'am. He tried to . . . to . . . have his way with me.

Rainey is amazed that, as comfortable as she is about sex, her children handle the subject with kid gloves around her, as if the mere mention of any sexual advances or activity will send her and her William into some kind of conniption. If they only knew! She works diligently to bring herself back into the very serious present.

William's calm voice breaks the awkward silence that follows Willia's declaration.

"You told him to stop," he says, his voice a cross between question and statement.

Willia nods.

"And then when he wouldn't stop, and I wouldn't give in, he decided to try to slap me."

Both Rainey and William can barely stifle their amusement at her emphasis upon "try."

"I grabbed the nearest thing to me, and stabbed him with it. Well, you'd have thought I'd grabbed a butcher knife, the way he carried on.

"Anyway," Willia concludes, her elegant shoulders raising themselves into a dismissive shrug. "Miss Latham thought I might do well to complete this semester's studies by mail. So, Papa, may I work in your office during the day? Reckon I need to earn my keep."

Later, in bed, after a conniption, William and Rainey discuss their girl.

"We don't have to worry about our girl Willia, huh?" Rainey says against William's shoulder.

"Guess not, " William says into Rainey's hair. "She's a tough one. Wonder where she got that from?" They laugh; William declares he has never met a tougher lady than his wife.

"Wonder." They will never have to worry about anybody hurting Willia.

They are some lucky parents.

And she began to rock back and forth in the Adirondack, holding her arms across her stomach as if to guard against a bitter blast of cold wind. There was no bringing back her baby. The reality of that stark statement hit her full in the face, and knocked her back, and sent her reeling --

It is 1927.

It is glowing hot because it is August.

She is cursing. She is in pain. She is laboring to bring forth the child who will be Willia.

She cannot remember having ever hurt so badly in her entire life. Will hadn't hurt her like this. Will just slid out, like her stool after a good dose of castor oil. Perhaps Step's assault had been good for that one thing.... Like a child down a sliding board.

This is pain; it is real; and she can't stand it.

And so she curses. The words roll off her whited tongue like marbles across gravel, smooth against rough; calm wind against coarse rocks. Each time a nurse comes in to check on her progress, she holds the curses against her teeth like pearls, she stops the flow of the words between her lips as if holding a silk scarf against a strong breeze.

"How you doin', Miz Davis? You holdin' on all right?"

She will only nod her head; she holds inside her mouth a power that she will share with no one. She will not cry, she will utter no sound save for the vile curses, and they are for her ears only.

And when the end draws near, and the doctor is there, and two nurses are urging her to "bear right down" and to "push," she utters no sound; she holds onto her personal storehouse of curses as she does their bidding. She will not give in to the pain.

But perhaps only someone so beautiful could bring forth such deep, cutting pain. Perhaps her newest treasure does not want to face a world that might mar her beauty.

And, ah, what a beauty. At exactly eight pounds, this baby will be her largest. But for now she cannot take her eyes off her. Look at those little eyes! They are scrunched tightly closed right now, but they have the shape of almonds. What color will they be? She won't hold them open long, but from what Rainey can see, it's hard to tell right now what their color will be. And she is going to have William's gorgeous darkness. Look at all those little curls in her hair! Why, she is simply the most beautiful child God has ever let come forth on this Earth!

All pain is forgotten, having now receded in her mind as a prelude to this moment.

Oh, doctor, don't take her yet! She's clean enough! Please?

It is 1927, before the age when it is not fashionable to breast feed one's child. Rainey puts this new child to her puny breast to feed her for the first time. And so they are bound, and their life together begins.

She is Willia Evelyn Davis and she has made her debut on Sunday, August 14 at 10:39 in the morning. Well, that's sermon enough for Rainey this morning, yes indeed....

And Rainey and Willia sleep, cleaned up and removed to their separate beds....

Somebody was screaming at the top of her lungs. Rainey was standing in the middle of the bedroom she shared with William in this beloved little house on stilts.

"Why, God, why? She's supposed to be here! She was still a baby, Lord!"

And so the screamer was Rainey, and she let forth the awesome power of her grief, her face becoming a baptismal fount of saltwater and sweat and snot as she submerged herself in the depths of the horror of not having Willia with her anymore. No more lively, rollicking conversations from out of nowhere. No more flamboyant attempts to make Rainey dress like a 30-year-old. No more sudden phone calls to ask Rainey about that raisin cookie recipe because "I got a taste for them."

Rainey railed against the reality, and walked through the house as she screamed in the face of the starkness of her daughter's death and the circumstances leading to it. She had been given no chance to ask Willia if she was all right, no opportunity to say, just once more, "I love you, baby." She would never again gaze at that silky brown face and marvel at the natural beauty of its heart-shaped contours, those exotic eyes, that electric smile that was a sparkling commingling of mischievous hilarity, benevolent intelligence, and preserved innocence. She had been cheated out of the chance to see once more Willia's elegant walk, her regal bearing.

Ultimately, Rainey decided that death was rude. You looked at what was left of your loved one, and you were ignored by that loved one. No amount of wailing, no protracted screams would arouse your beloved's attentions ever again. Rufus in his boiled shirt with his artificially rosy cheeks. Evie in her simple white shift, her face awash at last in peace. Willia in her blue shirtwaist with her fake lips and earlobes. If Rainey had been looking at remains, then what had happened to the part of Willia that was departed from them? Where was she? Just where the hell was she? Rainey gasped. I hope that's not where she is. Oh, God, why can't I know? Where was that blessed assurance now?

And in that bleak moment, when time for her ground to a mocking halt, Rainey knew that she would never again believe that blessed assurance could be hers. She gasped again at her blasphemy, and spat into a handkerchief as if to cleanse her mouth.

She threw herself across the sofa that had been the scene of Doug's first proposal and screamed and wept until she had no further strength. At last, she slept fitfully, awakening several times as if all that she had been through would somehow turn out to be one obscene nightmare. Sometimes she sat upright quickly as if she would rub her eyes and see Willia nearby. And each time she lay back down, psychically ill beyond belief, beyond all utterance, beyond all endurance. Finally, her powerful, raging fury spent, Rainey fell into unconsciousness, and in that state, an aspect of the girl-woman who had given birth to Willia, her lost child, crept back into the woman. But that girl-woman was a somber replica now, and she would never again lend her carefree demeanor to the woman she had become.

Death was rude.

It was on Saturday morning that the front yard of Rainey's beach house was beset by pigeons. They swarmed the ground, in her yard alone, it seemed. Rainey stood at the window of her dining room, her arms folded tightly across her chest. It was her habit, when she was deep in thought, to stand at the picture window at her Person Street home, or at this smaller, sea salt-streaked window, contemplating the matters at hand. She'd stood at this window repeatedly during these last two days, when she wasn't walking along the shore, as if her feet were glued to the rug below the window.

Perhaps she looked away for a moment in her reverie; perhaps she was just caught up in her contemplations. But a thump at the window brought her back to the present moment, and she found herself staring in amazement at the bustling gray congregation below. Into the middle of their gathering, a spotless dove swooped downward.   Its feathers seemed to gleam in the morning sunshine. All the pigeons turned their attention to this lone dove, and suddenly, as it burst into flight, the pigeons flapped their wings as if they, too, would take flight. As if rehearsed, the dove soared straight into the sky, swooped back downward, never landing, and swirled about. Its processional seemed joyous and filled with the freedom of flight. The dove never left the frame of Rainey's picture window. Occasionally, the pigeons would join the dove's antics, but the dove seemed to be flying for Rainey's benefit alone.

And suddenly, Rainey could not see the dove. Her vision was thickened with tears. She understood. Willia was at peace, Willia was safe, and Willia wanted Rainey to know, and to feel peace and resolution, too. Rainey nodded at the dove in flight, as her tears flowed, unchecked. Her nod seemed to be a signal to the dove, for it flew away to the northwest then, taking its lively retinue along with it.

For Rainey, the dove was a message from Willia and from the God she'd all but decided to abandon. Now she could look back in love. Willia would eternally be her first daughter, her funny one, her tiny beauty. Willia would be ever young, and ever a delight. Perhaps, one day, Rainey would be able to laugh heartily at memories of her daughter's antics. But for now she would be able at least to smile through tears, and, ultimately to be grateful to God that He had allowed Willia to brighten her life for those 32 years. Rainey would move through the rest of her life with a void in her soul, yes, but also with an abiding sense of pride that although Willia's life had been brutally abbreviated, she, Rainey, had been blessed with the privilege of having been her mother.

On Saturday afternoon, Rainey was haunted. Willia was safely and irretrievably away, never to return in any form recognizable as Willia. The sun shone brightly that afternoon in its uniquely May way, a jewel in the midst of an unbroken sea of blue.

She was ready to go home, too. These two days at Tesima had been her strangest ever. She had cried and slept and cleaned and rearranged and hated herself for having to drink the two pots of tea and eat the buttered toast. Her baby couldn't have any tea and toast. Her baby would never again have tea and toast. She continued to hate Buck Crowder for taking away Willia's opportunity to share tea and toast with her, but vile satisfactions welled up inside her that he would never again know any of the pleasures he had stolen in life. She imagined that Buck Crowder's putrid soul had stoked the fires of hell for a millennium.

But there was the dove to restore a reasonable facsimile of peace within her. She hoped she would be able remember the implicit message of its appearance in those inevitable moments when she was overcome with grief and rage.

She now felt an odd yearning to care for those remaining in her family. A tribute to Willia? Perhaps. But now Rainey felt a nesting instinct that was irresistible and compelling.

She put her train case on the front seat next to her and climbed behind the wheel of her powder blue Pontiac. She bowed her head beneath the weight of a wave of grief and remorse. Part of her died on the 6th of May, and the vile flower that had sprung from that open dead place had blossomed into a compulsion to kill. Again. No matter what Aunt Mittie told her all those years ago, she had allowed Step to die -- worse, she had helped him along -- and she had therefore killed him. Finally, she shook her head and the weight of the bun at her neck brought her close enough to reality that she could start the car and back out of the driveway.

Now it was down Ocean Drive, straight down to the old Topsail Highway, and on out to highway 43. It was a trip she knew so well that she decided to use the time to plan her activities -- her healings -- for the rest of the summer. Having spent the surface force of her grief at the Tesima house, she could now look forward to coming back to the house in the summer, with William, with the children, and with the grandchildren, but never alone. She shook her head against that horror. She could never come back to Tesima alone again, for alone she would have to face the hideous demon that Willia's death would always be for her. She must concentrate on the beauties of Willia's life, as best she could.

And suddenly there was fog, though the day remained clear, and she felt besieged by silent, brooding ghosts.

She had no idea where she was. She held tight to the steering wheel as if it were her only refuge, her only tie to a world that had turned against her. Every road sign rose twenty feet tall, leaning into her windshield in mocking deference to her confusion. The door of every roadside store or service station was a gaping mouth, laughing at her idiocy, welcoming her into madness. She grew dizzier with each car that whizzed past her, and the air that swooshed between her car and the others sent her into a mental tailspin.

This place, wherever it was, seemed like long ago, like a visual whisper trying to remind her of something that was just on the outskirts of her memory.

Finally, having slowed to 20 miles per hour, Rainey pulled off the road. She was sweating as if she were working in her garden under the relentless watchful eye of the sun. She leaned her forehead against that cool blue steering wheel and waited for the fog to clear inside her head. For a long minute she sat there, enclosed in silence, waiting . . . waiting.

An eternity later, someone knocked on her window. Rainey jumped, though the sound of that knock was oddly comforting. A young Highway Patrolman stood outside, his sunglasses flinging twin images of her confused face back at her. She rolled her window down quickly.

"You all right?"

Well. She couldn't tell this strange white boy that she didn't know where she was going. Lord, he'd have her committed to the Cherry Hospital and her head would be spinning for sure!

"I'm all right, Officer. Just trying to fight off a little headache is all."

"You sure?"

"Yes. I'm fine. Thank you."

"Okay, now. You let somebody know if you need some help, hear? Ain't no need of you being in pain and suffering and not telling somebody." The patrolman's kindly, patronizing tone, as if he were the loving father speaking to his tiny child, brought Rainey's sense of direction back to her with chilling force. She knew where she was, and where she was going now as if she had never experienced any doubts. And she knew that she was no child to this man who was young enough to be hers.

"Thank you," she said with steely politeness and rolled up her window. The patrolman became a faint, irrelevant phantom in the dust cloud as she glared into her rearview mirror.

On her trip back to Raleigh, back to her people, back to life, Rainey Elizabeth Clark [Herndon] Davis reflected on her 60 years. She had accomplished much, though it would never be recorded in history books, nor would any of it be remembered by any with whom she was not truly connected. But she could be proud of many accomplishments: she had made a good marriage with a wonderful man, she had taught many sweet children well, she had fought the fight for her own children, even though sometimes the fight would not be considered good from a moral stance, and she had stood strong for her family. She was a loyal friend and kinswoman. She had reared three children who were loved and liked by many. Rainey would never forget the throngs of sympathizers who had come to console them when Willia died. She had reared three people with whom she would have been friends had they not been her children.

And so, at last, as Rainey Elizabeth Clark [Herndon] Davis drove along the rural roads between Topsail Island and Raleigh, she knew that her life, though it had not been a riotous celebration, had been a success. She could live out her remaining years satisfied that she had done her jobs well. Her last years would be a tribute to the loved ones, especially her sweet murdered baby.

Happiness, fleetingly just away from her grasp as it was, might never be hers to claim, but she could some day hope to resume some semblance of her contented existence, which, to her mind, was a reasonable compromise for her.

Commencement, Rainey's Epilogue

I want to die while you love me
And never, never see
The glory of this perfect day
Grow dim or cease to be.

Back at the lovely house on South Person Street once again, most of Rainey's people waited for her to return.

She first saw William pacing across the floor and smoking a Camel, leaning sometimes on his newly acquired cane, in deference to his newly acquired limp. Directly behind him in their parlor, Olivia and Arthur sat on the sofa with their daughters, idly playing at reading a Dr. Seuss tale. Martha Alice was worrying a doilie on Rainey's wingback chair, and staring pensively out of the picture window. Red Art and Laurence smoked at cigarettes, too, and looked at the floor and at Martha Alice. They all heard her powder blue Pontiac pull into the slim driveway, and they all jumped to attention. Douglass came up the hall then, hitching his slacks into place from a recent foray into the half bath by the kitchen.

She was back.

They met her at the door, their mouths filled with questions to which they would not give voice. Their arms reached out, tentatively, to meet her shoulders, and their eyes caressed her with loving relief and welcome. Her granddaughters, feeling no constraints, rushed to grab her at her legs. Her hands reached down to stroke their neatly braided hair, and they kissed her hands.

Rainey stood at the threshold of her front door that brilliant May afternoon, basking for a minute in all the fierce and unconditional love she felt in front of and around her. She was back with her people now, and she felt whole. The gaping wound of Willia's death, though it would always be tender, would stitch nicely in the midst of all these beloved folks.

Rainey sighed loudly and smiled, holding out her arms before her.

"Y'all love me, huh?" She laughed and wept as they crowded into a circle around her, crushing her granddaughters, and nearly knocking her back onto the porch with their rush of affection.

It was good to be back among her folks.

About Lauren Sanders-Jones

A native of Raleigh, North Carolina, **LAUREN MARLENE JONES** has had a passion for writing since she completed her first paragraph in Marina Bell's second grade class at Crosby-Garfield School. Lauren graduated from Hampton University, where she majored in English and became a member of Delta Sigma Theta Sorority, Inc. She earned her master's degree in English at North Carolina State University, and has taught at several colleges, and even a high school, in the Raleigh – Durham area. Since 2008, she has resided in Charlotte, NC.

In the early 1990s, Lauren decided to take on the pen name Lauren Sanders-Jones in order to pay homage to the family of her mother and lifelong best friend, Marlene Sanders Jones, a master educator, organizer, and Delta who is now deceased, and who nurtured Lauren in every aspect of her life. Lauren got her maiden name and writing gift from her father, the late Charles Robert Jones, a journalist who at age 16 published a book of his original poetry. Her father's membership in Phi Beta Sigma Fraternity, Inc. was part of Lauren's inspiration to create Rainey as an early member of Zeta Phi Beta Sorority, Inc., Sigma's official sister organization. (Lauren's great aunts, Ruby Edward Sanders McKinney and Cornelia Rand Sanders Haywood, sisters of her maternal grandfather, Ernest L. Sanders, Sr., a member of Omega Psi Phi Fraternity, Inc., were Zetas.)

Lauren is the proud mother of three beautiful, brilliant, and fascinating young adults: Kristen Danielle Fuller, who with her husband Lawrence, blessed Lauren with her first grandchild, Isaiah Baxter Fuller; Adrienne Carol Tucker; and Justin Charles Tucker. Their surname comes from their father, Lauren's former husband, Ronnie Ray Tucker.

Lauren Sanders-Jones has these works in progress: *Defying The Mortal Coil: Book One of the Cypher Chronicles* (© 2011) and *After the Interruption, A Novel Aftermath To Reasonable Joy* (© 2011).

Front cover design and book layout: Lauren Sanders-Jones
Back cover concept: Adrienne Carol Tucker
Frontispiece and back cover photograph of Mattie Mae Hill:
Heritage of Black Highlanders Collection, UNC-Asheville Ramsey Library
bhcP77.10.4.2.16a.
Typeset Fonts: AvantGarde BK BT; Gabriola

Oakwood-Raleigh 218

DougBarter- fiace to Willa

Made in the USA
Columbia, SC
02 March 2021